Reasonable Adults

ROBIN LEFLER

KENSINGTON
PUBLISHING CORP.

www.kensingtonbooks.com

KENSINGTON BOOKS are published by

Kensington Publishing Corp.
119 West 40th Street
New York, NY 10018

ISBN: 978-1-4967-4133-2 (ebook)

ISBN: 978-1-4967-4132-5

First Kensington Trade Paperback Printing: November 2023

10 9 8 7 6 5 4 3 2 1

Printed in the United States of America

For Mom, who showed me what is possible

And in memory of Potter, a gentleman among Doodles

Reasonable Adults

Chapter 1

My toes are three minutes away from complete destruction. Attempting to insert a little pep in my step, I click across the Regan-Caulfield PR Professionals reception area. The black leather ankle boots I'd recklessly ordered after having my heart, if not broken, kicked in a sensitive area, are destined for the dark, dusty recesses of the bedroom closet. Much like my hope for a healthy adult relationship.

It's just after eight thirty on a gloomy Wednesday morning when I mince my way through the near-empty office to my desk. Most of my coworkers are probably still trying to wash off last night's escapades. I drop off my bag and detour to the kitchen for coffee, taking a moment to bask in my mature superiority. Here I am, ready to light my productivity fire, bouncing back so effortlessly after a horrendous betrayal by someone I cared about at least a medium amount. Settling into my IKEA office chair, I glance around to make sure no one is in the immediate vicinity before reaching up to give myself an actual pat on the back, which turns into a casual triceps stretch as my boss rounds the corner.

I report to a child. Gavin Boden is twenty-four and manages the Public Relations Associates in the Up-and-Coming Division. Or, the PRAs in the UCD, if you're into corporate acronyms like Gavin is.

"Morning, Rigsby."

"Hi, Gavin."

"We've got our triple O this morning. Can you bring a breakdown of the projected ROI for your RFF? K thanks." My eyes do not roll and I am amazed at my self-control.

"Sure can." I make a note—*justification for funds request at 9:30 One on One.*

"Oh, and Rigsby?"

I look up from my notepad to see him squinting at me judgmentally.

"You're going to change before the lunch with Party Thyme, right? The luxury herb crowd has presentation expectations."

"The people who flavor thyme to not taste like thyme?" When they came in for their kick-off session the cleaners had to shampoo the dirt out of the conference room carpet. The CEO wore a leisure suit and rubber boots. Rubber boots covered in *manure.*

"Gavin, come on. I'm all for a relaxed work environment and letting everyone be who they want to be, but you don't come to a meeting in your fertilizing boots." Within the incredibly tight confines of my own footwear, I flex and extend my toes, trying to get the blood flowing. "I really don't think they care what I'm wearing."

He sighs at my closed-mindedness. "They were communicating their *vibe*, their essence. You need to tone down the middle-aged city worker thing and embrace . . . I don't know, urban chicken farmer. Or passionate cultivator of a vanity balcony garden." He huffs and sits at the desk across from mine.

"Passionate vanity gardener," I echo. My brow furrows as I picture myself in denim overalls and a wide-brimmed straw hat, standing on a balcony overlooking the city center, adventurous bees humming around my head fifteen stories above the sidewalk.

"Listen, Kate."

Oh God. He was going to try to enlighten me.

"I need to enlighten you a bit. Drop some truth, you know?" He makes eye contact long enough to confirm I do, indeed, know, before tenting his fingers and kicking back to stretch his gangly legs across the aisle, dropping his feet onto my desk.

"When you joined us six months ago, Rigsby, I saw something in you."

"I've been with the company for two years, but hey, who's counting."

He points at me.

"That," he says. "That attitude is what's holding you back." His sockless, Sperry-clad toe nudges my coffee cup, sloshing some onto a stack of annual reports.

"You're cynical and afraid to push through the uncomfortable moments that make life worth living. Your negative worldview is preventing you from doing your best work. From truly shining. Where's your inner *passion*, Rigsby? What makes you *tick*? This is a creative, competitive environment." He spreads his arms as if to embrace the buffet of opportunity before us.

"I know we're in a time of HR sensitivity, but I feel like we know each other well enough that I can be blunt with you."

We do not know each other at all. This must be what it feels like to watch a car speeding toward you with no idea whether it will stop before flattening you into a thirty-one-year-old pancake.

"You're not getting any younger."

There it is. I am a pancake. A violently angry pancake.

"Sharks are swimming through that door every day, and you're floating around like a . . . I don't know—an indifferent manta ray. If you want to get ahead, if you want to progress, if you want to grow as a professional human, you're going to have to strip all this down"—he gestures at me from head to toe—"and build yourself back up stronger, hungrier, and, let's be honest here, physically more put together."

"I'm sorry, what?" He is not a car. He is a bus. The bomb-laden bus from *Speed* and there's no Reeves/Bullock combo to stop him.

"You know Madison, yes? On the Short Lunch team? She came up with the imagery of the burger eating a clock? Anyway, Madison is a makeup *pro*. She's watched, like, a million online tutorials and I bet she could give you some pointers on looking a bit fresher."

I glance at my watch and see hardly any time has passed, yet it seems like I've been stuck in this chair, mired in the terrible dropping of truth bombs, for years. I want to quit on the spot. I want to yell and stomp my foot and break a planter of artificial succulents over his stupid head. But I need the job. I breathe deeply and compose my features into an expression as close to neutral as possible.

"Noted, Gavin. Thanks for bringing this to my attention. I'll certainly take it under advisement. Now, if you'll excuse me, I'd like a few minutes to prep before our next meeting."

"You got it. Glad we had this chance to connect." He actually gives me the one-two guns before kicking over my coffee as he takes his feet off the desk. A puddle appears on my lap, soaking into the beautiful ivory wool sweater-dress less than a week old.

"Oops. Good thing you're going to change anyway, huh? Serendipitous." He freezes mid-step.

"That's a great word," he muses. "I can use that. See, Rigsby. When you're in touch with your heart-mind connection the gems just fall in your lap. Life is a treasure. Huh. I can use that too." He pulls out his phone and starts making notes as he walks away.

Brown liquid pools under my keyboard, dripping onto my leggings. I watch it for a moment, mesmerized, shell-shocked, and unsure of what to do next.

A calendar reminder pops up on my screen, snapping me back to reality. There's no time to go home and change out of my coffee-drenched, luxury-herb-inappropriate clothes before I have to walk into a room with Gavin and act like everything is fine.

The dress I managed to scrounge up after sending out an SOS in the #badassbitches Slack channel is a diaphanous affair with pink heirloom roses the size of my head spewing across a pale green background. It's supposed to be floor-length, but hits me mid-shin, leaving an awkward gap between the thin material and my now clunky-looking, foot-murdering boots. While long, it contributes absolutely no warmth, and I find myself pining for either a blanket or a very large portion of hard liquor.

While Gavin seems to believe I'm embracing retiree-chic a few decades too early, my standard vibe is more conventionally professional with the occasional nod to trendiness. I guess compared to the fresh-faced, effortless cool of my youthful colleagues, I'm hitting the more reserved end of the fashion scale. This outfit is so far outside my workwear comfort zone it may as well be in orbit.

My twenties were pretty kind to me, filling out my adolescent string-bean physique into something softer, curvier. I'm not short or particularly tall, though I can reach things on the top shelf of my cupboards if I stretch. When filling out an online dating profile, I'd pick the "average" body type option.

Not that I'm average in all respects. A guy once had me repeat my coffee order because he was so startled by my eyes (hazel) that he missed the details. And my hairdresser always compliments me on the healthy sheen I maintain on my naturally dark chestnut tresses ("You must not do much with it").

Any fashion concern I may have had disappears when Tim Fletcher, co-founder and CEO of Party Thyme, arrives at our lunch meeting in what appears to be a white paper hazmat suit. It crinkles as he sits and, despite absolutely no part of me wanting to think about him naked, I can't seem to identify the sign of any underlayers. No T-shirt collar peeking out. No telltale dark shadows where one might expect pants to be.

There are fist bumps all round as he explains that Josh Meadows, Party Thyme's Chief Taste Officer, is running late because "he's mega-deep in testing."

Tim's upgraded from the poo boots to black slip-on athletic sandals with socks that might once have been white. His big toe sticks through one. There's a brown crescent under the nail that I hope is dirt. Even Gavin looks momentarily ruffled before managing to pull his ultra-smooth schmoozing face back on. We'd chosen this specific restaurant because they recently started offering Party Thyme cocktails and mocktails. I am deeply hopeful that no one figures out who we are.

Forty minutes pass as we sip endless sparkling water enhanced with Zesty Lemon Thyme. Thyme for Chocolate. Rosemary and Thyme. Hibiscus Rose Thyme with A Hint of Bitters. I am constantly on edge, worrying that some will spill on the paper suit and we'll discover just how robust it is. More than once I wonder how this came to be my life.

Josh finally shows up as I'm ordering tea, desperate for something warm and not made of thyme. He's wearing real clothes, though the overall aesthetic isn't far off from his business partner's. His worn jeans have dirty handprints smeared across the thighs and he's wearing not one but two plaid flannel button-ups over a T-shirt advising me to GET HIGH AND LAY LOW.

The waiter delivers a mug of hot water with an organic muslin bag of Comfort Thyme propped cheerily beside it and I can barely suppress my groan.

"I think you're going to dig the subtle notes of lemon verbena in the Comfort Thyme," Josh says, noting my new beverage choice as he sits down. He scootches his chair closer to mine, pulling out his phone. "The organic honey crystals come from this totally rad hivery that has children's choirs come in to sing to the bees." His eyes are wide with wonder and what seems like genuine excitement. "They swear the energy of the kids makes the bees happier and the honey more balanced." To prove it, he opens a video of a ragtag children's choir standing beside a giant beehive, belting out "Twinkle, Twinkle, Little Star." It's hard not to be charmed, but I manage to hold on to my dour mood. Josh watches the entire video, whispers "Amazing stuff," and slides the phone back into his pocket. Admittedly, I'm tempted to ask about the science behind serenaded bees, but it seems like a slippery slope. Besides, Josh has already pulled a scrap of paper from his back pocket and is making notes, muttering about a "reverse collab with *thyme-flavored honey*" like he's about to change the world.

Across the table Tim rolls his eyes and elbows Gavin in a "get a load of this guy" move. "The Josh-ster wants to focus on, uh, local luxury, you know? And I keep being all 'Dude, but look at the big wide herb-loving world unfolding before us,' Why stay in Toronto when we could work with happy freakin' bees in San Fran?"

Aching to move things along so we can get out of here, I ask Tim to tell us his "from the ground up" story. This is usually great material for positioning interviews and media spots, but I'm also praying for a ten-minute reprieve from listening to Gavin and Tim trading stories of how hard it is to be the child of wealthy, overly attentive parents.

"So, Tim," I interrupt, "you were on track to be a chemical engineer. What made you decide to strike out into entrepreneurship instead of completing your degree and getting into a more traditional field?" I'm poised to take notes to turn into a pitch for some culinary reporters I'd spent the last three months wooing with free tickets to Toronto Maple Leafs games and *Iron Chef Canada* tapings.

Tim snorts into his drink. "Uh, yeah." He takes a sip of water laced with Kola Thyme. "I think you may have misinterpreted the information I provided in the kick-off session."

Josh makes a sound in the back of his throat, and raises his eyebrows at me. "Brace yourself," he murmurs.

I place my pen on the table and use one of my favorite unbiased business responses:

"Can you tell me more about that?"

"I wasn't actually in school for chemical engineering. It was, like, more of a hobby."

"Okay, no problem. We can work with that. So, you've always had a passion for science?"

"Yeah, not so much."

I look at Gavin, hoping he'll wade into the fray, but he's busy swiping at his phone, trying to figure out if he and Tim actually dated the same blond Lauryn in 2017.

"Um, alright. Let's circle back then. How did all this come about?"

"Oh man, this is a great story. I think you're going to be able to do a lot with it. Maybe get that pen ready."

I get that pen ready.

"So, I was a coke dealer, right? And—"

Despite my best efforts to maintain a neutral, professional face, I can feel my eyebrows practically hitting my hairline.

"Those are the chemicals in the 'chemical engineering' bit. Clever, huh? Anyway, I was doing that, hustling, makin' a buck and I started to get some higher-end clientele. So, I thought to myself, 'Self, what can we offer these fine people that will blow their very high minds while enjoying increased profitability and market gains?' And it came to me that night in an actual, literal dream. Party Thyme. A flexible herbaceous additive great for cocktails, cooking, and air purification." He takes a moment to bask in his genius, then jerks his thumb at Josh, who's migrated toward the bar to investigate the storage of said herbaceous additives.

"And I knew Josh-y boy was, like, right into horticulture and food science. It was a no-brainer. I handle the business, he takes care of the product. Easy peasy money in the bank, right?"

Gavin has tuned in and nods enthusiastically as Josh rejoins us, balancing a trio of cookies on a small plate.

"This is fantastic," Gavin says. "Rigsby, you got all that?"

I give him a thumbs-up. My notes end at "coke dealer."

Josh slides the plate in front of me. "They were hiding some lavender shortbread in the back," he says quietly. "You gotta try it with the Comfort Thyme. Bliss."

"Guys, we can do amazing things with this story," gushes Gavin. "The ingenuity you show, Tim, the resourcefulness. Bro, you're about to flip the luxury herb market on its head. Also"—he turns his phone around to display a picture of a gorgeous, leggy blond—"same Lauryn. That bitch. No offense, Rigsby."

"Sure." I mentally apologize to women everywhere.

He hoists his glass of Lemon Ginger Thyme and vodka in a toast. "*Thyme* to party."

"Nah man," Tim says, lifting his own drink. "The company's called Party Thyme. But I feel you. Let's do this thing."

"To a future as bright as the stars and as beautiful as Mother Earth," Josh adds.

From the corner of my eye, I catch Gavin and Tim exchanging an eye roll. Josh reaches forward to clink his glass against Tim's, apparently oblivious.

I'm raising my mug when I feel something brushing against my ankle. Tim's dirt-encrusted toe is stroking the bare skin between my shoe and dress hem.

He winks. "Really looking forward to working with you on this, Kate."

Kill me now.

In the comforting embrace of an idiot-free home, the day plays back in my mind like one of those sports-fail reels.

I pour a generous glass of wine, relocate to the couch, and prop my feet on the ottoman, positioning the bottle within easy reach for refills. I need to start avoiding people. I mean, not entirely. I know what you're thinking. "a burgeoning alcoholic shut-in isn't really the life improvement choice we were going for here." But the day would have gone much more smoothly with less human interaction. That, I think, we can all agree on.

I turn on a nature documentary featuring unlikely pairings of animal best friends and sip my wine as a skunk playfully chases a fox around an ornamental shrub. *Just one more*, I tell myself, topping up my glass. Know your limits, etc. Plus, it's a Wednesday. Not exactly the ideal time to hit the party button.

My phone vibrates somewhere under my left butt cheek and I fish it out. Ros, my best friend, university roommate, and head of Public Relations for a hoity toity downtown firm, has DM'd a video of a prancing baby llama. A soft open. She's got my attention. Moments later a photo from the account of Treetops Creative Retreat appears. A shimmering lake and a heart-stoppingly beautiful luxury cabin nestled in fall foliage, with the caption *Inspired. Living. Empowering and fulfilling Business Development Director position open to those with a seeking heart and talent for seeing the beauty in every moment.*

She throws in some pointed commentary. **You could use some empowerment.**

I mean, she isn't wrong. I click the link to the company's full website.

Specializing in short- and long-term retreats in the heart of Muskoka, Treetops is a luxury resort for artists whose process is emboldened by an environment steeped in comfort, support, and well-being.

I snort and tap out a message to Ros.

K: **This Treetops place sounds like a summer camp for the rich and entitled to build mahogany popsicle stick houses.**

A nearly instant reply pops up, interrupting a video of an internet-famous bear waving at tourists.

R: **Yeah, but I bet they cook for you. And maybe you could find someone suitably distracting to take your mind off Chaz. A little summer camp romance never hurt anyone.**

K: **1. I'm almost certain that is untrue. No one escapes sum-**

mer camp romance unscathed. 2. It's October. The season for cold, dead hearts.

R: But did you see the salary?

She includes the link to an actual job posting. The compensation for a November-through-January contract is unbelievable. A blue button flashes at the bottom of the screen. Apply Easily, Right Now. And what do I do? I hit that button. The fields magically populate with information saved from some previous failed foray into side hustles—Technology! After a quick, bleary-eyed scan, I shrug, raise my now-empty glass in a toast to rash decisions, and tap Submit.

Who would date a guy named Chaz, you ask? Me. I did. *For two years*. And then, just when I thought we were approaching the time for a well planned but emotionally stunted middle-class marriage? Disaster.

Picture this: Yours truly, Katelyn Meredith Rigsby, shows up at the cologne-heavy law office where my hardworking boyfriend has been putting in shockingly long hours. I open the door, thoughtfully prepared (okay, purchased) dinner in hand, only to discover him on his knees, providing some very, *very* personal services to a client.

He'd tried to explain, trailing me down the plush carpeted hall to the elevators as he buttoned his custom-made shirt. "Mrs. Strauss was anxious about speaking in court. I employed a proven relaxation technique to ease her mind."

Did I love Chaz with the fire of a thousand suns? No. But I'd had myself convinced we could coexist for the foreseeable future in a mutually beneficial arrangement. I now realize that's maybe not the right attitude with which to make life-altering relationship choices.

I sigh and wonder anew what it would feel like to punch Charles "Chaz" Hoberack in his stupid, perfectly symmetrical face. I've never hit anyone before but am always willing to try new things in the spirit of self-betterment.

A loud yawn from the other end of the couch pulls me back from the sad meander down self-pity lane. A large, curly, strawberry-blond head lands in my lap, tipping over my, thankfully now empty, wineglass. "Get enough beauty rest, handsome?" A gleefully wagging tail sends the evidence of my post-breakup pity party flying to the floor. Empty pizza box, empty peanut M&M's bag, mostly empty box of tissues. You get the idea. I refill my glass halfway, eye the dregs of the bottle, and dump the rest in as well.

"Eric! Control your enthusiasm!" I cry as seventy pounds of Goldendoodle clambers onto my lap and plops front paws onto my shoulders. With his big brown gaze a mere eyelash length from my own, I can't hold out.

"A treat?" I offer, halfheartedly. Eric bounds, wholeheartedly, as you may have guessed, to the cupboard. While I'm in the kitchen, I crack a fresh bottle of wine to bring with me back to the couch.

I scroll through my Instagram feed, accompanied by the rustic soundtrack of canine teeth on elk antler. Baby. Baby. Beach at sunset. Puppy. Penguins. Ad for leakproof underwear. Chaz on a magazine cover. Cat wearing mittens on a hardwood floor.

I pause, squint, and scroll back up. It was not a hallucination. Chaz is striking a power pose, leaning against a desk in an unfamiliar office, basking in the glow of professional lighting and wearing the yellow and cornflower-blue silk tie I got him for Christmas even though it cost six times more than any scrap of fabric has a right to.

Charles Hoberack, New Partner at Shingleton, Oberstein, and Mason, Talks Money, Property, and Mitigation

He'd gotten a new, larger desk.

"Unbelievable." I send the post to Ros, noting that Chaz probably needed the surface area for all the additional perks he offers his clients.

Spiraling down a rabbit hole of internet sleuthing, I click on the profile of everyone who's liked or commented on his post. I'm not going to sugarcoat this: It's a lot of people. A lot of women—the kind who roll out of bed looking like a dream, with morning breath that smells of roses and effortless success.

A new comment appears.

CamAboutTown So well deserved <3 <3 <3 I can say from experience, Chaz goes above and beyond for his clients.

Oh hell no. I enlarge the profile picture to make sure I'm seeing this properly. I am. CamAboutTown is Camilla Strauss. Up until last week, that is, when Chaz finalized her divorce and she was once again Camilla Giannova. Camilla was the Woman on the Desk. A key player in the ruination of my prettily packaged, if emotionally problematic, life. I'm overflowing with what I recognize is a completely unreasonable level of hatred for this woman I've never even met. Seen her in the throes of $300-an-hour passion? Yes. Proper introduction? No. I didn't stick around for that.

I take a swig of peppery Shiraz directly from the bottle, vigorously wipe my teeth with a finger, fluff my hair, and start recording some of my thoughts on the matter. I may be alone in my apartment, but why should I suffer in isolation? This is why God created the internet.

Chapter 2

At six thirty my alarm blares, pulling me out of a slumber I have no wish to leave. The pounding in my head overlays a deep sense of unease. I drag myself to the bathroom and slump in the shower, letting the spray power-wash some of the night's residue out of my mouth while also providing much-needed hydration.

I stumble into sweats and sneakers and take Eric out into the cold morning air. He sniffs the trees joyfully. He prances down the street without a care in the world. I try to channel some of his zest for life, but it makes me want to puke in the shrubs so I resume my careful shuffling.

Back at home, it's kibble for Eric, black coffee and dry Cheerios for me (multigrain, because health is important). I stare blankly into my closet. *I'm too old for this shit.* I wonder if I could get away with working from home today, then remember we have an offsite strategy session in the afternoon that's marked "BCNO" in the invite. Translation: Business Critical, Not Optional.

Monochrome seems safe. Black pants, black turtleneck,

black boots with a chunky heel, which cradle my feet in much-needed comfort, and, for some flair, a black and navy blanket scarf that I drape over my shoulders. Hair up. Lipstick on. Still look like death, but hey, beggars can't be choosers. I give myself a quick once-over with a lint brush and leave Eric in his chair by the window.

"See you soon, big guy. Keep those pigeons in line."

> 9:10 a.m.
> Gavin: Please come to my office.
> Kate: Sure. Can it wait a few minutes? Just in the middle of something.
> Gavin: No

I close the door behind me and turn to face Gavin. Lainey from HR is perched on the black leather guest chair. My stomach does a little flip that can't be attributed entirely to the smell of body spray hanging in the air.

"Hi, Lainey. What's going on?"

"Morning, Kate. Take a seat." She gives me a small, tight smile and looks at Gavin, who's pacing behind his desk like a hyena I saw on a visit to the zoo. I was less scared of the hyena.

I lower myself into the second, less comfortable, wooden guest chair, trying desperately to figure out what I've done. Did I say something stupid at lunch yesterday? I rack my brain but come up empty.

"Have you ever considered that this isn't your world and these aren't your people?" Gavin spits out the moment my butt hits the polished oak seat. "We work hard, incredibly hard, to build up and protect reputations. And what do you do?"

I keep quiet since I have no idea.

"You hop online and start spewing slanderous remarks about our clients."

My entire body spasms with shock.

"Wait. What? What are you talking about? I would never—"

A vague memory starts worming up from the boozy depths of the night before. Hazy at first, but taking shape with each horrifying second.

"Where's your phone?"

"I forgot it at home." On the coffee table. In front of the couch where I sat last night and drank too much wine. Oh, Jesus.

Gavin spins his monitor so Lainey and I can both see it. My Instagram profile is open. He clicks on a video and my own voice assaults my ears.

"Some of you may know this man, a newly minted Partner at Shingleton, Oberstein, and Mason." Even as I start to hyperventilate, I notice that my editing skills are superb. There's an excellent cutaway from my bleary-eyed face to the picture of Chaz leaning on the desk. I didn't even know I knew how to do that.

"What you may not know," drunk Kate continues, *"is that he offers his clients services that can't be found on the firm's usual menu."* Blood rushes in my ears, blocking what comes out of my mouth next. Judging from the extreme tongue action on screen, it wasn't helpful.

Gavin hits Pause and my face freezes mid tongue-waggle. I am very close to throwing up.

"Shingleton, Oberstein, and Mason is our largest Reputation Management client. Or they were until eight o'clock this morning when they fired us." He runs both hands through his already unusually ruffled hair and takes a deep breath.

"You don't care about this business. Our clients are barely even real people to you. Do you ever pay attention to how much they struggle? The amount of sheer perseverance it takes to get where they want to go? And they succeed because they're doing what is important to them. They have a calling and they're chasing it down like Usain fucking Bolt. Our job is to help them every step of the way. To hold their coffee while they sprint to the finish. And to shield them from people like you."

I hit a new emotional low. I have never felt like such a trash ball of a human. What was I thinking? How could I do this? That person on the screen isn't who I am. I don't even know her.

"You don't belong here, Kate. You're fired."

My bed welcomes me back into its low-thread-count arms. The following six hours are spent groaning in dismay and attempting to smother myself with an embroidered throw pillow the size of a tissue box. Neither activity is particularly soothing, so by dinnertime I'm on the couch watching *Grey's Anatomy* reruns. For the emotional catharsis, of course.

I briefly consider calling my mom, but that would mean telling her what I've done. About Chaz and my job and my absolute lack of a future. I can hear her "I told you so" already. Except she'd never be so overt. It would be cushioned in words that sound like a hug and I'd inevitably hang up, ready to pack it in and head back to the comfort of my childhood bedroom.

Putting the phone down, I try to focus on McDreamy. No dice. My brain is bouncing around like a deranged kitten.

I'd left home, a city of forty thousand, for The Big City in a fit of totally uncharacteristic spontaneity when I was eighteen. Growing up the only child of a primary school librarian and the area's most sought-after tractor mechanic, I was convinced I was exactly where I'd always want to be: in a town where I was comfortable, with friends I'd known since I was in diapers, safe in the knowledge that I too would be a librarian and live out my days alongside my high school sweetheart, Jordan Robertson, in the century home on Otto Street that I'd been eyeing for over a decade. Except, it turned out I'd made some assumptions. Big ones.

For example, Jordan hadn't been kidding all those times he'd said he was going to follow his dream of becoming an international rock star. I'd always figured we'd graduate high school and some switch would flip in his brain, making a job at the bank suddenly seem incredibly interesting. He could still do shows on the weekends. Best of both worlds! But for Jordan, there was only one world. The one in which we moved to Toronto and I worked full-time while he strummed away on his guitar in our tiny apartment, waiting for that sweet, sweet stardom to show up.

Spoiler: it did not.

I kept the faith for nearly two years. For twenty long months I served endless coffee and eggs, fighting exhaustion and waiting for this man-boy I had loved ever since he'd winked at me across the cafeteria in grade ten to realize this wasn't where we were meant to be. That *my* dream was much more realistic and financially sound. And when that didn't happen, when the third-hand couch in our apartment had formed to the shape of his buttocks and he still refused to get anything resembling a job, my patience hopped on a train out of town and I went with it.

But since life would never sedately take me from point A to point B, after a few months of loafing around my parents' house, I was back in Toronto, living that student life. And, big twist, it turned out I wasn't actually that into classic literature and library science. More critically, I *was* interested in business and marketing. Because I was now a Big City Woman who could do impressive corporate things and take on the world in my modern-day business attire.

Unfortunately, as much as I'd loved my marketing courses and international business studies, once I got into the real word it was all a bit of a letdown. Not a complete flop, but despite each new job feeling like it was going to be "the one," the ladders I wanted to climb haven't shown up yet, and the good ol' glass ceiling is barely even in sight, let alone shattered by yours truly.

But in the meantime, I've done a great job convincing everyone at home that I'm the bee's knees of the PR world. I love the city! My work is so rewarding! Right.

Eventually, I stopped going home every weekend, then missed the occasional holiday, slowly losing touch with nearly all my childhood friends, and now, six years later, it feels too awkward to reach out, to admit I was wrong. That things are suddenly crumbling faster than a day-old gluten-free brownie.

One of the many problems with effectively maintaining a mirage for this long is it's pretty hard to walk back without shattering the very friendships you hope to rekindle.

But this is fine. I can figure things out. I'm a capable adult who can solve problems and do the grown-up things. Besides, last I heard, Jordan was living in his uncle's workshop and rotating tires all day. By comparison, I'm still winning. Not that it's a competition.

I need a plan. I need change. I need an adventure! I punch a mental fist into the air while my actual fist grips my lunch, a chocolate chip cookie the size of my face.

A giant bite disappears into my mouth. Note to self: stock up on cookies. Eric hovers nearby, ready to assist with cleanup. What I truly need is a job.

Crumbs rain down into the cracks of my keyboard as I scroll through page after page of job ads. They all look terrible. I'm considering whether I can bring myself to work at a car dealership looking to "diversify their staff demographic" when destiny rears its timely head in the form of an email. Subject line: *Scheduling an Interview—Treetops Creative Retreat.*

> *Dear Kate,*
> *Thank you for your interest in the Business Development role at Treetops Creative Retreat.*
> *We are very dedicated to finding the perfect candidate to join our small team of professionals. It is critical that the individual we invite to join us fully and deeply embraces the culture of creative enablement for the luxury-minded artists to whom Treetops caters. We're seeking a big picture thinker with microscopic detail-level focus, driven by an innate passion for seeing people reach their full potential.*
> *If this sounds like you, please select a time in the*

*calendar link below for a chat over video conference
with myself and Treetops' Chief Revenue Officer, Brooke
Kerrigan.*

*We look forward to exploring how this opportunity
aligns with your long-term career goals.*

Janet Kanduski
VP People
HIT Properties

I click on the link in Janet's signature and it all comes flooding back. "Oh. Oh shit."

I think I mean *Oh shit! What excellent timing. Great work, me!* but with a smidge of *Oh shit. What have I done?* thrown in for good measure.

I navigate back to the full job description, occasionally brushing tail fur off the keyboard. Eric sprawls beside me, getting his requisite twenty hours of beauty sleep.

Business Development Director, Treetops Creative Retreat

Treetops Creative Retreat is seeking a passionate, dedicated, resourceful individual to bring a fresh outlook to connect Treetops to new clientele. For the appropriate person, this position will allow near-total creative freedom in an inspiring environment.

The role requires complete immersion in our retreat environment* in Otterburne, Ontario, to ensure the messaging put forth is an accurate reflection of the feelings our residents can expect to experience while in our care.

*A well-behaved pet may accompany the successful candidate.

The money they're offering is borderline obscene.

"Hrrrrrrmmmmmm." I tap my lower lip in thought and turn to my confidant.

"Eric, here's the deal. I made a terrible mistake and may have ruined all my career options in my chosen field in this city, possibly the country." I poke him in the ribs with my toe. "Are you listening? This is important."

His eyelids slowly blink open. He yawns, heaves himself upright, and turns to lie down again with his face on my knee.

"Thank you. So here we are, jobless, aimless, and deeply ashamed, but with an opportunity in our laps. Literally, actually." My laughter is slightly hysterical as I gesture to the computer propped on my other leg. Eric huffs out a breath that could be interpreted as exasperation, canine laughter, or, you know, just a dog breathing.

"We're at a metaphorical fork in the road of life. Do we travel down the path that takes us to necessities like money and the opportunity to make connections that may, in turn, lead to further opportunity and, dare I say, more money? Or do we mosey down the dark alley of unemployment insurance and grocery-store kibble?"

Eric is asleep again, snoring gently as I select a time for my video conference interview. We certainly have nothing to lose.

I meet Roslyn for lunch. I'd chosen my favorite all-day breakfast spot, hoping that perfect waffles and mediocre but endless coffee would act as an emotional bandage. Inhaling the combination of caffeine and grease, I spot an empty booth and swoop in triumphantly to grab it ahead of a group of inattentive high school kids milling around the entrance waiting to be seated by a server. Suckers.

My phone buzzes in my back pocket.

Mom: **Are you still coming home next weekend?**

My fingers drum the table. I bite my lip.

Me: **I don't think I can swing it. Work is CRAZY. Maybe next month? I'll check out my calendar and let you know.**

Mom: **Okay. Hailey will be disappointed. I ran into her at the grocery store today and she was asking after you.**

Hailey and I had been inseparable growing up. We still exchange the odd text or meme, but I hadn't spent any real time with her in years. I slump back in my seat. Our friendship had seemed so bulletproof, but it ended up another casualty of my failed quest for the better life.

Me: **I'll text her. It would be great to see her next time I'm in town.**
Mom: **Don't work too hard, poodle.**
Me: **Ha! I'll do my best.**

I slide my phone into my bag and meander down a winding trail of self-doubt as I wait for Ros.

I'm such an idiot. Is she going to yell at me? What is everyone saying about me? What if she tries to *tell me* what everyone is saying? PR is a tight-knit, loose-lipped community. Ros has probably heard all kinds of terrible things. I don't think I can bear it. I will cry. I will vomit. I will become a hermit under a bridge that not even the other very, very lonely hermits want to interact with because the horribleness of my past actions rolls off me in waves. I resist the temptation to lay my forehead on the cool, crumb-dotted, baby-blue table.

"You okay? You look like you might puke." Ros slides into the booth across from me. She is not alone.

"You brought Gary?" I moan, as a very handsome man in a perfectly tailored suit plops down beside me. Gary's been part of our tiny gang since he'd subbed in on our now defunct pub trivia team on a whim three years earlier. He's been working in New York for the past eight months doing big-time marketing exec things that pay more in a day than I make in two weeks.

"Big guns," Gary explains. "It's time for them." He straightens his cuffs with a tug. "It's Mom's birthday this weekend and my client canceled our kickoff at the last minute—their issue, not mine, I'd like to note—so I just happened to be in town at the exact moment you chose to self-destruct. It's fate."

I kick his shin under the table, then wrap him in a hug.

"It's really good to see you, Gare bear." His grimace at the nickname eases some of the turmoil in my stomach. Plus, he smells great. Like citrus and leather. It's hard to languish in the pit of stress with my head floating in a cloud of premium cologne. His soon-to-be-wife, Jemma, was getting a good one. Also an extremely finicky, send-the-wine-back-after-a-sniff, type-A-personality-with-a-Marvel-movie-obsession one. She has the patience of a saint.

"I was going to surprise you at work, but then Ros let me know about . . . things."

Ros's wide-leg black pants and white Peter Pan–collared shirt made her look like Hip Corporate Barbie, except this particular blonde would destroy you with a single withering glance for commenting on her stellar looks. Glancing down at my decade-old hoody and jeans, I feel like a kid in the principal's office. Or worse, like I'm about to get a lecture from my youthful, "not mad, just disappointed" mom.

"You're a fucking moron sometimes," she says, reaching across the table to give my arm a gentle squeeze.

Gary nods.

"It's true," he says. "But we love you anyway. You keep things interesting."

I exhale loudly.

"I know. I do. But honestly, I don't even remember doing it, and normal me would never, ever, ever do something so heinous. You know that, right?"

"We know," Gary says. "But, Kate, we need to talk."

I assume he's going to tell me that I'll never work in PR in this city again. That I'm universally disliked and blacklisted. I'm in no rush to hear it.

"Let me eat before you stomp on what's left of my very fragile ego."

When our food arrives, I focus on systematically destroying my waffles, dripping in syrup—the real kind from a tree—and topped with strawberries. Pure joy on a plate.

Ros daintily consumes half of her poached egg on a tomato slice, then pins me down with her sharp blue eyes. Gary sets down his third cup of coffee, asserting (again) that it's been over-brewed, before folding his arms and leaning toward me. I freeze with a forkful of whipped cream halfway to my mouth. Already consumed waffle performs a backflip in my stomach.

"Kate," Ros says, "this is some tough love. I'm telling you this because I care about you and it's time you face reality."

"I know, Ros. Really. You don't need to do this."

"I do. You're wasting the best years of your life on garbage relationships and a career you couldn't care less about. You're following the dotted line through a mediocre adulthood and it . . ." She trails off for a second before putting her shoulders back and plowing on. "Well, it clearly sucks." Gary nods. She deflates a bit, relieved to have gotten that tidbit off her chest.

I shove my plate away. "What is *that* supposed to mean? Jesus. You don't think I'm having a hard enough time right now? You want to stage a casual intervention over waffles?" I tend to get shrill when I'm on the defensive, and the couple at the booth next to ours look over, apparently pleased to get a show with their meal at no extra charge.

I start to grab my bag and coat, ready to get the hell out of there. I give Gary a nudge, signaling that he needs to move so I can escape. He doesn't budge. Just raises his eyebrows at me and rotates to more fully block me in.

"I know you've got your life all figured out, Roslyn, but that doesn't give you permission to dictate how I live mine."

"I'm not trying to dictate anything. I want you to be happy." She reaches over and wraps my hand in both of hers. "Can we please talk about this like reasonable adults?"

I glare at her but she must see weakness in my eyes because she relaunches her attack.

"In all the time I've known you, you haven't committed to anything. Not really. You tick the boxes, but you don't get emotionally involved. You could do so much better. In your job, in relationships. You just need to find your passion!"

"Are you a motivational poster? *Find my passion*? You know what I'm passionate about? Paying my bills on time. Having a roof over my head. Being able to afford Eric's premium dental kibble." I stick my arms into my coat before realizing I'm holding it backward. Once I've disentangled myself, I drape it through the handles of my messenger bag, elbowing Gary in the process. He still doesn't move from the bench.

"I'm passionate about not having to call my parents for a loan when my car breaks down. About being able to bring someone home for dinner; someone they're impressed by."

"Hold up," interrupts Gary. "You think your parents like Chaz? You truly believe your father, who values high-quality internet fishing videos, two-for-one burger night, and scoring a deal on flannel shirts was impressed by that jackass?"

"Of course he was! Everyone's impressed by Chaz. That was the whole point!"

They stare at me expectantly, waiting for the moment I'm shocked to realize that this isn't a great premise for a long-lasting, meaningful relationship.

"Listen," I say, sighing heavily and putting my bag back down. They're never going to let me leave without seeing this through. I rummage through the basket of creamers, looking for the highest fat content and cursing my inability to deal with conflict. "Some people have to look ahead and decide what matters to them in a relationship. Maybe that's not always love. Maybe it's stability and networking opportunities."

"You're saying your boyfriends are a business plan?" The pitch of Ros's voice and the height of her left eyebrow indicate she does not approve.

I'm so exhausted I finally give in and lay my forehead on the table, feeling crumbs digging into my skin.

"So what if they are?" I drag my body upright, brushing off my forehead with my sleeve.

Ros's gaze softens. Gary props his chin on his hand. Classic thinking pose. "Have you considered just taking some time away? Finding some breathing space to figure out what you really want?"

I tell them about the Treetops interview and Ros puffs up with pride at being the one to have inadvertently saved me.

"It seems too good to be true, but I'm not exactly drowning in options." I stir a third cup of coffee I neither need nor particularly want.

She pulls out her phone. "Let's get you prepped for this interview."

By four that afternoon, I'm set up at a makeshift desk fashioned from my laundry hamper. My chair is the bucket I use to mop the kitchen floor, overturned and large enough to accommodate one butt cheek.

The books that frame my head on the screen have keywords on the spines that my interviewer will subconsciously pick up on and associate with me. *The **Perfect** Cup of Tea; Wine Pairings: An **Artistic** Approach; **Big Picture Thinking**; Finding Passion in a Cold World; Living Your Most **Creative** Life.*

I'm practicing my casual fake laugh when Brooke and Janet sign on to the call. I quickly check my hair and arrange my face into something less desperate. Let the games begin.

The women beaming through the internet into my living room are diametric opposites. One is in her sixties, with frizzy brown hair highlighted with silver. Glasses hang on a multi-colored beaded cord around her neck. She smiles broadly and waves with enthusiasm, expressing her hope that I am having "a most stupendous Thursday."

In the box next to her, calling in from what appears to be

her bed, lounges a royal purple silk robe–clad ice queen. She appears to be in her late forties and has the most expensive-looking hair I've ever seen. It's as smooth as glass and a kind of grayish-blondish miasma that must take a full day of salon time to perfect. She acknowledges my presence with a slow blink, then looks down at something off-screen, smirking. She doesn't bother unmuting herself to say hello.

Janet, the cheerful one, introduces herself and provides a brief overview of Treetops but doesn't go into much detail. "I expect you've already done all the necessary research—no need to rehash things."

I nod confidently while wondering what she thinks I should already know.

Thirty minutes pass in a flurry of standard interview questions that I'm pretty sure I hit out of the park. I've always had a knack for interviews, and Ros's prep session really hit hard on the "fake it till you make it" approach. Not lying, of course, but massaging the truth into a more appealing shape.

Janet's head is bobbing like she's listening to her favorite song. Probably Enya.

"What makes you the right candidate for this role?"

"I've always dreamed of having an opportunity that would allow me to leverage my full suite of skills in marketing and communications, while also discovering new facets of myself in business development. Building strong, long-lasting relationships with clients leads to repeat business and referrals—that's true of any industry. I believe putting forth powerful messaging that communicates the unbelievable luxury experience awaiting the artistic community, and also the opportunity for them to make incredible on-site memories and creative strides, will position Treetops an unstoppable force in the retreat market."

I'm already planning the epic self-congratulatory meal I'm about to order from the pizza place across the street when a curveball is thrown.

"One last question before we sign off," Janet says, making a note. "This has been a Treetops interview question for decades now, and while it may seem a bit offbeat, we do appreciate a well-considered answer." She pauses, awaiting confirmation I understand.

I nod, intrigued.

"What color is the number four?"

"Pardon? I think the connection must have stuttered. Can you repeat that?"

"Of course—what color is the number four?"

Pivot, Rigsby, pivot!

"Oh, ha ha! Wonderful question." Terrible fucking question. I scan what I can see of the rooms around them and notice Brooke seems to have a thing for Tiffany blue. Plant pot on the bedside table, throw pillow, even specks of it on her cloudlike soft-knit blanket.

"Blue," I say with finality as if no one could ever suggest that the number four could be lilac, or brown, or no color at all because it's a goddamn number.

"I see," Brooke murmurs, participating for the first time since they signed on. But she doesn't sound convinced, so I go all in.

"Specifically, something close to robin's-egg blue, but with a touch more mint."

"I see," she repeats. "Why?"

Shit.

"As Janet asked this, it struck me that you feature quite a bit of the hue in question in your surroundings. The pot housing the aloe, the cushion beside you. This, of course, kept the color front of mind and it seemed to almost jump out at me and say 'Yes, hello! I am number four.' I couldn't say why, but it intuitively felt true."

I'm going to be so pissed if someone else lands this because the number four is magenta.

Turns out the number four is, in fact, blue and by the time I'm whipping up a lunch grilled cheese on Monday, I have a job. When the sun sets on Wednesday, the ink is drying on the agreement to sublet my apartment to a Swedish medical student who has just arrived in the city for an internship.

An alarming chunk of my savings goes toward outfitting myself for winter in northern Ontario. I asked Janet if she could provide a packing list for me, like when you go to summer camp, but I think she thought I was joking, because no such list materializes. The internet provides several suggestions and I end up with a suitcase full of high-tech-sounding fabrics that wick away moisture and insulate against sub-zero temperatures.

The night before I leave, Ros and I stand in the hallway of my apartment, surveying the pile of bags beside the door.

"You're really doing this," she says in disbelief, raising a sweating glass of Chardonnay to her lips. I wonder what the hell I'm doing, walking away from the life I've spent over half a decade building. It's far from perfect, but at least it's mine. *This will blow over, and you'll come back stronger. Probably.*

"I am really doing this." I finish my wine in a single gulp and go to pour another.

Chapter 3

Eric's tongue flaps in the frosty air as we travel along a tree-lined highway heading farther and farther north. I crank the heat another notch in my beloved Toyota Camry, but can't bring myself to close the window. He's so darn happy.

We've been on the road for three hours, the traffic going from the six-lane standstill of a major city artery to a gentle trickle along two lanes, until we found ourselves on a near-deserted winding road carved through never-ending forests of what might be pine and maple and probably some other wonderfully majestic tree life. Signs posted every few kilometers remind me to be cautious of the herds of moose that are apparently waiting to leap in front of my vehicle. You'd think they'd have better things to do.

I park along the back edge of a large lot behind the Otterburne public library, nestling in between a Mercedes SUV and some kind of high-end electric hybrid minivan. I'd been instructed to wait in town for pickup and transport to Treetops, which seemed a little weird, but presumably, they don't want a field of cars messing with the views.

Clipping on Eric's leash I pause to give him a pep talk.

"I have assured these people you are a very well-behaved young man. Don't make me look bad. Do you understand?" His tongue swipes sandpaper kisses up my cheek and glazes my sunglasses with slobber.

I reinforce my messaging.

"No jumping on people, no stealing food, and most, *most* certainly no head-butting male guests or employees in the junk when you say hi."

He barks, either in affirmation or at the squirrel running across the roof of the car behind me.

We perform an exploratory lap of the parking lot's perimeter, and promptly at five o'clock a shiny silver panel van swings in and pulls in front of where I'm lounging against my car's sun-warmed hood.

The van is unmarked, and as the side door slides open, I feel my body tense in preparation for a sprint to safety. Am I about to be kidnapped?! Was Treetops Creative Retreat an elaborate ruse to get desperate single women to the middle of nowhere and then spirit them away into the wilderness for undoubtedly horrific reasons? Will someone cut off my ear and send it to Chaz with a ransom demand? Would he pay it?

A tiny blonde in black jeans, hiking boots, and an appropriately forest-green Treetops Creative jacket pops out of the van like a jack-in-the-box.

"Hiya! You must be Kate! I'm Tania, Guest Co-ordinator at Treetops! Welcome to beautiful Otterburne! Is this Eric? Oh, aren't you a handsome devil!" She crouches down to rub the exposed belly of my trusty guard dog, who'd rolled onto his back to better receive pats—or certain death—though the chances of burbling-fountain-of-welcome Tania being a kidnapper/dog assassin seems fairly low by this point.

"Yes! Hello!" I try matching her enthusiasm but feel like I'm just yelling in her joyous nature-guide face. Tania has never had her heart thoroughly insulted by a smarmy lawyer. She's too glow-y. I try again. "Nice to meet you. This *is* Eric and he does believe himself to be the handsomest of devils."

She beams up at me from Eric's side before standing and dusting off her hands on her pants.

"Let's get your bags loaded and we'll head on in. I can't wait for you to see the place in person. Fall up here is so magical. Winter can be a bit . . . much? But fall"—she sighs like a woman in love—"fall you're going to absolutely *die* for. At least, for the time it sticks around. Did you bring snowshoes?" She strides to the back of the Camry and starts heaving luggage out with unexpected strength.

"Snowshoes? Ah, no. No one mentioned them." I look around at the admittedly chilly, but snow-free late autumn day. "We probably have a bit of time before snow hits, no? It's barely November."

"Oh yeah, of course!"

My shoulders slump with relief and I grab my laptop bag and Eric's bed. I may have lived in Canada my entire life, but a snow bunny I am not.

"We've got a couple of weeks until it really sticks, so if you do want to order snowshoes, or anything else, you can have them delivered to the post office. Mike will pick them up in town when he does his Friday run. Mike's our Head of Landscaping. He's, um, quiet? Absolute genius with a chainsaw though."

"Chainsaw?" I echo, somewhat alarmed, but Tania doesn't seem to hear me as she arranges Eric's bed on the floor of the van.

"There we go! A bed for the prince!" She makes a final adjustment and stands back.

"Are you all set? If you forget anything here, we can arrange for someone to grab it later on. I'm sure Brooke mentioned we do require all new hires to remain on-site for a minimum of three weeks, so you won't be able to come yourself. But hey, you'll probably be too busy to even want to leave, right? Okay! Here we go!" She swings into the van with a smooth, well-practiced leap while I stumble behind, tripping over Eric's leash as he rushes ahead to join his new bestie.

I am certain no one mentioned three weeks of introductory isolation and am experiencing a range of feelings—frustration, disappointment, rampant panic—at the idea of being effectively imprisoned by my employer. I consider my options. It's not too late to jump back out of the van and head home. But then what? It's not like I have a mountain of lucrative prospects waiting. No, this will be fine. I mean, three weeks at a luxury retreat is something people hand over big Scrooge McDuck–style bags of money to experience and I'm being paid to be here.

I allow myself to crack a hopeful smile. How bad could it be? I envision myself posting snarky captain's-log-esque reels, and oohhhhhh how people would laugh in the face of my misfortune. I can see it now, the DMs pouring in from friends I haven't talked to in years aside from casual birthday wishes and effusive congratulations as they've gotten married, had babies, and sent those babies off to school for the first time. I try not to think too hard about how much I'd like the chance to really catch up with them. To have coffee on someone's front porch while their kids bike up and down the sidewalk.

I climb into the passenger seat and buckle up, glancing back to make sure Eric had found his spot. The cargo area is full of produce from an apparent grocery run and he's curled up on his bed next to a box marked FREE-RANGE, ORGANIC, WELL-LOVED CHICKEN.

Scrawled below the label is a handwritten note:

Betsy, Matilda, Alice, and Okra, RIP. Thank you for your delicious sacrifice.

I snap a picture to include with my first update, to be captioned "Is this in poor taste? PUN INTENDED."

Tania's voice cuts through my reverie. "If you want to send any texts or anything, now's the time. Once we get out of town there's no cell reception except in the middle of the lake, and that's spotty."

Three-week isolation. No cell reception. Chainsaw-wielding maniacs. Cool cool cool cool cool.

"There's Wi-Fi in the main house, of course, but we, uh, don't exactly invest in the top speed plan? It's good for the guests to be able to really, truly disconnect. And it can be a nice break for us too!"

I press my forehead to the cool glass of the window as the van accelerates, and hope an errant moose will put me out of my misery.

I try to keep up some idle chitchat as the road winds back and forth deeper and deeper into the forest, but with every bend and sudden hilly descent, I have to fight the urge to puke on the freshly vacuumed floor mat. This must be a common issue, or I've turned a particularly obvious shade of green because fifteen minutes into the drive Tania takes pity and rolls the window down so I can stick my head out and gulp fresh air. Eric watches longingly and sniffs at the breeze blowing into the back, but stays close to his chickens. Priorities.

"No worries!" chirps Tania. "We're almost through the worst of it. But if you need to throw up let me know and I'll pull over in a flash. I just picked the van up from the detailing place and that's the last cleaning before she goes into storage, so it would be great if we can keep it tidy."

"Understood. But, don't you need the van through the winter? How do guests get in?"

"Great question!" She beams at me and I feel unreasonably clever. Man, she's great at her job. "Once we get the first couple snowstorms under our belts the access road isn't drivable any-more, so we park ol' Nat here"—she pats the dash fondly—"at an off-season facility in town. If we do have any winter guests, we have other means of getting them in. Usually some combination of ATV, snowmobile, snowshoeing, or skis if they're after some adventure. But our regulars tend to just get dropped off by helicopter. It's a bit of an up-sell but *super* convenient. The noise is, of course, a disruption to the Creatives, but by January we usually only have one or two around anyway."

Hold. The. Mother-effing. Phone. My mind races as terrible dots connect. Inaccessible roads. *If* we have winter guests.

"Um, hey, Tania?" I say as casually as possible while calculating whether a duck-and-roll out of the van would kill me or just result in some subtle maiming. "What's the average occupancy rate in the winter?"

"Hmmmm, like between ten and fifteen percent? It's kind of nice, to be honest. We used to go full out from May through September, so the lull is a great time for the staff to refocus and connect to their craft again. Of course, quite a few of us are seasonal, so a bunch go home or to work out West at the high-end ski resorts. It's a bit of a skeleton crew October onward. Well, this year we started paring down a bit early, but, you know . . ." She trails off.

I don't want to be overdramatic. My life doesn't flash before my eyes or anything, but I do have a clear mental picture of my employment contract. Specifically, the compensation portion I so confidently reviewed and declared "totally achievable."

> *Base salary (25%) shall be paid out in even, monthly increments over the course of the contract.*
> *Variable compensation (75%) to be paid at conclusion of contract based on meeting/exceeding performance targets as detailed below:*
> *Occupancy rates maintained at 55%+ December through February*

I blame the celebratory glass (okay, half bottle) of Pinot Noir I hoisted in a toast to my incredible resiliency before scrawling my signature across the dotted line. Never again, Pinot. We've had some good times, but we're done. I chew my thumbnail and do some quick math to figure out just how bad this is.

Newsflash: It's real bad. If I use up the rest of my savings, I can just squeak by with car payments, Eric expenses, and rent for my apartment for a couple of months after this contract ends. I may as well be bartending in the city. This is a total waste of time.

And then, the trees part and through the fiery golden fall foliage, I see paradise. I must have gasped because Tania looks at me with a knowing smile. "Yeah. I know, right? Welcome to Treetops."

Chapter 4

My door is open before the van rolls to a full stop. Eric bounds around the parking area sniffing trees and claiming them as his personal chunks of the wilderness. I gape. I cannot honestly say I have ever before been struck completely dumb by the grandeur of nature combined with immense wealth, but here I am. Opening and closing my mouth like a fish when I should be helping with my bags, controlling my supposedly well-behaved canine, or figuring out how to increase the number of winter guests by what may as well be seven hundred million percent. In that moment, none of it matters.

The parking area is set well above the rest of the property and I have a clear view of the layout below. The sun has just started to set and the lake reflects deep pinks and purples from the slowly darkening sky. Tiny ripples, mere suggestions of waves, lap at the shore. A loon calls out.

Across the water, hills densely covered by pine and spruce tower, promising dark, quiet, potentially menacing adventure. Along the tree line at the right side of the property stand a handful of small cabins, each with a slightly different aesthetic, but all blending beautifully into their surroundings. And at the top of a gentle rise, surrounded by precisely ruggedized but approachable landscaping, is the main cabin. Mansion? Cottage-castle?

I know from the website that the building can accommodate twenty-five guests throughout sixteen rooms and suites, plus staff. Somehow, despite the absolutely ludicrous size of the building, it manages to look inviting and cozy. It's built into the hill, with two stories aboveground, and I can just make out the corner of another peeking from the hillside toward the water. A second-floor wraparound porch is surrounded by a glass railing so as not to impede the view of the lake while guests lounge in the Muskoka chairs spread along its length, offering the choice of group or solo seating arrangements. I wonder whose job it is to keep all that glass fingerprint-free.

Gravel crunches under my boots as I walk across the parking lot toward the main entrance. Eric thunders up behind me, sounding like a small pony, but skids to a stop, nails scraping across the slippery wooden decking of the porch, as the door swings open ahead of us. A bear of a man blocks the entrance.

"Nope. You are not bringing that in here."

I peer at the figure, backlit by cozy firelight pouring from inside. He's wearing the black pants and green collared shirt of a Treetops employee with a gorgeous ivory cable-knit cardigan layered on top. A clipboard is tucked under his arm and he brandishes a handheld vacuum like a sword to stop our progress.

"Come on, Kevin." Tania appears beside me and surreptitiously pulls small twigs out of Eric's curls. "We're supposed to welcome Kate like a guest so she gets the full experience. Besides, Eric is such a good boy. You won't even know he's here. Right, Kate?" She shoots me a meaningful look.

"Yes! Absolutely!" I agree enthusiastically. "Eric's taken the Good Canine Citizen course." And was expelled. "He is an excellent dog." True, depending who you ask. "Very respectful." Blatant lie.

Kevin huffs. "He can wait for you in the mudroom. Brooke wants you to stay in the main house, but I'm going to have to move you out to one of the standalone cabins. I will not have this . . . this . . ."

"Dog?" I offer.

"This *creature* tracking in Lord knows what kinds of filth." He visibly shudders at the thought, but finally steps aside to let us into the warmth.

The interior is just as breathtaking as you might expect. A towering fieldstone fireplace is the centerpiece of the common area. The lofty ceiling is held up by huge dark honey-colored wooden beams that glow with the warm, gentle light shining from a chandelier made from a seemingly impossible number of antlers. The furniture is a bit more, um, classic, than I expected, but the room is a beautifully curated mix of antiques and incredibly high-quality, if dated, pieces made to feel both luxurious and functional despite their age. Here and there I spot patches or scratches. The room exudes nostalgic cottage comfort and the imperfections seem to enhance that. Except for the drooping, stained section of ceiling in the corner by the staircase. That's not cute.

Tania leads a morose Eric into exile in the mudroom off the main entrance and goes to unload the van, abandoning me with Kevin. He glides silently across the shiny hardwood floor in his shearling-lined moccasins to a side table and pours something from a lidded ceramic jug. A steaming mug is plunked into my hand before he moves across the room to vacuum an already spotless corner beside the fireplace. I sniff at what seems to be mulled cider.

Once the whooshing of the vacuum stops, I attempt polite conversation.

"So, Kevin, what's your role here?" It could have been a trick of the light on knitwear, but his chest seems to puff ever so slightly.

"I am the Environmental Specialist. I also manage the day-to-day operations of the facility."

"Oh cool! You guide the nature walks and stuff? It would be great to tag along and get a better sense of the area. I bet you have some awesome wildlife stories. I'd love to see a fox. Are there many around here?"

"God. No." He picks nonexistent lint from his sleeve and tucks the vacuum lovingly into a cabinet. "I am in charge of the *creative* environment. I nurture the glimmering and fragile light of each artist through the provision of an ideal atmosphere that caters to the specific requirements of their craft as it is channeled through their unique person."

Silence. I try to think of something appropriate to say.

Kevin snorts at my inability to translate pretension. "For example," he says, gesturing at my woeful ineptitude, "what's your output?"

"My output?" I fear his eyes might get stuck, they roll so far back.

"Yes. Your *output*." He stresses the word like saying it slowly and loudly will somehow make the meaning clear. It does not.

"Good lord, girl. Your output! Your craft. Your art. What do you give back to this beautiful earth in gratitude for providing you the chance to live on it?"

"Ooooohhh. Of course, yes. My *output*. I assume you mean other than my gift for generating revenue, eh?"

This falls very, very flat. My output is not comedy, apparently.

"Words?" I offer tentatively. I mean, I can write a witty caption like you would not believe.

"Ah. A writer. Commercial fiction, I take it? How common. Alright, well it's something, I suppose." He examines me for a moment with piercing gray eyes and nods once.

"You would be best suited to the Borealis cottage. It gets the most morning light off the lake, which shines directly onto the coffee deck and into the interior workspace. You are most productive early in the day, though I suspect you're a slow starter and will find that light energizing.

"Borealis is set slightly apart from the other buildings, which will allow you to immerse yourself in the sounds of the forest by day, but it is closest to the Gathering Fire so you can easily step out to join in the evening socials. You require space and clarity to create your best work, but recharge and generate new ideas by spending time with people, and this location provides ample opportunity for both. Finally, once the Gathering Fire has been extinguished, that particular spot provides the most spectacular view of the night sky. I believe you would benefit from prolonged periods of self-reflection while lost in the glory of the stars."

For someone who has just proclaimed their output to be words, I am at a loss. Kevin is either psychic, a talented internet stalker, or the most intuitive human I've ever met. *Alright*, I think. *I can sell this.*

"Kevin, that's incredible. How did you—"

"However," he interrupts, "Borealis is reserved for paying guests. You will be in Employee Hut Four. It has a small fenced area to the rear, which will contain your hound. And you will keep that beast contained or restrained at all times or I will demand your removal from the property. I have things to do. Tania will show you around when she gets back."

With that, he walks down the hall and disappears.

And that is how I find myself residing in one half of a school portable, being warmed by the sad wheeze of an electric fireplace and Eric's body heat. Thank heavens he's a spooner. I lie on the bed, cocooned in a blanket that smells vaguely like someone else and I can't decide if that's comforting or completely disgusting. I lean toward the latter.

Tania said the other half of the portable is being used for storage, but I swear I can hear scrabbling. Rats, raccoons, and larger, toothier things dance through my head.

"What have I done?" I ask Eric, but he's already snoring.

Chapter 5

Tania arrives at my door promptly at eight a.m., breath hanging in clouds in front of her in the chill of the morning. I have just enough time to cram a granola bar into my mouth and chug some tap water before we dive into the day, leaving Eric cozied up back in bed after breakfast and a quick trip outside.

In the warmth of the Big House, she produces a laptop, a three-ring binder labeled PROCESS and my very own Treetops polo shirt and name tag. I'm officially part of the team. Joy.

"Okey dokey, so Brooke is going to call in for a chat with you in about fifteen minutes, then we'll start on the facility overviews and nail down the details of your onboarding schedule!"

I am deposited in a small, bright meeting room on the second floor.

"The Wi-Fi can be a bit touchy, but if you log out and back in it should work! Probably."

"This is going to be great," I tell myself as the door closes behind Tania. I set my laptop on the table and connect to the Wi-Fi, then log into the meeting and await Brooke's arrival.

"They're excited to have you here. You're excited to be here. This is a reciprocal, productive journey that we are embarking on together. Teamwork makes the dream work. You can do this."

Pep talk complete, I'm pulling a notebook and pen out of my bag when a ding signals that someone else has signed into the meeting. Brooke is driving, phone mounted to her dash, and it sounds like she's in a wind tunnel. She hits a button to roll up the window as she takes a quick sip from her rose-gold travel mug, somehow avoiding leaving a ring behind despite her coral lips.

"Brooke, hello! So nice to see you again."

She looks at the camera as if startled to hear my voice.

"Oh, um." She rummages around blindly on the passenger seat, grabbing a crumpled piece of paper I recognize as my résumé and holds it against the steering wheel. She glances at it over the top of her sunglasses. "Kate, is it?"

"It is!"

"And you're the new Business Development hire?"

"Yes?" I hate the uncertainty creeping into my voice. The awkwardness of the reintroduction fuels my need to smooth it over. "It's breathtaking here. Are you planning to come out for some of the onboarding process? It would be great to do some deep dives into your vision for Treetops and discuss how that aligns with my ideas." I'm kind of surprised she isn't here right now.

"Me? God, no. I couldn't possibly. We'll have a regular cadence of video conferences and, of course, email and the like on an ongoing basis. I have no doubt that the team there will be able to give you a real 'boots on the ground' perspective of things." She does some more rummaging and produces a tube of lipstick, which she smooths over her lips, staring into the rearview mirror as she dabs them gently with a fingertip.

"Oh. Um, okay. Yeah, I'm sure that will be fine."

Finished with her touch-up, she looks into the camera, managing to fit a whole lot of judgment into a two-second glare, before turning her gaze back to the road. "So, Kate, we need to talk about your numbers. As you are no doubt aware, we currently have five guests in residence, which is far below our ideal. I'm going to need you to flesh out a plan to meet your contracted quota and submit a detailed roadmap so we can get ramped up."

"Of course—I have some ideas I'd love to run by you if you have time now. I think there's a whole demographic we can reach out to that we may have been overlooking."

She signals and changes lanes without looking. A horn blares. She doesn't even seem to register it, flicking her hair back over her shoulder. "No, thank you."

". . . No?"

"As mentioned, please email a complete proposal, targeting our ideal customer, by, ohhhh"—she waves a burgundy-nailed hand around vaguely, as if pulling a deadline from the air— "Friday? Tania can provide you with our ICP—that's Ideal Customer Profile—if she hasn't already."

"This Friday? Two days from now? I think if you could allow me a bit more time to get a solid understanding of Treetops' strengths, identify areas for improvement, and research competitors, I could provide a more insightful report with actionable suggestions."

Brooke waves her hand, batting away such a ludicrous idea.

"Treetops doesn't have any direct competitors, and, if anything, our weakness would be that we care too much about supporting our artists." It sounds like she's reading from a brochure. She screeches into a parking spot and checks her makeup again in a small mirror she pulls from her well-supplied bag, wiping away a fleck of mascara from beneath her eye. "The approved methods for sales and marketing efforts are outlined in the Process Manual. Treetops is built on tradition and proven paths to excellence. You will respect this tradition and follow those paths."

She detaches the phone from its mounting point and for a

moment all I can see is the ceiling of the car. It's beige leather with black piping. I hear the door open and Brooke's stern face is back, hair whipping around in strong fall wind.

"I'll look forward to reviewing that proposal by Friday. As per your contract, we'll need to see a minimum average of fourteen guests for the month of December. We'll reconnect next week." She punches a button and disappears, but not before I catch a glimpse of the sign behind her for La Mirage, one of the most exclusive health and well-being resorts in Toronto.

I am in an alternate universe. I am asleep. This is a dream. A nightmare. A hallucination. This is impossible. *What have I done?* I wonder yet again.

I sit there for a moment, staring out the window at the swaying trees and steeping in a deep sense of disbelief. Already feeling the inevitable failure starting its slow creep toward me, I sling my bag over my shoulder and pull the door open. I'm intent on getting back to Employee Hut Four to check on Eric and maybe, if time allows, have a small temper tantrum.

I rush through the door of the meeting room and run facefirst into a very solid chest. My nose mashes against a cleansmelling, pale blue button-down shirt. My carefully applied rose-tinted lip balm leaves a greasy pink smear beside the chest pocket.

"Oh God! I'm so sorry!" I propel myself backward far enough to see the owner of the shirt and firm pecs hidden within.

Dark chocolate eyes surrounded by lashes I would kill for move slowly between the maimed shirt and my appalled face. I can feel the burn of tears and am immediately annoyed and embarrassed, which just makes them flow faster.

"Hey, are you okay?" A large, warm hand lands on my arm. I suddenly feel ever so slightly better.

"Yeah. Yes. I'm fine. Just one of those days." I swipe the back of my hand across my cheek and glance at the hand still resting gently just above my elbow before looking back at those eyes, which are set above a very nice nose, which leads to . . . wow.

Two days of dark scruff tinged with red have my hand itching to reach out and caress his cheek. A jawline that could stop traffic if we had that here. He lowers his hand and extends it for a shake.

"Matt." His hand is smooth and warm. I hold it a moment too long. Awkward.

"Nice to meet you. I'm Kate, and I really am sorry about your shirt."

He looks down at his chest consideringly.

"You know, I think it adds a certain unique quality to an otherwise pretty standard garment."

"Well, then I'm sorry for assaulting you so early in the morning. I mean, at all. Assault isn't appropriate at any time of day. Or night for that matter. I'll stop now. Sorry." I'm backing away quickly, as if physical distance will cool the burn of mortification. I just need a bit of space to collect myself and I'll be fine.

"Have a great day! Enjoy your stay!" I'm speed-walking down the hall, calling over my shoulder. Except I'm going the wrong way.

I turn to see him still standing in the hall, arms crossed, leaning casually against the door of the conference room, observing with an amused half smile on his face. Taking a deep breath, I square my shoulders and retrace my steps, giving him a curt nod on the way past. He reciprocates with a tip of an imaginary cowboy hat and a slow smile.

After much wandering of hallways and hitting of dead ends framed by windows with incredibly picturesque views, I muddle my way back to the dining room. Tania is nowhere to be seen but I hear the murmur of voices coming from the kitchen. A low butcher-block counter and hanging pots and pans create a big-city-chic divide between the two spaces while still allowing diners to catch a glimpse of the action. Just behind one of the dangling copper pans, Tania is leaning up against the counter beside someone chopping carrots into precise matchsticks. The someone is quite handsome in a your-older-brother's-goofy-friend kind of way. Not traditionally good-looking, but project-ing that confidence so many women find irresistible.

"We can't just keep going like this, Jay. We have to do some-thing." Tania reaches out and grabs a piece of carrot, crunching into it with the most aggression I've seen her display to date.

Jay sighs. "We don't have to do anything. Let it play out, T. We don't owe them."

"How can you—" Tania cuts off as she sees me walking in.

"Sorry. I can come back."

"Oh no, it's fine. We were just talking about the dinner menu. The guests can be so finicky!" Her laugh is a bit breathy. She shrugs her shoulders a couple times, as if to physically shake off the conversation, and regroups.

"Kate, this is Jay Higgins, our head chef."

Jay raises his non-knife hand in greeting.

"How was your call with Brooke?" Tania asks.

"It was, um, interesting. She certainly knows what she wants." I'm very proud of my ability to filter. "Does the man-agement not spend much time here? Brooke was saying she's rarely on-site."

Jay has moved on to chopping cilantro, and the sound of the knife seems to get louder. He snorts but doesn't weigh in. Tania shoots a quick glare in his direction.

"The board feels they can most effectively contribute from a distance."

"But couldn't they get a better sense of what needs to be done if they had someone here? Or at least with regular visits?"

"The board has its head up its collective ass," says Jay, not looking up from his pile of herbs. "And they *do* have someone here."

Tania looks exasperated. "Anyway. Kate!" She claps her hands in what I've decided is her signature camp-counselor-style move. "I have here"—she produces a piece of paper from a folder with a flourish—"your official Treetops onboarding schedule for today!"

I feel like I'm supposed to be jumping up and down with excitement to match her enthusiasm. It's as if she just announced we're going to Disneyland. Or a bar. I take the paper and see what the day has in store.

"Wow. This is very, uh, thorough. This is one day? Not, maybe, the week?"

"Brooke wanted you to get a full understanding of what Treetops has to offer as quickly as possible. But the good news is, you can bring sweet Eric along with you on the outdoor excursions. And I'll be around most of the day if you think he needs some company. I'm happy to hang out with him whenever I can."

"That's really kind and much appreciated. Thank you. I actually wouldn't mind just running over to check on him before we kick off the next part of the day, if that's okay?"

"For sure! Take fifteen minutes and we can meet at the main entrance. I'll take you on the official tour."

I return to Employee Hut Four and find Eric engaged in a staring contest with a red squirrel perched on the exterior window ledge. His nose is pressed to the glass and a cloud of condensation puffs onto the surface with each exhalation. His tail wags as I walk in, but he's got more important things to do than greet his person. I let him out for a couple minutes of chipmunk patrol, make sure he has water and drop a treat into his bowl, promising to return for him shortly. It's nice to see at least one of us is embracing our new surroundings.

The next hour is a whirlwind as I learn about everything guests can do at Treetops when not producing creative output. They can relax in the spa grotto, the meditation chamber, or the fitness den. They can take a cooking class with Jay or a personal training session with Jurgen. Outputs aren't flowing like they used to? Consult a nutritionist, therapist, chiropractor, or a Reiki master (but only in the high season).

I learn that at peak occupancy, Treetops needs twenty

employees—a mix of maintenance, health and wellness professionals, and other "service specialists"—to operate efficiently. Most of those come in daily from town, but up to fifteen can stay on-site. Right now, in the low season ("The perfect time for rejuvenation of ourselves and the resort!" chirps Tania), there are seven resident employees and a smattering of additional "specialists" that come in as necessary. I start to think about what it will be like to be trapped here with the same six people for the winter, but quickly decide that can be a problem for Future Kate.

While each area of the Big House has a fancy name, there's a decidedly dated feel to it. I get the sense that things have been a bit slow revenue-wise for a while. Based on the faded moose-covered wallpaper border in the dining room, no one's splurged on upgrades since approximately 1998.

We emerge from one of the Focus Rooms where artists can spend their time in isolation, allowing the creative juices to flow without interference from the outside world. It's how I imagine a middle-management office at an insurance company would look. A beige-walled sensory-deprivation chamber with a painting of a loon to fancy things up. It's a distinct contrast to the welcoming, comfortable vibe of the Big House's common spaces, but when I mention it, Tania is quick to point out a bronze plaque: WHEN THE PAGE BEFORE US IS BLANK, WE ARE FORCED TO TURN OUR GAZE INWARD AND EXPLORE THE CREATIVE BOUNTY THERE.

"There's more to see but I think that's enough for now." Tania pauses and reluctantly pulls a piece of paper from the folder she's been toting around. She holds it out to me. "You can use this room for the quiz."

I am terrible at disguising my emotions, and my confused annoyance must be projecting loud and clear because poor Tania looks sorry that she's the one having this conversation. She tries to revive her earlier enthusiasm but from the uncharacteristic frown lines creasing her forehead, I get the sense it's a struggle.

"Don't think of it as a quiz, per se. It's more of a . . . um . . . reinforcing tool! To make sure you retain the information we've covered. You know, they say you need to review material something like seven times before it sticks?! So, consider this round two!"

I take the paper and look it over.

There's a spot on the page for a grade. "You're going to mark this?"

"Well, yes, but I'm sure you'll do a fantastic job! Okay! I'll just leave this timer here." I'm having flashbacks to university exams. She slides by me and sets what looks like a pocket-sized digital clock, or a small bomb, on the desk. She waits for me to sit down before pressing Start.

"I'll be back in twenty minutes. Good luck! Not that you need it!" She throws me a double thumbs-up before gently closing the door.

Question One: If a guest indicates they are experiencing a creative roadblock, which three services might you suggest? Provide detailed explanations for each choice, along with current pricing.

"Fuuuuuuuuuuuck," I groan, lowering my forehead onto the desk and lightly bouncing it off the shiny wooden surface. *Bonk. Bonk. Bonk.*

Tania opens the door a crack. "Everything okay in there?"

"Just peachy! Going great!" I call back cheerfully before grabbing my pen and diving in. "Fake it 'till you make it," I mutter.

Chapter 6

I don't know what the passing grade for the quiz is, but I must have inched past it because I'm allowed to continue the onboarding adventure without donning a papier-mâché dunce cap.

At ten thirty I grab Eric, layer on outerwear and head to the Gathering Fire. Lengths of rustic log benches are arranged in a hexagon, surrounded by seasonal flowers. At the center is a large, charcoal-darkened firepit.

The rest of my tour group is made up of a single guest: a pale kid in his early twenties who speaks directly into his woolly scarf and won't make eye contact. I ask his name, and he mumbles something that sounds like "Adam" at his toes.

I think things are shaping up to be pretty low-key, bordering on boring, until a gray-haired woman rolls in on a red banana-seat bicycle, smoking a cigarillo. She pulls up beside Adam and leans forward, arms dangling across the center of the handlebars as she takes a drag and surveys us.

A whiff of vanilla and tobacco slides toward me on the breeze.

"Let's do this thing," she says, twirling her finger in the air in the universal teenager-and-biker-club signal for "roll out." And so, we begin Exploring Art in Nature with our guide, Heidi.

She pedals at a walking pace up the driveway. Adam and I follow like dutiful ducklings. About halfway up the drive, out of sight of the main house, she pauses. I surreptitiously tug Eric away from her bike's rear tire as his back leg raises.

"I'm Heidi Jutland, ceramics artist and forty-nine-year resident of Otterburne. Apparently, I'm also your Girl Scout leader today on this wilderness adventure. I'm here because I'm paid to be. What about you?"

Adam and I exchange confused looks. He says something unintelligible.

"Are you speaking English? Or some idiotic form of hipster? Get that damned scarf off your face. It isn't February. Your nose isn't going to freeze off."

He obliges, tugging the fabric free, and repeats himself. "I said, do you mean, like, here, now, on this walk? Or like, here at the retreat?" He pauses. "Or, like, on Earth?"

I get the impression he's surprised at his own depth.

"Christ on a cracker. Why are you paying top dollar to spend time in the woods with me, instead of holing up in your bedroom to do The Work? What do you think this place is going to get you that you can't figure out on your own?"

He suddenly becomes very animated, mittened hands punctuating his speech.

"Dad wanted to send me to some kind of army camp, right? But my mom was all 'Oh no! Not my delicate child!' so we totally pulled one over on the old man. Told him this was a far north survival experience." He looks around, face falling a bit. "It's kind of lame though, isn't it? I was expecting more chicks." His eyes meet mine and open wider. "No offense, ma'am."

Ma'am? Jesus Christ. "But"—I hate myself before the next words even exit my mouth—"what's your output?" According to my brief scan of the Process Manual, there is a screening procedure in place. Perhaps a superficial one with a low, low bar for quality, but prospective guests are asked to provide a portfolio of work to show they can at least pretend to be artists for the duration of their stay.

"I make videos."

"What format?" asks Heidi. "Film shorts? Commercials?"

"YouTube."

"YouTube," she echoes.

"Yeah, it's this online platform where anyone can upload content—"

"I know what it is. I just hadn't realized we were considering cat videos an artform these days." She shakes her head woefully.

"Nah. I don't do cat videos. I'm going to go viral with celebrity sightings with a twist."

"A twist? What's the twist?"

"I don't try to talk to them." He looks at us expectantly.

"I don't get it," I say after a moment.

He leans closer, like we're being let in on a secret. "I get a video of them living their lives. It's like a nature documentary. Like when dudes hide out in the jungle to capture footage of rare animals. That's what makes it art—I'm not in it to, like, get acknowledgment from this upper echelon of society. I want to give the Everyman insight into their behaviors when they think they aren't being watched." His eyes are wide, head bobbing in excitement.

"Well, I'll be damned," muses Heidi. "It sounds like you're straddling a pretty muddy legal line, but that's what makes the best art. It's about the risk. Thinking out of the box. I like it."

"What about you?" she asks, turning to me.

I'm trying to wrap my head around the idea of stalking being art and it's a real struggle.

"Me? I'm actually the new Director of Business Development. Coincidentally, I am also being paid to be here!"

"Huh. Alright then. But the same question still applies. What are you hoping to find here that you can't at home?"

"The answer is still money."

"We're not going a step farther until you give a real answer. You might be responsible for the death of Scorsese over here if we don't get moving soon. He looks like he's going to turn into a human popsicle at any moment."

It's true. He's got his scarf wrapped back around the entire lower half of his face and he's stomping his feet to get the blood pumping.

"I want to be wildly successful in my field. I thought stepping outside my comfort zone by leaving the city was an interesting first step." Huh. Look at that. Great self-reflection, Self.

"Better, but still mediocre. Work on that." She stands up on her pedals to get some forward momentum, bumping across the uneven semi-frozen mud of the path before committing to a consistent pace.

She calls back over her shoulder. "Observe the fall colors. Inhale the scents layering the forest—lake water, decay, frost, moose shit. Consider that everything out here is dying even as it is born—including your best ideas. How are you going to nurture them long enough to make them reach some of their potential?"

I nod but start thinking about lunch before I've fully observed even one tree-worth of fall colors. I hope Chef Jay believes in feeding the creative spirit because I'm starving.

Eric is positively overjoyed to be out for a romp and as soon as we're clear of Treetops property I unclip his leash. He bounces circles around me before putting nose to ground and catching a whiff of some kind of novel woodland creature. He bounds into the tree line but stays in sight. Admittedly, being out and about, not feeling obligated to keep up a conversation, feels great. The morning clouds have started to disperse and rays of sun poke through the increasingly bare trees. I venture so far as to unzip the top quarter of my vest.

Heidi pedals slowly but steadily ahead of us, down a dirt path wide enough for an ATV, snowmobile, or particularly brave car to pass with the branches scraping its sides. She pauses every minute or so to point out wonders of the natural world.

"This mushroom will be consumed by something higher up the food chain any day now, but do you see it shrivelling? Is it giving up the ghost because its fate is inevitable? No! It's pushing through the leaves, displaying this crust of frost like goddamn armor." She surveys Adam and me, green eyes narrowing under the rolled edge of her beanie. "What does your armor look like?"

I stand there, staring blankly at the precocious little fungus, and picture myself charging into battle covered in empty, clinking wine bottles.

A sizable hill looms ahead and I vaguely wonder what will happen when we get to it. Will Heidi pedal up? Make us push her?

But then it doesn't matter because there's a bear.

Eric sprints out of the forest and beelines to me. Behind him lumbers a great black beast, two or three times Eric's svelte bulk. I freeze. Heidi and Adam have gotten a ways ahead. Do I yell? Will yelling make things worse? I vaguely recall reading somewhere that you're supposed to make yourself big and intimidating if confronted by a bear, but only if it's a specific kind. Brown or black. If it's the other color, you curl up on the ground like an unassuming rock. If you get it wrong you will almost certainly be eaten or severely mutilated. Shit.

By the time my brain wanders down this useless path of possibly totally fabricated wilderness safety skills, Eric has parked himself behind me, and Heidi and Adam have taken a moment to notice I'm not with them. The bear has ambled out of the trees and as it turns in our direction, I notice the giant pink tongue lolling out the side of its mouth. And the jangling of tags, presumably attached to a collar buried under its prolific fur.

"Delilah!" a man's voice hollers from down a path I hadn't

noticed, snaking into the trees through a patch of bare rasp-berry bushes.

I feel like an idiot. The fluffy black dog is clearly not an artist-eating bear. It looks pretty dopey, in an expensive, classy way. Overgrown Bouvier? Newfoundland dog? Whatever it is, it's quite grand. Eric's nose tentatively peeks past my leg. I think he might be feeling a tad sheepish too. His tail starts to wag.

"Delilah!" the voice calls again. I can hear feet crunching through the leaves. "You wretched beast, come back. You're going to get covered in burrs. You know she *hates* when you get messy. And who's going to have to deal with the temper tantrums? Certainly not you." The voice fades to an aggravated mutter with occasional well-enunciated swears. Delilah is pay-ing no mind, sniffing at a questionable puddle before taking a drink. When she raises her face, muddy strands of drool dangle from her lips. She looks very pleased.

By this point, Eric has decided he's miscalculated and the bear-dog is a great candidate to be his best bud. He's play-bowing in her direction, slowly making his way closer in fits and starts, with the occasional spin thrown in for good mea-sure. Playing it cool is not his specialty.

A man emerges from the shrubbery lining the path, dressed like half of my former colleagues at Regan-Caulfield. Gray toque, thick-framed rectangular glasses, a dark blue plaid flan-nel shirt topped with a soft denim jacket. Black slim-fit pants sagging over his butt in a fashionable way, like they haven't been washed in three months. Dark brown, chin-length hair drapes across his forehead and I wish I had a clip or subtle-yet-stylish hairband to offer. An expensive-looking camera dangles from a leather strap around his neck and a large duffel is slung over each shoulder, clinking as he moves. He looks harassed and I wonder if maybe his day is going even worse than mine.

Delilah continues to ignore poor Eric, who is now drop-ping sticks at her feet in a desperate attempt to buy her love. She traipses over and sits expectantly in front of the man, eyes trained on his jacket pocket. He blows out an exasperated breath.

"You get treats *when you come when you are called.* Not when *I* come to *you.* You know I despise your very being, don't you? You're supposed to be a professional." Her tail thumps on the ground. The guy cracks a smile, but just barely. I catch a glimpse of artificially bright white teeth beneath his scraggly attempt at a mustache. He looks at me, shrugs. "The handler couldn't make it this weekend. Said she'd be a perfect lady."

"Taylor!" someone shrieks from the woods. Not a panicked shriek. This is the shrill cry of entitlement. The guy takes a breath, holding it for a five-count before exhaling like he's blowing out a cake full of candles. He lets the duffels slide to the ground, wincing at the sound they make as they hit the rocky path.

"Over here, Christine. On the main path." He lowers his voice and adds, "In the depths of my purest hell."

A statuesque, model-level attractive human steps gingerly from the woods wearing what I guess you could call hiking boots, but with a stacked heel that adds four inches to her already ridiculously tall and lithe frame. This isn't normal. I look around, waiting for a film crew to pop out and yell *"Gotcha!"* The dogs circle each other, sniffing butts while they wait for their humans to make a move.

"Dammit, Taylor. Could you not wait for two minutes?" She takes a delicate sip from a pristine white travel mug, grimaces, and thrusts it at Taylor, barely waiting for his grip to tighten before stepping away and taking out her phone. He fumbles, trying to balance leash, dog treats, and the cup, but manages to make a full recovery. His relieved sigh is cut short by a new set of demands. "Call Renaldo. I need a massage. We'll post it and link to his page. He should comp the trip."

The woman's inky black hair is halfway down her back, cascading over a black leather jacket that looks like it costs as much as an entry-level sedan. Her makeup is, as the kids might say, on point. I am immediately jealous of her eyeliner skill, but also confused about why she's choosing to display it here, in the middle of the woods.

Her eyes scan our ragtag party. "Well, this is too fucking crowded. You said we'd get isolation here, Taylor." She marches toward him, closing the distance until a perfectly manicured, gold-tipped nail hovers an inch from his nose. "You promised a new level of art. My followers have expectations." She shudders, looking at our surroundings with disgust I'd save for a trip into the sewers.

"You know I loathe this place."

At that moment, the sun breaks through the clouds, allowing gentle rays to brush across her flawless skin. The accusing finger falls to her side, hand resting on her hip, hair blowing gently in the breeze.

"Hold!" Taylor cries, backing up a few steps to snap a series of quick shots. She shifts poses, her hand going from her hip to shoulder to running her fingers through her hair as she smiles warmly into the sun. I wait for a chickadee to land on her shoulder and sing to us. Instead, Delilah lies down at her feet, facing the sun so it picks up the traces of deep auburn in her fur. A brief gust of wind sends some perfect, fiery leaves floating down. A gentle sigh of appreciation escapes Heidi's lips. *Click. Click click click click.*

As soon as the camera lowers, the smile disappears and Christine backs away from the dog, brushing invisible fur from her leg.

"Let's go to the lake," she says in a nasal, sing-song voice. "Switch things up from the grit and harsh light of the city." She crosses her arms across her chest, somehow managing to scowl and pout simultaneously without creasing her forehead. Botox, or dark magic? "And this, this *thing*!" She juts her chin toward Delilah. "I hate it. Why is it even here?"

Taylor sighs the sigh of the put-upon employee. "I know it's hard for you, doll, but new sponsors demand new looks. They asked for something a bit less bitch— er, softer. More 'of the people.' And people have dogs." He lowers his voice, cutting an eye to their audience. We all pretend to be focused on the view of the lake through the trees. "Think of the money," he whispers.

"Okey dokey," says Heidi, elbowing Adam in the side to stop his gawking. "Let's let these nice people get on with their day." She puts her foot on a pedal, ready to move onward and, I assume, upward to the top of the mega-steep hill ahead.

I do some side-to-side stretching, limbering up, getting my hips ready to scale a veritable mountain. Eric, beside himself with the joy of being in the wilderness and making all these new friends, decides he can't hold back a moment longer. He launches himself at Delilah, yipping with delight as she turns. Unfortunately, she chooses that moment to engage and the two dogs take off, racing in circles around us. "Bend your knees!" I call to everyone, my city-dog-park habits holding hard.

Delilah hip-checks Eric and sends him flying into Christine, who does not have her knees bent for balance and protection. She falls butt-first into the only mud puddle in the vicinity.

"Are you fucking kidding me?"

"Ohmigod." I rush forward to help her. "I'm really, really sorry. Are you okay?" I extend a hand to help haul her up, but Taylor's already at her side, an arm around her waist, hoisting her to standing, and I retract my arm slowly, feeling like a schmuck.

"Yeah, I'm great," she says sarcastically, looking at her muddy jeans in disgust. "What the hell is wrong with you? You can't let your dog run around completely out of control!" I look at Delilah, confidently sniffing Eric's butt.

"They were just playing. If you want to nitpick, Delilah is the one that shoved him. She's quite a bit larger. He didn't stand a chance." I recognize this isn't helping but can't stop. "I am sorry though. What are the chances you'd fall in the only puddle on the whole trail? It's bad luck."

Is this how parents feel when there's a playground altercation? If so, I'm never procreating. My palms are sweating inside my mitts.

"Look, babe, I really, truly couldn't care less how sorry you might think you are."

Babe?

"Christine," Taylor says soothingly, "why don't we go and get you cleaned up? We can head over to the waterfall later and get some more shots." He tries to put a hand under her elbow to guide her away, but she rips herself from his gentle grasp with a glare.

"Shut up, Taylor," she snaps. She stomps a few steps, then turns and strikes a killer runway pose. "And you." She points at me and I half expect it to be followed by a threatening throat-slashing gesture. "Keep your fucking dog on a leash."

It must be hard to stride through Canadian Jumanji in heels. I'm surprised, and a little disappointed, she doesn't sprain an ankle.

Taylor clips on Delilah's leash, black leather that matches Christine's jacket, and is gone without a backward glance. So much for making friends.

"That was amazing!" Adam trills, phone in hand, sagging against a tree like he's just run a marathon or had excellent sex. I hope a bird poops on his head.

"Yeah, super good. I had a great time being verbally assaulted by wilderness Barbie."

He snorts. Friggin' teenagers.

"Do you know who that was?"

"Yeah, that was Taylor. And Delilah. And a woman with a very poor attitude."

"Oh God." He's cackling now, one arm supporting himself on the tree as he doubles over. "You just"—*gasp*—"shoved"—

guffaw—"Christine Morrow *into a mud puddle*." He's sitting on the ground now, hopefully getting a soggy rear end.

I stare at him, arms crossed. "Yeah, except that wasn't my fault. And it was a terrible experience for everyone." I point to Heidi, who's leaned her bike against a tree and is lighting up something that smells much more herbal than a cigarillo. "Look, poor Heidi has to self-medicate to calm herself."

The sweet smell of weed rolls toward me and I inhale more deeply than is strictly necessary. She holds out the joint in my direction and I politely decline because I am a responsible business professional. Heidi shrugs.

Adam stares at me. "You don't know who she is."

"I do. Christine."

"Oh man. This is amazing." He starts pacing back and forth, phone held up to the sky in an attempt to get some sliver of a signal. "Gahhh. No internet. In this day and age. How is that even possible?"

"Trees. Signal obfuscation. Satellite coverage holes. I don't know. Does it matter?" I try to remind myself that he's a guest and I should maintain some measure of politeness, even if I want to smush his face into a pile of moldering leaves.

"It does. Because if we had internet, I could show you that Christine mother-effing Morrow is like, *the* influencer. Or was, at least." He lowers his voice, I assume in case she's still in the vicinity and comes back to cut his tongue out with her talon-like nails.

"I don't care if she's the freaking Queen of the Mooses. Moose? Meese? Whatever. I did not appreciate her reaction to that situation and would like to move on with my day."

"Yeah, okay, but you should probably know—"

I hold up my hand signaling he should stop. "Moving on with my day."

"But—"

"I appreciate your concern, but I'm good. Let's continue,

Heidi, if you would." I roll my hand in a *proceed* gesture and wait to be instructed.

Adam shrugs, slipping his phone back into his pocket. "Your funeral," he says under his breath, but still very clearly.

God, I hate youths. And people in general.

Heidi blows out a cloud of smoke. "That concludes today's session of Exploring Art in Nature. Please feel free to fill out a comment card conveniently located at the check-in counter. Check ya later, City Slicker." Clambering onto her banana seat, Heidi looks at me. "That woman may be a grade-A bitch, but she's got passion. You should work on that. Passion is always better than being a limp dishrag when it comes to your true purpose."

She sets off back toward Treetops trailing fragrant smoke in her wake. Adam lifts his phone to the sky again. "Gonna search for a signal," he says, walking down the path toward the actual paved road that goes into town.

"Don't get mauled by bears!" I call after him. "You can't sue us if you do." Pretty sure, anyways. Act of God, et cetera.

Eric has tuckered himself out and sits beside me on the path. He has his ears perked, listening to the sound of birds singing and small forest animals scurrying through the undergrowth. He looks entirely relaxed and deeply pleased with his life circumstances.

"Well, I guess that's something," I say to myself before giving him a pat on the head and meandering toward what I hope will be a substantial lunch with an aggressively caffeinated accompaniment.

I end up with a whole wheat wrap full of "superfoods" and seriously lacking in delicious condiments of any kind.

Jay looks wounded when I ask for some mayo. "There's a light olive oil and balsamic vinaigrette massaged into the kale twenty-four hours in advance to tenderize the leaves."

It seems that part of my "fully immersive experience" is not eating the same food as the guests, who are chowing down on steaming bowls of sweet potato and squash soup with a side of house-made bread and hand-whipped butter.

"Whose hand does the whipping?" I ask after reading the menu. No one answers. I presume this is outsourced.

My health food and I head back to Employee Hut Four. I gift Eric the dry ends of the wrap. He doesn't refuse them, but he's also not overly impressed with my offering. I wonder if it would be out of line to send Janet in HR a recommendation that new employees should be advised to bring their own full-fat mayonnaise, in addition to equipment fit for a polar expedition.

Eric's positioned himself on a green shag mat by the sliding patio door, guarding against any ingress by chipmunks. I decide to take a moment to sit with him in a puddle of warm sunlight, trying not to consider how many bare feet have traversed this mat before me. The shag is more comfortable than it looks.

Chapter 7

I'm twenty minutes late for the Artist Update Presentations. I woke up on the mat with dog hair in my mouth and my heart hammering against my rib cage as I realized I'd messed up. Again.

Eric is deposited happily with Tania as she winterizes a garden bed at the side of the property. She hefts bags of mulch like someone three times her size. I make a mental note to start working out.

I race back to the Big House and jog up and down hallways on tiptoe until I find the Georgian Room, where the five guests currently staying with us are providing details of their progress. They present to the Artists in Residence, who act as their mentors, along with anyone else who is interested in hearing what they've been up to. Like, say, the newest employee, who needs to gain a deep understanding of what makes these people tick and, more critically, why they spent so much money to be here.

I crack the door open intending to sneak in as quietly as possible, but some idiot has arranged the room so the door is positioned directly behind the person presenting. I arrive immediately at center stage and give an awkward half wave before scuttling to the side and grabbing a seat near the back.

"They did it on purpose," a deep voice whispers in my ear. It's the guy from the hallway. Matt. My eyes fly to his chest and see the greasy pink smear from my lips. I blush hotly. It seems so intimate, his minty breath fluttering my hair, an outline of my lips on his chest. My heart starts beating much faster than is appropriate. I reach down to pull a notepad and pen from my bag, taking some calming breaths in the process.

"They made it as awkward as possible to be late because"— his voice takes on the timbre of a self-help tape, rumbly and soothing—"*you are here for the art. By keeping it waiting, you are only denying the very thing you seek to nurture.*"

Despite the corner of his, really very nice, mouth turning upwards ever so slightly, I can't tell if he's being serious. "It's effective," I whisper back. I give him a polite smile and try to ignore the heat of his bicep against my shoulder. A guest, I remind myself. A temporary distraction. Part of my brain briefly pursues a fantasy where we reconnect in the future and become embroiled in a passionate affair. I give a mental salute of farewell to that dream, shoving it aside to focus on work.

At the front of the room a middle-aged, suit-clad guy is pacing back and forth in front of a wall-size photo of what appears to be a pile of coins. His forehead is wrinkled as he listens to feedback from the gallery.

A woman with dyed bright red hair bundled on top of her head taps her lower lip thoughtfully. "Gord, it's a beautiful start. You've nailed the harsh emotion of the Great Depression, with a glint of hope for the future. But I wonder, could you do more?"

"More. You want me to do *more*, Clarissa? The emotional sacrifice this subject demands is killing me. *Literally.* I can feel the malignancy growing inside me each and every day that this piece is not completed."

Now that he mentions it, he does look a little gray. I look at Matt and whisper, "Are we allowed to ask questions?" He gestures his arm forward in invitation. I can't help but notice his forearms, sticking out from the rolled-up sleeves of his shirt. They're muscular, tanned, and covered in golden hair that catches the dim light. His fingers are also long and beautiful and it's hard not to think about how they would feel against my skin. *Whoa. Rein it in, Rigsby.* I give my head a little shake and raise my hand.

"Um, yes. You there," says Gord, pointing to me.

"Hello, Gord. I'm Kate Rigsby. Your work seems very passionate, yet well planned. Is it part of a larger project?"

I can feel, if not hear, the collective groan from the audience as Gord launches into a detailed lecture about the construct of society and how he is capturing the essence of corporate greed and its inevitable, if temporary, downfall. The medium is vintage American coinage and hot glue, and he expects this to be a seven-piece series—one for each of the deadly sins. Based on Clarissa's dramatic jaw drop, this is an unexpected twist.

Eventually, Gord sits down and we're treated to updates from three more guests. It seems I missed the first one entirely. I do not ask any more questions.

"Matt, would you like to begin today's supplementary content?" red-haired Clarissa calls from the front.

I hear him let out a gentle sigh before standing and moving to center stage.

"Good afternoon, everyone. For those of you who don't know me, my name is Matthew Reid. I've been a visual arts mentor at Treetops for two years now.

"Today we're going to delve into the concept of heat, and how we can bring burning passion to the visible forefront of our work."

Of course, not a guest. My head tilts slightly to the side as I take in the full view, now definitely mourning the loss of any future potential. I have a longstanding "no dating coworkers" rule, but man, it's a hard one to self-enforce right now. Long legs, those strong arms, and—I try not to groan as he reaches up to point at something at the top of the screen and a hint of stomach peeks out from under the hem of his shirt. Someone to my left doesn't have such self-control. I sneak a glance and catch Audra, one of the guests, hand resting on her chin, staring at him like a lioness presented with a hunk of raw meat. I'm surprised a puddle of drool isn't forming on the floor in front of her.

The session concludes with a Moment of Centering where Clarissa encourages us to reach deep into our core and "check in with our purpose." I disregard this advice and sneak a sideways glance at Matt, who has settled back into his seat. He's looking at me and winks. My stomach flutters. This is ridiculous.

As soon as we're done centering ourselves, I stuff my notepad back into my bag and hightail it to meet Tania for a tour of my office. I've been looking forward to this all day.

"Hey, Tania," I say with all the casualness of an infatuated ninth grader. "What's the deal with Matt?"

"Matt? He's not super social with the team, but a nice guy." She shoots me a look from the corner of her eye. "Why?"

I rummage through my bag to avoid making eye contact. "Oh, no real reason. I just keep running into him and he seems . . . nice."

"Nice?"

"Yeah. Nice. Friendly." I don't understand why this is so difficult. "I was just wondering if he's, uh, nice to all the new employees." Gah. There needs to be a better way to ask, *Is your coworker known for his promiscuous ways?*

"Matt is, um, professional?" Tania steers us along a hall toward a staircase leading down.

"Oh, great," I say with an enthused nod. "Ditto. Always professional."

"You know," Tania adds thoughtfully, "he asked me about you too. He's never done that before."

Oh *really*?

We head down the creaking stairs and I brace myself for the big reveal.

My office is in the furnace room. There's a door leading outside, which would be a nice feature (the only nice feature) if it wasn't also funneling a frigid draft directly onto my desk with enough gusto to rustle the notepad resting there. Someone has erected a ten-foot square of drywall and installed exactly enough pot lights to make it appear as though I am not in a bunker should I have the need to video conference. But I am in a bunker.

"Is this some kind of hazing ritual?"

Tania shifts nervously from foot to foot. I feel bad for making her uncomfortable. This isn't her fault. I try again.

"I mean, I guess this is the safest spot to be if a tree falls onto the building. So that's great."

"Yes! Absolutely. And in the case of a tornado as well!"

"Do you see a lot of those here?"

"I, personally, haven't experienced one, no. But global warming is changing things. Maybe we'll get more!"

You know things aren't going well when you're hoping for more tornadoes.

Tania takes me on a tour of my desk, which features a ten-year-old desktop computer that looks like it came from a garage sale. A peeling *Simpsons* sticker adhered to the side of the monitor suggests I CHILL OUT, DUDE. Solid tip.

"I'll leave you to it then! If you need anything, Kevin's office is just up the stairs and down the hall. I'm heading into town for a meeting but should be back in a couple hours. See you later!" She flits out the door.

The sage-green office chair might have been new when I was in high school. It doesn't immediately break when I lower myself into it, which I take as a good sign.

I log on to the computer and feel an unreasonable sense of relief when the Google homepage loads. I'm about to take a few moments to catch up on my personal emails when a warning appears.

> *Valued Employee,*
> *Treetops reserves the right to monitor all activity*
> *that takes place over the company-provided internet*
> *connection. This includes, but is not limited to, lists of*
> *websites visited and individual keystrokes.*
> *Thank you for your understanding and responsible use*
> *of this perk.*

That can't be true. Or it might be true, but who has the time to look at those records? It must be a bluff. Right? My fingers still hesitate before moving over the keyboard to compose an email to my parents.

> *Hi guys!*
> *Got here safely and am going through a super*
> *thorough onboarding process.*
> *Eric is settling in like a champ and making new*
> *friends. He is, of course, on his best behavior, as you*
> *would expect from him on any given day. He is a very*
> *good dog.*
> *Love,*
> *Kate*

After hitting Send I manage to control my willpower for all of four seconds before I'm asking the Google gods about Christine Morrow. First stop, images, so I can prove Adam wrong. I mean, come on. What are the chances of a) a celebrity being in Canada; b) a celebrity being in Canada in winter(ish); and c) my dog cavorting with that celebrity's dog resulting in catastrophe and an instant feud? Zero. I click on the first thumbnail, featuring a smoldering brunette in eveningwear lounging on the sidewalk outside a decrepit red brick building. The chances are ze— Shit. It seems the chances are at least slightly more than zero, because I'd recognize that look of disdain anywhere.

I go back and scroll through the top results:

Morrow—Banished to the Wilds? *Click*.

If the sun is going to come out, it won't be to-Morrow for this bad girl of the runway.

"Christine has been banished," a source close to the fashionista turned social media superstar tells us. "No one wants to work with her until she figures out how to treat people like, well, people instead of . . . you know. Poop."

A statement from Holden McNab, Morrow's agent (her sixth in the last three years, by our count), gives a different story. "Christine invested in a luxurious, isolated property years ago and has been so in demand that she's barely visited. She is taking some time there now to connect with herself, with nature, and with the inspiration that drove her to social media in the first place. She will emerge more centered and fiercely beautiful than ever before."

BigTimeCeleb.com wishes Ms. Morrow well and hopes she emerges soon. The gossip world just isn't the same without her.

Ditto, BigTimeCeleb. If she's out traumatizing the rest of the world, at least *I* don't have to worry about her.

I spend an hour flipping through the Process Manual. Most of it leaves me befuddled, though I do take special note of the section banning inter-employee relationships. Not that I care. Totally not applicable.

When the sun goes down my office becomes a cold cellar. I turn off the lights, wondering if I can score a space heater somewhere, and head up to the staff room to find some food.

Dinner ends up being the best part of my never-ending day because it turns out no one expects us all to sit down together as a group. Also, the food has taken a decided turn for the better, and the scent of spices and butter wraps around me like a hug. Chef Jay provides a staff buffet with little steel takeout tins you can fill and take back to your sweet employee digs, or home with you in the case of people who come in daily. I pile coconut rice and pineapple curry to the brim of my tin and balance a tiny cup of vanilla cardamom pudding on the lid.

The pudding is starting a precarious slide toward the floor as I attempt to hold my food, keep my bag on my shoulder, and pull the door open at the same time. My foot catches the door as it starts to swing closed and I execute what should have been a flawless kick to fling it back the other way. Except that Kevin chooses that critical second to apparate in front of me.

"No," he says sternly, pointing at me like he wants to add a *bad dog!* "I've just had these doors refinished. The Hawaiian beeswax and hibiscus oil can take up to three months to properly cure. If you mar it . . ." He sucks air in between clenched teeth, his dark, lustrous mustache quivers.

Setting my bounty down on a convenient table, I pluck a napkin from a stack, put it over the pudding, and stuff the cup into my coat pocket praying it will stay mostly upright.

With possibly slightly exaggerated care, I pull my sleeve down to cover my hand and use the soft surface to pull the door handle. I give Kevin a jaunty wave as the door closes behind me.

"Have a great night!" I call.

He stands motionless, a disapproving statue guarding the fortress of pristine artistic integrity, until the door is fully shut. There's a loud *click*. Kevin has locked me out.

Soft light glows behind the curtains of Employee Hut Four and I can see Eric's nose pressed up against the glass, his eyes covered by the faded fabric. We have a joyful reunion and I let him out into our yard. It features a patio just large enough for a folding lawn chair, a tiny table holding an overflowing ashtray, and a patch of brown grass the size of a picnic table. After three years in a six-hundred-square-foot apartment, he finds this to be akin to his dedicated dog park. You know, with the added bonus of the endless wilderness on the other side of the bright orange snow fence. It's a shame the job itself is a complete shit show.

My overflowing suitcase has spewed its contents onto the floor between the living space and what could loosely be labeled the kitchen but is actually a chipped three feet of countertop that holds a microwave and kettle, with a mini-fridge tucked underneath. I try to channel Tania, clapping my hands camp-counselor style. "Okay! Let's do this! Unpack. Settle in. Sanitize. Make this house a home!"

Fifteen minutes later I'm curled up in bed watching pre-downloaded episodes of a Hollywood real estate show. "For inspiration," I explain to a dozing Eric. I try not to think about how often I justify my choices to my dog.

By nine o'clock my eyes won't stay open. I set an alarm for six thirty, switch off the light, and am instantly asleep.

Chapter 8

It's still dark when my alarm blasts me into wakefulness. I imagine for a moment that I am on a strange vacation and not meandering, spruce-lined path to bankruptcy and a life spent sleeping on Roslyn's couch.

Dragging myself out of bed with the comforter wrapped around me like a giant floral burrito, I scrounge for food. The side pocket of my purse yields a granola bar that expired only three months ago. There's a single packet of instant coffee that some kind soul left behind when they cleared out. While it doesn't taste anything like actual coffee, it does provide enough of a boost to get me showered and out the door.

I'd decided that I should try to maintain Eric's schedule as much as possible as he settles in, so we start our day with a walk.

Despite the hour, there are a couple people out and about, and I give a wave as I pass. A short, slight man clad in the type of coveralls I associate with mechanics is walking toward the tree line that separates the employee housing from the main resort area. He carries a chainsaw casually in one hand. Orange safety goggles are perched on his salt-and-pepper hair. He changes trajectories when he sees Eric and veers toward us.

Eric can sense a potential belly rub a mile away and meets him halfway, practically throwing himself onto his back in the grass while maintaining a full-body wiggle of joy. The man's face lights up as he puts the chainsaw on a nearby bench and crouches down.

"You must be Eric," he says. "You are clearly a good boy. Oh yes you are!" Eric is mad with delight at this point, his tail thumping the ground with abandon. The man clears his throat and looks at me a bit sheepishly as he stands.

"Mike. I'm the groundskeeper. You must be Kate."

I try to hide my amusement as we shake.

"I am, and I see you're already familiar with Eric."

"Oh yes, he's the talk of the town. Well, Tania is pleased to have him around at least. She spoke highly of him."

Eric sits beside Mike, leaning heavily against his leg, and is rewarded with additional strokes on the top of his curly head. His tongue lolls out the side of his mouth.

"I believe he feels similarly about Tania. Unfortunately, not everyone here seems to be a dog person." I look around, hoping Kevin isn't watching Eric peel himself away from Mike to pee on the bronze inspirational plaque just outside the Gathering Fire (WE LIVE. WE BREATHE. WE CREATE AS WE BREATHE, AND, THUS, WE LIVE. —GRAHAM SUTHERLAND, FOUNDER).

We stand there for an awkward moment before giving up on further conversation.

"It was great to meet you!" I say, starting back toward the driveway. "Good luck with, uh, groundskeeping today."

He turns to his chainsaw with a casual wave thrown back over his shoulder.

My stomach is growling again by the time we get back. Eric looks morose as I say goodbye, but settles onto the mat by the back door and takes up his morning guarding duties.

Staff breakfast is available from six thirty to nine each morning and is, as I understand it, a come-and-go-as-you-please kind of setup. Imagine my surprise when I open the door at 8:05 to a panel of faces projected onto the wall. The tables have been pushed to the side and two rows of chairs spread across the room. Fifteen employees in Treetops green polos balance breakfast on their laps. There is one empty seat, front and center.

"Oh, come on," I mutter. Plastering a smile on my face I scurry to the chair and desperately eye the buffet off to the side. The smell of pancakes wafts into my face from my neighbor's plate.

The giant head currently speaking to us belongs to a man old enough to have a generous smattering of wrinkles and pure white hair. His well-groomed beard matches perfectly. He reminds me of a slightly stern, business-minded Santa Claus. Professor Claus.

"And that is why it is absolutely vital we maintain strict adherence to the doctrines that have brought us so much success, not only monetarily, but in a much more valuable currency—" He cuts off and stares at his audience expectantly.

"Output," the room says back.

He beams. The internet connection stutters, freezing him in place. Someone coughs. A spoon clinks against a mug. I'm starting to wonder if I should offer to reset the modem or something when, suddenly, he's back.

"No questions then? Okay. Then I would like to invite Brooke to take back the proverbial reins of the meeting. I believe she has a new initiative to announce."

"Thank you, Graham. As usual, your remarks were spot-on. It is always such a pleasure to have our Founding Father join us for inspiration and guidance." Her tone indicates she takes zero pleasure in his participation.

"Very kind, Brooke. Let's remember though, I may have built Treetops from the ground up—not literally, of course, I hired skilled labor. Ha ha. And I may be Chairman of the Board, but the magic that happens there every single day has very little to do with me anymore. All of you"—he points a large finger at the camera—"are the lifeblood that keeps our artists coming back for more." He starts clapping and doesn't stop until we all join in.

"Mm-hmm. Excellent." Brooke uses her notebook like a judge's gavel, banging the edge onto her desk. "I would like to share the details of an exciting new program I've developed called Observe and Report. OAR for short."

"Very clever, Brooke!" inserts Graham.

She gives a tight smile. "Thank you. Now, OAR will provide a mechanism for employee-centric feedback that will allow for rapid improvement, growth, and personal development. I know, that sounds like a big promise for such a little acronym."

She gets a polite twitter of laughter but most people look, if not concerned, not particularly excited to hear more.

"OAR's core principle is that it can be difficult to recognize areas requiring improvement within oneself. Therefore, OAR encourages frequent candid commentary about the work being done at Treetops. Moving forward, each employee will be required to submit no less than two OARs per month."

Someone near the front of the room raises their hand.

"Yes, you there." Brooke gestures vaguely at the room. "What is it?"

"Can you provide an example of what you would consider an appropriate and useful submission?"

"Absolutely." She shares her screen and a template appears.

"If I were to submit an OAR today, I would fill out the date, time, and location fields you see here." She begins typing.

"Verbally would be fine, Brooke, if that's easier."

"I think the example will have more staying power if you can experience it fully. As you can see, I've selected today's date, 8:05 a.m., and Staff Dining Hall."

A sense of unease starts to build in my stomach.

"You'll note there's a field here for additional situational details. In this case, I could add something like 'quarterly town hall meeting.' Now comes the part that I believe we will find most beneficial."

She begins to fill in the Employee Name section. *K.* Okay, okay, probably Kevin. *A.* Not Kevin. Really? REALLY?

> **Employee Name:** *Kate Rigsby*
> **Observation:** *New employee, Kate, was observed arriving 25 minutes late to a business-critical meeting.*
> **Takeaways:** *Though likely not intentional, this gives the impression that Kate does not value the business she is here to help grow. One might assume this employee is, at best, disorganized, and at worst, showing a flagrant disregard for her obligations.*
> **Suggested Area(s) of Focus:** *Time management, professionalism*

Beside me, Tania gives me a deeply apologetic look. As I glance around in disbelief, Heidi shoots a subtle thumbs-up my way. Everyone else faces front and center but I'm pretty certain Kevin, standing near the buffet, is smiling into his tea.

"I'm sure you can all see the value in OARs. After being reviewed at Head Office, the report will be sent on to the person mentioned therein. Of course, the identity of the individual sharing the infor—"

"Snitch," someone coughs. Brooke seems to glare at the corner where Jay and Matt are sitting but can't pinpoint the offender.

"The individual sharing the information will be kept anonymous unless there are extenuating circumstances."

She glances at her watch. Light glints off diamonds as her wrist rotates.

"That's all for today. Thank you for sharing this time with us and I look forward to continuing our journey on the path of excellence together."

The screen goes black. I see red.

As people start to file out, the gentle hum of casual chatter fills the room. I'm glued to my chair by rage and injustice.

Tania rushes to my side and words pour from her mouth in an apology waterfall.

"Ohmigod this is all my fault I'm so sorry I can't believe I forgot to tell you about the town hall I am the worst I'm so so so so sorry that was so terrible." She looks like she might cry.

Now I feel bad that she feels bad about playing an indirect role in my public humiliation.

"It's fine. I'm not mad at you. But this," I say, gesturing to the building around us, "this is bullshit."

Tania looks around wide-eyed, apparently concerned someone might be in range of my potty mouth.

"Bull. Shit." I enunciate. I think through my options briefly before asking, "Can you give me a ride back to my car? I'm done. This place is insane."

"No, Kate, please. Please reconsider. Brooke was—" She glances around and lowers her voice to a whisper. "Brooke was way out of line to single you out like that. No one here is going to take that seriously. They probably won't even remember it past lunchtime."

"You realize you're all part of some strange cult, right? Or maybe you can't see it because you're living it, but this is like upside-down world. Nothing makes sense."

Jay pauses on his way back to the kitchen. "Don't worry about any of that. It's typical Brooke craziness. We've all been through it." He looks at Tania. "Are we still good for tonight?"

Bright pink spreads across her freckled cheeks as she nods. I look back and forth between them and almost smile. Then I remember I am enraged.

"Why am I even here? As far as I can tell, no one *wants* new business. Treetops has been relying on the same block of a couple hundred repeat visitors for years. The only growth has been when they directly refer people. I don't even need to be here."

Tania opens her mouth to respond, but I cut her off. I'm on a roll.

"I refuse to suffer through any more public indignities! I am a human, Tania. I may not be a great artist. My *output*"—I sneer the word—"is very likely mediocre. But you can't just hire someone to do a job, give them two days—No! Not even two days! One and one-eighth days—to prove themselves! And a root cellar for an office! This was supposed to be an interesting, lucrative adventure, and It. Is. Not." I stomp my foot for emphasis.

"Oh, is life here not everything you were hoping for?" asks a smooth voice behind me. Kevin sidles up, a fragrant mug of herbal tea steaming in his hand. "We're just a bunch of kooky artists, right?" He waggles the fingers on his free hand. "How hard could this be?"

I resist the urge to kick him in the shin and run away.

"You're just like the rest of them—these so-called business people. You show up here unqualified, unmotivated, and looking for a hilarious anecdote to share with the gals back home. No wonder you all fail."

"You don't know me." Jesus. I'm fifteen again.

"Thank heavens for that," he says, walking away.

Despite my desperate pleas for my body not to betray me, I can feel the heat of imminent tears as I stare at Tania, making sure she's as appalled by my treatment as I am. Since it's Tania, of course she is.

Suddenly I am very tired.

"I'm going to pack. It shouldn't take long."

She starts to interrupt but I hold up a hand to stop her.

"I'd appreciate a ride into town, but I understand if you don't have time. I can figure something else out. Thanks for all your help over the past couple of days. And you're right, fall here is gorgeous. It's a shame about the people."

I sling my bag over my shoulder and walk slowly out of the

building and down the paved path toward Employee Hut Four. The morning is overcast and a dense fog hovers over the lake, but every so often a sliver of sunlight breaks through the clouds and lands like a spotlight on some beautiful natural feature. A tree with golden leaves falling like giant snowflakes. A red squirrel aggressively chattering at Audra as she makes her way to breakfast. A body on the dock.

I stop dead, no pun intended, and blink hard. *It's been a stressful morning*, I tell myself. I'm probably seeing things. More likely than not it's someone out tanning . . . in November. In a wetsuit.

My heart starts to race. I drop my bag on the ground and sprint across the lawn to the dock. I leap with shocking athleticism over the benches surrounding the Gathering Fire instead of taking the time to go around. Skidding along the damp wood of the dock, I slow as I get closer. It's a man, that much I can tell. He's wearing a scuba suit, complete with flippers and goggles with a snorkel attached. Water is pooled around him. His lower face is covered by a ginger beard that looks vaguely familiar. His skin is like marble. He isn't breathing. A harpoon is sticking out of his chest.

"Ohmigod. Ohmigod." I look around but no one is in sight.

"Help!" I yell. "Someone! Help!"

I stand up and turn to run to the Big House but trip on a coil of rope. My arms windmill as I fall backward into the waist-deep water. The cold takes my breath away. It feels like I landed in a pit of knives. Knives made of ice. I get myself upright and am wiping silt and hair out of my eyes, trying to figure out the shortest route to dry land, when someone says, "Hey, are you okay? Give me your hand." I start to reach out, and then freeze as my vision clears. It's the dead guy. He's leaning off the side of the dock, harpoon bobbing as he tries to get closer without falling in himself. I back away as fast as I can, but end up losing my balance and falling again.

"Listen, I'm sorry, okay? But you gotta get out of there. You're going to get hypothermia."

I run both hands over my face and look around. Belatedly, I see a video camera and tripod set up on the beach, red light blinking, pointing right at us. I stare at him. "Seriously? SERIOUSLY? What IS this place?" I let out a strangled scream of frustration and allow myself a couple seconds of aggressive splashing and kicking at the water, then I grudgingly accept his help and we work together to haul my soaking, shaking body out of the lake. He grabs a blanket from a backpack and as he wraps it around my shoulders I realize where I've seen him. He's the artist whose presentation I missed at the Artist Update session. His photo was on the screen ever so briefly. Heinrich the Performer.

"You gotta get inside and get warm. Come on." He hoists me to my feet.

We start walking back to land and I see people running across the lawn toward us. I sigh. Sure. Why not enjoy just a bit more embarrassment before I go.

"I gotta say, that was great. My expectations for today weren't high. Creative energy is running a bit low, you know? Dying every day sucks something real out of you. But man, you made 297 one for the books. Thank you." He sounds like he means it.

"You're w-w-welcome, I g-g-guess," I chatter, just before I'm engulfed in a crowd of concerned faces.

In no time at all, I'm nestled in a duvet in front of a roaring fire in a guest room. I'm nursing a giant mug of tea laced with brandy. It is disgusting but very thoughtful. Every fifteen minutes someone pops their head in to make sure I haven't kicked the bucket.

Heinrich, it turns out, is working on a long-term performance piece entitled *The 365 Deaths of Heinrich the Performer*. He's been dying for the camera every day for the past 297 and arrived at Treetops two weeks earlier for a change of scenery and inspiration. Everyone's so used to it now that they don't even notice. New guests are given a heads-up and invited to observe the proceedings. No one thought to tell me.

I'm about to doze off when there's a gentle tap on the door. I turn, expecting Tania for the fifth time. "I'm good, really. You can stop fussing. I'm not going to sue."

"You might consider it, but I think your employment contract has some strict liability limitations," says someone who is definitely not Tania.

Matt slides in and closes the door behind him.

"Oh, hi," I say awkwardly. My hair is wrapped in a towel and I'm cocooned in a Treetops green triple-layer organic bamboo robe that I'm one hundred percent taking with me. It's substantial but makes me ultra-aware that I have nothing on underneath. Last time I looked in the mirror my lips were still gray.

"You know it's not really the right time of year for swimming," he says as he perches on the edge of the bed.

"Yeah, I had no idea. Life lesson, I guess. God, this is embarrassing." I bury my face in my hands.

He gently peels my fingers away, and when I raise my eyes from my lap, his face is very, very close to mine.

"This may not be your best day, but it does not define you. It does not define what you're capable of." His breath smells like chocolate mint Girl Scout cookies. His pores are tiny.

"That's a great line. You must get a lot of use out of it."

An easy smile spreads across his face. His teeth are unnaturally straight. He sprawls backward, half lying down, propped up on his elbows. His chest strains at the buttons of his shirt and I can't help but wonder what he'd look like without it.

"Yeah, people love that one. It's not total BS, though, you know. One bad day doesn't warrant a suicide attempt."

"It wasn't a—oh, you're joking." I consider for a moment. "But it would have added a real dramatic twist to Heinrich's footage."

Matt lets out a hoot of a laugh and sits upright. "You clearly have all your faculties about you and don't need me hovering here." He stands to go and I'm way too disappointed about it. He stops with one hand on the doorknob.

"Have dinner with me tonight."

It's tempting, especially after the glimpse of perky denim-clad butt I caught as he walked to the door. But it also seems suspicious.

"Why are you being so nice? You barely know me."

He shrugs. "I know starting a new job is hard and you're having a rough couple of days. I know you were kind to Gord today." His head tilts and he looks at me consideringly. I have to stop myself from shifting around or straight up hiding under the blanket. "I know you're adorable when you're flustered," he continues. "And I'd very much like to know more."

"I'm leaving," I blurt. "This afternoon, I mean. I'm going back to Toronto."

He leans back against the door and crosses his arms over his chest. "You just got here."

"Yeah, it's not a great fit. It's better to go now than drag out the misery."

"Is it so bad?"

I stare at him in disbelief. "Were you not at the meeting this morning? I'm Kate Rigsby, receiver of the inaugural OAR. Kate Rigsby, worm in Kevin's culture apple. Kate Rigsby, professional clown."

"I'd argue your clown skills are a bit below professional grade. We've had pro clowns here before. You're not them."

"What I am, is done. I'll head back to the city and enact plan B."

"What's plan B?"

I open my mouth to answer and realize there is no plan B. I have no job prospects, nowhere to live. Even my friends think I'm a failure.

"That's depressing," I say under my breath.

"Why not figure out a plan B that involves staying here?" Matt says.

I mull that one over. "Wouldn't plan B here be the same as plan A except executed better?"

"So, consider it plan A, subsection B. You've set a bit of a low bar, performance expectation-wise. Should be pretty easy to blow them away now, don't you think?"

I want to say it's a stupid idea. That I could come up with ten other options that would almost certainly guarantee a better outcome. But since I refuse to move back in with my parents, I've got nothing.

"I'll consider it," I say grudgingly. "But I will almost certainly come up with a better idea by tomorrow morning."

"Ah! So you *will* be here tonight! I'll pick you up at seven then."

What the hell, I think. As a soon-to-be ex-employee, I'm hardly breaking the rules. What's one more night? Gives me more time to pack.

"Fine."

I try to hide my smile.

Chapter 9

Eventually, as the sun disappears behind the trees along with any remnant of my pride, I eject myself from the comfortable arms of the Big House and return to the frigid hut to start packing. I can't afford rent, so there's no point in asking for my apartment back. It's going to have to be Ros's couch until I figure something else out. I start working on a speech for her, but everything ends with me sounding like an idiot.

"Funny story! Remember how I was fired from my last job? Well, I've chosen to leave my current employer before we go down the same failure-bound road. Yes, I was only there for two days, but it was a very long two days and I think, after hearing about it, you will agree I made the right decision. No, I do not have any new job prospects. Yes, Eric is coming too. No, his manners have not improved."

I decide there's no use thinking about any of this until I absolutely have to, which gives me at least sixteen hours to ignore the state of my life and focus on my date with Matt.

It takes some counterproductive rifling through my suitcase

to find lacy underthings and what I consider to be the perfect casual date shirt. It's dark gray, clingy, but not actually revealing aside from a V that dips down the back, stopping just short of my bra.

After way too much hair removal and applying of lotions and primping in the closet of a bathroom, I declare myself ready.

At seven o'clock sharp there's a knock at my door. Eric goes wild and I hold him back with one leg while Matt edges in, looking somewhat concerned. He's wearing the same clothes as earlier, with the addition of a jacket and navy beanie. A backpack is slung over one shoulder.

"He's just excited," I reassure him. Eric is now jumping up, trying to put his paws on Matt's shoulders so he can get some eye contact. He likes to connect with our guests.

"Is he always this enthusiastic?" asks Matt. He's leaning back equal amounts to Eric's push forward, and I'm mildly concerned they're both going to fall over.

"Pretty much. He believes in living life to its fullest." I grab Eric's collar and pull him over to the mud-brown couch. He jumps up into what he's decided is his spot and stares at me accusingly as I block his path back.

Matt extends an elbow for me to take. "Shall we?"

It's freezing outside and we walk quickly back to the Big House and slip in through a side door. My mind is racing with possibilities. Has he arranged a romantic interlude in a private dining area? Ooooooh, I wonder if Treetops has one of those picturesque wine cellars where high rollers can eat their dinner surrounded by millions of dollars' worth of fermented grape juice.

"After you." He opens a heavy wooden door and reveals . . . the staff dining room. Two employees I recognize from the ill-fated town hall that morning are chatting at another table. Matt is starting to steer me toward the buffet area when a voice calls my name across the room.

"You're here!" Tania cries. She's sitting with Jay and his sous-chef, Serge, classy-looking cocktails in front of them. Her eyes dart between me and Matt, her eyebrows raised in surprise. In the blink of an eye, she's recovered and out of her seat, dragging a neighboring table over to join theirs to accommodate us.

Matt looks at them, a strange expression on his face. "Um, Kate and I were actually . . ."

Jay is up, helping to grab chairs. "She was starting to worry you'd snuck out under the cover of darkness."

That actually sounds like a great idea and, given the turn the evening has taken, I'm kind of wishing I had. So much for a casual farewell fling with the neighborhood dreamboat.

"Thought about it, but Mike isn't going into town until the morning and I wasn't feeling the hitchhiker vibe." I look at Matt, hoping he has a way to get us out of this, but he's taken a sudden deep interest in a loose thread on his jacket.

"This is great," I say with at least twenty times more enthusiasm than I feel. I plop down in the proffered chair. What's one more disappointment?

Serge places a frothy pink cocktail in front of me with a flourish. I sniff at it.

"Cranberry gin fizz with a sprinkle of rosemary sugar," offers Jay. "He wants to take advantage of your fresh taste buds."

Serge, short and sturdy with glossy black hair and a smattering of subtle freckles across his nose and cheeks, slides an index card across the table, a serious look on his face. "You will rate the drink from one to five across three categories and provide constructive commentary in the space provided. Here is a pen."

I look around the table, trying to decide if this is a joke. Jay and Tania hold up their own completed cards. Alright, then.

"Serge takes the art of the cocktail extremely seriously," Jay explains. "We are his guinea pigs." He takes a swig of what looks like green juice and grimaces. "Too much ginger, man."

"On the card." Serge gestures impatiently.

Jay sighs, and for a moment the only sound is the scratching of pen on paper. My gaze bounces around the room, searching for a topic to break the quiet. The silence presses in, making me jumpy.

Matt bumps his shoulder against mine and puts his lips close to my ear. A whiff of cedar and fresh linen dances up my nose and sends me reeling. No one has any business smelling this good. "Take a deep breath. Everything's fine."

My hand is gripping the edge of my chair and his fingers brush against my wrist. I wonder if he's saying it as much to reassure himself as he is for me. Despite him being a fairly long-term employee, I'm not picking up a lot of buddy vibes with the group.

Play it cool. "Mm-hmm. Yeah. I love a comfortable silence." I move to take a casual sip of my drink and a sprig of rosemary stabs me in the eye. I jerk back, sloshing liquid onto my lap. Sigh. So cool.

Jay slides his comment card across the table. Serge tucks it into a folder. I swear I can hear the clock ticking.

Leaning back in his chair, Jay crosses his long legs in front of him. He's wearing jeans, which I find surprising since professional chefs on TV wear those puffy, pajama-looking pants. I'm wondering if it would be weird to ask whether that's an industry requirement or a preference, when Tania finally, blessedly, breaks the silence, saving me from myself.

"Hey, did Brooke approve the new stove?"

Jay snorts in disgust. "What do you think?" He pushes himself upright and takes a hearty swig of his drink, making a face as he sets it down on the table hard enough to make Serge wince.

Tania is aghast. "How are you supposed to do your job with the piece of junk back there?"

"Great skill and determination?" Jay sighs, resigned. His eyes land briefly on Matt, and he pauses for a moment before continuing. "This isn't a surprise to anyone, right? She never wants to invest in improvements. I guess the one positive is that meals cooked over an open fire are endlessly charming in the winter. You know, as long as the guests don't have to freeze their output-producing asses off to make it."

"I don't get it," I interject, leaning forward to rest my elbows on the table. "That seems like a no-brainer on the decision-making scale." I think for a second. "Unless you asked for one of those hoity-toity things that, like, the Kardashians probably have. They don't even call them stoves. Ranges? I think they're ranges."

"Oh, Kate," says Jay bitterly. "You're so new. So naïve. It's refreshing."

Matt stays quiet. I can feel the warmth from his skin jumping across the tiny space between his arm and mine.

Serge shoots Jay a warning look. "Maybe we should talk about this later. Kate doesn't need to hear our issues."

The group reverts to awkward silence, Tania wringing her hands, Matt studying the tablecloth like he's going to find the answer to life's great mysteries in the pale yellow, poly-cotton weave.

Jay takes another sip of his drink and grimaces. "Really, man. Too much ginger. Way too much."

Serge wings an index card at his head.

My stomach growls audibly. It's been a long time since lunch and I'm sure the emotional roller coaster I've been riding has burned endless calories.

"We should eat!" Tania announces, jumping up from her chair and heading toward the buffet. I follow eagerly, the men-folk trailing behind.

Jay lifts the lids off the trays to reveal a feast. He positions himself in front of the food and clasps his hands. "Ladies and gentlemen, this evening we have local venison in a maple, balsamic, and rosemary glaze. Sides include sweet potato and parsnip mash, green beans, and freshly baked herb focaccia. Dessert is an apple crisp with the optional addition of local, hand-churned vanilla ice cream." He bows slightly and steps aside, allowing us access to the culinary paradise beyond.

Matt claps him on the shoulder as he passes. "Great work, man."

Jay's eyes widen slightly in surprise, but he smiles back.

Tania turns a charming shade of pink as Jay hands her a plate and their fingers touch. I pretend not to notice until the charged air returns to normal as we move away.

"Jay, huh?" I ask, nudging her gently with my elbow.

She sighs wistfully and gives me a half smile. "Maybe?" She bites her lower lip and looks at him discussing his ratio of balsamic to maple with Serge. "I think so, yeah." She pauses, cocks her head at me. "You and the man of mystery, huh?"

I pull a face. "Is there a secret agent here somewhere?" My eyes land on Matt for a second, studying the sharp line of his jaw, his stubble, and I'm about to release a sigh full of shoulda, coulda, wouldas when his eyes lock on mine and I stop breathing altogether.

"Mm-hmm." Tania balances a bonus piece of focaccia on top of her plate and maneuvers back to the table, giving me a moment to collect myself.

Over the next hour, I learn that Tania was born and raised in the area. Her parents still live in Otterburne. Her dad's the local dentist and her mom runs the community center, bringing people together for chair yoga, paint nights, and kids' playgroups.

"I thought I was going to be a kindergarten teacher, but I started working here after high school and never left. There's just something about it, you know?" She looks around, and I imagine she's seeing everything surrounded by a rosy halo.

"Brainwashed," I cough into my sleeve, earning a laugh from Jay. I take a sip of my second drink—cranberry apple cider with maple bourbon caramel drizzle—and start to wonder if maybe this is the evening I needed after all. Matt's finger trails down my forearm where it's resting under the table, and I'm certain sparks are flying in its wake. I take it back. Not the evening I need. Not even close. I shift around in my chair, trying to edge closer to him without being obvious about it.

"I, on the other hand," offers Jay, "was lured here from Vancouver by the promise of culinary freedom and endless opportunity for growth."

"Sounds familiar, minus the food thing," I interject.

He laughs, shaking his head.

"Only half of that actually materialized, but running my own kitchen and being able to dive so fully into hyper-local ingredients has been amazing." He shrugs one shoulder. "Who needs career growth, anyway?"

Voices pile on top of each other, making clever remarks about everything from the growth of their waistlines thanks to Jay's cooking to concern for the growth of his ego after all the praise heaped upon him by guests.

"Serge, what's your deal?" I ask. He's been quiet most of the time, studying people's reactions to his liquored-up potions.

"My parents are deeply concerned about my life choices. They were hoping for an engineer or corporate lawyer," he says, smiling into his glass as he takes a sip of sparkling water. Despite his passion for crafting artisanal cocktails, Serge, it turns out, isn't a big drinker.

"Don't be modest." Jay elbows him. "Tell the whole truth."

Serge sighs, color rising in his cheeks. He shakes his head. "No one wants to hear all that."

"Fine. I'll tell them. Before succumbing to the lure of his true passion, Serge was on the path to be a grade-A scientist. A real nerd's nerd. He's got his . . ." Jay trails off, scrunching his face. "Shit. I forget what it's called. But this guy right here, this unassuming person of refined palate and distinguished taste, was going to design robots to take over the world. Build his own little army of mini-Serge's to deliver drinks, lulling society into a tipsy stupor."

"It's a joint major in mechatronics and physics. And I'm cutting you off. You've clearly had enough this evening. Mini-Serge's. Hmph." He looks around the table at our questioning faces and sighs again. "You can do a lot with a mechatronics degree, and it's quite lucrative. It just isn't how I want to spend the next forty years." Dragging his finger through the condensation on the side of his glass, he says, "Don't you ever feel like you're doing things for all the wrong reasons, but it's too much work to change the path you're on?"

Preach, Cocktail Master.

"Well, I was interviewing for jobs in Silicon Valley."

"As you do," interrupts Jay.

"As you do, yes, and one day I just decided it was better to suck it up and make the leap now, rather than in five or ten or twenty years. Kind of like ending a bad relationship, I guess." He runs a hand through his hair and raises his head, smiling at us.

"I keep thinking I should invite my parents here for a weekend, but somehow I don't think it would help. It's cool though. One day they'll have grandkids and won't give a hoot about me."

We've circled the table giving backstories and it's down to me and Matt. I certainly don't feel like sharing my trash fire of a saga. I turn to Matt. "How does one become a professional art mentor? Seems pretty niche."

"It's kind of the family business," he starts, and I may be projecting my bitterness onto him, but he sounds . . . off.

A phone dings from his pocket. It's such an unexpected sound here, even after just two days, that it takes me a moment to place it.

"Sorry, I need to get this." He excuses himself and leaves the dining room.

Tania, Jay, Serge, and I take sips of our drinks and look around the room for a couple of minutes, making polite but stilted small talk before deciding to call it a night. I pass my completed cocktail appraisals back to Serge and help clear the dishes.

"This has been nice. Thank you." And I'm not lying. They're lovely people and the food was delicious, and none of this disaster is their fault.

"Are you sure you need to go?" Tania asks. "Maybe a few more days will get you settled in?" She looks exceptionally doubtful, but I appreciate the sentiment.

"It's not the settling-in that's the issue," I say, smiling because it's all almost over. "Did you have a chance to ask Mike if I can tag along to town with him in the morning?"

"I did, and it's fine, of course." She bites her lower lip and looks like she's trying to hold back whatever is coming next.

"Just tell me."

"I don't want to overstep." She looks pained at the very idea.

"Tania, you are one of the kindest, most genuine people I have ever met. If you have something to say it must be important." I sit down in one armchair of a pair, arranged for morning coffee around a low circular table, and signal she should take the other. "Now spill it."

Hands clasped in her lap, she leans toward me and speaks in a low voice, as if she's worried we'll be overheard.

"Treetops isn't doing well."

"No shit."

"No, I mean, like, I don't know how we're still operational. Every request for upgrades or repairs we make, even for necessary equipment like the stove, is denied. Every single time. We're making do, fixing stuff ourselves. And I know Mike paid for the last round of snowmobile repairs himself just so we can get guests in."

"I don't know why you're telling me this," I say gently. "The imminent demise of the business isn't a great selling feature for me."

"That's not what I'm trying to say."

I can see she's getting frustrated, though her version of frustration is still very friendly, like she's coaching the village idiot toward the right answer.

"Listen, the others, they'd kill me—" She catches my horrified expression. "Not literally! God! Who do you think we are?"

I try to keep my face neutral but suspect I look constipated. Luckily, she ignores me and plows ahead.

"Like I was saying, they'd think I'm crazy for saying this, but we need you. Like really, really, really super need you. If we don't get more guests, I don't know if we'll make it through the season."

"I'm sure it's not *that* bad. And don't take this the wrong way, but there are other resorts. Lots of opportunities for people with your skill set. If you're this worried, maybe start sending out résumés."

Tania sits back in her chair and gets as close to a glare as she can muster. It's almost concerning.

"You haven't been here long enough to get it. Forget me for a second. Have you thought about what keeps Jay here? He's been offered three jobs in the last year working with superstar chefs in New York, Vancouver, and Toronto."

"Well, he said he likes running his own kitchen, so . . ."

"And Serge. You heard him. He turned down a job at NASA. You think it's solely a love of cardamom-sugar-infused rye that keeps him around?"

"No, but—"

"Kevin and Mike could go anywhere, do anything, but they're here. They. Are. Here." She hits the arm of her chair with each word. "This place is special. These *people* are special. What we're doing, it seems ridiculous, I get that. But when it comes down to it, we're showing people how to find out who they are. What makes them so uniquely *them*. And who cares if some are entitled and snooty. Everyone deserves to understand what makes them tick, even if the first step is just a quiet weekend in the woods to listen to whatever their heart is trying to tell them."

Her cheeks are flushed, her voice strong but wavering around the edges. "Won't you at least *try* to help?"

I stand, knowing I'm being a bitch, feeling bad about it. But not bad enough to purposefully excavate an even deeper pit of despair trying to hit impossible targets.

"I'm sorry, Tania. Honestly. You care about this place an awful lot, and that's commendable. But whatever, *whoever*, Treetops is made for, it sure as hell ain't me."

I look around hoping to see Matt, but he still hasn't returned, so I throw my coat on and head for the door. I need to pack.

He's on the walkway between the Big House and the employee huts, blowing into his cupped hands and rubbing them together to keep warm.

"Thanks for dinner," I say, walking past without pausing.

"Hey, wait! What happened?"

I stop and spin around to face him, ramping from generally disappointed to specifically directed anger in seconds.

"What happened?" I stare at him, incredulous. "What *hasn't* happened, Matt?" I start ticking horrors off on my fingers. "I left my job, my apartment, my friends, and, let's be honest, my dignity behind in a desperate bid for a successful future, and I got this. A hut that smells like dirty boots and stale weed, the boss from hell, hypothermia—"

"You didn't get hypothermia," he cuts in.

"Shut up. Hypothermia," I reiterate. "OAR'd in front of the entire company, then you swoop in with your smile and your sneaky abs and cookie breath."

"Cookie breath?" His brow furrows as I plow onward.

"I get asked on a date that ends up not being at all a date, then abandoned on said non-date, I hurt Tania's feelings, and now I have to go live on a couch that I *once threw up on*." I'm stomping back and forth on the wooden walkway as Matt stands off to the side looking like he's weighing his fight-or-flight options.

"So, what happened, Matthew, is both everything and abso-fucking-lutely nothing." The wind falls out of my rage-y sails and I am exhausted. I take a deep breath, pushing the air back out in a frosty cloud of angst. "Anyway, it was . . . fine, I guess, to meet you. Have a nice life." I start walking down the dimly lit path toward the packing disaster that awaits.

"Hold on a second." He holds up a hand, pausing my escape.

"Things aren't going your way. I get it. This has been an all-around bad experience for you and I will admit that this evening wasn't the showstopper I'd planned. I wanted to send you off with a bang."

The corner of my mouth twitches and I can't help but raise an eyebrow at his word choice.

"Shit. No pun intended."

It's hard to tell in the darkness, but I think he's blushing. He runs his hands over his face.

"Listen, I thought we could duck into the dining room to grab food and then go down to the theater, where you could choose from the horrible yet nostalgic selection of nineties VHS tapes. I have wine. The internet says it pairs well with popcorn and M&M's." He swings his backpack around and unzips it, pulling out a bottle of wine and revealing enough candy for six people. "But then it seemed like you were having fun with the group and . . . well, I kind of started hoping that if you spent some time with them and forgot about this afternoon for a bit, that . . . um, you might decide to give us another chance." He rubs the back of his neck, inspecting the ground with unnecessary intensity.

I start to feel a little ashamed.

He nudges a stray leaf with his boot, giving me a moment to immerse myself in the all too familiar feeling of being a jackass, before locking his eyes onto mine.

"Well, anyway, I'm sorry everything sucks so badly right now. For what it's worth, I think you would have done very well here." He passes the wine to me. "You can come up with a better plan B than the puke couch." Shoving his hands into his coat pockets, he gazes at me through his stupidly long lashes. "It was more than fine to meet you. I wish it had been under different circumstances."

He walks away into the darkness, breath puffing out in little clouds.

Well, shit. Way to go, Rigsby.

At least I have wine.

Chapter 10

My suitcase won't close. Two days ago, it zipped shut like a dream, but today, on the frigid morn of my escape from Crazy Town, no dice. The zipper won't budge, leaving me staring woefully at the crumpled, overflowing mess within. It provides an excellent visual metaphor for my barely contained feelings. Title: *Emotional Baggage—The Spill.*

I woke up puffy-eyed, with my mouth tasting like regret and mildewed hockey equipment after solo-ing most—okay, all—of the wine from Matt. It seemed like ill-gotten spoils and I did consider dropping it off on his doorstep. Then I realized I didn't know the location of said doorstep and one thing led to another and it was open. Even I know you can't return an open bottle. That would be tacky.

You'd think that three hours of soul searching, ugly crying, and looking for answers in the fibers of the Hut's beigey brown carpet would have led to a crystal-clear list of next steps. It did not. Shocking.

Despite the suitcase being packed to bursting, I'm far from

convinced abandoning ship is the right move. It's a move, certainly, but it seems that of late I've been doing a lot of zigging and zagging and it's not turning out *super* well. Matt's confused, annoyed face hurtles to the front of my mind, followed closely by Tania's sad one. A sneering Kevin is threatening to round out the trio of disapproval so I shake my head aggressively enough to make my neck hurt a little and move to look outside, distracting myself with the potential for a moose sighting.

Staring at my reflection in the dark window, I realize there is someone who might be able to help me. I curse the lack of cell service for the seven hundredth time and pull a pair of worn-only-once socks from the gaping suitcase. Grabbing my coat off the antler hook (yes, real antlers) by the door, I stomp toward the Big House.

"It's six in the fucking morning." Ros's scratchy, sleep-laced voice is music to my ears. "This had better be your kidnapper or a super sexy police officer trawling through your contacts to notify someone of your demise."

I lean back in my office chair and close my eyes. I'm almost certain if I open them I'll be able to see my breath, despite being indoors.

"To be honest, I don't feel like I need any third-party assistance in the demise department." My throat is getting all tight and blood is rushing to my face. I'm going to cry. Again. Ugh.

"Whoa, whoa, whoa, there, little adventurer. Internet rock-chucking David who takes down unprofessional lawyerly Goliaths with a single well-placed shot. It's been what, three days?" I can hear the rustling of sheets as she sits up and the click of her bedside lamp turning on. She draws in a dramatic breath. "Was it a scam? Are you being held in a shack in the woods against your will? Being forced to wash the bearskin cloak of some wilderness crime-mastermind in the frigid lake waters until your hands turn blue?"

I wipe my eyes with my sleeve. "I'd laugh, but you're not

that far off. Except I don't think you'd wash a fur in the lake? Maybe, like homespun underpants made by one of the other sister-wives."

"So what happened and how did it lead to you needing to wake me up in the middle of the night to talk about it?" More rustling. "Coffee," she mutters. "Must get to the coffee."

I launch into the whole ridiculous story as her coffee machine gurgles productively in the background. The job is stupid. Kevin hates me for no reason. There's a real-life actual celebrity next door who, brace yourself, also hates me. Brooke seems to think I am completely incompetent, and I don't know why she hired me in the first place because it seems like she has zero interest in actually making Treetops successful.

"Which, *by the way*, has a direct and horrific correlation with my ability to secure the stupid bonus that made me come here in the first place." I'm pacing now, back and forth along the length of the desk, a small two strides, repositioning the phone base every three passes so it doesn't crash to the floor.

"To summarize," Ros says, slurping coffee. "Everyone hates you and the job is hard?"

"Well, no."

"No? Because that's the story I've been listening to for the last fifteen minutes."

"Not *everyone* hates me. I am a generally likable person."

"Okay. Who likes you?"

Matt's face appears in my mind, handsome and smiling. It's quickly replaced by the dejected Matt of last night. Nope.

"Um, this woman who seems to flit around like a humming-bird, doing a million things in a very chipper way. Tania. But I think she'd like everyone who isn't an ax murderer, and really, she'd probably try to find the good in them as well."

"Who else?"

"The guests seem to think I'm okay."

"And your job is to bring in more guests, correct?"

"On paper, yes. But Brooke—"

"No. Your contract states you're there to develop business. To increase guest headcount by some percentage. And, I assume, to maintain some kind of long-standing brand image while doing it. Is this accurate?"

"You're using your business voice and it's weirding me out. It's like two octaves lower than your normal voice."

"Did you or did you not call me for a consultation?"

"Fine. Darth Vader away, oh wise one."

She breathes noisily into the phone for a few breaths, getting into character, before picking up where she left off.

"Are you going to let this woman win in *one meeting*? You're running for the hills after forty-five minutes of frustration?"

"No, wait," I try to interrupt. "There has been substantially more aggravation than just her."

"But who cares about other people? You're there for three months. Three months, Kate, that can set you up with flexibility and a low-stress launch pad to figure out what to do when you get back. Are you trying to tell me that you, who dated that mother-effer Chaz for nearly two years—which was incredibly painful for me personally, by the way—can't put up with a shitty boss you don't even have to see in person *for a few weeks*?"

"But there's no way to succeed! She's stuffing me into a sales and marketing box that was built when the Olsen twins were still in diapers. No one could make these numbers, Ros. Not even you."

"For the love of all things holy. Have you not been working in PR for the last decade? You just need to spin this differently. Make her buy it."

She's quiet for a minute, and I can almost hear her brain checking out all the angles. It pays to be friends with the smartest kid in the class.

"Brooke has zero effs to give, right?"

"She gives superficial effs. Effs provided for show."

"Is she going to check your work?"

I try to envision Brooke reviewing my guest profiles and promo plans from her bed or salon chair.

"Probably not, unless she's feeling particularly spiteful. Which isn't out of the realm of possibility."

"You're very noncommittal these days." Ros huffs. "I'm adding in a small risk factor for spite." The click of a keyboard.

"Are you making a spreadsheet?"

"Does . . ." She fades out and I hear more typing, a gentle grunt, then she's back. "I was going for a 'Does a chicken lay eggs' type joke, but funnier. It's too early though. Brain can't make the funnies and save your ass at the same time."

"I love you."

"It's a shame I'm already married to my job. Don't take this too personally, but I think we're better off as friends."

"That cuts deep."

"Use that pain and tell me how you're going to play this game and get that money, girl. Here's what I think you should do . . ."

We brainstorm. We laugh. I stub my toe on the leg of the desk and swear loudly enough to make someone yell "Everything okay down there?" from the top of the stairs in a way that sounds more like *Keep it down!* than any real concern for my well-being. And finally, after an hour, I have some semblance of a plan that is only seventy-five percent likely to get me fired.

I sheepishly notify Mike that he can head into town without me, which isn't nearly as awkward as I'd built it up to be in my head. He even offers to hang with Eric while I go about my important business activities. Eric is, of course, jazzed, and I leave them to bond over the mutual destruction of tree parts.

I'm working up the courage to face the rest of my colleagues when I hear someone coming down the creaky, horror-movie basement stairs to my dungeon/office. I position myself in front of the computer and peer intently at the calendar on the screen, presenting the ultimate picture of productivity.

"You're still here." Kevin is wearing another gorgeous sweater today. This one is deep burgundy with green flecks running through it. It reminds me of the fall leaves and red wine. If the person wearing it wasn't so entirely repellent, I would love to run my hand over the sleeve to feel the texture.

I paste a professional smile on my face. It hurts.

"Kevin! So lovely to see you. Yes. I am, indeed, still here. Until the New Year, actually. Tough to do too much useful biz dev in two days, right?" I lean back and cross my legs, turning my chair to face him. I very much hope it doesn't choose this moment to fall apart. "I see that you, too, are still here. What's on the agenda today? Rearranging furniture to allow better flow of creative energies? Crafting some output-inducing candles from near-extinct flora and fauna?"

What am I even doing? I'm thirty minutes into deciding to make this gig work and I'm already sabotaging myself. I breathe deeply, inhaling the smell of moist concrete and the collection of mucky old boots lined up against the wall.

Kevin looks down his nose at me. Down his nose! "You're young . . . ish," Ouch. "So maybe no one has ever told you—it's not best practice to mock your superiors." He places a finger on his perfectly groomed beard. "I wonder if that's what brought you here. Blatant disregard for social niceties and lacking the fundamental talent to make it in your chosen field. Which, by the way, I seriously doubt is anything to do with business development."

My stomach drops. *Deflect! Dodge! Be cool, Kate. Be cool.*

"You're absolutely right, Kevin. I was out of line. Apologies." I arrange my features into what I hope looks like an appropriately repentant, yet helpful and eager expression. A tall order for an early thirties woman with a hangover.

"What brings you to my office on this fine fall day?"

He unceremoniously plops a heavy yellow envelope on my desk. The kind favored by lawyers, and moms preserving their children's artwork to roll out at their weddings.

"This needs to be delivered and it appears you need something productive to do."

He looks at me expectantly. I wait for more information. He offers none.

"To whom? By what method? Do you want me to give it to Tania to mail on her next run into town? Or Mike?" He winces at the mention of Mike. Innnnteresting.

"If I wanted Tania or . . . someone else . . . to take it, I would give it to that person. I have placed it on your desk. It must be delivered to the neighboring property immediately." He crosses his wool-snuggled arms and stares me down.

My chair wheels give a piercing squeak as I shove back from the desk. I stand and grab the envelope, resisting throwing in a salute. Helpful Kate to the rescue!

"Where am I taking this thing? A neighboring bear cave? Wolf den?"

"You're to deliver it to Ms. Christine Morrow."

I have a flashback. Mud. Stacked heels crushing the flora. Amazonian social media princess threatening to end me. So, yeah, pretty much a wolf den, then. Cool.

Chapter 11

I'm setting off for my survival adventure when I hear the helicopter. It's such an aggressive, out-of-place sound that for a moment I think we're having an earthquake. I catch a glimpse of its shiny white body through the trees. It hovers over the lake for a moment before meandering down the shoreline. By this time, I'm jogging up the driveway to get a better view from the top of the hill. I've never seen a helicopter up close before. It looks expensive. Very shiny.

Matt is up ahead, a khaki duffel bag slung over his shoulder. He's wearing dark-wash jeans, and a charcoal bomber jacket, and cuts an appealing figure from my vantage point. I've never known anyone who travels by helicopter, but the way he's strolling makes me think this isn't an unusual occurrence.

I jog to catch up, casually falling into step beside him, hands stuffed into my pockets. He looks at me, eyes widening in surprise, before reverting his gaze to the path ahead. The frozen ground crunches gently beneath our feet and I keep an eye out for errant patches of ice.

After fifteen seconds of waiting for him to say something, I lob an easy one.

"So where are you off to? Do they have doughnuts there? I asked Jay if he'd make some and he looked like I'd stabbed him right in his local-produce-filled heart."

Need an expert in awkward rambling? Kate Rigsby's your girl.

I look Matt's trim figure up and down. "Do you eat doughnuts?" He flicks a look at me from the corner of his eye. God, his lashes are obscene.

"Are you asking me to bring you doughnuts? You should be able to find plenty back in the city." He tilts his head to the side ever so slightly. "Speaking of which, shouldn't you be on your way by now?" His keeps it light, but it still stings.

We're approaching a clearing where the helicopter has landed, its rotors still spinning. Up close it gleams like the frosted opal eyeshadow I'd dabbled with in grade nine. It looks much better on the helicopter.

I take a deep breath and the words that have been tumbling around in my head for the last sixteen hours spill out. I have to yell to make myself heard, which amps up the embarrassment. "Listen, Matt. I'm so sorry about last night. It's been a tough couple of days but that's no excuse for . . ."

But I've lost his attention and as I follow his gaze I see why. A dark-haired angel is leaning against the helicopter. Her complexion hurts my eyes, it's so damn perfect, and that pain makes something click in my head. It's not an angel. It's the devil herself, Christine Morrow. I stop dead and look between her face and Matt's.

She barely acknowledges my presence and if it weren't for the flicker of a sneer in my direction, I'd be pretty convinced I was invisible. Taylor wrestles with a mint green suitcase, that, if his effort is any indication, weighs as much as a baby elephant.

I cock my head toward Matt. He gives me a well-this-is-awkward look and seems to be about to speak when Christine tosses her mane of hair and yells, "Jesus Christ. Get on the fucking chopper. We're going to be late."

As Matt walks past me I suddenly remember why I'm braving the cold in the first place.

"Wait!" I call, swinging my backpack around and pulling the envelope out. I wave it in the air.

Christine scoffs, dismissing me with a flick of her wrist.

I can't hear her, but it's easy to read her lips. "You're joking. An autograph?"

I shake my head aggressively to indicate that is not what's happening here. "Paperwork," I yell. "From Kevin." She looks at me blankly. "Kevin Ramsay? From Treetops?" I gesture in the direction of the Big House. She inclines her chin in what I interpret as permission to approach, though she could have been preparing to spit.

I crouch, mindful of the spinning rotors above, and scurry toward her like a supplicant approaching a royal. My cheeks burn with equal parts embarrassment and anger.

"I hate this. I hate this. This sucks," I mutter to my shoes. Finally, I get within passing distance and thrust the envelope toward her. She gestures to Taylor, who steps forward and accepts my offering.

I thwap it into his hand. He reverses three steps and passes it to Christine, who looks like she wishes he'd sanitized it beforehand. She wings it through the door of the helicopter and takes Matt's proffered hand, stepping up and into what looks to be quite a luxurious interior. Taylor scrambles in after her.

Matt shrugs in my direction. I can't read the expression on his face but it's not particularly pleasant. A little like he bit into a wormy apple. "Later, Kate. Good luck."

I back away to safety and stand there, bewildered, which seems to be my go-to state these days, as the three of them settle in. The door is closed and as the rotors pick up speed, I back away from the noise and chaos. Through the small window, Matt delivers a tiny salute. After he leans back in his seat and presumably forgets I exist, I flip him the bird. It's not one of my most mature moments, but as far as I can tell, this isn't even real life, so who cares.

When they disappear from view, I lose whatever cool I have left.

"Arrrrrgggggghhhhhhhh!!" I yell up at the sky. At the trees. At the birds with their pleasant fucking chirping. Embracing the tantrum, I stomp and kick at the ground and generally act like a complete lunatic until I'm out of breath and a rock works its way into my shoe, making additional stomping an unattractive option.

I sit on a boulder to deal with the rock-in-shoe situation. I should be crying, but I'm out of energy and the idea of sobbing in the middle of the woods seems too melodramatic a follow-up to the universe-cursing.

Pulling off a sneaker, I shake a pebble onto the ground, heave myself to standing and do some of the deep, centering breathing I imagine they taught in the Ab-Sculpt Yoga classes Chaz got me last Christmas. They never seemed to quite line up with my schedule, so I'm winging the breathing thing, but it kind of works.

I think back to my call with Ros, hearing her confident voice in my head. I have a plan. I can do this. Matt is a distraction. I don't need distractions. Forget it. Forget him. Move on.

Heading back to Treetops, I stomp heavily along the leaf-covered path to warn any wildlife that something large and in charge is coming through.

A mantra. That's what I need.

"It's only three months. It's only three months," I mutter, then pause. Three months is a long time. "It's only twelve weeks." Ick. That sounds much worse. Increments of time aren't working. I kick at the leaves in front of me, sending them whirling through the air. "This probably won't kill you. You'll likely be fine. This is a character-building exercise." Yeah, that's better. "This probably won't kill you . . ."

*   *   *

My afternoon is filled with apologizing to Tania for being a miserable human (for which she somehow forgives me instantly), reading the stupid Process Manual in great detail, and avoiding further interactions with Kevin, which at one point involves staying in the bathroom for twenty minutes while he arranges and rearranges a bowl of rocks and sand on a table in the hallway. There is a sixty percent chance he is just messing with me.

I arrive at my second meeting with Brooke high on chocolate-dipped shortbread and indignation, toting the requested sixty-day plan that I've managed to fling together in the two days since we last spoke. It is the most boring thing I have created since an essay describing the eating habits of the earwig in grade seven. Including only vintage ideas pulled directly from the playbook, it makes almost no sense in the context of present day. My stomach lurches a little as I open my presentation and click through a few slides, getting ready for the pitch of a lifetime.

Brooke calls in from a café and keeps asking me to repeat myself because "Your voice just can't compete with the fervent energy of my environment."

The meeting goes about as you'd expect.

I had planned for her to be online so I could wow her with engaging 1990s clip art and stock photos from the early days of the internet, but end up having to read the plan out loud, attempting to casually describe the imagery I'd included.

"Picture a demure woman referred to us by existing clientele, utilizing the tips and tricks learned in that morning's workshop to pen a quiet, satisfying poem on the dock."

No response.

"Imagine, if you will, a midforties business-casual duo ensconced in an intimate breakout room, planning the next phase of their wonderful mixed-media series, supported by all the inspiration and supplementary services Treetops has to offer."

Chewing sounds. I try to guess what she'd pick for a snack. Maybe a croissant? Bran muffin? Heart of a mourning dove?

As we're wrapping up, I still haven't gotten a full sentence out of her. Desperate, I throw out the suggestion of expanding Treetops' reach through social media and an updated website. This, at least, stirs up some modicum of passion.

"Absolutely not. It's not budgeted."

"Would it be possible to see the budget breakdown for the duration of my contract? It would be helpful to know what I have to work with."

"You have everything you need. The printed materials are stockpiled in sufficient quantity from the last run. I see you've booked time next week to start reaching out to established clientele by phone." She sighs. "Krista, use the drive you're attempting to apply to new thinking and dedicate yourself to performing the tasks already outlined for you."

"Mm-hmm. It's Kate, actually. It's just"—pausing, I make sure my voice conveys my complete lack of confidence—"you brought me here with a pretty specific, um, mandate to increase business and it doesn't seem like, er, well, like there's much interest in actually doing that?" I channel the spirit of insecure yet entitled Regan-Caulfield co-op students. "If the Board wants to see a noticeable change in bookings in such a short period—"

Suddenly, I hear a male voice murmuring in what sounds like a French accent. Brooke giggles and it's such an unexpected noise that I hold the phone away from my ear, staring at it until the sharp voice I'm growing so used to comes back on the line.

"I have to go. Please remember you're entirely new to this industry. Take the opportunity to learn the basics and perhaps after your contract ends you can move on to a position that— Oh, you flirt! Just one moment, darling—you can move on to something that allows you to do"—she stalls and I can imagine her waving a hand around—"whatever it is you're trying to do. Follow the outlined processes. That is your job."

"Understood, Brooke. I will interpret the processes and execute my strategy accordingly."

"Fine. Good." *Click.*

In the privacy of my office, I give myself a supercool high five. (Looks a lot like a clap, but with different intention). Onward and upward. Or at least, not immediately straight down.

The Friday Gathering Fire takes place that night. I expect it to be a quiet event where we all stare into the flames and wait for inspiration to be reflected back at us. Mostly I want to know whether there will be marshmallows available for roasting or if I need to bring my own.

I'm due for a reward in the form of sugar and, ideally, a stiff drink.

Employee Hut Four is a stone's throw from the Gathering Fire if you cut through a little patch of trees, but the promise of a broken ankle seems a bit high, so I take the long way around on the meandering stone path. The chill of the night cuts through my jeans, and I wonder if I should go back for my snow pants.

Eric pauses to thoroughly assess the scent profile offered by a stump just out of view of where Mike, Jay, and Tania are setting up. Mike's piling wood *Tetris*-style in the fire pit. Jay's laying out what appears to be a full bar and buffet of snacks. I squint, trying to get a closer look, but no 'mallows reveal themselves. Tania arranges a blanket and tin cup at each spot along the log benches.

"We'll figure something out, T. You gotta stop stressing about this. It's not doing you any good," Jay is saying.

"What about Falcon Ridge?" asks Mike, fiddling with some kindling.

"What about it?"

"I heard they're short-staffed. If we can get through the off-season here, I bet they'd take us in spring."

I'm frozen in place, straining to hear more.

"It feels like asking them to adopt a family of dysfunctional orphans," says Jay, carefully dropping cinnamon sticks into a steaming carafe. "Maybe it's time to head back to civilization."

Tania looks pained. "But where does that leave Treetops?"

"Exactly where they seem to want it," growls Mike. "Dead in the water."

"Maybe Kate's going to change things. You know, now that she's decided to stay."

I hold back a cheer, but allow myself a tiny fist pump at Tania's vote of confidence.

"Come on, T," Jay says, picking up her hand to give it a gentle squeeze before going back to creating artful piles of cookies. "She seems fine, but she's destined for failure."

I bristle. True, I'm not off to the most successful start, but I just got here. Cut me some slack.

"Besides," he continues, "who knows how long she'll stick around." He adds a drizzle of something to the plate, a couple shots of whipped cream. The sound of the aerosol can make me jump. "We could go out west, or to Toronto. Maybe this is the bump we need to get out of here."

Well, crap. Just how imminent and magnificent do they expect my failure to be? I may not be awesome, but I don't think I can singlehandedly drive the place into the ground in the next three months unless I accidentally burn it down.

I instantly regret putting that thought into the universe.

Mike looks up from the fire that's just starting to catch and crackle, tendrils of smoke waving into the night air. "And she doesn't seem particularly motivated. She doesn't know us. Why should she care?"

Tania puts a blanket down in the last spot and faces the group, fists clenched at her sides. "We should tell the Board. Maybe they don't know what's happening. They could fix everything."

"They know," Jay says forcefully. "How could they not? All the requests they shoot down, no matter how much justification we give? They just don't care. We're small potatoes in their farm of assets. They're probably using us as a tax write-off or something."

"I love it here." Tania sounds like she's close to tears.

Jay wraps an arm around her, rubbing her arm before moving back to the bar setup. "I know. We all do. Or did, at least."

Everyone goes quiet, focused on their thoughts.

Eric spies a squirrel chattering at the base of a tree on the other side of the clearing and drags me around the corner into full view. I try very hard to make it seem like I haven't been eavesdropping. "Oh, hey, everyone! Am I late? How can I help?"

Tania pastes on a smile and pats Eric on the head, and the conversation turns fully to the preparations. I'm counting cutlery, working up to asking just how bad they think the situation *really* is, when guests start to trickle in, chatting politely. They nestle into the seats carved out of fallen tree trunks. We're at a 1:1 ratio of guests to employee attendees and a vision of money being flushed directly into the septic tank is quite vivid.

Promptly at seven, Clarissa stands and addresses the group. "In the light of the fire, by the soft gleam of the moon, doubts can do one of two things. They can swell and turn into monsters lurking in the darkness, just outside our periphery, growling and sending waves of uncertainty crashing over us, making us feel small and creating black holes that suck our creative energies. Or doubts can present in their true form—that of tiny little bugs ready to be scourged by the flames. Let's get to the scourging." She raises her tin cup in a salute. Someone hits Play on a list of acoustic renditions of Top 40 hits.

The stars are so much brighter than in the city. It would be beautiful if I wasn't freezing and falling asleep on my feet. I'm getting ready to grab a handful of cookies and excuse myself when Heinrich the Performer appears with two mugs of Jay and Serge's very boozy cider. He offers me one, which I reluctantly accept.

"How did today go?" I ask, taking a generous mouthful and

resigning myself to another few minutes of social interaction. "Traumatize anyone for life?"

"Unfortunately, no. *Death by a thousand papercuts.* I went over to Falcon Ridge and convinced them to let me use their copy room, so I kind of had to fill them in on the plan."

"I don't know what Falcon Ridge is," I say, thinking back to Mike's earlier comment about it being understaffed, "but it sounds like a superhero hideout."

Heinrich smiles, a huge, death-obsessed, ginger-bearded teddy bear. "They'd probably like to think it's similar. Corporate retreat. You know, team building, facilitated brainstorming, nice business center, endless mediocre coffee. Saving the world one bar graph at a time."

"Ugh. Sounds terrible."

"Maybe to people like us, but business is booming. It's actually a pretty nice place. Great property, lots of amenities. They said they're basically at capacity through to Christmas. I had to stop filming at one point to make twenty copies of a flow chart detailing the decision-making process of fourteen- to eighteen-year-olds as it pertains to vending machine choices."

I get a little stuck on "people like us," my brain struggling to put me and Heinrich in the same category.

After a couple more minutes of chitchat, he excuses himself, declaring it bedtime. "Tomorrow's still a bit of a mystery. I'm hoping inspiration strikes in my sleep."

"Okay, sweet dreams!" I call, instantly cringing at my own words.

I'm about to retreat to the Hut and call it a night when Jay materializes, refilling my cup. I stifle a groan. *Just let me go to sleeeeeeep*, I moan in my head. Since when am I so popular?

"You look like you're failing at the doubt-scourging. Probably just need more fuel."

"Thanks, but I think if I drink much more of this I'll spontaneously combust."

"That's a real risk. We'll just throw you in the lake— Oh, wait. You did that already."

"Har har." We stand in companionable silence for a moment, staring into the flames and dodging the occasional cloud of smoke gusting into our faces. Audra's voice floats toward us from the other side of the fire, insisting that Serge compile "a goooorgeous drinks recipe book focusing on the complex flavors and subtle health benefits of each libation."

"So, how's it going? Three days in and . . . ?"

He lets the question dangle and I take a moment to consider my answer, torn between pleasant lies and the truth. Wondering if Tania said anything about our conversation the night before.

"It's . . . not entirely what I expected." I weigh my next words. "It seemed like in the town hall meeting, Graham cared about this place and was proud of what he'd built, but then Brooke . . ." I trail off.

"Then Brooke," Jay says, nodding.

Another sip of punch has me throwing caution to the increasingly frigid wind.

"What's her deal? It seems like she's got the Treetops Process Manual memorized, but at the same time she's always a bit, um, distracted?" I don't know Jay well enough to say what I really feel, which is that Brooke can spout dated corporate party lines all day but is clearly checked out.

Jay looks torn. "Yeah. It's kind of complicated."

"I'll take what I can get." I stare at him expectantly.

His fingers tap out a little rhythm on the side of his cup as he makes a decision. "You can't tell anyone I told you. It'll ruin my aloof chef image. I'm supposed to be above stuff like this."

"Scout's honor, pinky swear. Your secret moment of gossip, erm, I mean, professional intel sharing, is safe with me." I get the impression that this is a limited window of opportunity and pray he won't come to his senses before spilling the beans.

"Brooke was awarded management of Treetops in a settlement." He takes a deep breath and lets it out in a puff. "A divorce settlement."

My confusion must be obvious because he adds, "From Graham Sutherland."

"She's his ex-wife?" I blurt out, more loudly than is appropriate for a clandestine conversation.

He shushes me and pulls me a few steps farther away from the crowd. Eric looks up from where he's dozing but relaxes once he confirms I'm not abandoning him.

"She still reports to he Board, headed by Graham, which seems super fucking awkward to me. But hey, no one's offering me hundreds of thousands a year to do basically nothing. Maybe I'd be fine with it too."

Hundreds of thousands, plural? I choke on my punch and manage to stop myself from asking if Graham is currently available and looking for his next ex.

"And then there's Matt."

My attention snaps back to Jay with laser focus, but I try to keep it casual, gulping my drink before saying, "Oh yeah. Him. What's his story?"

Jay takes a swallow of punch and is opening his mouth to speak when a thoroughly lubricated Audra swoops in, wrapping herself around him like a python on a tree limb. "Chef Jayyyy," she says in the singsong voice of drunk women everywhere, "I was just telling, Char . . . Clarin . . . Cralissa? I was speaking to this woman over here about the fine, fine quality of the amusebouche at dinner tonight, and she is absolutely *insistent* that you make it all yourself! And I said to her, Marleena, how can that beeee?" She's still holding his arm, stumbling back toward where Clarissa stands beside Tania, who is unsuccessfully trying to hide her laughter behind purple mittens. Audra is slated to check out the next morning and I wonder if someone should start making her mocktails, heavy on the water.

My own cup is woefully empty and I have to remind myself this is a work event for New Kate. Responsible, productive, forward-thinking Kate does not drink to the point of drunkenness with Treetops guests, or employees for that matter.

The light from the fire catches on the glistening dregs of something sitting on the bottom of the cup. I stick my finger in and look more closely, wondering how likely it is that someone has drugged the punch.

Serge, the cocktail master, is walking past with a jug of what I hope is water and I catch his sleeve with my other hand.

I hold my finger up close to his face. "What's this? It's from the punch."

"Ah! Thyme for the Holidays—it's from this awesome new luxury herb outfit—"

"Party Thyme," we say simultaneously.

Chapter 12

Ten days later, I haven't been murdered by the locals and am feeling like things are on a very slight upward swing. Eric is at one with his new environment. I wouldn't be surprised to learn he has named each of the neighborhood squirrels as he simultaneously plots their demise.

Footsteps crunch outside my front door, and I fling it open with one hand while rummaging through a basket of outerwear with the other. Tania's promised to take me on a tour of some side trails this morning, assuring me that the chances of being attacked by a bear, wolf, or aggressive otter are very low. I haven't decided if I believe her, but the promise of a winter waterfall is too much to pass up, even at seven o'clock on a Monday morning.

"Just a second!" I call, mashing a turquoise pom-pom toque onto my head and running a quick swipe of ChapStick across my lips. "Do you have survival supplies? Tinfoil blankets? That dehydrated food astronauts eat?" I'm only half kidding. I clip on Eric's leash and move to step out the door.

Where an elfin, peppy blonde should be, there is Matt, all lanky muscle and butterfly-inducing warmth. He's holding a bakery box and he looks exhausted. Lifting the box with one hand, he shrugs a shoulder.

"They were out of freeze-dried ice cream."

He climbs the two steps to where I'm standing like an idiot and hands the box over, fingers brushing mine and sending an electric sizzle up my arm. The scent of fried dough and sugar wafts under my nose and I'm pretty sure I look like a cartoon character, body levitating with joy as I inhale. He's schlepped baked goods from whatever port of civilization back to the frozen north. For me. Our eyes meet and I shake the giant heart emojis from mine, taking a mental step backward while my body insists I get *closer*. So much closer.

"You don't call. You don't write. Flying off into the, um, midday sun with people of questionable character." I glare at him with poorly pretended annoyance. He doesn't owe me anything, though I'm desperate for an explanation. When I (super casually) asked Tania where he'd disappeared to, she said he was working on a side project and left it at that. It was only my desire to hold on to some last shred of dignity that stopped me from nosing around further.

The sun rises over the tree line, hitting Matt full on the face. He winces, shields his eyes. He's probably spent the last week doing shots from Christine's flawlessly spray-tanned belly button. Isn't that a big-city artists and models activity? The idea is picking up steam when he gives me another slow, warm smile that melts at least three layers of emotion-protecting armor. At the thought of heat, my brain tweaks and I realize we're standing there jawing with the door open.

"It's taken me days to bring this place above freezing. Get inside! Close the door!" I frantically tug his coat sleeve until he's over the threshold. With the door closed, he seems very close, very large, and very, very appealing. He smells like cold air, cedar, and something I can't place, but it makes me want to lick him like a man-sized ice cream cone.

"I called last night to see if anyone needed supplies, and Kevin mentioned you hadn't run into the woods screaming yet." He looks around my humble abode, taking in the empty wine bottle still sitting on the tiny kitchen counter. "He asked that I bring a crate of Febreze and a six-month supply of lint rollers to, and I quote, 'mitigate a small portion of the chaos that girl and her beast will rain down upon our senses.'" He eyes my suitcase, which is still lying in the middle of the floor, contents spewed around it like an erupting volcano. "I like what you've done with the place."

"'Doodles barely even shed!" I protest as I hustle over to kick a couple of bras under a pile of T-shirts. "Kevin's angora sweaters drop more hair than poor, misunderstood Eric." Said canine headbutts my knee, indicating that while idle chitchat with sexy menfolk is all well and good, we have plans. I peek out the window to see if Tania's arrived yet.

Another whiff of sugar dances toward me and I give up trying to resist its call. Ignoring Matt's amused gaze, I slowly lift the lid. The icing shimmers in the frosty morning light. There are five doughnuts, but a greasy circle on the cardboard indicates that at some point a sixth had been nestled in with its delicious friends.

I shoot him a look of betrayal. "You stole one of my doughnuts."

"Technically they were my doughnuts at the time. If you feel they've been tainted I'm happy to take them up to the Big House. I'm sure others would appreciate the sugar hit."

Shielding the box with my body, I turn to put them on the counter.

"No need to get dramatic. They have a good home here, poor little plundered half-dozen." I face him again. "For which I am profoundly grateful, by the way. Thank you."

I give a now very impatient Eric a doggie biscuit, whispering, "I'm just having a bite before we go!"

It's nearly impossible to choose, but the plain Jane with chocolate frosting is too much to resist. My fingers close around the fluffy dough. As my teeth sink through the generous coating of sticky icing, my eyes close and I can't help but groan. Heaven.

I hear a soft chuckle and force my eyelids up enough to glare halfheartedly at Matt, who is leaning far too comfortably against the closed door. My brain sizzles with thoughts of all the interesting things that could be done against that door. I shove them away. *How inappropriate, Katelyn.*

"Can't a girl and her donut enjoy themselves, in the privacy of their home—I may add— without judgment?"

"I'll leave you two alone then." He laughs again as I maintain eye contact and take a huge bite, shooing him away with my free hand.

"Take your voyeuristic tendencies elsewhere. Jay would probably let you watch him massage the kale!" I call through a mouthful of perfection.

He opens the door and steps off my tiny front porch.

As he walks away shaking his head, I can see the side of his mouth quirked up in a half smile.

Eric and I stand in the open doorway, destroying the Hut's cocoon of warmth. I shove the last piece of doughnut into my mouth and suck icing residue from my fingertips as Matt rounds the corner behind a row of spruce trees and disappears from view.

I pour a mental pail of ice water on the warm fire burning in my belly (and quickly spreading elsewhere). Coworker, I remind myself. Cavorting about in helicopters with social media supermodels. Certainly, one hundred percent bad news. My eyes land on the box of doughnuts sitting innocently on the counter. The wine bottle. I find an instant crack in my resolve. Maybe ninety-five percent bad news. Still lots of bad news, though. Plenty.

Tania arrives, all pep and early morning enthusiasm. It's easy to imagine her as a highly paid fitness instructor, clad in head-to-toe athleisure, loudly assuring full-capacity stroller boot-camp classes that they can do anything they put their minds to.

Today, though, Tania is snapped into a red and black plaid lumberjack-style coat, jeans, and a beautiful chunky knit cream toque with a furry pom that sways gently in the wind, like a small friendly creature atop her head.

"Sorry!" she chirps. "I got sidetracked by Heinrich. He misplaced his noose. We had to make do with an extension cord. Ready to go?"

Eric's tail thwacks against the fake wood paneling that covers the walls as he drags me toward adventure.

I pop two more doughnuts into plastic bags and slide them into my coat pockets. For emergencies.

"Ready as I'll ever be."

The walk proves more refreshing than terrifying, and I get some great photos of the waterfall tumbling down across ice-glazed rocks, trees pressing in on either side. I didn't know this *National Geographic* level of natural beauty existed so close to home, and it kind of blows my mind.

I deposit an exhausted Eric back at the Hut and head to my office, thermos of tea in hand. Likely as not, I'll end up shoving it under my shirt to stay warm instead of drinking it. It's nice to have options.

After my last call with Brooke, I got an email notifying me that our weekly meetings were being changed to written reports. She either trusts me to toe the line or wants evidence of my ineptitude in writing for easier firing. Good thing I'm turning into an excellent double agent.

Every day I put together stacks of mail—actual mail with envelopes and stamps—to go out to the list of past visitors. This package includes a brochure detailing our services and highlighting the achievements of our Artists in Residence, as well as past guests who have made it big after spending time at Treetops. The most recent was here in 1989. Margie LeFoy hit the pros with an exhibition at the Art Gallery of Ontario, stretching painted colored strings around a room in a fashion reminiscent of high-tech laser security in action movies.

After mail duty, I reply to any inquiries about future book-ings, of which there are few, and then do a walkabout, chatting with guests and making vague lists of things that need repairs or updates—water stains on the ceiling, new ceiling fans for the guest rooms to help circulate heat, the newest model of hand-held vacuum with a special pet hair attachment. Occasionally I submit formal requests for funds to address these. So far, I'm zero for four on approvals. The vacuum was the biggest per-sonal hit. I was going to give it to Kevin for Christmas as a peace offering.

The afternoons are when the magic happens. And by *magic* I mean *subterfuge*. In keeping with Brooke's explicit directive, processes are being followed. For example, today I'm taking a deep dive into Section 8, Subsection C.

> *Staff are encouraged to leverage existing network con-nections to stimulate bookings growth. New guests must be screened against the Ideal Customer Profile to ensure a suitable fit in:*
> a) *Belief in the Creative Spirit*
> b) *Quality of Output*
> c) *Openness to upselling of onsite services*
> d) *Additional growth opportunities through referrals*

It goes on to suggest reaching out by phone, fax, or pager number (if available), but I decide to get a little wild and go with email. I craft a pretty solid template, pitching Treetops as a place to get away from the hustle and bustle of the city, connect with each other, and emerge stronger, armed with in-novative new ideas and action plans to forge a path to success. I also include the spa services list and sample menu, because who doesn't love a little pampering?

I blast through my list, adding personal touches to each message before saying a prayer that the keystroke-monitoring goons are three mimosas deep or getting a fresh gel manicure, and hit Send. Just like that, the startup community from Toronto to Vancouver becomes aware of Treetops.

Chapter 13

Days turn into weeks. I get into a groove that starts to feel tolerable, if not exactly comfortable. I sweet-talk Jay into increasing his waffle output from Saturdays only to a minimum of two days a week, with the potential for a third if I get Tania to ask for me.

Matt and I fall into the habit of having lunch together a couple of times a week, where we engage in casual buddy conversation with absolutely no flirting. When his hand brushes mine as he reaches for the pink Himalayan sea salt it's totally an accident. My smiles are hardly more coy or involving more eyelash flutters than they would with Ros or Gary. Purely chill, platonic coworker vibes here, everyone. Nothing to see.

Gloria Miller and Minnie Gluckstein have been coming to Treetops every year for a decade and their vibe is decidedly unchill. Their files paint a clear picture of two friends using their time at Treetops to full effect. Bar bills spanning multiple pages, spa records that look like they just showed up and declared *One of each!* and a smattering of output-focused sessions. Gloria tending toward craft enhancement and Minnie going for more inspiration and motivation through one-on-one creativity nurturing sessions. There's a note from the year before, after Minnie's Igniting the Fire Within workshop.

> NOTE: Mrs. Gluckstein indicates "moderate disappointment" with the content of this session. She "had hoped it would have more of a focus on sexual awakenings" and suggests we consider this as an option for next year.

I stop by the common area for the joint purposes of introducing myself and pilfering a wool blanket from the giant wooden chest that sits by the fire. The heating system in the Hut is leaving much to be desired as real winter temperatures set in.

The women are settled at either end of the couch, feet snuggled beneath them.

"Look there, Glo! Why that tree must have grown a foot since we were here!" says the one closest to the fire, pointing out the window with great certainty. How she can tell one tree from the next, I have no idea.

She's dressed in head-to-toe green and gray camouflage long underwear, a soft-looking black pashmina wrapped around her shoulders. The other woman, who must be Gloria, sporting an equally enthusiastic amount of cabernet velvet, snorts at her. "Or you've shrunk a foot, Granny!"

She cackles joyfully, rising from the couch when she sees me, hands on generous hips.

"A new girl! Tell us immediately, without even a moment of consideration, what should be the theme of our visit? Last year it was 'Excess,' so don't pick that."

They stare at me. I stare at them.

"No thinking!" Minnie has moved to where we're standing and swats my arm none too gently.

"Tomfoolery," I blurt.

Their eyes widen. I narrow mine and nod confidently.

"Delightful!" they cry in unison.

Gloria grasps my hand in both of hers and shakes it vigorously while letting me know "We're here to hone our most treasured skills—gossiping and avoiding our husbands! Oh, and for the poetry, of course."

When she lets go, I feel the crinkle of paper against my palm. A twenty-dollar bill.

I do not run when Kevin appears, but I do exit with a high level of enthusiasm, leaving them sipping spiked cider, soaking up his magician-like insights as to which accommodations will best support their goals for the next three days. I pause in the hall to eavesdrop.

"Ladies," he greets them. "So wonderful to have you back with us." He pauses and I know he's staring at them with his finger on his chin. Intuiting. "I believe this year you are on a journey of connection. Connection to the output, of course, but also to the greater experiences to be had in the nurturing, supportive, and safe space provided at Treetops. To best enable you to meet, and, I expect, exceed, your creative goals for the week, I have you staying in the main lodge. Mrs. Gluckstein—"

"Oh please, Kevin, after all these years you absolutely *must* call me Minnie."

"Absolutely right," Gloria chimes in. "Kevin, you understand us better than our husbands ever will. You have our full permission and encouragement to use our given names."

I re-position myself so I have eyes on the entertainment.

"As you wish, Gloria." He nods in her direction. "Minnie." Another nod. "As I was saying, you will be in the main lodge on the third floor. Mrs. Mil— Gloria, you are booked into the Maple Room, and Minnie, you are in the adjoining Spruce Room. These face away from the morning light to allow for a longer, deeper sleep and a natural awakening, without any interference, when your body has fully recharged. I believe you will find the gentle sounds of the wind in the trees and snow settling on bare branches to be extremely soothing on a subconscious level. Additionally, there is a small common area with bar service just outside the rooms. Serge has been working on a variety of seasonal martini variations in anticipation of your stay and is desperately awaiting your feedback."

"Nectar of the gods!" Minnie cries. "I am incredibly parched from the ride in."

"Let's not keep him waiting." Gloria stands, smoothing the lush fabric of her leisure suit. "You know my output requires a visit from the libation muse before it deigns to be released from the deepest crevices of my mind. Onward!"

I get myself out of the way to avoid being trampled.

"Enjoy your stay, ladies," says Kevin. "You are booked into the spa starting at eleven a.m. tomorrow. A full schedule awaits you in your rooms, along with your luggage."

Kevin may be a grade-A jerk but he puts on a great show.

I'm trying to decide if it would be easier to burn four hundred brochures than mail them when Mike pokes his head into my office to ask if I want to ride into town with him. My three-week isolation period is over.

"Freedom!" I cry, leaping from my chair with enough vigor to send it, wheels squealing, crashing into the wall. "I need my bag. I need my phone. I need—"

"I'm not leaving for an hour," he interrupts. "Gather all your whosits and whatnots and meet me out front at two."

I take off running for the Hut like this is a jailbreak.

"And for the love of God, woman, put on a hat!" Mike calls after me. "It's winter, not a damn fashion show."

By 1:50 I'm standing beside the Treetops truck, bag in hand, vibrating with excitement.

"Leaving so soon?"

Ugh. Kevin. I turn to face him and lean against the truck, the picture of casual confidence.

"And separate myself from your shining charm? Never. Just

going for a jaunt into town with"—I watch his face closely—
"Mike."

His right eye twitches and his shoulders slump ever so slightly
in his sky-blue cable-knit cardigan.

"Ah. I thought it was Tania's day." He's clutching something
in his hand. His jaw clenches repeatedly as some kind of inter-
nal debate rages.

Mike comes around the corner of the Big House and pauses
mid-step when he sees Kevin. I can see the wheels turning as he
tries to decide whether to retreat.

"Nope. Not today. But I see Mike coming now so if you need
something you can ask him in just a second!" I smile brightly at
his wide-eyed look of panic.

"That's fine," he rushes. "Kate, stop in at the Squirrel's Nest
and pick up these items."

I look at the list he's extended toward me and raise an eyebrow, waiting.

He sighs heavily. "Please. I would very much appreciate your
assistance in this matter." He gives the list a little shake of ur-
gency as Mike makes his choice and clomps toward us.

I wait one final, beautiful second before taking the list from
him.

"Of course, Kevin. Anything for a pal like you."

He's gone, jogging through the front doors of the Big House,
before I finish speaking. I check out the list.

5 x Yak Single—Dark Cherry
3 x Yak Single—Cactus
3 x Black Sheep Merino Silk—Goldenrod
4 x Black Sheep Merino Silk—Darkest Night

Is this an underwear order? If anyone's going to sport merino-
silk blend undergarments it's Kevin. A mental picture forms,
unbidden. I shudder and tuck the list into my coat pocket.

The truck door clicks as it unlocks and I heave myself up. By

the time the driver's door opens, I'm fully buckled and leaning forward as if the sheer will of my excitement will propel us
onward.

"You're like one of those ninety-year-olds on their first air-
plane ride," Matt says, and my head swivels so fast I worry it
might disconnect from my neck.

"You're not Mike." I'm confused.

"Correct," Matt says, putting the key in the ignition. The
truck rumbles to life, startling me out of my frozen state.

"It's just, I could have sworn Mike was the one who said he
was taking me into town. And, like, fourteen seconds ago I saw
him walking over here. But now you're here and he's gone." I
gasp dramatically and put a hand over my mouth. "You've murdered Mike! This is where the whole wilderness retreat thing
takes an even more terrible turn and I'm trapped in a thriller
that was masquerading as a rom-com. Good lord." I swoon
against the window. "My heart can't take it."

"A rom-com, huh? Who's the lucky guy?"

Crap.

"Kevin," I huff, cheeks burning. "Enemies to lovers. It never
would have worked out though. Obvious reasons."

"Like the fact that he truly despises you?"

"I was thinking more the clear divergence in our lifestyle
preferences. You know, dog hair and whatnot. But yeah, the
deep-seated hatred also comes into play."

"Mike asked if I'd do the run." Matt's eyes flick to the rearview mirror, and when I crane my neck around I can see Mike
standing outside the front door of the Big House, arms crossed
over his chest, waiting. "He needs to talk to someone."

My excitement drowns out any nerves about being close to
Matt and I hit the dash with my palm. "Let's roll! I have big-
time town things to do."

The sun shines blindingly onto a frost-coated world but
doesn't seem to be putting out enough heat to melt anything. By
the time we're speeding along the main road to Otterburne, my

extended proximity to Matt has overshadowed even the thrill of new scenery, and my mind has taken about thirty detours into filthy territory while trying to hold up my end of a boringly polite conversation. *We could just pull over into this little wooded area. Bench seats are a great option, but then there's also the back of the truck which happens to be a convenient height—*

I realize Matt's looking at me, waiting for the answer to a question I've completely missed.

I clear my throat and try to think pure thoughts. "Pardon? Sorry. Thought I saw a moose."

"I asked if you're ready for the storm. It's supposed to hit hard this weekend. If we have anyone planning arrivals on Friday or Saturday we should see if they want to come a day early or postpone. It'll be dicey coming in and out."

"Shoot. The O'Donnells are supposed to get picked up in town Saturday morning, and there's a girls' getaway coming Sunday through Wednesday. Though I think the girls in question are about seventy-five. 'Women's getaway' just doesn't have the same ring to it. Sounds like code for a gynecologist's appointment." I pause, try to figure out how to backtrack from my unfortunate reference. "It's a fact of life. Like prostate exams," I offer, in case he needs a more manly comparison. *Super smooth, Rigsby.*

He makes an *ew* face. "Thanks for that."

We drive on in silence and I regret that I may have conjured visions for him of my lady parts in the context of them requiring medical attention. Good thing I have no interest in pursuing any activities outside of this very satisfying, totally platonic friendship. *Lies, lies, lies,* my brain sings.

"So how did you end up here?" I ask after a couple of minutes of listening to radio personalities debate whether a hot dog is a sandwich. It's not, by the way. "You said at dinner the other night that it's the family business, but . . . I guess I don't get it."

He raises a smooth eyebrow. "Where would you like me to begin?"

"You must have done something before all this." I circle my hand through the air. "Tell me about your life pre-Treetops."

He turns his head to look at me, just for a second, before facing the road again. The sun brushes across his face, highlighting a faint scar above his left eyebrow. My fingers itch to touch him. I wedge them under my thighs.

"Would you like the light chitchat coworker version?"

I mull that over for a second. "Can you cobble together like a midweight option? I'm interested and caring, but also semi-maxed-out on the emotion front right now. You probably don't want me to cry."

"I didn't pack any tissues. Midweight it is."

He runs a hand along his cheek as he figures out where to start. His nails are pink with those perfect little white half-moons at the base. I wonder if he takes advantage of the spa discount for the men-icure package, but it doesn't seem like the right time to ask.

"I grew up in Toronto. I had a guinea pig named Pig-Pig-Pog and a goldfish—which I suspect, but cannot prove, was a series of fish—called Hoops."

"Oh wow. We're really going back. Okay." I angle my body so I'm facing him as much as the seat belt allows. "Were you into basketball? Or Cheerios?"

"I think I wanted to name it Poops. Hoops was a compromise."

I nod. Makes perfect sense.

"My mom was a chef. A good one. Great, actually. She had her own spot down by the St. Lawrence Market and worked wild hours, but always made sure I was taken care of." He slides a look in my direction. "Don't go thinking of some sad, lonely kid sitting in front of the TV, eating microwaved chicken nuggets while his mom created delicacies for the masses."

"I wasn't." Totally was.

We come around a wide bend, startling a deer nibbling grass at the edge of the road. I hold my breath until it decides to run back into the trees instead of onto our laps by way of the windshield.

"Art has always been part of my life. Mom focused on the food, but she also painted. On her days off, we'd find a spot in the city to sketch together or go to museums. She saw beauty in everything."

He sounds sad, and I get a sense of where this story might be heading.

"Dad's into a whole slew of things, as you might guess."

Might I? I nod knowingly.

"We've never been close. He traveled a lot when I was young, and they split up when I was six."

We pass a sign indicating we're fifteen kilometers from Otterburne.

"Skipping ahead, I got an Audi when I turned sixteen, and an all-expenses-paid trip to whatever university I could get into. I went to University of Waterloo for my parent-mandated business degree but did a double major and stuck art in there too, then went to Western for my MFA."

I try to look suitably impressed. "Sounds important."

"I guess." He pauses, looks at me. "You know what an MFA is, right?"

I roll my eyes. "Yes. God. I may not be the queen of output but I'm not a heathen. Mediocre Food Artistry. Everyone knows that. Though, to be fair, I think you could have aimed a bit higher."

His forehead crinkles charmingly. "I don't know how your parents survived your teenage years. You must have been unbearable."

"And still am, if you ask my father." Pitching my voice into low Dad tones I say, "You can't avoid difficult conversations with humor, Katelyn. You must face them head-on, like a matador faces the bull. Pretty sure he heard that on the radio once and just went with it."

Matt snorts. "With all due respect to your esteemed father,

who I'm sure is only looking out for your well-being, I'd argue the matador is all distraction and flourishes and the bull is the one doing the charging. You know, if you wanted a more accurate analogy."

My eyes bulge slightly as I lean toward him, glowing. "That is my argument exactly! Man, I bet he would love it coming from you though." The words play back through my head. Oops. "I mean, not that you would have a reason to meet him. Or that I was thinking about that outside the context of this conversation." Yup, that's better.

Inhaling deeply, I put on my game face. "Aaaanyway. Ready to return to the Matt Origin Story. I'll wipe my nose on my sleeve if I have to."

"For what it's worth, any family that has you as the output is probably worth meeting."

I'm staring at him and can't stop myself. We swing around a bend and the sun beams through the window onto the lower half of his face while his eyes stay shaded by his ball cap. The light picks up the red in his stubble. Would his kids have red hair? *God, Rigsby, stop it.*

I'm just overwhelmed by the freedom of being away from Treetops. My wild emotions have absolutely nothing to do with the hunk of man sitting in close proximity, smelling like heaven and looking like . . . well, also heaven.

He clears his throat and dives back in.

"When I graduated, Dad offered me a job at his company. I've always been more interested in the ways art ties into people's lives than in trying to make a living painting. I declined and went to work at a charity finding ways to make art accessible for kids, and also give them a safe space to spend their time. It was beautifully broad. Not just visual arts, but also theater and dance and cooking." He brakes for a chicken-sized bird that has parked itself on the yellow line before continuing. "Mom would come in to teach a class whenever she could. I loved it. The people, the work, hell, even the building. We were in this big old factory that was converted into studios and common areas and test kitchens. It was amazing.

"We were expecting a funding boost that would let us expand nationally. I was planning locations in Winnipeg, Calgary, Vancouver, and then I wanted to figure out how to support smaller satellite branches to service smaller, more remote communities."

I'm nodding, because it does all sound wonderful, but what's actually incredible is how talking about this place changes Matt. Having been exposed to a slew of young, passionate CEOs rocketing toward their destinies, it's easy to identify that charisma here. Matt is a born leader. Romantic urges aside, I'd follow him anywhere.

He trails off and rolls his shoulders back, and I brace myself for the hard part.

"But then our main funding was pulled and we had to close. And, at the same time, Mom got sick. Cancer. It was quick, which I think was better. She was fine, and then she wasn't. She died four months after she was diagnosed." His fists clench around the wheel. "It was a lot, all at once."

I'm terrible in these situations. There are so many things to say, and none of them are any good. I try not to feel too relieved when he picks up again without waiting for my reaction.

"I was twenty-nine and had my own life, a career I cared deeply about. And then it was just . . . well, just me. And then Dad, who's fine, but not very into the supportive parent role. Anyway, he offered me the chance to hide out here while I figured out what to do next and, um, I guess I'm still working on that. It's taking longer than expected. Sometimes it seems like it would be easier to do what he wants. Be the next HIT Properties CEO in waiting."

I must have made a sound because he looks at me. I clear my throat and gesture for him to continue while my mind does some feverish mental gymnastics. Family business. Treetops. Property mogul. Dots are being connected and it's not looking good. Romance with an employee is not great, but manageable, professionally speaking. Seducing the potential heir to the luxury getaway throne? Whole different hornet's nest.

I try to sound calm. "Just to backtrack a moment. Graham? Like, the Big Boss? Large head on the screen at town hall? He's your father?"

He sees the look on my face. "You didn't know."

No beating around the bush. I appreciate that almost as much as the charming flush that rises from the neck of his sweater as he sees me putting it all together. The reason the other employees aren't super keen on him. Why he keeps to himself. How he can get away with flitting off with That Neighbor Woman.

"Does this story somehow tie into your helicopter privileges? Or is that just your charm at work?" I'm trying to keep it jokey, but it comes out a little more shrill than I'd have liked.

"Christine? She's my half-sister. Mom was wife number four." He waggles four fingers in the air. My head falls back against the headrest as I attempt to process this particular fact nugget.

"Before Kizette and Brooke, after Shoshana." His eyes crinkle in thought. "I can't remember the first two."

"You all have different last names?"

"He believes in the power of feminine energy and matriarchs as, and I quote, 'oases of positive transformation.' Christine and I each have our mom" last names to harness that power."

"Right. Oases." My mind is racing.

"He's a sucker for creative genius, and love in general." He puts on a posh, artsy voice. "I think it speaks to the passionate nature of his innermost self."

Pushing all my confusion and desire for detail aside, I jump back in like I'm not reeling from this barrage of information that changes so many things. "Oh, so he's like a well-groomed mullet. Property mogul in the front, bohemian in the back."

He laughs, and the sound has the same effect as a glass of mulled wine and a good book. I'm calm. I'm happy. I'm smiling dopily when I should be building huge walls around my sad, damaged heart. Getting involved with this guy now, when I'm already subverting every other well-documented rule my employer, who happens to be his dad has laid out? Terrible idea. It's like I'm begging for a disciplinary review.

I try new mantras. *Money before honey. Cash before pash. Bills before thrills.* I keep this up much longer than necessary, trying to distract myself from the way he's looking at me out of the corner of his eye. Like he doesn't know I'm terrible at life. Like he likes me. You know. *Likes* me.

Chapter 14

Matt drops me off in front of the town's most charming, and possibly only, bakery while he goes to pick up some supplies for a project of his own. Something that involves lumber and chicken wire.

I take a detour to my car to make sure it's intact. It is, and for a few minutes I sit in the front seat, basking in the sun and the feeling of being somewhere familiar.

Back at the bakery I request the biggest latte available, paired with a brownie the size of my face, and take advantage of the speedy Wi-Fi, catching up on celebrity gossip and spending an inordinate amount of time scrolling through social media.

Eventually, I'm nibbling the final corner of my brownie and wondering if I have room for a croissant when I decide I should be a responsible adult and listen to my voicemails. I'm tucking a buttery, pastry-filled bag into my purse when Chaz's voice assaults my ear. It's so loud I'm sure the sweet-looking ladies next to me can hear every word.

"I CAN'T BELIEVE YOU DID THIS. DO YOU KNOW

WHAT YOU'VE COST ME? I WON'T LET YOU GET AWAY
WITH THIS, KATE. FUCK. I'M GOING TO RUIN YOU."

Smiling politely, I walk quickly out the door. My hands are
shaking so badly I nearly drop the bonus latte I got for the road.

Outside I collapse against the sun-warmed bricks of the bakery and try to calm myself. What can he do? Sue me? I guess,
but good luck getting anything out of it. Destroy my career? Did
it all by myself, thank you very much. I can feel myself spiraling
into a pit of mental darkness and despair, despite the sun and
my newfound freedom. Lost in thought, I stay slumped against
the wall.

A shadow falls across my face.

Matt is standing in front of me, blocking the sun and causing
near-instant shivers to rack my body as it registers the sudden
lack of heat. Rays of light beam from around his head like some
life-size angelic stained glass. With his worn jeans, scuffed work
boots, sunglasses, and ball cap, the feelings he's dredging up are
much more on the devilish side of things. The light catches the
scruff on his chin and I wonder what it would feel like against
my skin. He makes a great, if temporary, distraction.

"Are you choking? Why aren't you speaking? It's usually impossible to get you to be quiet."

I consider faking a throat obstruction just to feel his arms
around me, but relegate that to the "unnecessarily dramatic"
column of Kate's Possible Life Choices.

"Nope. Fine. Just, erm, caught up in the beauty of this fine
day."

He gives me a look that calls BS. He checks his watch—gold
face with a black leather band. "We should head back. I have a
workshop at four thirty. Did you get through your list of exciting town activities or were you too busy soaking in the majesty
of your surroundings?" He starts walking down the sidewalk
and I push myself off the wall to follow.

The memory of Chaz's voice rings in my ears.

"I managed to listen to my messages." I shrug, pasting on a

smile that hopefully looks more natural than it feels. "I can do the other stuff next time. It was nice to get a change of scenery, if nothing else."

Matt stops walking, and his hand lands on my arm, pausing my forward momentum. On reflex I look behind me, making sure some pedestrian immersed in their phone screen isn't going to body check me. But this isn't Toronto and there's hardly anyone in sight.

"That's it? You checked your messages? You must be extremely popular if that took you an hour."

"I also got this latte, a one-pound brownie, and a croissant for the trek home." I hold the steaming cup up as proof.

He snorts. "I've seen you with desserts. That brownie would have lasted four minutes, max. Are you sure there's nothing else you need to do?"

I think of the extensive snack shopping I'd been looking forward to. In the aftermath of Chaz's message, I feel too queasy to appreciate a casual stroll through a well-stocked junk food aisle. Even the thought of a chocolate bar the size of a small terrier can't tempt me into the grocery store now. I dump my full latte into a nearby garbage can.

"Let's get going. Don't want you to be late for Matt's Art Minute." As I stick my hands in my coat pockets, I notice a piece of paper edging its way out, gleaming white against the fabric. I'm shoving it back into the depths from whence it came when I remember what it is: Kevin's list.

I groan. This is supposed to be a fun, light-hearted outing during which the guy I'm not even remotely interested in falls in love with my winning personality and stunning girl-next-door looks, but instead, it's one disappointment after another.

"I have to pick up Kevin's underwear."

Matt's face scrunches in confusion. "Nope." He shakes his head. "Does not compute."

I hold out the list. "Kevin voluntold me to pick up this stuff for him."

He takes a moment to scan the items and shakes his head again.

"I see you haven't clued into Kevin's true creative output."

"Don't tell me he's a luxury underwear model. I can't take it."

He checks his watch again. "We've got time. And Clarissa can kick it off if I'm not back. Let's go."

Warm, strong fingers wrap around my mittened ones and pull me down the street. My heart skitters in my chest like a hyperactive chipmunk. When he lets go five seconds later, confident I'm not making a break for the truck, I do a terrible job of not being disappointed.

The door to the Squirrel's Nest swings open, accompanied by the gentle ring of a bell that sounds more like wind chimes. A world of string lies before me. Wool. Embroidery thread. Normal thread. Twine. There's a wall of knitting needles, crochet hooks, pattern books, and approximately one thousand varieties of beads.

A woman in white skinny jeans, a chunky knit sweater the color of rubies, and thick-framed tortoiseshell glasses emerges from behind a mountain of multicolored balls. A handwritten sign poking out the top advertises Premium Korean 100% Organic Wool—$2 off.

"Can I help you?" she asks. She straightens her name tag (Lindsay). When her eyes land on Matt I can almost feel her wishing her phone number was printed on it as well. In her twenties, she's got that effortlessly cool vibe that I desperately wish to emulate but can never achieve. Her shiny chestnut hair tumbles loosely around her shoulders. Her nose does not run from being out in the cold.

"Hopefully," I say, stepping into her line of vision. She seems startled by my sudden appearance. I get it, try not to hold it against her but am a little perplexed by how much I don't want her interacting with Matt. *Mine, mine, mine.*

Extending the list toward her, I say, "Do you have these things in stock?"

Lindsay purses well-glossed lips as she reads.

"This is a beautiful selection. Is it for you?"

I can't decide if I'm offended that she sounds so doubtful. "No, I'm not well versed in the, um, string knotting arts. Just picking it up for a, uh, friend." Matt snorts and I elbow him.

"It's for Kevin Ramsay," Matt explains.

I give him a look. "Is he famous in yarn-working circles or something?"

Apparently so, because Lindsay's eyes widen behind her glasses. "Oh!" she breathes. "Of course. Just give me a minute."

I turn to Matt as she disappears between two giant rows of shelving, overflowing with natural fibers. "Explain, please."

His cheeks are pink from the warmth of the store, and his brown eyes dance with laughter. "He's just really good at knitting. His sweaters? They're art."

"Well, yeah. But why do people know who he is? My grandma knit me a very cool vest with a penguin on it and no one got all breathy when I mentioned her name." My brow crinkles in consternation. "Fame via knitwear? Who knew?" This explains why he struts around like a wool-clad peacock each time a new garment makes an appearance. The man has skills.

"Local fame," he clarifies. "It's not like you're going to tune into the Kevin Ramsay Netflix special to hear his commentary on the youth of today while he designs and creates a custom garment, live onstage."

I freeze for a moment, picturing the spectacle he's so clearly described.

"Got it!" Lindsay announces cheerfully. "Had to run into the back for a couple of the gem tones, but it's all there, individually wrapped, of course." She hands the bag to Matt, smiling with enough warmth to burn his clothes to the ground where he stands.

I snag the goods from Matt and step in front of him, reinserting myself into the conversation. "Great! Thanks so much for your help. How much do I owe you?"

"Oh no, Mr. Ramsay has a running tab here."

After promising to tell Kevin just how much Lindsay admires his work, and another three rounds of thank-yous and have-a-great-days we finally move toward the exit.

The sun has disappeared, replaced by a herd of aggressive-looking clouds.

"What now?" Matt asks.

What now, indeed.

We're standing a foot apart, which isn't far at all, now that I think about it. I'm looking up at his face, taking in the shape of his mouth and the curve of his jaw. The little lines that appear between his eyebrows when he's thinking about something. The way his eyes are locked on mine, getting closer, closer, until I'm breathing in the mint on his breath and his lower lip is brushing across mine. My eyelids start to close and it's going to be so, so good, except . . .

"We can't." I take a quick step back, banging into a grumpy-looking guy carrying an armload of groceries. "Sorry!" I call too loudly, accompanied by an apologetic wave. All I get back is a glare, which isn't nearly as bad as the vibes I'm getting from Matt.

He's got his hands in his coat pockets. I can't tell if he's mad at me or just cold. Probably both.

"I'm sorry. I feel like you're making these truly lovely attempts to move things along here"—I motion to the space between us—"and I keep applying the brakes. Kind of aggressively. It's just . . ." How much do I tell him? Not the whole story, obviously.

"I just got out of a relationship," I try.

"Ah. That old nugget." He doesn't sound particularly pleasant or convinced.

"No, listen, it's not like I'm hung up on him. He's literally the worst. It's more that the end of, um, all that is what led me here and I'm trying to focus on the job. It's turning out to be more of a challenge than I anticipated." The job? Focusing? What am I even saying?

"It's fine. I get it."

"You do?" A little surprising, since I don't get it myself.

"Yeah. You thought a quick fling would be fun when you were planning to get out of Dodge, but something less fleeting isn't in the cards. Understood."

"No! That's not what I meant."

He turns, starts walking toward where he left the truck.

"No hard feelings, Kate."

I don't budge. He stops and looks over his shoulder at me.

"You ready? I need to get back."

"Yeah, sorry. Of course." I take a couple of steps, then halt. "No, actually. Not ready." It's starting to get exhausting, all these ups and downs, and I want to make my position clear. There's a bench at the edge of the sidewalk, framed by adolescent trees and planters brimming with shiny festive greenery and adorned with sparkling red bows. It's the last week of November, I realize as I sit down. Time to start Christmas shopping. Or, it would be, if I was going home for the holidays. Brooke dropped that little bombshell in our last meeting, along with a not-so-subtle hint that my inquiry about vacation time was off-putting in the face of a lackluster performance thus far. Apparently "someone," aka Kate Rigsby, needs to stay on-site for holiday bookings. I haven't figured out how to break it to my parents. One more thing to worry about, but not right now.

Matt reverses course, stands in front of me a polite distance away, relaxed, feet hip-width apart. There are little crinkles at the corners of his eyes that suggest this is a façade. He's done with the conversation, isn't looking forward to an awkward drive home, and is probably itching to get as far away from me as possible to avoid further torment. I pat the bench beside me. He doesn't move. I put some more oomph into it and stare directly at him, eyebrows raised. He sighs, sits.

Rotating so I can look at him, I consider whether I should take his hand in mine, decide against it. Partially because he's resting one arm along the back of the bench so his hand is right behind me, and I like it there. Also, it would be awkward to try to and relocate it.

He clears his throat and I realize I should get the ball rolling. A mental sports commentator chimes in from a distant corner of my brain, whispering into his mic in a British accent. *This is a critical moment for Rigsby. Is she going to go all in and risk everything for the big win, or take the safer path to a mediocre outcome as we've seen so many times in the past?*

"I like you. More than I want to, if I'm being honest." I look down at my lap, brush some imaginary dust away. *She's going for it!* My fingers clench in my mittens. Yes, she is.

"I also, quite desperately, need to find a way to do the impossible and increase business enough to get the bonus at the end of this horrendous rainbow. And, well, I'm already, um, treading a bit close to the line in terms of how that's going to happen. If I break the Cavorting Clause and someone reports it—"

"The what?"

"The Cavorting Clause." No reaction other than a slight twitch of his lips.

"In the Process Manual?" If I close my eyes, I can see the words as they're printed, in faded Comic Sans. "Section 4, Employee Behavior, Subsection 3b: 'Treetops employees shall not engage in personal relationships with coworkers, guests, or strategic business partners.'" My eyes pop open. "Though it doesn't specifically call out the progeny of the CEO, I'm sure it's implied."

"There's a manual?"

I am agog. Agog! "You've got to be kidding. *Is there a manual?*"

"Well, it's not like a Bible at a hotel, is it? There wasn't a copy in my bedside table when I arrived."

"You've been here for years! How have you completely

skipped past the concept of this book that guides every facet of day-to-day life without experiencing severe repercussions?"

His head tilts, considering. The tips of his ears are red from the cold. "Nepotism?"

"Motherfucker," I mumble into my scarf.

He bursts out laughing.

"It's not funny," I insist, but I can feel the pressure lifting from my chest. "Here's what I wanted to say, so stop giggling and pay attention. I like you. I want to figure out if whatever this is can be more than it is right now, if that's still of interest to you in nine weeks."

I hold my breath.

His hand moves from the back of the bench, cups my chin lightly. His thumb runs gently along the little indent below my lip. I am a puddle.

"Nine weeks? That probably won't kill us."

Ignoring the wave of strong, hormone-induced feelings overtaking my body, I stand. "Exactly." Heart-to-heart complete. "So, buds for the next nine weeks and then, well, then we'll see?"

I remove a mitten and extend my hand toward him for a shake, all business. He closes his hand over mine, folding my fingers shut, and goes for the fist bump, complete with explosive fireworks to close. My skin tingles where his palm had pressed against it.

"You got it, pal." He wraps an arm around my shoulders for a quick, friendly embrace before checking his watch. "Shoot. We gotta run." And then he takes off, loping gracefully to the truck.

I trail behind, huffing, the paper bag of precious wool bouncing against my hip. *Was that a goal? Waiting on the official call from the refs.*

Chapter 15

There is no part of me that wants to go looking for Kevin, but I need the room assignments for the group of three coming in tomorrow, and in an uncharacteristic move, he hasn't deposited the details on my desk when I'm not around. We're getting better at avoiding each other as much as possible, utilizing carefully timed drops and other employees as messengers. Also, I have to deliver his bag of wool. I haven't seen him since my trip into town yesterday and I want the opportunity to experience this rare moment of undying gratitude in person. I was hoping I wouldn't have to hunt him down to get it.

The door to his office is, as always, closed. I've never tried to open the door, so I couldn't say if he usually locks it, but today it glides silently open, revealing the enemy's inner sanctum.

The room is small, only about ten feet square, and smells faintly of vanilla. A beautiful rolltop desk is pushed up against one wall, the writing surface covered with four stacks of neatly arranged folders. A single window looks out over what Jay calls his kitchen garden, though this late in the year it's just a frozen patch of dirt surrounded by chicken wire and naked trees waving in the wind. Judging by the flakes that have started to float down, the dirt won't be visible for long.

The dark, low-pile hotel-style carpet that covers most of the hallways and office spaces has been topped with a lush cream area rug I didn't think people in real life could ever own without it being instantly destroyed. Three walls are dark beige (but probably called dove gray or warm taupe). The fourth is burgundy but mostly covered by a large bulletin board on the left and whiteboard on the right.

A neatly handwritten grid on the whiteboard shows the names of upcoming guests along the top, and topics down the left side. Lighting, Productive Hours, Suggested Supplements. The bulletin board is covered with what look like printouts of pictures from the small inkjet printer perched on a pedestal table beside a cozy brown leather wingback armchair and footstool.

I start toward the desk, hoping to find the information I need sitting conveniently atop one of the stacks of folders.

"What are you doing?" Kevin says from the doorway, his tone even more frigid than usual.

I nearly drop the wool that's crushed under my arm, compromising the fibers and rendering each overpriced skein functionally useless. I'm annoyed at the feeling of guilt that washes over me. *I'm* not the one who didn't do their job in a timely fashion. Inhaling deeply, I turn to face him, the usual pained smile on my lips.

"Just looking for the room deets for the group coming in tomorrow so I can get things teed up with the mentors. You know how Clarissa gets if she doesn't receive adequate notice."

"Do you have no respect for personal boundaries? No regard for privacy?"

I open my mouth to answer but he cuts me off before I can get a word out.

"Brooke has truly outdone herself this time. Usually, the Development people she brings in are lazy and selfish but have some modicum of decency. Of respect!" His cheeks are rosy with emotion, mustache quivering in outrage. Yikes.

"Whoa there, bud." I put my hand up in the universal sign for halt. "You're the one who didn't deliver the information I need to do my job, requiring me to come searching for it so another valued member of our team can do *her* job well and our guests arrive to a properly prepared and personalized environment. So if you want to just take that accusatory finger and turn it right around, I think it'll be pointing at the source of today's act of disrespect."

I cross my arms over my chest and wait for an apology that doesn't come. Instead, Kevin storms past me, the tail of his tiny-stitched scarf brushing against my black technical fleece zip-up, leaving blue and white fibers in its wake. He grabs a folder and flips it open, pulling the top page out and thrusting it toward me.

"Here."

I take it, issuing a grudging "Thank you." I'm about to turn for the door and beat a hasty retreat when I have an idea. *Focus on the work,* I remind myself. The riches, not the bitches. I mentally hum a bar of "Jesus, Take the Wheel."

"Kevin," I venture, carefully stepping toward him. "What else is in that folder?"

"What? Nothing." He snaps it shut and stands with his back to the desk, blocking my view.

"It's just, if I understand your process, I can market your skills more effectively. Right now, we promise a personalized creative environment, but if I could explain some of the expertise that goes into those assessments, well"—I make a chef's-kiss motion—"people love a highly trained service professional." My gaze floats over the walls, taking in the strange combination of abstract art and watercolor landscapes. "Also, I have this bag of wool shorn from prized Nepalese yaks."

I dangle the bag from a finger, swinging it gently back and

forth. His eyes follow, narrowing, before he reaches out to snatch it from me.

"You're welcome," I say, a picture of magnanimity. "So? Do you have any applicable certifications? Degrees?"

His jaw clenches. "Thank you," he chokes out, then continues, "I am among the best in my field."

"So just the double major in hurtful observations and standoffishness, then?" I give myself a mental kick in the pants. *Stifle the sass, Rigsby.*

I try again. "You are excellent. There's no denying it. But how?" I edge closer, eyes locked on the folders on the desk. If I could just get a peek inside one . . .

Reading my mind, or possibly my less than subtle body language, Kevin gathers the folders into his arms and hugs them tightly to his chest.

I sigh dramatically. "Just let me see! Or tell me! There's no reason for this to be a secret!"

"My process is my own. Now get out." He shifts the stack of folders to sandwich it under his arm and moves to stand at the open door, waving me through it.

"I thought we could bond over your brilliance, but fine. Have it your way. We will soldier on in mediocrity."

Moving through the doorway, I catch a glimpse of the name on the folder sticking out from behind his elbow. My hand moves in before my brain even completes the thought, snatching it from him with speed and accuracy completely unfamiliar to me. I have it open before he can react.

"What the fuck, Kevin." My eyes move between the pages and his face. His mouth opens and closes as he searches for the right words to explain why he has pictures of my apartment in Toronto. Pictures of me at events for Regan-Caulfield. With Chaz. Of Eric surrounded by half-chewed books.

"It's not what it looks like."

"Are you sure? Because it looks like you're a stalker." I back toward the door, not taking my eyes off him. If this were an episode of *Law & Order*, he would start chasing me down the hall at any moment, intent on keeping his terrible secret. But I don't feel like I'm in any particular danger. The more I look at the pictures, the more I think I understand. Or at least, I hope I do, because no one else seems to be around and I'd rather not be murdered, rolled up in this expensive-looking area rug, and buried by moonlight in the fallow kitchen garden.

"Cheater!" I cry, pointing at him. "You research everyone and pass it off as this magical intuition!"

He puts the remaining folders down on the desk again and leans against it, pressing his fingers to his eyes, as if staving off a headache.

"It's not cheating," he says, sounding pained. "It's years of experience. Decades of investigatory skill, combined with the deeply concerning trend of people sharing their most personal moments online for anyone to see."

I take the liberty of collapsing into the nearby leather arm-chair and put a fingertip to the picture of the living room in my apartment back home. "My sublet ad?"

"Yes."

The work functions. "Regan-Caulfield events page?"

A grudging nod.

The picture of Eric gives me pause. "This is on my Instagram, but that's private and you most certainly do not follow me."

"You had it as a profile picture on Facebook, and your privacy filters let anyone see those. Also, when you applied for this job, you temporarily made your Instagram account public." His head tilts to the right, like an inquisitive bird. "Curious, really, given some of your most recent content."

My stomach lurches. If Kevin had seen my post about Chaz, it would certainly go a long way toward explaining at least some of his feelings about me. But now is not the time to worry about it. Shake it off. Move along. Nothing to see here.

"Are you a cop?"

He rolls his eyes.

"You are! Or were?" Forgetting my concern for my reputation, I am legitimately excited to discuss his career in great detail. Like many of my contemporaries, I'm a sucker for true-crime stories.

"Did you solve murders? Arrest serial arsonists hell-bent on burning all the toilet paper in all the Walmarts of Ontario?" I inhale, bracing myself for his upcoming confirmation that my next guess is spot-on. "You were an undercover narcotics operative cracking down on the world of illicit substances. Taking them down from the top!"

"Dear God. Please stop talking." Through gritted teeth he says, "I am—was—a private investigator. Retired"—he gestures to our surroundings—"obviously."

"A PI! Shut up! You—man of mystery and interesting, mildly concerning secrets. That's so cool." I sprawl back in the chair and kick my feet up onto the ottoman before Kevin's sharp look at my shoes has me putting them back on the floor.

"Well, shoot." I lock eyes with him, feeling the manic gleam in mine. "I can work with this."

He gives his head a single, sharp shake. "I do not give you permission to leverage my personal history for business gain."

"Is that not what's happening here?" I wag the Kate Rigsby folder in the air.

"Because I am left with no choice! What else am I supposed to do in this godforsaken place—" He stops himself, and takes a moment to rearrange the scarf around his neck, carefully draping the tail to display the waving ocean-like tones to full effect.

"This is none of your business. You have crossed personal and professional boundaries. Now get out."

I flee, taking my folder with me, but not before noticing one he's still holding particularly tightly. A photo peeks out from the edge, showing a quarter of a head with wrinkle-free skin and hair I'd recognize anywhere. *Brooke.*

* * *

I head down to my office, sidestepping puddles of melted snow that have accumulated on the cement floor where people have stomped through with boots on. Wrapping myself in my new blanket borrowed from the living room—I'd gone with cream wool, striped with bands of blue, yellow, red, and green—I sink into the creaky chair and open my email.

> *Ms. Rigsby!*
> *I checked out the information you sent and I agree, one hundy-p. Treetops is exactly what we're after for our year-end retreat.*
> *I've copied Trev from our events department (Crazy, huh? We have a whole department for parties now!). He'll be in touch to work out the details. Oh, and I hope you don't mind, but I passed this over to a couple of other dudes and dudettes who are looking for something similar.*
> *Peace and Thyme,*
> *Josh Meadows*
> *Chief Taste Officer, Party Thyme*

I scan through the follow-up note from Trev (Director of Good Thymes), wondering if we can accommodate a group of twenty for four days, three nights.

My stomach is swooping.

"This is amazing." The math is fuzzy but promising. This could make my month. Then I realize the cat's going to be clawing its way out of the bag. "This is bad. Incredibly bad." My knuckles are pressed against my mouth so hard I can feel teeth cutting into my lips. Getting the booking was step one, but now I need to figure out how to pass off a corporate retreat as a legitimate output-generating artistic experience.

I pace back and forth. Eric, who I have taken to sneaking into the basement to warm my feet, is tucked under my desk. He tracks my progress like he's watching the world's most angsty self-talk-filled tennis match.

"How did this happen?" I mutter. "Because you're a brilliant idiot, intent on going down in a glorious fireball. Holy moly. Holy. Moly." A smile stretches my face enough that it hurts. "It might actually work."

I stop in my tracks and stare at the ceiling. It's creaking as someone crosses the floor above me, heading toward the stairs that lead down to my dungeon.

A foot appears on the top step and my heart stutters. No one can know about this yet. My arms flap like the wings of a panicked hen as I rush to the desk and click to a different window. I perch casually beside the phone. I am the picture of calm. You know, aside from the sweat beading on my forehead and the hives that are probably breaking out on my arms at this very moment.

"You down there, Kate?" Jay stops when his knees are in sight.

"Yup!" I screech. Super casual.

"The boss is on the phone."

I slap a hand across my mouth to stifle a hoot of panic. "Do you know what she wants?"

"You know I'm the chef, right? Not your assistant?" After a beat, he relents. "She's about to get on a flight and wants to know the status of the something or other. Log into the video conference. She sent an invite."

My knees buckle as he clomps back up to the main floor. This is it. I'm done.

I click the video link in the meeting invite.

Brooke's face glowers at me through the screen. It looks like a normal level of dislike, as opposed to "I saw evidence of your complete idiocy via the advertised email monitoring and am about to smite you." So that's something.

She's in an airport and despite my panic, I'm desperate to

figure out where she's going. Based on the oversized straw hat perched on top of her suitcase, somewhere much warmer than here.

Her sharp voice rips my attention away from the fuzzy gate announcements running in the background.

"When we spoke last week, you indicated you were targeting five new bookings. How did that go?"

She knows perfectly well how it went. My failings are documented in great detail each and every Monday as part of my required reporting. An excellent way to kick off the week.

"Unfortunately, we missed that goal. I reached out to guests who have enjoyed stays with us throughout winters past." Winters past? Who am I, Dickens? I give my head a little shake, feeling my dangly gold and amber earrings bounce jauntily. A panicked giggle threatens to burble out of my mouth, so I cough instead. Take a sip of yesterday's water. Putting the cup down, I notice a spider is floating in it. Blech.

"The Millers decided on Jamaica this year instead of their customary pre-Christmas retreat, and they invited the Robertsons along. Others were, uh, unresponsive." I steel myself and plow on. "What I'd like to do, Brooke, is cast a wider net. There is a much larger market out there that we are missing entirely. It's still early enough that if we go all-in on some targeted campaigns immediately, we can get some solid traction for Christmas and the New Year." I hold my breath.

"This has been discussed already. We have proven practices—"

"But they aren't working!" Frustration boils over before I have a chance to build an extension onto the fortress that usually attempts to contain my unprofessional thoughts and opinions.

She glares at me coldly. I'm surprised the screen doesn't frost over and crack.

"Maybe *you* aren't working. If you cannot follow the simple directions that provide a pathway to success in your role, I'm afraid I won't be able to keep you on. Other applicants would be thrilled to embrace this opportunity to learn the ins and outs of the luxury hospitality business."

No doubt. They probably won't lust after your stepson or assault the neighborhood internet celebs either. I channel my most grown-up, shit-eating self.

"Brooke, I understand your frustration. You've given clear directives and, while I have been following them, you're right— I have also been veering off into the weeds in search of a way to make my mark here. You are the expert, and I am so grateful to have this chance to learn from you."

She looks slightly mollified. "You should note that I am extremely influential in the industry. Should this go well, my name can open doors."

Inspiration strikes. Or I have completely lost my mind? I shove things around on my desk, looking for the page I'd ripped out of the Process Manual at breakfast while shoveling fluffy scrambled eggs into my mouth.

"I, uh, noticed an area of the Process Manual I'd like to explore a bit further, but only if you believe it would be worth the time." I swipe a stack of brochures onto the floor, cringing at the *thwump* they make as they land. Where *is* it? Brooke interprets my silence as me awaiting permission to continue. She gives a single nod, eyes focused on something in the distance. Probably one of those ten-minute pedicure booths. Finally, I see it, sticking out from underneath a box of brochures. Swooping down, I scan the words to find what I need. There.

"In Section 18, Subsection 2.11, there is mention of soliciting endorsement. Specifically, it states *Sales and Marketing may engage with existing contacts and utilize that engagement to further the reputation and success of the Retreat.*"

Let's roll the dice of life, shall we? Brooke is scrolling through her phone, barely listening.

"What I was hoping, Brooke, was that you would allow me to leverage our stellar reputation to try to entice some kind of endorsement, or, as mentioned in the handbook, *engagement* with some of my premium-level contacts. It could really shine a spotlight on us."

Brooke's face indicates this is an asinine idea and she believes I have no contacts, premium or otherwise, but she must have had an extra shot of green juice this morning because she throws me a bone. "If this additional activity is completed on your own time and without using Treetops resources, you may make an attempt."

Mother Teresa, everyone.

"Understood, Brooke. I am deeply grateful for the chance—"

A cheery, overloud voice interrupts. "Now boarding group A for flight 657 to Málaga–Costa del Sol."

"Finally. I need to go." She disappears from the screen and I can't help that a small, desperate part of me hopes her plane will crash before she figures out what I'm up to.

Chapter 16

By dinnertime, the snow is calf-deep. Even someone who hates the cold as much as I do would have a hard time not feeling a little bit of magic walking through the curtain of huge flakes floating down to join their fallen comrades. There's no wind to speak of. Just snow falling straight down.

The warm lights of the dining room shine from the stone walls of the lower level of the Big House. It's dark by five o'clock these days, but the bright snow reflects whatever light there is and makes it possible to be outside without feeling completely blind.

Something about the first snow of the year and the imminent Party Thyme booking makes me feel lighter. I throw caution to the wind and let Eric out the front door of the Hut without his leash. I lock eyes with him, do a quick feint left, and then take off running right. He yips with joy and romps along beside me. We do a lap of the fire circle before collapsing into the snow. I make snowball after snowball and chuck them as far as I can, watching them plop down and disappear. He chases them into the darkness and immediately comes back for another.

Out of nowhere, something thumps into my arm. I whip around and see Matt coming out of the trees, a half-formed snowball taking shape in his gloved hands.

"Oh, you think because I'm from the city I can't win a snow-ball fight?" I shove myself to standing and sprint to the Gath-ering Fire, taking cover behind one of the tree-trunk benches. Quickly, I pack together a tiny arsenal. I shoot my head up for a quick check of my surroundings and am immediately under fire.

"I haven't always been an artist, you know," Matt calls out conversationally. "I was a pitcher in high school." His voice is coming from somewhere to my right. I sneak another peek as another snowball whips out of the darkness and knocks my jaunty pom-pom toque off my head. "A really good one!"

"Yeah? Well, I am not particularly good at any sport, but I am"—I pause to chuck a volley in the direction of his voice—"very passionate about survival. And"—another throw that, from the deep laughter that follows, lands nowhere near my target—"I have a secret weapon. Eric! Get him!" Three seconds later Matt's on his back in the snow, trying to fend off the en-thusiastic licks of an overexcited, snow-encrusted canine. I mo-sey over, grab an armload of snow, and let it fall directly onto his head. "Winner!" I declare, arms raised in victory.

Mike is walking past with some fallen branches over his shoulder. He nods toward the Big House where the door is just opening to reveal an angry-dad-vibe-exuding Kevin. "You might want to relocate."

"Retreat!" I whisper, grabbing Eric's collar. Kevin stares into the still-falling snow and starts stomping directly toward us. I can't get back to my place without crossing the open space be-tween us. This is how a deer must feel when it's been targeted by whatever lecture-giving wildlife exists in this area.

"My place is this way," says Matt, nodding his head to the right. I follow him through the tree line and along what I assume is a well-worn path when we're not mid-blizzard. He clicks on a light that's cleverly built into his toque and I immediately feel the need to have one of my own. An early Christmas present to myself. Wilderness tools! In the cone of light emanating from his forehead, I can see the branches on either side of us starting to sag under the weight of the snow, forming a fairy-tale overhang that spits us out into a clearing.

Matt does not live in half a portable. He doesn't even live in an entire portable. Matt, goddamn him, has a house.

The 1960s A-frame is nestled in a clearing a couple hundred feet from the Treetops property. The house is brown and cream and makes me think of the snippets of the Swiss Alps I've seen on travel shows. It's positioned sideways on the lot, so one side of the sloping roof faces the road, and the other the lake, while the front looks onto the woods that stand between here and Treetops proper.

"Nepotism again?"

He doesn't answer and I put it down to the noise of the snow under our feet drowning out my voice.

I trail him along the front of the house, feeling like I'm in a snow globe. Is it possible to be drunk on winter? Because I think I am. Mind you, the very fine ass ahead of me doesn't help with any feelings of steadiness.

As we round the back corner the lake comes into view, a swath of darkness surrounded by freshly fallen snow. It looks like you could step in and be transported to a different world. Growing up—hell, up until I got to Treetops—I'd thought cottage country's charm ended at the same time as swim season. I can't believe how wrong I was. It may be freezing, but it's still magical.

I'm taking it all in when I notice Matt's not in front of me anymore. I look around until, squinting against the snow, I finally spot him twenty feet up on the balcony that juts off the back of the house. He's shucking his jacket to reveal an ivory wool sweater. He rests his forearms against the balcony railing, which looks a little less robust than I typically expect from a safety structure. Shielding my eyes from the snowflakes fluttering directly into my face, I'm immediately impressed by the strong lines of his . . . uh . . . that is to say, the house.

I am impressed by the strong lines of the house.

He waves me around to a set of stairs that lead up to where he's standing.

They creak and sway gently as I climb. My fingers grip the rail for dear life. Two heart attacks later, I make it to the top and stand beside Matt, chest thumping so loudly I'm sure he can hear it.

"Wow," I breathe. The views are even more spectacular from here, where an overhang protects us from most of the snow. The shore has been cleared of trees along the width of the property, and I can imagine the unobstructed sight lines to the trees and cliffs on the opposite side that must be visible by day. It feels like being in a bird's nest with no one around for miles and miles. Except Matt, of course, who pushes up his sleeve before reaching into a cooler and pulling out a beer, offering it to me with a raised eyebrow.

"Seriously? It's the middle of winter, you're shirking outerwear, and you want to pop the top on a frosty cold one?" My tone is light, but I can also feel my teeth starting to chatter the longer we stand still.

He chuckles softly. "Cocoa then?"

He slides open the patio door and when the light flicks on, I realize we're standing in his bedroom. The roof slopes dramatically on either side. One wall is covered with cabinetry that must have cost a fortune. The other side of the room holds a tidily made bed. My thoughts bounce between *Did he plan this?* and *Skip the cocoa. Give me a lengthy and detailed tour of any and all horizontal surfaces.*

For a moment, Matt pauses beside me, arm pressing against my shoulder. I can hear him breathing, feel the gentle movement of his body. Inhale, exhale. Inhale, exhale. How is he keeping so steady? I sound like a hyperventilating teenager. My heart is pounding hard enough that I can see the front of my coat moving.

We're reaching awkward silence territory when he pulls his beanie off and looks at me with a wry smile and a shrug. My fingers twitch as I repress the urge to run them through his hair.

He clears his throat. "Well, this is awkward. Neutral zone this way."

I follow him through the small room and along a tiny hallway. I stop for a moment to study the pictures hanging there. There's a framed photo of a striking woman with dark, curly hair and a wry smile holding a frowning little boy.

Matt comes back to where I'm standing and looks over my shoulder. "I've never been a fan of having my picture taken."

The next image on the wall is a painting of the Toronto skyline from the lake, the curved bow of a canoe poking its nose into the bottom of the frame. "Did you paint this?" I ask, getting close enough that my breath steams up the glass. "It's beautiful." He's managed to show the energy of the city while giving a sense of peace, a feeling of being just slightly removed from the urban chaos waiting there. My head tilts a little to the side as I consider. Or is it the feeling of being slightly removed from everything? Excluded from the world in front of you?

I can feel his eyes on me as I study his work, not for the art itself, but to try to get a better understanding of the man who painted it.

He stands beside me for a moment before nudging my shoulder with his own. "Let's go downstairs. We can finish the tour."

I pull myself away and trail after him, but look back over my shoulder at that little boy in the photo.

The living room is everything I've ever wanted. An entire wall is covered by bookshelves. A pair of cozy-looking armchairs are nestled together, close enough to share an oversized ottoman. A gas fireplace sits in the center of the room. Clearly an update, it's open on all four sides, spilling cheery firelight and warmth into the living space and through the other side to the most charming kitchen I have ever seen. It's like stepping into every dream country kitchen renovation the internet has thrown my way. Pale wood, white cabinets, plants perched on shelves beside vintage cookbooks. Stepping closer, I run my fingers along their colorful, well-worn spines. I can feel his gaze hot on the back of my neck.

"This is beautiful."

"Mom and I used to come here sometimes when she needed time to work on new recipes. She made it look like magic." He stares at the sink, and it's easy to imagine a woman standing there, apron around her waist, a glass of wine on the counter, swaying to some music. "She always seemed to know exactly what someone needed to make their night whatever they wanted it to be. Fun, adventurous, romantic."

"She sounds amazing."

He gives his head a shake, sending a dark lock of hair tumbling onto his forehead where it begs to be brushed back.

"And this would pain her very much, but . . ." He pulls a tub of instant hot chocolate mix out of a cupboard, along with a bag of mini marshmallows so old the elastic wrapped around it is broken and fused to the plastic.

A few minutes later we settle onto the small couch, thighs a hair's breadth apart, mugs steaming. Eric's curled up at my feet and the smell of wet fur permeates the air.

"No cable and my film selection seems to have stopped being updated sometime in the late nineties, but I can offer you some classics. Would you prefer the cinematic mastery of *Jurassic Park* or the timeless charm of Will Smith and Jeff Goldblum in *Independence Day*?"

I take a sip of marshmallow-laden, bordering-on-too-sweet cocoa and smack my lips together. Perfect.

"Matt, I want to be honest with you."

He puts down his mug and turns to look me in the eyes, all seriousness. "Okay." He looks concerned.

I put my hand on top of his. In a totally friend-zone way. Like I'd set my fingers atop the strong, capable hands of any ol' pal. I ignore the electricity that zings up my arm, making my lips tingle. "No one could possibly choose between *Jurassic Park* and *Independence Day.*"

We end up eenie-meenie-ing it and *Jurassic Park* takes the win.

By the time the ground is shaking with the footsteps of an approaching T. rex, Matt has his arm around me and my head is resting on his chest. He's stroking the spot between my neck and shoulder in gentle, tiny circles and I am very close to purring like a cat.

My body involuntarily arches toward him, asking for more. I really badly want to touch his naked abs and find out just how many there are. My guess is eight, minimum, which should be absolutely ludicrous, but, in this moment, snow falling outside, fire roaring beside us, seems like just the right number for a sexy fairy tale of a night. I raise my chin to look at him and find him staring back at me with those ridiculous eyes, lashes low. My teeth sink into my lower lip and I have just enough time to register that I'm being an excellent seductress before his mouth is on mine.

He starts out slowly, softly, cautiously. Occasionally backing off ever so slightly, giving me an out if I want it, which I absolutely do not. He tastes like chocolate and poor choices, but I'm beyond caring. We've been dancing around each other long enough. Knowing he's into me, and that after our talk in town *he* knows I'm full of reciprocation and longing . . . well, it's not making things easier. If I'm going to come out of this Treetops experience worse off than when I arrived, I'm going to take the perks I can get. And if one of those perks happens to be epic levels of sexual chemistry culminating in this night, so be it.

Finally, *finally*, I run my fingers through his hair. It's long enough to create some drag, and I can't help but give it a gentle tug, eliciting a quiet groan that flows from his mouth into mine.

"More, please," I whisper as his lips dance butterfly kisses across my face, his stubble rasping my cheek.

He pulls me around so I'm facing him, straddling his lap. His lips are on my neck and he's reaching underneath my Treetops polo, laying a trail of fire along the lace edge of my bra. Well, that escalated quickly. Nice to know he can take direction.

I run my hands over his shoulders and press him backward so I can take in the view. It's like I'm sitting on a *GQ* cover. My fingers slide downward, grab the hem of his sweater, and pull it up and over his head. I take inventory. "Holy shit. How often do you work out? Where do you work out? Is bear wrestling the equivalent to a gym membership up here?"

"You need to move past this bear obsession," he says, nuzzling my earlobe before giving it a nip. "We use otters. Much more slippery." He glides a finger down my ribs, tickling me gently, and in that moment of distraction, unhooks my bra with his free hand. He slides my shirt over my head. My hair tumbles out of its messy bun and I give it a quick run-through with my fingers, hoping no one gets stabbed in the eye with a stray bobby pin.

Before I can worry too much, I'm on my back with him suspended above me, and I'm tracing the outline of his impressive triceps. I always assumed the artistic life was quite French and involved the consumption of much bread and wine and hard liquor for inspiration. Reality suggests otherwise.

But then his mouth plants gentle kisses down my chest and his hands pin mine above my head and I stop thinking about much at all.

Fingers run under the waistband of my jeans and pop the top button. I can't stop squirming. I want more. I want all of him. *I need, I need, I need* echoes fuzzily through my head. And then he stops.

"This isn't what you want," he says in a shaky voice, backing off, letting the cold air edge between us.

It takes me a few seconds to hear his words, and before I can assure him there is nothing in life that I want as much as this, as much as him, he's putting his shirt back on.

"We agreed on nine weeks." He hands me my bra.

I'm suddenly incredibly self-conscious and turn my back to him, slipping my clothes back on with trembling hands.

"Right, yeah. Okay."

God, I'm an idiot. Of course he doesn't feel the same way. I bet he goes through this all the time. Women coming in and getting unreasonably attached to his good looks and charm, throwing themselves at him. He'd been letting me down gently, agreeing to the nine-week wait, knowing it was never going anywhere. And now here I am, pushing the schedule and messing up his easy getaway at the end of my contract.

I grab the mug of cold cocoa and take it to the kitchen counter, pausing in the shadows to try to get my emotions under control. He stands there watching me in the flickering light of the TV.

"Are you okay?" he asks.

I start to say *Yeah, I'm fine* and then stop myself. I'm not fine. This is not fine.

"No, Matt, I'm not okay." I bang my hand on the counter and turn to face him. My mind is racing. What did I do wrong? Where did I misunderstand the situation? I'm so, so tired of feeling like I can't do anything right.

I point to the couch. "What the hell was that? Explain this to me, because I'm clearly missing something. How is this so easy for you?" I cross my arms over my chest.

He walks over slowly and unwraps my arms from my body. Hooking a finger into the waistband of my jeans, he pulls me up against him. I look up, intending to glare fiercely, but his mouth closes over mine and he walks me back until my back presses up against the nearest wall, and . . . wow.

The gentle sweet kisses of two minutes ago would be incinerated by the heat he's putting out now. One hand cups my ass, lifting me slightly, while the other wraps itself in my hair. My head tilts back, and he nips and probes and touches me until I barely remember my name, let alone that I'm mad at him.

He pulls away.

"Tell me you think this is easy for me," he demands.

Very firm physical evidence pushing against my stomach suggests this is not, in fact, easy for him, so I'm completely stymied when he once again backs off, leaving me flushed and panting.

"If it's so damn hard"—pun intended—"why are we stopping?"

He mumbles something.

"What?"

"Because I like you."

"For fuck's sakes. Are we twenty?" Am I trapped in a quarter-life purgatory of career and relationship stasis? I tug my shirt back down and bundle my hair into its elastic prison.

"You like me. Cool. I figured that out. There were signs." I direct a pointed look to his mouth, then the front of his pants.

"No, Kate." He stops, running a hand over his face and through his hair, making it stick up in a way that is far too endearing for the moment. "I *like you* like you." His voice is rough, like it pains him to say the words. The warmth and playfulness of earlier is gone. He's dead serious.

"Alright. Whatever. If you want to talk about this using grown-up language at some point, let me know. Thanks for the drink." I move to the front door and have my coat zipped before realizing my boots are still on the balcony upstairs. The one that requires me to walk through his bedroom. Of course. Perfect.

My foot lands on the first step as he speaks again.

"Wait. Please. Just a minute." His voice is hoarse, but gentle. *Stay strong, Rigsby.* I falter for just long enough, and he leaps on the opportunity like a romance panther in the night.

"You want grown-up language? Fine." I hear a deep inhale.

"Kate, I think you're amazing. You're brave and smart and ridiculously entertaining."

I hear him moving, covering the ground between us until he's standing beside me, his hand on the rail an inch from where my fingers clench the banister hard enough to turn my knuckles white.

"I will admit to being entertaining, but it's hard not to laugh at someone who fails as often and as hard as I have been lately."

Even I can hear how forced the humor sounds.

The warm weight of his hand settles on top of mine. I can't look at him.

"Let me finish."

I stand perfectly still, eyes locked on the stair in front of me even as tears blur my vision.

"Do you know how many people go through life just taking the next step that's expected of them without ever truly considering what they want? What they need?" His thumb slowly strokes mine. "School. Job. Long-term relationship. Marriage. Kids. Just checking boxes."

"I didn't get to marriage, but you're basically describing my life up to now, so maybe switch tactics."

"But you're here. You took a leap of faith—"

"Desperation."

"It doesn't matter why you did it. You jumped. And I know you're having a shitty time here and the job sucks and Brooke is awful. But watching your resilience, your creativity, and the way everyone is drawn to you . . . I don't think you understand how special you are."

"I am not a special snowflake."

"That's not what I mean and you know it. Stop being obtuse."

"Stop mentoring me!"

Ugh. When will I stop defaulting to teen angst during arguments?

"That's not what— You know what, fine. Have it your way.

Live your life believing you're mediocre. Don't prove to your-self that you're capable—and deserving—of so much more than what you're taking on."

I start up the stairs. I can feel his eyes drilling into my back. He sighs. "I don't want to be just a distraction from your bullshit day. You may not know what you're worth, but I think I do. And it's a hell of a lot more than a quick fuck. You asked for nine weeks to get yourself sorted and really make a go of this job. You owe that to yourself. If something goes sideways, I don't want you to point to tonight as the moment where every-thing went wrong."

A fog of emotions, so varied I can't pick one to focus on, makes me weak in the knees. I'm annoyed, certainly, and em-barrassed to have this kind of attention on me. But he's also said a lot of really nice things. Like, *really* nice. The step I'm balanced on suddenly feels like a tightrope. One wrong step and the whole thing will crash and burn.

He puts a toe on the edge of the stair and pulls himself up so his face is level with mine. Lips brush across my cheek, and then he's moving into the kitchen. When his footsteps grow faint, I risk taking a backward glance. He's staring out the picture windows, close enough that his breath is fogging up the glass. *Portrait of a Pensive Man in Winter.*

I make my way quietly up the stairs, through his pristine bed-room, and back to the cold comfort of Employee Hut Four, knowing that every step I take away from him feels wrong, but maybe he's on to something. Maybe this is the part where Kate Rigsby makes the right choice, even if it's a hard one (pun still intended).

Chapter 17

There's no time to stew on the situation with Matt because, suddenly, things are turning around for me on the business side. Prepping for the arrival of Party Thyme, which will take us to ninety-percent capacity for the duration of their stay, has taken over my life.

I've realized there is no point trying to skirt the issue and I am going to need all the help I can get to pull this thing off. So, on a cloudy Friday morning, I call my first staff meeting.

I gather Tania, Jay, Mike, and Kevin in the dining room so we can sample the batch of cranberry and dark chocolate muffins that just came out of the oven.

"We don't usually dedicate this many paid resources to tasting a proven recipe," Kevin says, taking a delicate nibble from the edge of a muffin top.

"And you know your attitude is much improved with a snack," Mike replies dryly. "Enjoy your muffin and let Kate tell us why we're here."

Kevin huffs indignantly but doesn't object. If I didn't know better, I'd say he was pleased to have Mike's attention.

"Thank you all for coming," I begin. "I know you're very busy." What I actually know is that we have five guests right now, and twice that many staff floating around looking for things to do. I went down to the library bar earlier to check stock levels for Serge and found the massage therapist napping on the couch.

"We have a new booking coming up in a couple of weeks that I'd like to discuss with you all, as I believe it will take some effort to prepare for and execute."

My audience looks at each other like they can't believe I'm doubting their abilities.

"I know you've all been doing this way longer than I have, but this reservation is a bit different from what I've experienced here so far. Maybe I'm overreacting, and if that's the case, we'll call this meeting a snack break and move on. Agreed?"

Jay nods. "Sure. Whatcha got for us?"

Time for the big reveal.

"It's a three-night stay for a group of twenty. Seven shared rooms, six private."

Jay's eyes widen. "Holy shit."

Tania beams at me. "That's a full house! Oh my gosh, Kate!"

"There are some dietary restrictions we'll need to talk through, Jay."

He nods, already making notes. "I should get us a deer," he mutters.

"Mike, Tania, they'd like to ski in, so I'll need you to help me sort out logistics there. Many have equipment but some will need to rent. I'll send you the specifics."

"Got it," Mike says, swigging coffee.

Tania is practically bouncing up and down in her seat.

"Are they interested in additional activities? We could do ice fishing if the conditions are right, or bring Heidi back in for guided hikes?"

"Almost certainly. Can you get me a list of options for this time in the season? I'll see what they'd like to supplement with."

Kevin clears his throat.

"A group of twenty? Who are they?"

Knowing this moment would come doesn't make it any easier. I hedge.

"A group of young, professional creatives. They meet all the criteria as outlined in the Ideal Customer Profile." I start checking things off on my fingers. "Belief in the Creative Spirit. Quality Output. Open to upselling. Referrals."

I'm still getting a suspicious squinty-eyed glare.

"But *who are they?*"

I squirm, but Mike says, "You know he'll just look it up. You may as well spit it out and be done with it."

With a sigh, I spill. "A corporate group."

Silence replaces the excited chatter.

"But, guys, honestly, they're not what you're picturing. Party Thyme has an incredible culture of creativity and truly believes in putting good vibes into the world . . . you know, through luxury herbs perfect for cooking or cocktails." I cough nervously and await judgment.

"You're bringing Party Thyme here?!" Jay jumps up and grabs my hands. "Those guys are, like, luxury herb rock stars! Holy shit." He turns to Tania, kissing her full on the mouth. "Serge!" he yells, jogging into the kitchen. "Serge! You're gonna lose your mind, bud!"

Tania, while blushing furiously, is still quiet. Kevin stares at me.

"Well." Mike stands, pulls his gloves on. "Let me know if you need anything else from me." He walks out the back door that leads to the patio. A gust of frigid air blasts over us as he exits.

"This is amazing," Tania starts cautiously, "but . . ."

Kevin cuts to the chase. "Does Brooke know what you've done?"

"Not explicitly, no."

He rests his elbows on the table, drops his forehead into his hands, and starts massaging his temples.

"Listen, we're desperate here. You think I don't see the money we're hemorrhaging?" I can hear the frustration creeping into my voice, the volume rising despite my efforts to stay calm and professional. "Brooke told me to follow the rules and I am. Party Thyme meets the criteria. They're building something amazing and they want to be inspired to do more. That is our business." I stare at Kevin, daring him to tell me I'm wrong.

He pushes back from the table and smooths the front of today's sweater—navy blue with deceptively cheery snowflakes dancing across the chest.

"Send me the guest information at once. Full names, residential addresses where possible. I usually have much more time to prepare for such a large project, but I'll do what I can. You'll need to confer with Clarissa on mentorship."

He pauses, one hand on the door. "Perhaps you aren't entirely useless after all."

I stare after him as the door swings shut, mouth open. "Did he really say that?"

Tania wraps her arms around me and jumps up and down, rattling my teeth.

"We need to celebrate," she announces. "My place at eight. Bring that handsome dog of yours."

We arrive at Employee Hut Two covered in snow from the brief walk. Eric shakes himself dry just inside, sending water flying in all directions. This is why we can't have nice things. Or visit people who have nice things.

Luckily, Tania's residence is only a small step up in quality from my own sweet digs. Instead of being half a portable, Tania gets a full seven hundred square feet, but other than that it's essentially the same. Grandma's-basement-style couch, microscopic bathroom, once-beige carpeting that should have been replaced a decade ago.

One piece stands out in that it has absolutely no business being within a hundred yards of any of the hand-me-down garbage in the room. It's a privacy screen separating the bed from the rest of the living space, but it's unlike anything I've ever seen. Branches are twisted together and attached in other invisible ways, leaving spaces like natural puzzle pieces in between. Those spaces have been perfectly fitted with colored glass. It looks like something from a fairy tale.

"Whoa. Did you make that?" I have no idea how anyone would even begin to craft something like this.

"Lord no. I don't have the patience. Mike did it."

"Chainsaw Mike? What is he doing here puttering around with the landscaping when he can do *that*? He could be raking it in selling those things."

"Ah. Well, that's a bit of a long story."

I kick off my boots and hang my coat, feeling warm and fuzzy inside. I'm with a friend, after a huge business win, having a nice evening of chitchat and wine. I've missed this.

Eric settles onto a folded quilt on the floor while Tania and I take up either end of the couch. She tucks her feet up so her chin rests on her knees, looking like she's about fourteen. She raises her glass. "A toast. To big wins, fine canine companions, and new friends." We *cheers* and take a healthy glug of wine, sitting in companionable silence.

"This wine is great. The liquor store in town must be stocking some pretty premium options for cottage-goers in the off-season. Or have you been borrowing inventory from the dining—"

Her cheeks turn a charming pink.

"Ah. Or has a handsome and talented chef been by bearing gifts of fine wine?"

Tania's enormous grin says it all.

"Details, please," I say, crossing my legs and leaning forward, the picture of rapt attention.

Half an hour and another generous wine pour later I am fully caught up on the glorious romance of Tania and Chef Jay. Girl meets boy. Boy woos girl with specially prepared snacks to take on her drives into town. "He said he wanted to make sure my blood sugar levels were healthy on those dangerously winding roads."

Girl falls for boy who pays close enough attention to know she likes a sandwich cut into triangles instead of squares. "Who notices that stuff?" Tania swoons at the memory of such thoughtfulness. And finally, boy brings excellent wine over to Employee Hut Two, and it is quickly forgotten, only to be enjoyed the next day by yours truly.

"Are you worried about breaking the rules? You know . . . the no canoodling betwixt employees thing?"

Tania moves down to the floor to sit beside Eric, who has finally dried off and is considerably more cuddle-able than when we first arrived.

"I mean, yeah, of course. But I report to Kevin and—" She catches the look on my face and laughs. "Honestly, he's not that bad. He wouldn't spill the beans about me and Jay, and I don't think anyone else actually pays attention, so . . ." She shrugs. "You gotta take a risk sometimes for something big, you know?"

Wines swishes down my throat. "I do know that, yes."

She scritches the spot under Eric's ear. "I haven't seen you much lately, buddy. Your mom's been keeping you to herself."

"Between you and Mike I'm worried he's going to abandon me for greener pastures. But also, I've been trying to keep him out of trouble. I don't think my relationship with Kevin needs more hurdles. And God forbid he get into puppy shenanigans while you or Mike have him. The wrath would rain down upon you and you would be smote!" I sip my wine, considering. "Is that the appropriate use of 'smote'?"

Tania shrugs. "One, this good boy could never be trouble. And two, Kevin wouldn't talk to Mike if he was on fire and Mike was holding a hose, so don't worry about any smiting over that way."

"What's their deal, anyway? Kevin can't take the obnoxious, output-inhibiting sound of a chainsaw?"

Tania gets up and empties the rest of the wine into our glasses. Her lips purse and she looks a little conflicted.

"They have . . . a history."

"A history." My favorite game: speculation! "They grew up in the same town and Kevin bullied Mike? Mike was Kevin's boss at a fine furniture store and fired him for being obnoxious and then in a horrible twist of fate they both ended up here?"

Tania shakes her head and stares at me, eyebrows raised. "No."

"You mean they have a *history*?!" I am flabbergasted. Mike is so quiet and nice and dog-loving. Kevin is . . . Kevin. "I need a minute. Mike and Kevin? Really?"

"Really. I know you and Kevin have your differences."

I look at her sideways. "That's putting it mildly."

"He's always been particular, but he used to be pretty pleasant to be around most of the time. Ever since they split it seems like he's taking a lot of anger out on everyone else."

"Did they meet here?"

"Oh no. They came here together, oh, two years ago maybe? Mike says he always wanted to move up here, work on his art, and live quietly. Kevin was the one who initiated it though. For the longest time they stayed in the city because of his job, but when he saw the posting here, he applied, got it, and whisked Mike away to live his dream life." She sniffs. "Super romantic, huh?"

I ask the obvious question. "What happened?"

"They had some kind of falling-out in the spring. It was terrible. Horrible." She shudders at the memory. "Mike didn't speak to anyone for weeks. Practically disappeared into the woods to work. Kevin started snapping at us all the time. We thought for sure he was going to leave, but"—she shrugs again—"I like to think he's got a plan to fix things and is just waiting for the right time."

We sit for a moment, contemplating the injustices of a romance gone south. A soft knock on the door tears my attention away from the dregs of my wineglass.

"Who?" I start to ask. But I see the look on Tania's face and know.

"Is *that* the time?" I say dramatically. "My goodness. Eric, we need to get you home to bed or you'll be absolutely useless for chasing squirrels in the morning."

Tania lets Jay in and he stands around looking sheepish while I put on my many layers for the two-minute walk back to my place. Huh. My Place. Funny what a half bottle of wine and some friendly conversation can do for a girl's outlook.

"Have a pleasant night, kids." I can't help but smile looking at them. They're so damn cute and so, so excited for me to be gone. "Don't stay up too late!" I call over my shoulder, but the door is already closed and I see two shadows merge into one through the curtain.

A sigh puffs out of me, big and fluffy in the cold night air. "Must be nice."

Chapter 18

Josh Meadows and his freshly expanded Party Posse ski back into my life wearing more neon than I've seen since the early nineties. Tania brings them in Thursday morning, acting as their guide and professional wolf/bear repeller. I'm surprised but deeply relieved to see Tim isn't among them. The memory of his crusty toe on my leg is still alarmingly fresh in my mind.

Mike has already gotten back with their luggage in the 4x4 and is unloading an impressive array of duffel bags made of everything from calfskin leather to hemp, and in one case, a sweatshirt tied into a compact bundle to hold its contents in place. A Hacky Sack is edging out of the neck hole.

"Miz Rigsby!" We execute an explosive fist bump.

"Josh, we're so excited to have the Party Thyme team at Tree-tops." I scan the group. "Will Tim be joining us later?"

"Tim has some other priorities this week." His forehead crinkles and his glow dims for a moment. He shakes his head, dislodging the negative energy. "But, dude, it was such great timing when you reached out. Connie and I have been wanting to book something like this for ages—calendars blocked and everything. Get away from the grind and reconnect with ourselves, get to know everyone a bit better. We just haven't been able to find a spot that really hits the vibe, you know? But now look at this!" He spreads his arms and grins up at the gray sky.

A petite, dark-haired woman slides forward, neon-green goggles perched on her head. "Connie Yu, Chief Organization Officer," she introduces herself, extending a mittened hand for a shake. "We've been growing so quickly, and it's tough to get past the business side of things and really lock in a relationship with the new peeps."

Josh nods enthusiastically and inhales deeply. "This place is mag."

"It is. And I think we've nailed an itinerary that balances re-centering the self and filling your personal bucket, while also building out relationships based on the commonalities and exciting differences that brought each individual into your group." Who am I? What am I saying?

Josh stares at me. "Miz Rigsby, I do believe you've found your calling."

I try not to look alarmed. Despite my brain's absolute insistence that Josh is wrong, something warm curls up in the vicinity of my heart. Probably too many saturated fats with my waffles. I smile at the Party Thyme crew and wave them forward. "All I hear calling right now is some sweet organic cocoa. Let's get you all inside and warmed up."

Kevin and Tania divide and conquer, each taking a group of two or three to do initial consultations, give out room assignments, and book supplementary activities. The rest of the Party Thyme team mills about, drinking cocoa and chatting. The energy in the room is as sunny as—well, the sun.

The crowd slowly disperses, with some guests hitting the spa, a couple people heading back outside for a hike, and a smattering of meetings throughout the afternoon. At some point, I vaguely register the coming and going of a helicopter, but am too busy taking Jay through a small mountain of last-minute dietary requests to worry about having Christine back within striking distance.

In the morning, we kick it into high gear. Tania leads sunrise yoga in the living room as a fire crackles in the hearth. After breakfast (cinnamon-apple baked oatmeal, yogurt parfaits drizzled with maple syrup from our very own trees, and my personal favorite, breakfast cookies), Heidi takes a group out for a hike aka Mindful Meditation in Nature.

For the next two days, guests flow into and out of a series of business-focused workshops covering everything from Creating with Intent to Investing in Your Output. Seeing them come together after each session, sipping Thyme for Energy–enhanced sparkling water and discussing what they learned, eyes bright, fist-bumping with newfound enthusiasm? It's a thrill I didn't know was missing from my life.

The big winner, though, is Kevin. He runs back-to-back personal consultations about how to arrange office space to maximize creativity and gets rave reviews from every participant. His grand finale is a workshop with the C-suite and upper management, introducing ways they can read their team members and "interpret the subtle indicators of stress, passion, or disengagement, allowing for effective and timely redirection of energy to maximize output while minimizing emotional turbulence." Josh locks Kevin in a bear hug at the end, insisting he's changed the way he sees the world.

I'm loitering in the lounge, taking it all in from behind the reception desk when Matt walks in, all lanky legs and dreaminess. Aside from polite interactions focused on organizing events for Party Thyme, we've barely spoken since That Night.

"How's it going?" he asks, surveying the scene in front of us.

My breath whooshes out, taking with it a portion of the tension that's been building over the past week. I try to limit the size of my smile, contain the happiness I know is written all over my face. I'm proud. And for a second, I wonder why I'm trying to hide that. *Later,* I tell myself. *Think about that later.*

"Really well. Attendance at the workshops has been strong, and Tania's living her best life, getting everyone set up with excursions and spa time and Lord knows what else. I think I heard Heidi pitching nighttime sled races. Do we have helmets?"

My gaze turns to the ceiling, where what was once an intermittent drop of water here and there has become an unrelenting drip from the shower in the guest room overhead, tinkling into a giant bucket discreetly tucked into the corner.

"I think the bigger question is, do we have sleds?"

"Huh. Yeah. Good point."

The bucket is getting full, but there's no way I can carry it out of here without making a scene, and likely a large mess. My gaze lands on the wiry, muscular forearms currently residing on the desk beside me.

"Can you sneak this bucket out?"

He sighs, but it seems to be directed more at the fact that there's a bucket to empty than my request. "I can. But I have a favor to ask in return."

While I'm fully aware the chances of the favor being sexual are low, my hope for the same skyrockets. "Yeah, sure. I mean, as long as it's not illegal. Or hiding a body. But, now that I've said that, body hiding is also very likely illegal. Anyhoo, what do you need?"

"Can you come by my place tomorrow morning? I need . . . advice."

"Advice."

"Yes." His face scrunches up in distaste. "It's complicated."

"Okay, yeah. Of course. Advice." My brow is furrowed, and I know he can see my brain tripping all over itself trying to figure out what's going on. "No hints?"

He bends his knees and smoothly lifts the bucket with one hand, sliding a backup from under the desk and into place with the other. "I think you should just see for yourself."

My teeth press into my tongue, hard, stopping any possibility of telling him all of the things I'd like him to show me.

One of the Party Thyme finance execs is holding his phone out, trying to snap a selfie with his teammates, and I head over to help, praying it's going to end up on social media, pushing more business our way. After performing my photographic duties, I prop a little sign against the plant I see Kevin gently misting each morning. TAG US IN YOUR PICS FOR A CHANCE TO WIN SPA CREDITS! #TREETOPSCREATIVE

By the time Jay's ultimate edition of the Gathering Fire wraps up their final night, we've got thirty stories and posts on Instagram, feeding into a network of thousands of potential guests. One in particular is getting like after like and share after share. The video is taken from farther out on the now-frozen lake. It starts by taking in the night sky, then pans down and across the length of the Treetops property. Mike spent the afternoon crafting a bar from ice blocks at the edge of the lake, a gleaming expanse of snow surrounding it, lit by fairy lights and an almost-full moon. The fire glows warmly, throwing just enough light on the guests wrapped up in cozy blankets, lounging in chairs or milling about with drinks. *Thyme to fill our buckets.* *#treetopscreative #getthere #perfection #luxuryherblifestyle #partythyme*

I'd done the math that afternoon. December occupancy is at seventy-five percent with three weeks to go. I try to control my giddiness, but every so often a stray giggle slips out.

The sun is barely cresting the trees when Eric drags me up the drive toward Matt's house, zig-zagging back and forth as he chases scent trails left behind by all the night creatures. As soon as we hit the property line, I set him loose and he's off into the bracken, crashing around with abandon. I meander along much more sedately, marveling at the size of some of the trees and running through my to-do list for the morning.

The Party Thyme crew is snowshoeing out after breakfast

and I'm trying to cobble together some kind of farewell speech when someone rounds the corner ahead of us, walking in our direction. I call Eric back to my side, a command he obeys. We're both surprised.

As we get closer, a giant black creature lumbers out of the trees and I realize it's Delilah and . . . Matt? I am extremely hopeful that International Social Media Modeling Sensation Christine Morrow is still asleep or buried under a landslide of hair product and makeup.

I lift a hand in confused greeting as Eric and Delilah exchange pleasantries.

Matt crosses the sparkling snow toward me. He's dressed for the cold in a black parka, a rust-colored knit scarf looped around his neck. His black snow pants are somehow cut to be incredibly flattering. Or maybe he's cut to flatter the pants. Either way, I get a little slack-jawed at the sight.

When he's near enough for us to talk without yelling, I gesture in the direction of the dogs, who are chasing an agitated squirrel through the trees.

"So, what's new?"

He makes a sound in the back of his throat that sounds like a growl. "An early Christmas gift."

"That's, uh, generous? In my family, we usually go for sweaters, a book. Maybe a bottle of wine. This is nice though."

The narrowing of his eyes and set of his jaw make it clear he does not agree. "It is not nice. It's selfish and inconsiderate. How do you think poor Delilah feels?" He thrusts a mittened hand toward the dogs, who are now tussling over ownership of a stick the length of my leg.

"She looks like she's coping."

We continue walking down the path. It's hard not to notice how nice this feels. How comfortable I am with him. How much I want him to wrap his arms around me.

"Taylor, Christine's assistant-slash-photographer-slash-devotee, flew in yesterday to drop her off." His voice cuts through my steamy domestic fantasy. "Christine was, of course, very busy and unable to deliver this generous and heartfelt gift herself."

"Did you mention wanting a pet? Maybe she's trying to turn over a new, thoughtful leaf." This seems extremely unlikely, but maybe it's a Christmas miracle.

Matt snorts. "Taylor spilled the beans after one beer. The guy they got Delilah from, for the shoot up here, saw the images and, 'knew Delilah had found her true place in the world.'" He shakes his head. "The only place Christine wants to be is a perched atop a well-padded bank account."

I nod. "Mm-hmm. Don't we all."

"The guy's trying to buy her affection, or at least attention, like everyone else. And my charming sister, of course, didn't decline despite her complete lack of interest in caring for another living being. She can't even keep a cactus alive." He huffs out a disgruntled breath. "So now I am part of some elaborate quest to maximize Delilah's impact on my dear sister's online engagement stats. I'm supposed to take pictures of her eating organic vegan biscuits and drinking Tibetan spring water, all so Christine can maintain her new 'of the people' image. Because people have dogs and don't turn down the gift of a ten-thousand-dollar pet." He stops walking and turns to look at me. "I had to sign an NDA."

I press my lips closed and try not to laugh.

His gaze cuts toward me. "It's not funny."

"It's funny."

I catch his mouth twitching but he manages to hold back his smile.

Eric is following Delilah closely as she trundles through the woods. Each time she pauses to sniff at a patch of snow he falls into a play bow. His tail whirls at top speed.

Despite the option to turn off the main path onto any number of more interesting narrow trails, Matt sticks with the main one that allows us to walk side by side.

"Delilah is lovely," he starts.

"You're not ready for this level of commitment?"

"She came with a care manual. Did you know she under-stands over one hundred commands? She's too good for me."

"That's probably true. She's a classy lady. What are you going to do?"

I'm focused on spotting any sneaky ice patches, but can feel his eyes on me. "No."

"No what? I haven't even said anything."

"I can feel your thoughts. I'm not taking her."

"But Eric loves her. And she, well, she'll grow to accept him. Over time. And with a lot of bribes."

"There are other options here. Much more sane ones." I scroll through my mental list of everyone I know. Who would be interested in a super classy, enormous, exceptionally trained, snobby dog?

My eyes widen as a well-groomed, bearded curmudgeon in knitwear appears in my mind's eye. A curmudgeon who could really use a grand, relationship-mending gesture. I am either a genius or a lunatic.

"I have a plan. When this works you will owe me one hundred liters of wine."

"I think I'll owe you more than that." His hand brushes mine, softly enough that it might have been an accident. But when I catch his eye, the look is all fiery intention. My heart starts racing and a lot of questions come to mind about the logistics of a winter romp. How cold would my butt get? How cold is too cold? But then we're walking again, turning back toward Tree-tops and the Party Thyme wrap-up.

Matt bends down to grab a stick, straightens, and hurls it through the air. He smiles at me as the dogs frolic after it, little lines crinkling around the corners of his eyes. I think I see his chest rise and fall with a little sigh as his gaze lands on my mouth. My body buzzes.

Seven more weeks.

* * *

After Party Thyme's departure, I sign into my meeting with Brooke, stewing in a mixture of dread and excitement. I'm not in bonus-making territory yet, but am on a curve that makes it look more possible if I can just get a couple of corporate bookings to round out the one-off artists coming in for mentorship. To be clear, by "a couple," I mean a three-hundred-percent year-on-year increase from last January and February. No big whoop.

I'm planning to coast through today's soul-crushing session on the wave of success Party Thyme brought. They may not fit the Ideal Customer Profile as Brooke interprets it, but their money (and there was *lots* of it) should be fairly compelling. I hope. Between the early morning walk and making sure Josh and Co. got back on the road without a hitch, I'd spent an hour answering what felt like an avalanche of inquiries—there were five—and felt cautiously confident that I might, despite all odds, hit my target for December.

Brooke's ten minutes late, and when she finally calls in, the background noise is atrocious. People are chatting loudly in what sounds like Spanish, music is playing, glasses and cutlery are clinking. She keeps her camera off.

"Hi, Brooke!" I try to project enough to be heard over the clamor. "Is this still a good time?"

"It's fine." Her voice is at odds with the party in the background. She sounds tense. Not her normal *you're interrupting my pedicure* tense, but, like, legitimately on edge.

"Great!" Great, great, it's all great. Sigh. "I think you'll be pleased with the numbers I have to share with you today."

"Go ahead, then."

The first slide doesn't bury the lede. It's a graph showing the impressive bookings growth achieved over the past month, superimposed over last year's numbers for the same period.

"As you can see here, we're getting a lot of traction with new guests. Over the past five days, we've received fourteen inquires and three new bookings—one couple, and two groups for visits in the new year." I click to the next slide.

"I believe this can be attributed to a new kind of referral. People are engaging with the social media posts made by our guests. I've made a point of asking where people heard about us, and almost every time they were made aware of Treetops via someone they follow online."

I stop presenting so Brooke can get the full effect of my earnest face. I practiced in the mirror and don't want to waste the effort.

"This data is extremely compelling. I strongly believe it's time to adopt the referral methods most relevant to today's clientele. These numbers don't lie."

There's a banging sound on her end. Like a fist on a table, making the plates jump and crash. "Enough," she said, almost spitting out the word. "I've been patient with you over the past few weeks while you attempted to get up to speed with how we do things, but this clearly displays your complete lack of respect, not just for Treetops and our methods, but for me."

"Alright. I understand why you might feel that way." I do not, but this is nothing new. "However, I reached out to Graham earlier this week." It might be my imagination or a poor connection, but I think I hear a small gasp. My head tilts to the side in interest, like a dog hearing the sound of a treat bag rustling.

"You did *what*?" she whisper-shrieks. A chair slides obnoxiously across the floor and I can picture her flying to her feet, probably wrapped in some kind of gauzy silk kaftan. "Excuse me," she says. Then louder, "*Get out of the way*." The music gets louder for a moment, and then a door slams and it's quiet, aside from her raging voice in my ear.

"Are you insane?"

I start to say it depends who you ask but think better of it. Which is fine as it turns out to be a rhetorical question.

"Graham does not have time for someone like you. Why would you think it's acceptable to take one moment of his day to listen to your uninformed, juvenile ideas?"

"I needed a quote for the blog. You suggested in your last email we add some content from prestigious guests, but after hearing him speak at the town hall I thought he might be able to add some words of inspiration to round things out." I decide not to mention I'd only gotten as far as a kind, but firm, admin assistant who assured me he'd pass on the message. I am immediately rewarded.

"YOU SPOKE TO HIM? I hope you didn't bring up anything that you've mentioned today." She sounds panicked. I can hear her breath coming in hitches.

"Well, the topic of bookings came up." In that I mentioned things are going well, though the admin may have only been asking about my day. Or the weather. "He was interested." I assume.

Little hiccup sounds are coming through my earbuds. I press on.

"Something else came up that I was a bit confused about. His admin said he hoped the guests were enjoying the new ATV. I mean, I know Mike would love one, but when you and I spoke about it a couple of weeks ago, I got the impression there wasn't that kind of budget available. Did something change?"

"Do you know how many properties HIT owns?" She doesn't wait for me to answer. "Thirty-one." I mouth it along with her before I can catch myself. "He can't possibly keep it all straight. In all likelihood, he was thinking of their place on Lake Louise. *They* have that kind of money." She takes a deep breath and exhales for so long I worry she's going to pass out on the floor of whatever bathroom she's holed up in.

"Karen."

"Kate."

"This whole interaction smacks of subversion."

"Honestly, Brooke, I'm only trying to do what's in the best interest of the business, as per Section 14, Subsection—"

I'm talking to my own image on the screen. Brooke's gone, likely making her way back to her no-dressing salad and a fresh double G and T.

Chapter 19

It's one of those intensely sunny winter days that, from the safety of the Big House, looks like you could go outside in a sweater. Except it's more degrees below zero than any environment not featuring penguins or polar bears has business being.

Today, seven prominent female executives and their plusones are arriving for four days and three nights of networking, collaboration, relaxation, and, just maybe, some fun. I scroll through the checklist on my phone for the umpteenth time since breakfast. This needs to be perfect. Between the seven women's accounts, we could reach over a million people on social media.

They've booked the entire resort to ensure privacy, serenity, and respect for the confidential nature of many of their discussions. All the Treetops employees have had to sign supplementary nondisclosure agreements.

I'm careening through the house, looking for Tania to confirm numbers for ice fishing. Rounding the corner into the employee dining room at speed, I come face-to-face with yet another reason to panic.

Christine Morrow is staring at the espresso maker like the power of her well-contoured glare is going to make it work. Joke's on her. That thing's been broken for weeks. We've all been sneaking through to get coffee from the guests' breakfast spread.

I've just decided to keep walking like I haven't noticed her extremely good-looking and ill-natured presence, when she turns.

"You there." She snaps. Her. Fingers. At me!

I inhale, trying to mainline the calming scent of cinnamon buns wafting from the kitchen. Nope. Not even the aromatherapy of sugary dough can quell my rage.

"Can I help you?" I cock a hip, cross my arms over my chest and hope she can't see the shake of my hands against the edge of my trusty clipboard.

"This machine is broken." She holds out her empty mug to me.

"It is."

I don't move. She jiggles the mug. I examine my cuticles.

"Service here is abysmal. People will be hearing about this."

"Hearing about what? You swanning in to harass the staff because you can't stand to make your own breakfast?" Matt strolls in and takes the cup from Christine. "Isn't the walk over more work than boiling some water?" he teases.

He ruffles her hair in a pure big-bro move and walks through to the kitchen. The sound of coffee beans being ground to delicious, caffeinated dust drowns out her whining about him messing with her tresses. He reappears with a steaming mug moments later and sets it in her waiting grasp.

With coffee in her hand, sprawled across one of the armchairs, she seems slightly mollified and I'm about to slip away when she says, "I have to film some video content today. I need the dog, and the lawn space must be kept clear, as well as the interior windows. I don't want people in my backdrop." She sips her coffee and crinkles her nose in distaste.

My whole body jerks in surprise. "Sorry, you want to film here? Today?"

"Um, yah. That's what I just said."

"You can't."

Her eyes narrow and she sets her mug down with much more force than is necessary, making me wince. As she unfolds herself from the chair to stand, I find myself backing up a step.

She looms over me. "What did you say?"

"We have guests coming in today who have paid for exclusive access. You can't claim the prime outdoor space as your own and forbid them from looking out the windows."

I wonder if I'm going to get punched, then notice that her gel nails are too long to let her close her hand into a fist. Wouldn't stop a slap though.

I clear my throat. "They're here for four days, but I can let you know when they've cleared out."

"Unacceptable. I have work to do and whatever *you*," she scoffs, "are doing, can wait."

"No can do," Matt chimes in. "You should have booked it."

"I don't need to *book it*," Christine sneers. "It's mine."

Matt rolls his eyes. "The HIT properties are not your personal playgrounds. Also, the dog has plans today. She's unavailable."

"What the hell do you mean? It's a *dog*."

"Ah, well." Matt spreads his arms in a *What can you do?* gesture. "As I'm sure you read in Delilah's owner's manual, she requires monthly grooming. She is currently on her way to an exclusive canine spa and treatment center, but will be back in four days. I'm sure we can slot you into her calendar then."

"Fine," Christine says. "*Fine.* I have partner ads that are a better use of my time anyway." She picks up her still full mug and struts out of the room, turning back at the door to add, "But don't think I'm going to forget about this."

She stares at me a moment longer and I'm expecting her to end on a witchy cackle or a thumb-across-the-throat gesture at the very least. When she pivots on her heel and walks away, I don't know if I'm relieved or disappointed.

We hear the slam of the front door, followed by it opening and slamming again with even more gusto.

"Canine spa and treatment center?"

"She went to the waterfall with Tania this morning." He smiles. "She'll probably be in need of an extended period of self-reflection and restorative calm afterwards."

He lowers his chin and looks at me consideringly. "And *you* need a cinnamon bun, then you can tell me how I can help this morning." His hand runs down my arm from shoulder to wrist, clasping it gently for a second before he lets go and walks back to the kitchen.

The butterflies in my stomach are meaningless, I'm sure.

Thirty minutes before the first half of the group is due to descend (literally; they're coming in by helicopter) I gather everyone together in the dining room. Standing in front of them, watching them shift impatiently from foot to foot, anxious to get back to work, I wonder what the hell I'm doing. This is meant to be a moment of inspiration. I want them to know that if we pull this off, it could mean everything to the business. To me. To my bank account. To my sanity. But why should they care what I have to say? I'm dragging them along on this wild ride of self-preservation, completely twisting the well-documented purpose of Treetops Creative Retreat to meet my own needs. Someone clears their throat. Showtime.

"Um, hi guys. Thanks for taking the time to join me here. I know you're all busy with prep for this group." I cast my eyes around the room, desperately searching for a friendly face. Jay is flipping noisily through his clipboard of menus for the next twenty-four hours. Kevin is making a cup of tea and clinking his spoon against the sides of his mug with about as much force as can be applied without breaking something. The two summer spa staff I've dragged in are whispering to each other and eyeing Matt. Meanwhile, Matt's chocolate eyes are on me. Encouraging. Empowering. And oh so dreamy. I let my gaze trail just a little farther down his body before getting back to the task at hand, feeling a little stronger than before.

"Alright. In case anyone missed it, this booking could be huge for us. Please make sure you've taken the time to read through the information Kevin has so thoughtfully and thoroughly prepared about our guests. We want this to be spectacular. So!" I insert a Tania-style hand clap. "Let's run through it. Chef Jay?"

"Got it sorted. Menus based on local produce, as usual. Dietary restrictions and preferences noted. I've got everything arranged for the ice-fishing trip—Serge's been working on some rad new cocktails for that one." He consults his clipboard. "There's one guest—Vicki Shelburn's plus-one—listed as TBD, so I don't have any specific info for them. Can you get that to me ASAP once they land?"

I nod and make a note. "Kevin?"

"Lodging recommendations have been noted and arranged. I do, of course, have plan Bs in place in case anyone disagrees with my assessment, which is extremely unlikely. Meeting rooms have been freshened and arranged for the specific number of attendees—both in the main boardroom and breakout areas. I've created personalized service menus, as per usual, including artistic mentorship opportunities, spa treatments, and outdoor exploration."

I confirm that the spa is prepped and everyone knows what to expect over the next four days.

"And that's it. I know these past couple of weeks we have been welcoming guests who push the boundaries of our standard customer profile, but these women have the same streak of brilliance we see in the artists that come through our doors every day. Well, not *every* day, but you know what I mean. They've chosen to apply their creative energies to building thriving businesses instead of a more traditional output."

I check my watch. It's go time.

"Let's do this."

It feels like an all-hands-in for some kind of team break situation, but everyone is already dispersing. I settle for a low-five from Jay as he passes.

The helicopter carrying the first half of the group arrives promptly at ten thirty. Tania and I, along with Serge and Mike for luggage-toting assistance, greet them as they trek toward us. Tania quickly bundles them into the Big House to warm up and get into their welcome session with Kevin. As they meander up the freshly shoveled path I hear them *ooh*ing and *aah*ing over the scenery, and there are at least a couple of pauses to take pictures.

The second group lands forty-five minutes later and we take our positions, welcoming smiles frozen on our faces as the wind tries to rip every shred of warmth from our bodies. I check them off in my head as they disembark.

Margot Ye, co-founder and CEO of a tech start-up catering to the construction industry, holds hands with her husband of six months as they duck under the rotors and jog toward us. Behind them, Felicia Indira, co-founder and CFO of an ethical makeup-sample-box subscription service sticks her head out the helicopter door, mashes a toque over her glossy black curls, and jumps out into the sun. Her mother emerges more tentatively, sporting a fantastic one-piece turquoise snowsuit. Felicia had called to change the booking yesterday, explaining, "Mom is visiting from Trinidad for the holidays. She'd be happy to stay with the kids, but she deserves a little adventure and pampering."

And finally, Vicki Shelburn, VP International Marketing for a gigantic beverage corporation. She steps down, gracefully tossing a scarf over her shoulder, gray-blond hair looking like it's being directed by a wind machine instead of an arctic gale, and calls something to the person behind her. Her yet-to-be-identified plus-one. A man steps down wearing very expensive-looking winter wear. He looks familiar.

I've been in the sun too long. I take off my sunglasses and rub my eyes. I blink hard.

"Are you okay?" Tania whispers, looking concerned.

"Katie!" calls Charles Hoberack II, dropper of divorcee's panties and destroyer of lives. Mainly mine. "What a charming surprise!"

I can't take my eyes off his stupid smug face. "Mm-hmm. This is great."

I have never been less okay.

Kevin gives the performance of a lifetime, tying the health benefits of an herbal body scrub to return-on-investment, and the sharpening of creative minds to making swift pivots in the boardroom. It is glorious.

The women head to a kickoff meeting while their guests mill around the Big House, taking in all the amenities and discussing optional activities with Tania. Chaz is taking full advantage of the open bar and has flung himself dramatically into the corner of a leather sofa, cocktail in hand. Ice clinks against the side of the glass. A fire crackles cheerily, warming the room to a near-perfect temperature. Garland and shiny glass ornaments decorate the hearth. Poinsettias in matte silver planters are scattered around the room. This morning, Kevin plucked up the courage to ask Mike about getting a Christmas tree. I swoon a little at the thought of spending the holidays here, then wonder if I can convince Mom to mail me some of her Christmas Morning muffins for a little taste of home.

"I suggested Turks and Caicos, you know," Chaz says to Margot's husband, Kyle, who has the poor luck of having set himself up to read by the fire within conversational distance. He tears his gaze away from the page to look levelly at Chaz.

"Yes, you mentioned," he says dryly. "A few times."

"I just don't understand why, with so many resources at our fingertips, they would choose"—he waves at the space around him—"this."

Mrs. Indira, Felicia's mother, plops into the armchair across from Kyle. "Well, I couldn't be happier. This is just wonderful."

She takes a sip of her hot chocolate and sighs appreciatively. "That lovely Tania has me set up in the spa this afternoon and I have a creative living consultation before dinner. And then! Do you know what I'm doing tomorrow? You'll never guess, so I'll tell you. Ice fishing! I have never been fishing before in my life— why would I? But I'm going to try it. Did you know there are little huts with heaters and they bring snacks and"—she lowers her voice conspiratorially—"*cocktails*!" She clutches her mug to her chest, radiating pure joy.

I move closer so I can speak to her without disturbing the rest of the group.

"Mrs. Indira, you're going to have a wonderful time. Your guide is also an accomplished photographer, so I'm certain you'll come out of the day with some beautiful keepsakes to go along with your memories."

"Oh please, call me Cece. We passed a large sign for a taxidermist on the way here. Perhaps I could have my fish preserved!"

Chaz finishes off his drink and puts it on a glossy wooden side table, directly beside a coaster. "Ice fishing? Sounds horrific."

I cast my gaze around for Kevin, hoping beyond hope that he'll swoop in and destroy Chaz with a single snarky comment. No luck.

"Turks and Caicos would have been so much nicer. I have friends there, you know, who would have taken excellent care of us. Deep-sea fishing, now there's a real excursion. Just man versus the might of nature, proving who is the greater beast through strength and perseverance."

I raise my eyebrow at him. I know for a fact that Chaz can't swim and is terrified of the water. He also hates anything that can be classified as "outdoorsy," relegating everything from beach volleyball to skydiving to the category of unnecessarily risky behavior unbecoming of a person of his social stature and breeding. Tennis and golf are acceptable if played as part of a business deal.

Kyle looks up from his book. "Don't they just attach a fishing rod to the boat and feed you beers until something bites?"

Cece chimes in, "I heard they'll even do the reeling so the refined city guests don't have to mar the skin of their soft hands."

"That's not at all accurate," Chaz insists, working himself up in the face of their dismissal. "You would know if you'd ever been. But it's quite an investment, so not many people get the chance. I've only managed to go three or four times myself."

While I put my energy into maintaining a serene, uninterested expression, Tania does a circuit of the room, confirming everyone's activity choices and handing out summaries. "A copy will be delivered to your room so you can easily refer to it while you're relaxing, which is also a critically important piece of this retreat." She pauses in front of Chaz.

"Mr. Hoberack! I noticed you've chosen not to participate in any supplementary offerings during your stay. This is, of course, totally fine. A goal of relaxation and getting back in touch with oneself is absolutely valid."

"I don't need you to tell me that my choices are valid."

Tania, bless her, lets it roll right off. "Of course you don't, sir. I will, however, leave this list with you in case you change your mind. I overheard you telling the group how much you value adventure and getting close to nature. The snowshoe hike with Heidi is wonderful and we've had quite a few moose sightings the past few weeks."

He leaves the heavy cardstock on the chair and walks away. "I need another drink."

As soon as he clears the doorway, Cece leans toward me. "You know, he threw up in the helicopter." Her smile widens. "Twice."

I resolve to focus on the other guests and avoid Chaz as much as possible, but he seems to be popping up everywhere.

"I think that guy is into you, in some weird, really off-putting way," observes Tania.

I try to laugh it off. "Oh really? I don't think so. He's just a big personality."

"You mean a big asshole?" mutters Jay, sidling up behind us and resting a hand on Tania's hip. "He sent his drink back three times. Three!" He lowers his voice further and I lean in to hear the details. "It was Scotch. With a single ice sphere. Poor Serge is going to develop a complex."

Aside from Chaz, things are going beautifully. The women are charming, pleasant and easygoing, seemingly giddy at the prospect of being in a setting so opposite to a downtown high-rise.

"There's something so refreshing about having these conversations surrounded by trees instead of panicked engineers and over-cologned investors," says Margot during the pre-dinner cocktail hour.

I see some people positioning their drinks artistically to get the live-edge bar and fireplace in the backdrop. Serge stands off to the side looking immensely proud.

Dinner goes off without a hitch. Jay serves up the requested plant-based menu, highlighting local flavors and ingredients. Freshly baked bread, winter-vegetable-stuffed ravioli tossed in olive oil, sprinkled with herbs painstakingly grown in a tiny greenhouse attached to the kitchen. Apple-cranberry crisp with vanilla-bean coconut milk ice cream.

I'm scrolling through our guests' social media accounts, tallying up the posts, tags, likes, and shares. I was right. This is going to be huge for us. I can feel a tiny flame of hope growing. Maybe, just maybe . . .

"You seem happy."

"Jesus! Chaz! You scared me." Clutching my phone to my chest with one hand, I use the other to prop myself up against the bar and take a couple of deep breaths. He's close enough that I can smell the whiskey he's been consuming all evening.

"I said"—he drags it out—"you seem happy."

I consider this for a moment, taken aback by the idea. Do I? Am I? Mental shrug. Who knows? And Chaz certainly doesn't care.

"It's definitely a change of scenery and a chance to work on a different skill set."

"And does your employer know about you?"

"What about me?"

"That you're a slanderous whor—"

I cut him off, holding my hand up. Looking around us for innocent passersby, I lean in and whisper-yell, "Stop. Right. There. You have no right—no right!—to speak to me like that. You may not like what I did, but you're the one breaking whatever lawyerly rules of conduct you agreed to follow when you were called to the bar."

"I have every right to speak to you however I want. You obviously don't know how the real world works. You think people care about the allegations you made?" He scoffs. "You're nobody. Nothing. You think you're fooling anyone, saying you're out here proving yourself, developing new marketable skills? You know you're worthless and you're so ashamed of yourself for failing to make it in the big leagues that the only option left is to hide out here with these so-called artists. Ha. Con artists is more like it. Lord knows what a background check would bring to light." He pauses, sips his drink.

"But even criminals have standards." He leans close, brushing his cheek against mine as he whispers in my ear. "I wonder how your employer would feel, knowing how low you'll stoop when things don't go your way." He tsks, making me wince. "I bet they value professionalism and appropriate conduct. It would be a shame if they saw evidence of your past actions."

My nails cut half-moons into my palms, and I can feel my teeth grinding together hard enough to make my orthodontist shriek.

Matt and Tania approach with Vicki. Chaz's demeanor shifts in an instant. I smile, trying to ease the frown off Matt's face.

"Ah! Tania. I was just telling Katie here how lucky all of you are to be nestled away in the bosom of nature like this."

Matt's eyes dart between Chaz and me before settling on me, questioningly. Vicki wraps her arm around Chaz.

"Mm-hmm." I nod enthusiastically, focusing on Tania. "Chaz was just saying how much he would love to sign up for tomorrow's ice-fishing trip. Can you make sure he gets on the list? He wants to get as much of a wilderness experience as possible. I can't think of a single person who loves communing with nature more than my pal Chaz here."

"Funny, Kate. Actually, I'd rather—"

"It's so sexy when a man embraces life and new experiences. Especially in the primal role of the hunter." Vicki shudders with the delight of it all and trails a hand down his arm suggestively. "Actually, I think I forgot something in the room. Will you come with me to get it?"

"See you at five!" I call cheerily down the hall after them. "That's a.m.!"

Chapter 20

Knowing that Chaz is off the property for at least a few hours has me feeling light and fluffy when Eric and I strike out for our morning stroll. It helps that I woke up to a slew of DMs asking for information about booking Treetops for corporate and personal getaways. If it's possible to swagger through freshly fallen snow up to one's shins while wearing three pairs of pants and five upper layers, then that's what I would be doing. Realistically, I'm pulling off more of a Frankenstein shuffle.

Eric manages his winter look much more smoothly, dashing around with effortless bounces that show off his highlighter-pink boots and complementary neon-yellow and -green canine parka beautifully. There's just the tiniest bit of retina-searing. Upon reflection, I could have picked less assertive colors.

Watery sunlight is fighting to get out from behind a wall of steel clouds and the forecast promises additional snowfall by evening. It's not the prettiest of days, but even in the gloom the lake and woods have a certain gothic appeal.

We're rounding the last bend to get to the neighboring lake's shore when Matt and Delilah jog up behind us.

"Shouldn't you be inside teaching someone how to access their inner Picasso? Minus the ear thing, of course. We'd probably get sued if people started disfiguring themselves after visiting us."

He laughs. "Van Gogh was the ear guy. Your mind works in mysterious ways."

"It's part of my charm."

I throw a stick for Eric that immediately disappears into the snow.

"How do you think things are going with the new group?" Matt asks.

"Really well. The execs seem to be loving it and their guests are mostly lovely and are jumping right into the experience."

"Jay mentioned that one of the guys has been hassling you."

"He's not hassling me. Well, not just me. He's been a jerk to everyone. Ask Serge. He sent his drink back three times!" I walk a bit faster. "I have no idea how he's got Vicki so convinced he's some kind of catch. Actually, I do have some idea but I don't want to think about it." *Good lord, stop talking.*

Mentally zipping my lips, I focus on making it up the hill we've started climbing, without falling on my face. There's a layer of ice under the snow that's trying very hard to lay me out.

Matt's sneaking looks at me out of the corner of his eye. I can feel him trying to think of how to smooth this conversation over. Pausing, he grabs my hand and holds it in his, turning my body toward him.

"Will you tell me, or someone at least, if he becomes a problem? I don't trust him."

Lord, he's sexy when he worries about me. Also concerning, because I really, reallllly don't want him spending too much time thinking about Chaz.

"Of course. But they're all leaving in a couple of days. I don't think he's going to be an issue." As long as he doesn't announce how unprofessional and generally awful I am or try to sue me. Ha ha ha ha. Ugh.

It's midafternoon and people are milling around, having a snack, chatting between activities. The executives have spent the day rotating between small breakout meetings and spa treatments. Margot burst out of her consultation with Kevin absolutely swooning over his suggestions and ready to spend more than I made in a year at Regan-Caulfield on updates to her home office. I wonder if we should start offering this as an end-to-end service.

Quiet murmurings and the turning of book pages are interrupted by the sound of a door slamming back against the wall as someone bursts into the room.

"She tried to kill me!" shouts a half-frozen Chaz. Melting snow drips from his hair and runs down his face.

Heidi's daughter, Kim, comes in behind him, brow furrowed in frustration.

"No one tried to kill anyone, sir."

"Don't sir me! Are you even a licensed wilderness guide? Huh? ARE YOU?"

"There isn't actually a regulatory body—"

"Only a complete lunatic would allow a novice driver to tackle those types of maneuvers. I am shocked no one has died or been seriously injured while under your purview."

He pauses for a breath and Kim rolls her eyes at me and Tania.

Matt steps forward from where he was talking to Kyle beside the fire.

"Let's all calm down. Kim, what happened?"

Before Kim can open her mouth Chaz jumps back in.

"What happened is I was encouraged—nay, pressured—into engaging in snowmobile maneuvers far beyond my abilities.

Proper instruction and guidance regarding safety protocols were not provided and I NEARLY DIED."

"You fell off your snowmobile. You got covered in snow. There was little risk and it wouldn't have happened if—"

"I HEARD THE ICE CRACKING. I was seconds away from hypothermia. Drowning. A crush injury if that stupid machine fell on me. A COMBINATION OF THE THREE!"

Cece slides in from the mudroom, still decked out in a bright red one-piece snowmobiling suit unzipped to the waist. She stomps to Chaz and points a finger at him, channeling megawatt mom energy.

"You, young man, are acting like a complete fool. You were given precise instructions you chose to ignore to get . . . what was it? Sweet GoPro footage for the bros? So why don't you let us see this little movie? It should make the situation very clear, no?" She plants her hands on her hips and, no lie, taps her foot on the hardwood floor. Audibly, like a ticking clock.

Matt takes the piece of paper Kim holds out and reads through it.

"Mister, uh, Hoberack, is it? You indicated on your Ice Fishing Experience questionnaire that your knowledge of snowmobiles and their use is at the expert level."

"Yes, well the question is misleading."

Matt holds up a second piece of paper.

"And here we have the waiver you signed, indicating you fully understand the risks associated with outdoor sports and adventure excursions, and that Treetops and its employees and/or contractors are in no way liable for injury. I'd also hazard to suggest that Kim is not responsible for your hurt pride."

"You know I'm a lawyer, right? That waiver would never hold up in court. This whole place is a joke."

Cece chimes in. "I do see quite a few people laughing. Not sure it's at this place, though."

It looks like Chaz's head might pop off his body he's so enraged, but just when I think he's about to explode, Vicki swans into the room in her Treetops robe, fresh from the spa.

"Ah! Darling, you're back! I can't wait to hear all about your day, and I'm absolutely gagging for a drink to round out my afternoon relaxation experience. This place is heaven." She starts to wrap an arm around him and stops, appraising his dripping form and flushed cheeks. "Hrmmm," she murmurs. "We need to get you out of those clothes." She takes off down the corridor, hips swinging. "Chaz, come," she calls without turning around.

The room is silent, everyone staring, waiting for his next move.

His eyes land on me.

"This isn't the end of the conversation, Katelyn." He bites off my name, clenching his teeth, and storms after Vicki.

By some silent agreement, people resume their activities and continue as if nothing out of the ordinary has happened. Cece places her hand gently on my arm.

"This is one of the best trips of my life. You have something really special here." Her words hit me in the gut. I feel something. Pride?

"It makes me incredibly happy to hear you say that. But more importantly, how was the fishing?"

Her face breaks into a huge glowing grin, white teeth shining behind dark pink lips. "I caught four!"

Kim is nodding happily. "She's a natural. The fish are just drawn to her."

"Kim has promised that lovely Chef Jay will cook them up for us this evening." Cece wraps her arms around herself in a hug. "But now I must go find that hardworking daughter of mine and convince her to take a break. It's all well and good to instill the values of perseverance and dedication in our children, but my word, she can't miss all this! A moment of relaxation allows the mind to breathe. And besides, she needs to see the fish!" She rushes away, scrolling through photo after photo on her phone as she goes.

The adrenaline from Chaz's meltdown starts to fade and the crackling fire is making me sleepy. Halfway to the kitchen for an emergency latte, I run into Matt, who's coming the other way, steaming cup of black coffee in hand. It smells heavenly and I find myself leaning into the fumes.

He offers me the mug.

"Help yourself. I can get more."

"It's a lovely offer, and I might just take a quick sip to power me the rest of the way to the kitchen"—I pause to do just that.—"But my heart is set on a vanilla latte and, maybe, if the stars are aligned, a cookie. Or brownie. Or anything with butter and sugar and chocolate. I'm not picky."

His eyes are fixed on mine and I wonder if maybe there's another acceptable pick-me-up option. I've got a two-hour break in my schedule that I'd earmarked for brochure mailing, but . . .

"What are you doing right now?" I blurt.

His eyes narrow and his gaze travels down my body.

"Having very impure thoughts."

Our eyes lock and I have the weird sensation that our hearts are beating perfectly in time.

The door to our left glides open soundlessly and Kevin steps out of his office to stand directly between us, breaking the spell. His eyes flit from my guilty expression to Matt, who's leaning casually against the wall, sipping his coffee. His soft navy flannel button-up is open over a cloud-gray merino shirt that looks so, so touchable. I sigh loudly. Matt's lips twitch upward into a smile. I'm fairly certain he flexes his abs in my direction.

Kevin looks pointedly at his watch.

"Shouldn't you be setting up for Expressions of Creativity in Everyday Life?" he asks Matt.

"Mm-hmm. Heading there now."

Kevin gives a curt nod and pauses in front of the closed door leading to the common area. Running his hands over the front of today's cardigan—burgundy with gray and ivory flecks, finished with intricate Celtic knot buttons—he takes a deep breath and squares his shoulders before stepping through, ready to face his adoring fans.

Matt moves to follow Kevin's path but pauses just before heading through the door to look over his shoulder at me. "Can you get away after the Gathering Fire has kicked off?"

"Once this group has their dinner wine and a couple of Serge's cocktails in them, they wouldn't notice if a bear joined the party, so yeah, probably. Why?"

"It's a surprise. Eric can come too. Meet me by Tania's, around eight?"

"Sure. No hints?"

"Dress warmly."

"That's not a hint. My default number of layers is now three, minimum."

He just smiles, slow and warm, and disappears through the door to teach the guests how to make their grocery lists more artistically fulfilling.

Hormones still fizzing, I get my latte and a zucchini chocolate-chip muffin, then head down to the dungeon to spend a bit of time answering the slew of booking inquiries that have been rolling in over the past couple of days. This morning I'd booked in a team of lawyers for an ice-fishing weekend, two girls' weekend getaways, and another corporate group referred by the Party Thyme crew. If, somehow, things continued on this track we will easily hit my contract booking minimum for January and February. Especially with groups booking the whole retreat for themselves.

Dollar signs and the glint of success dance before my eyes as I answer an email from a photographer asking if our space is available for photoshoots. Certainly, good sir.

Someone is wondering if we do creative bachelorettes. I take a moment to scope out her Instagram, which sparkles with diamonds in every season and rotates between sailing trips, post-workout selfies *(#inittowinit),* pouty selfies with her cat *(#meow),* and selfies with various women who all look eerily similar and have perfectly applied, subtly winged eyeliner that make me very jealous *(#bffs #workhardplayresponsibly)*. You bet we do creative bachelorettes!

Jay serves Mrs. Indira's fish in taco form after frying them up over the fire. Cocktails flow and phones are snapping photos willy-nilly. I sit back and soak it all in, exhausted but happy. Vicki keeps Chaz occupied on the other side of the fire. I like having the roaring flames between us, though I occasionally imagine him leaping through them like a circus lion to rip out my throat.

When everyone is suitably lubricated and settling in for the long haul, I excuse myself and fetch Eric from the Hut. I skirt the tree line to Tania's place, cursing the new moon's darkness as I trip over snow-covered rocks and roots.

Matt's sitting on Tania's front steps, looking like he's basking in the sun on a warm summer's day instead of the glow of an LED lantern. Delilah is sniffing a nearby tree, but graces me with a very human nod of acknowledgement before going back to her task. I bob up and down on the balls of my feet, trying to maintain some body heat as he rubs Eric's head in greeting before standing to pass me a battery powered lantern that matches his own. He gestures for me to follow him through the trees.

We walk single-file along the skinny path that leads to his house, the occasional branch smacking me in the face despite his efforts to hold them out of my way.

"Have you considered asking Mike to clear this for you? Or offering your guests safety goggles?"

"Nah. I don't want it to be too welcoming."

"Oh, yeah, of course not," I grumble, shoving more cedar out of my way. "Much better to have people arrive partially blind."

Once the trees spit us out, he heads for the lake. We slide a little on the way down the small hill where the shore meets the ice, and then set course for . . . where, exactly?

"Night ice-fishing?" I guess, though there's no hut in sight.

"No."

"Night cross-country skiing?"

"You know you're going to find out in about thirty seconds, right?"

"Nocturnal snowman-building contest."

He just sighs and keeps stepping through the knee-deep snow. My breath is huffing out like we're wrapping up a marathon, but he doesn't seem to be exerting any more effort than he would strolling down a sidewalk. If his ass wasn't so great, even in snow pants, I might have a harder time forgiving him.

Eric's bounding around Delilah but I've got my eyes down, squinting to focus on stepping in the holes Matt's feet have left, and am caught completely off guard when my next step lands on flat ground. For a second, as my foot keeps moving past where it felt the snow should catch it, I am convinced I'm about to fall through the ice to my death. The cutting cold of the water doesn't come, though, and when I look up, I see we're standing in a ten-foot circle of snow that's been packed down. There are two distinct piles of blankets with a thermos and mugs nestled between them.

I raise my eyebrows. "Slumber party?"

He moves to the blankets and starts spreading them out. Once they're arranged to his liking, he gestures me over. "Lie down."

"Um."

There's enough light that I can see the whites of his eyes as they roll heavenward, the puff of condensation as he sighs.

"Humor me."

"Should I take my boots off? What's the etiquette here?"

"Get. In. The. Damn. Cocoon." The words push through clenched teeth.

"When you put it that way." I lower myself onto the dark wool blanket, trying not to cover it in snow. "Of course, good sir. Your gallant offer is so enticing. Never have I received such a kind, gentle—" I squeal as snow plops onto my head and glare up at him. He wraps me quickly in another blanket and steps away to survey his work. Warmth begins to seep through my coat, and I spot a little light glowing within the fabric.

"Is this thing heated?!"

"I thought it would be better than listening to you complain about the cold for the next hour."

I grumble with pleasure and wiggle deeper into the pocket of warmth, pulling off my mittens. Eric finishes his survey of the area and comes to stand beside us, sniffing at the thermos before plopping himself directly onto the other blanket pile and rolling around, covering it in snow and eau-de-wet-canine.

"Eric, no! Get out of there!" I am mortified. Based on how Delilah huffs, she is equally disgusted. She turns in three tight circles before lowering herself into the snow, seemingly oblivious to the cold.

Matt's mittened hands rest on his hips as he surveys the scene. He turns to me.

"Scootch."

"Scootch?" The thought of opening the envelope of heat is not appealing, but my greater concern is being in such close proximity to this man for any length of time without my clothes falling off.

He unzips his coat and slides it off, tucking it in a bin off to the side of the clearing.

"Kate, it's freezing and your delightful canine has seat-scammed my respectfully distanced observation post." He kneels and prods me. "Lemme in."

I shimmy over, making room for him beside me, and lift a flap of the blanket, cringing as the cold air snakes in. Luckily, Matt doesn't dally and within moments I'm warm again. Getting warmer by the second, actually, as my body registers just how close he is.

"Did you say observation post?" I squirm around, trying to put some distance between us, but it just creates gaps, letting in the cold. I give up quickly, our hips nestled side by side, my back resting against his chest as he leans back, arms holding us both up. Show-off.

"Lie down." He follows his own instructions and I have little choice but to follow the path of the blankets. Before I can find a reasonably comfortable place for my head, his arm swoops around me, bringing me closer. We lie there, pressed together, my head on his shoulder. The soft fabric of his sweater smells like detergent and cold night air. It's impossible not to snuggle closer until the entire length of our bodies is touching.

"Okay, so what exactly are we observing? The secret night-time migration of the loon?"

"They left ages ago. Now, be quiet and look up."

"At what?" But even as I say it, I understand. Stars cover the sky so densely it's hard to discern any real space in between. "Wow," I breathe.

"Just wait."

My head rises and falls with each of his slow breaths. It doesn't take long before we see the first shooting star.

I bolt upright, pointing. "Did you see that?!"

He laughs, pulling the back of my jacket to guide me back down. "This is supposed to be the best night for seeing the meteor shower from here. We should be getting plenty more."

I nestle my head back onto his chest, still in awe. I can't remember the last time I just sat and looked at the stars. Not that there are many to see in the city. It's mostly satellites and airplanes. I didn't know I'd been missing all *this*.

We lie there in silence for the next hour, watching streaks of light fly across the sky. Eric snores gently in his own blanket nest, oblivious to the light show happening above his head. Delilah is awake, but looks thoroughly bored. I don't know if I've ever felt this content.

Eventually, not even the electric blanket and our many layers can combat the cold creeping into our backs from the ice and snow below us, and the wind is picking up, pushing in a veil of clouds that obscures our view. But neither of us moves to get up.

I tilt my head to look up at him, but in the dark, my view is limited to the dim outline of his jaw and a well-shaped earlobe sticking out from under the edge of his hat. There's a lot I want to say, but as the words run through my head they all sound ridiculous. Too emotional, too personal. Just too much for this quiet moment.

His head moves, slowly turning until our noses are practically touching, my head on his arm as his eyes search mine. He leans in a fraction of an inch, resting his forehead on mine. His eyelids close and mine follow suit. For a moment, we just breathe each other in, prolonging this perfect feeling.

A gust of wind edges between us, strong enough to roust Eric, who stretches and walks to the edge of the clearing. He lifts his leg and pees on the raised wall of snow. I burst out laughing, Matt snorts charmingly. I'm fairly certain Delilah scoffs before turning tail and sashaying toward home.

We stand, Matt sliding into his coat and jumping up and down a few times to get warm before gathering up the blankets and dropping them into the bin. He hands me the thermos.

"Jay's peppermint hot chocolate. A definite upgrade from last time."

There's an awkward silence as the ghost of that night at his place sidles in, but it's quickly pushed aside as we turn back to shore and I realize I can see the shimmer of the Gathering Fire and hear the occasional burst of aggressive laughter that is gratingly familiar. For a moment, I consider telling Matt about Chaz. About everything. But the words stick in my throat and before I can push them out, he's picking up the bin and stepping out of the clearing. He leads the way across the open expanse of frozen lake, taking us back to reality. *Tomorrow*, I resolve. *I'll explain it all tomorrow.*

It's late when I get back to the Hut, and the crowd around the fire is dispersing. I let Eric into the yard to perform his final perimeter check and am just starting to undress when someone knocks on the front door. Weird. I peek through the curtains but the window is foggy and all I can make out is the vague shape of a man on my steps. Clad in jeans and a thin tank top, I wrap a throw blanket around my shoulders, flip the lock and open the door, expecting a tipsy guest who's lost track of his own cabin.

"You need to head back toward the fi—" The words die on my lips as the cold air whistles in. The blanket drops from my grip and my arms fly up across my chest as my brain races to reconcile this horrible twist.

"What a welcome." Chaz leers as he steps forcefully into the room. He reeks of the high-end liquor he's been throwing back nonstop.

"You need to leave." I hate that my voice shakes.

The door shuts and suddenly Chaz seems huge. There were moments in our relationship when I felt intimidated by him, but never physically. He's a jerk, sure, but not this menacing character.

"Chaz." I say sharply, hoping to cut through whatever boozy haze is clouding his judgment. There's a sweatshirt lying across the arm of the couch. I grab it and hold it up to my chest, but don't feel like it's safe to take my eyes off him long enough to slide it over my head.

"Chaz," I repeat. "This isn't okay. You should go."

"*This* isn't okay? You know what wasn't okay, Kate? Barging into my office while I was with a client. Airing dirty laundry on the internet." He's getting louder with every sentence and moving closer to me until I can feel the couch pressing against the back of my knees and he's looming over me, breathing hard. "Did you know I was asked to leave the firm because you couldn't keep your mouth shut?" He's quiet now, but it's a dangerous quiet.

"I'm sorry, Chaz. Really, I am. I was angry and hurt and made a poor decision." I put a trembling hand gently on his arm and look into his bloodshot eyes. "But what you're doing right now? This isn't you."

He shakes my hand off and grips my wrist hard enough to make me gasp.

"You have no idea who I am. How could you?" He lowers his face until his stubble is scratching against my cheek and his hot breath is on my neck. "We're on different levels, Kate. You were lucky to have me for the time you did. Maybe you need to be reminded of that." Teeth close on my earlobe and I think I might throw up. Chaz runs his hand roughly up my side, under my shirt, pawing at my breasts.

"I saw you whoring around with the heir to the throne. What are you up to now? Trying to fuck your way to the top?"

"GET OFF ME! Have you lost your mind?" I'm flailing, trying to find a way around him but I'm pressed against the wall. For a second, he backs off and stares at me, but his hands stay against my skin.

Thoughts race by too quickly to latch onto any of them. Tears slide down my cheeks and I don't know if I'm crying from fear or rage at my complete helplessness. Through the blood rushing in my head, I register Eric barking frantically outside the back door and throwing himself at the glass.

Concern for Eric is what pulls me back to the moment. I put both hands on Chaz's chest and shove as hard as I can. He rocks back and falls over the coffee table. In a split second, he's sprawled out on the floor and for a blink, I wonder if he's hit his head and died. That would be just my fucking luck. But then he's glaring at me and hoisting himself unsteadily to his feet.

I take the opportunity to let Eric in. He plants himself between the two of us, hackles raised, showing teeth as he advances slowly toward Chaz. A low growl comes from the back of his throat.

"Get out," I say, voice flat. "Now."

"You're going to regret what you did," he says, ripping the door open to reveal a startled Matt, hand raised about to knock.

"Trust me, Chaz. I already do."

He shoulders his way out and strides into the night. I watch as Matt takes in my tearstained face and shivering body. He looks at poor Eric, who is practically vibrating with tension.

"That son of a bitch." He turns to follow Chaz, hands balled into fists.

"Matt, please. Just stay." At that moment my legs decide they've had enough and I crumple to the floor. Eric is at my side before I fully realize I'm not standing anymore. Rough dog kisses cover my cheeks and he presses his curly forehead against mine.

"You're such a good boy," I whisper. "A good, good boy. The best." Burying my hands in his fur, I sob uncontrollably, body heaving.

Matt's strong arms cradle me, lifting my limp form onto his lap. He wraps himself around me, smelling like mint and snow. Eric jumps up beside us and rests his head across my thighs. Slowly my breathing stops hitching every time I try to speak. Matt's hand runs up and down my back over the blanket he draped over me.

"We should call the police," Matt says into my hair.

"No!" I pull away and look at him. "We can't. Chaz is . . . he'll turn it all around and it will be a disaster for me. For Tree-tops."

"I don't give a single fuck who he is. He doesn't get to force himself on you. Terrify you. What if Eric wasn't here? Would he have left?"

That's too much to consider right now. I push it away. Shove it down to deal with later. I take a deep breath, shift myself off his lap so I can fully face him. The sweatshirt is in a heap on the floor, and I reach down, using the moment it takes to slip it on to try and collect my thoughts.

"Please, Matt. He was upset. He . . . —I . . . —" This is way harder than I thought it would be. "We know each other. From back home." *Get it all out, Rigsby.* I clear my throat.

"We were, uh, together. For a while. And—"

"And that doesn't give him permission to treat you like this.

I get that you might still have feelings . . ." He trails off. "Oh." His hands tighten where they're resting on his thighs and then, abruptly, he stands. "Shit. Well, I feel like an idiot. For the past two days, I've been worried some creep guest is eyeing you, but maybe that's what you wanted."

"What? Matt, come on!"

"Did you invite him here? To Treetops?"

"With his new girlfriend? Are you serious?"

"I was feeling pretty serious about you, yeah. This felt . . . different. I thought—fuck. It doesn't matter. I was just a distraction, wasn't I? While you waited for this asshole to come back and sweep you off your feet. But he brushed you off, huh? Choosing the horny CEO over you. That's why you're so upset."

My head is spinning. This is such bullshit.

"I'm upset because I'm scared. I'm angry. And you're standing there accusing me of feeling all this"—my hands move up and down along my torso, indicating how absolutely overflowing this cup of emotion is—"because I'm sad that sack of garbage doesn't want me?" My volume has crept up to a full-on yell and I take a breath, try to dial it down.

Before I can go further though, Matt speaks again, quietly.

"I saw you two in the bar at the Big House, Kate." He runs both hands through his hair, over his face. "If it's nothing, why didn't you just tell me when he got here?"

Well, there's the million-regrets question.

I'm silent too long, staring at the carpet trying to think of a way to answer that doesn't make me look like the complete disaster I am.

"Right," he says, opening the door. "That's what I thought." And he's gone.

Chapter 21

The C-Suite ladies leave the next day after lunch, heaping praise upon our exhausted heads and promising to tell all their friends about us.

Aside from a glimpse of his hungover face during breakfast service, I manage to avoid Chaz completely. As the helicopter blades thrum, Vicki pauses to hug Kevin and thank him for his "absolutely incredible gift. If it's even possible, Chaz gets a shade or two paler as they walk toward the helicopter door. Some kind, deranged part of my brain considers cutting him a break and offering to have Mike drive him into town. Then memories of the night before smash into me and I stand very still when I should be waving jauntily at our happy guests.

We have a bit of a pre-Christmas lull with some individuals and couples more in line with Treetops' traditional guest profile coming in for a night or two of peace before the holiday madness ensues. I refuse to continue calling it the Ideal Customer Profile. That ship has sailed. The free time is a gift and a curse.

I use it to catch up on inquiries and reach out to some well-regarded travel blogs while constantly stomping down the wave of emotion that rears up every time Matt's within range.

I haven't told anyone much about that night. Only that Chaz showed up, drunk and belligerent. I choose to completely ignore Matt's role in compounding the horror of it all. I thought he was good, and kind, and so much of what I'd been looking for. What I deserved after so much BS. But maybe this is still what I deserve. It's not like I'm guiltless in this whole situation.

I throw myself back into work, the one thing that, beyond all reason, seems to be going well. My email and Treetops DMs continue to be hit with requests for pricing and information. Most of them go nowhere but enough go through with bookings that it feels like real progress. Tangible growth. I never thought I'd say this, but I can't wait to plot it out in Excel. It's going to be one hell of a curve.

Two cups of coffee and a chocolate chip cookie—alright, three cookies—into Monday morning, I finish sending a quote to LifeCycle—creators of an app to track the freshness of your produce for ideal consumption times—for a five-day Refresh & Balance retreat and click on the next message in my inbox.

Dear Kate,

We appreciate your help booking our upcoming retreat for Logan, Howitzer, and Nagle. However, it has been brought to our attention that perhaps Treetops is not a good fit for our group. We have heard concerning reports of unsafe practices and staff acting less professionally than what we would expect from an organization of this sort.

Because of these concerns, we find ourselves unable to proceed with the booking. Please consider this notice of our full cancellation.

Regards,
Anita Fullsome

I groan, leaning back to distance myself from the words. They're polite enough, but the undertones are there. Chaz. He did this.

Feeling deeply uneasy I navigate to our Instagram account. There are enough positive or neutral comments on our posts that I'm lulled into feeling reassured, then *BAM*.

goodisgone57 Don't waste your time. Heard this place has lawsuits pending. They jeopardize the safety of their guests to make a buck. PASS. #danger #tourismtoavoid

And a bit farther down.

One_B1g_Fish Dragged here by the ol' ball and chain recently. Sucks. Terrible food, losers posing as "artists," and a spa about as nice as your parents' bathroom in 1992. #dontgo #awfulhotel

It keeps going. Not often enough to be blatant trolling, but in sufficient quantities that I get the point. True to his word, Chaz isn't letting this go. I spend a bit of time trying to drill into the individual accounts and figure out who they are, but it's pointless.

By that afternoon two more groups—with at least one Toronto lawyer in the mix for each—have canceled. My graph is looking much flatter than it did that morning, as are my emotions. I call it a day and head upstairs to hunt down Serge and volunteer to be a guinea pig for his new cocktail recipes. All of them.

Over the course of the week, my raging sea of emotions calms to a manageable level. More like a wave pool set to medium-low. Anger simmers, waiting for someone to step out of line, but I'm coping. Matt's been MIA, and I heard someone mention he was back in the city for a while. I hope he stays there.

A gaggle of chefs checks in for three days of inspiring cuisine experimentation with Jay, ice fishing (which is quickly becoming one of our top-selling and highest margin excursions), and absorbing Serge's tutelage on pairing herbaceous cocktails with dessert items. They seem perfectly content to hang around the kitchen discussing how much rosemary is too much and sipping beer brewed in town.

There are four other solo guests in residence, along with Georgia Yates's bachelorette party, and the day disappears in a haze of polite conversation, coordinating extra mentoring sessions, and confirming the plan for the chefs' fishing trip with Kim. Since the Chaz debacle we've doubled down on safety protocols just in case, and Tania and I pass a cheerful hour sipping coffee and watching the chefs learn how to maneuver their snowmobiles while heckling each other.

Earlier in the day, Georgia's maid of honor, Abby, shyly asked if it would be okay for them to have a bit of a traditional bachelorette party that evening in the library. "You know, BRIDE TO BE sash, penis straws, the usual. Nothing crazy though. Georgia wouldn't go for that." They've been so delightfully, and unexpectedly, respectful and dedicated to embracing the creative retreat side of things during their stay that I agreed, not thinking much of it.

The sun is dipping behind the trees when I decide to take Eric out for a quick walk before full dark. The late afternoon is calm with little wind and while it is still incredibly cold, I'm finally starting to enjoy being outside, even when I lose feeling in my toes within twenty minutes. *I need to get better boots next year,* I think before remembering I won't be here next winter.

My phone has a countdown to the last day of my contract and while it started out in the same spirit as a prisoner counting down to release, it's feeling a bit different these days. I watch the numbers tick by with a mess of emotions. Apprehension at the idea of being broke, homeless, and without a plan for the future. Blind hope that Brooke will clue into all the effort I've been putting in here and give me at least part of my bonus as a goodwill gesture.

This is closely followed by anger. At myself. At Brooke. At Chaz. At Matt. Then at myself again. Most confusingly though, I'm sad. *It's no good dwelling on it,* I tell myself when some part of my brain tries to figure out why I'm pausing a little longer to watch the sunset, or opening my mouth to tell Kevin that his sweater is even more stunning than the one from the day before.

After getting Eric settled at home, I decide to luxuriate in the three-square feet that make up my shower, leaning into the spray until the hot water runs out six glorious minutes later. Collapsing onto the couch, I decide to continue the self-care with an hour of downtime. I flip mindlessly through some magazines I'd pilfered from the lounge, popping dark chocolate chips (liberated from Jay's kitchen) into my mouth every two pages.

Eventually, I heave myself upright, chug a glass of frigid water, and head over to the Big House to make sure the guests have everything they need for the night. As soon as I open the door, I hear it. The rhythmic thudding of heavy bass makes the pot lights vibrate. Dread spreads through my chest as I jog toward the staircase down to the library. The heavy door is cool against my hand and I pause for a moment, wondering if I can just pretend none of this is happening and go back to my couch and a glass of wine. At that moment I hear the unmistakable sound of breaking glass. No going back now.

It is mayhem. Penis-shaped balloons are tied to all the expensive stained-glass table lamps. Glittery streamers loop around the library ladder and meander along the back of furniture. Some idiot has set up an ice luge—who even has time to make an ice luge?! The classy Yates party ladies are a thing of the past. Egged on by a hooting band of merry chefs, Maid of Honor Abby kneels down to receive her shot of . . . Fuck. Is that the forty-year scotch? You'd think these food people would know better. At least we can invoice for everything they consume. Someone stumbles into a balloon, pulling down the lamp it's

attached to. The shade shatters. We will also invoice for everything they break. Possibly also emotional damage.

A pretty solid *I'm not angry, just disappointed* speech is forming in my head when Matt appears beside me. He surveys the
scene. I think he looks a bit pale but put it down to the strange
lighting and the shock of a three-foot-long penis balloon hitting
him in the face as people start playing volleyball with it.

"Kate, you've got to get them out of here. *Now.*"

"No shit. I was just going to start encouraging them to wrap
it up."

"No, I mean like, right now."

"Yeah, got it. You can go."

"You don't understand—"

"I don't understand," I repeat, feeling the anger that's been
simmering for the past few days bubbling like a volcano. "*I
don't understand?*"

He backs up a step and the alarmed look on his face is both
gratifying and intensely annoying.

"You"—I poke him in the chest—"are the one who doesn't
understand one goddamn thing about me. How *dare* you treat
me the way you did. You think I didn't get the emotional shit
kicked out of me enough by Chaz? You had to get in there too?"

Nineties hip-hop anthems get even louder as someone cranks
the volume. Angry tears pool on my lower lashes.

"I have had enough of being made to feel like I am worthless. I am done being treated like garbage." I glare at him, taking in the obvious strain around his eyes and mouth. The bags
under his eyes. It would be easy to forgive him, to forget it ever
happened, but then where would that leave me? Chasing yet
another guy who thinks he's better than me. No. Not this time.
"You hurt me. Badly." My arms are crossed over my chest to
hide shaking hands.

"Please, Kate. We can talk about this later." He turns to look
at the door he'd just come through. He's jittery, looking around

wide-eyed like he doesn't even know where to begin. "We have to talk about what happened. About what a complete asshole I am. But not now. Now *you have to get these people OUT!*"

The playlist comes to an end, allowing his voice to carry over the din of laughter and conversation, making everyone pause and turn to look at us.

The overhead lights flick on, illuminating a tall woman with gorgeous gray-blond hair that's been tossed around by the wind, but in a romance-book-cover way.

"What the hell is going on?" She's got bags under her eyes and her lipstick is smudged, but I'd know that hair anywhere.

"Brooke." I look around, taking in the decorations, the broken lamp, the woman on her knees in front of an icy shot delivery system. My shoulders slump. "So nice to see you."

Chapter 22

The usually irresistible smell of waffles wafts down the stairs to my office, where I've been sitting since five thirty this morning, wrapped in two blankets and chugging coffee. There was no sleeping last night. Not after Brooke stormed in like a parent returning early from vacation to discover a high school party in full swing. I'm waiting for the adult equivalent of being grounded and having the car keys taken away.

On a normal morning, Eric would be curled on my feet, keeping them at least a couple of degrees away from frozen, but I didn't want to risk bringing him in. A spreadsheet is open in front of me, peppered with graphs and charts and every piece of job-saving data I can come up with. Hopefully it'll be enough to convince Brooke not to toss me to the unemployment wolves.

Starting at seven thirty people start to casually stop by to chat. No one ever swings past my office. It's on the way to exactly nowhere.

Jay drops off a vanilla latte and a freshly baked shortbread cookie, giving my shoulder a gentle squeeze before heading back to the kitchen.

A few minutes later, Tania pops in to ask if it would be alright if she walks Eric.

Serge, embracing the drama, sends a flask of Baileys down, dangling at the end of a string while he stands peering over the ledge at the top of the stairs. Keeping his distance. Good idea.

Around eight thirty I see a face peering in through the tiny window in the door, but the glass is too frosty to make out who it is. The doorknob starts to turn, then stops. The person walks away. I hustle over and peer out. Matt's retreating back makes a tempting target. I resist the urge to chuck a snowball at his head, but just barely. And really only because I don't have gloves on.

Just as the clock on my computer blinks to nine o'clock, Kevin saunters down the stairs. The anxious butterflies that have been camping out in my stomach for hours ramp up their activity until I think I'm going to throw up on his pristine house shoes.

"Brooke would like to see you in the Oak Room."

My face squishes up. "Do I have to? Ugh. Don't answer that. It was rhetorical." I begin my death march.

"Keep your head up. You've done good work." My head whirls around trying to figure out who spoke. It was Kevin's voice, but Kevin would never offer anything sounding remotely like encouragement. When I look back, he's surveying the area that's been my office, paying absolutely no attention to me. Probably planning a renovation to erase any evidence I was ever here.

It's a gorgeous day and the sun shines through the window in the boardroom, warming it to the point of uncomfortable. I unzip my sweater and sit down across from Brooke, who completely ignores me. She's typing industriously and pauses every few moments to consult her notebook. Her writing is bubbly like a high-schoolers and easy to read upside down. I see keywords like *unprofessional conduct* and *multiple OARs—starting first day.*" Whelp. I guess we know what direction this is taking.

As I sit sweltering, wondering when the hell she's going to acknowledge my presence, my fear fades and is replaced by rapidly building anger. Just as I'm about to reach a breaking point and walk out, Brooke looks directly at me. She says nothing. Fine. We engage in a staring contest. I blink first. Typical.

"Tell me why I shouldn't fire you."

Like she's not going to fire me anyway. Whatever, I'll play.

"There are a number of compelling reasons, actually." I plug in my laptop to display my presentation on the wall-mounted monitor.

"I believe I've found my niche here. Note the spike in bookings. Projected revenue is up sixty percent year on year." I click to the next slide.

"You'll also note the uptick in add-ons while guests are with us. On average, our guests are now selecting between one and four additional services after check-in, leading to an average of twenty-five percent more revenue per booking than before I started."

As I run through my list of accomplishments and justify some failures as trial and error, I realize something. This isn't just me spouting what I think Brooke wants to hear. I believe what I'm saying. I've put more hours, more suffering, more of myself into this job than anything I've done before—and I love it here. The people, the terrible weather, even Employee Hut Four with its faulty heater and gangrenous carpets. I want Treetops not just to stay open, but to be an industry benchmark for success, and more than anything, I want to be a part of it. A big part.

Brooke tents her fingers and looks at me through a quarter-inch of eyeliner.

"Do you know why we hired you?"

"Because I interview very well and was willing to sign your terrible contract?"

"Close, actually. No one else would sign. You were interviewee twelve." Placing her hands flat on the desk, she glances at her notebook. "You think you have new ideas? You think you're saving us? You're mediocre, if that. Your business plan is a joke. The revenue you're so proud of bringing in is going to cost us money when the high-end clients cancel because our quality of experience is going down due to riffraff."

She holds up perfectly manicured fingers, pushing them down as she counts off my transgressions.

"Multiple OARs. Negative reviews online have increased tenfold in the last month." I silently curse Chaz as she continues. "Unprofessional behavior. We have strict guidelines about employee relationships that you have flouted." She gives up on the counting, but not on the lecture. "Our trusted and valued neighbors have complained about you and your dog not once but several times. And, as if I needed any additional evidence that you are completely unfit for this role, last night's gathering in the library was completely outside the realm of what Treetops was created for. What a fiasco!"

She stands and starts gathering her things, sliding them into a leather satchel that probably cost more than my entire wardrobe.

"I'm sorry that you've deluded yourself into thinking that you belong here. You will be invoiced for damages incurred last night, and the amount will be deducted from your final paycheck. Should anything be left owing, someone will be in touch to collect it via wire."

I'm still sitting in my chair. Even though I knew this wasn't going to be pretty, this is beyond. Brooke pauses at the door.

"I wouldn't dawdle. Mike will be taking you into town in two hours. I expect you have packing to do."

Chapter 23

I crash land at Ros's place two days before Christmas. I called her from halfway down the 401 when the fact that I had nowhere to stay slapped me out of my post-firing stupor. In true best-friend fashion, she gushed about how she was so grateful I called when I did. And would I possibly be so kind, so generous, so absolutely *wonderful* as to stay with her for a while so she doesn't have to take sole responsibility for the aloe plant a client gave her? I accept with just the right amount of hesitancy and extreme gratefulness, only breaking into hysterical sobs twice before hanging up.

When I arrive, she's trying to wedge a box of Niagara Riesling into the fridge between a bag of spinach and a tub of plain yogurt. An array of gossipy magazines is fanned across the counter.

She turns to me.

"What do you need? Snacks? Reading material? Can we take out a hit on someone?"

"Would you just pour me a glass of that wine and listen to me rant for a while?"

"Ah yes, the classic wine & whine. Good thing I bought cheese."

We set up a laptop on the coffee table and call Gary, waiting the six minutes it takes him to find a drink and arrange a suitable charcuterie board of his own. "You can't rush these Brooklyn spent-grain crackers from their packaging, you savages!"

Snuggled into the corner of Ros's comfortable, alarmingly white couch, nibbling brie and a nice smoked cheddar, I regale them with the events leading up to and including my untimely departure from Treetops. They gasp at all the right parts, call Brooke a number of unflattering and creative names, and suggest we murder Chaz as soon as possible.

"But what about Matt?" Ros asks, ripping open a bar of organic eighty-percent dark chocolate we found in the back of a cupboard while looking for crackers. "Why aren't you holed up at his place playing hide the paintbrush?"

I get up to refill my glass. Eric noses the spot I vacated, searching for cheese particles. Ros gives him a look and he goes back to his designated dog zone on the floor.

Gary yells from the computer, "Katelyn Rigsby the First, you sneaky, idiotic minx. You didn't tell him you were leaving, did you?"

"There wasn't time."

"Lies! Subterfuge!" Ros chucks a flowery throw pillow embroidered with the words BITCHES GET RICHES at my head.

"Fine, fine, I was scared," I admit, batting the pillow away. "When the thing with Chaz happened, I was overwhelmed, and then Matt was such an asshole about it. He tried to talk to me—to apologize—and I wouldn't let him. I was embarrassed and . . . I dunno."

Ros stares at me over the rim of her glass as she takes a sip of wine. Gary snorts into his whiskey.

"Ugggghhhhh. I have a lot of feelings, you guys! I am a mess of emotion and despair and also desperation. I'm not making good choices! And really, he should be with someone better."

"Truth-bomb time," Ros says.

"I decline your kind offer." I plug my ears but she just keeps staring at me until I tune back in to the truth channel.

"He made mistakes. You made mistakes. Mistakes were made. Whoopdy-fucking-doo. You're both human. You, certainly, are among the best people I know. It sounds like when he doesn't believe he's been lied to and cheated on, he's pretty cool. Also, he apparently knows he was an asshole and tried to fix it fairly immediately. Now it's your turn to apologize for running away and being emotionally inaccessible."

My mouth drops open. "I will not! Did you miss my whole story? I am the one to pity, not him!"

"Oh, don't worry, I pity you plenty."

I nudge her folded legs with my foot, narrowly avoiding spilling her wine onto the couch.

While she's confirming the fabric is unmarred, Gary chimes in, voice gentle. "Don't you think life is hard enough right now without adding in heartbreak? Just call him."

I do not call him. I think about it. Hell, I have nightmares about it. But it's too late, too awkward, and just too much to ask of myself. So I stew in my disappointment and try to find reasons to pin more blame on him, which only serves to point the finger of failure back at myself. Who wouldn't listen to his apologies? Who didn't try to talk to him before fleeing? Who treated him fairly terribly on a number of extremely hard to think about occasions? One guess, and it's not Eric.

I spend the holidays lying in Ros's bed drinking nine-dollar bottles of wine so generic it's only labeled WHITE. Ros made the pilgrimage to her grandmother's house in Windsor, leaving me to my own puffy-faced devices. She invited me along, but I figured if I couldn't face my own parents, I could hardly foist my sullen mood onto my best friend's sweet little grandmother.

My phone is on silent, stuffed beneath a pillow and an emergency bag of Skittles. I don't even like Skittles, but somehow eating a family-size bag of candy I barely enjoy seems right.

I haven't gotten the courage to tell my parents about my latest failure. As far as they know, I'm still at Treetops. I pout, imagining Kevin enjoying my mom's Christmas Morning muffins while Jay tries to figure out how to duplicate the recipe. I call my parents on Christmas Day, putting on the chirpiest Tania voice I can manage and assuring them that Life. Is. Great. The Greatest. I am so happy and successful. I promise to visit soon, crossing my fingers under the blankets.

My subletter is much more accommodating than anticipated. Turns out, she's fallen madly in love with a doctor from work. "You know what it is like, Kate." Her lilting Swedish voice bounces with the promise of fresh romance. "He asked me to move in! I am more than happy to do this now—it is a win-win, I think you call it?" She's not too far down the love rabbit-hole to forget to confirm she'll get a refund on the remainder of this month's rent. Even though it's only a few days, my bank account screams in protest, but given the choice between being destitute in my own space or able to afford brand-name processed cheese slices on Roslyn's couch, I embrace a new level of thriftiness and move home.

On New Year's Eve morning, a frazzled FedEx driver delivers a box wrapped in kraft paper dotted with green pine trees. One corner of the cardboard is thoroughly crushed. "Sorry," the driver says, shrugging as he hustles back to the elevator. "Feel free to submit a claim! Happy belated holidays!"

Settled deep into a corner of my couch, I peel back the wrapping paper and carefully cut the tape securing the top flaps of the box. I pull out a bottle of bubble-wrap-snuggled wine, a tag tied around the neck:

> *Pairs well with bright futures and good friends. Also, cookies. —Tania and Jay*

A box of what were once Christmas cookies, now reduced to crumbs, comes out next. I lick my finger, picking up some of the sweet dust and pressing it to my tongue as I make a valiant and useless effort not to cry.

Next comes a small, tissue-wrapped package. Nestled in the paper is a tiny wooden carving of Eric, paws raised mid-prance. Tears. Tears everywhere. I cradle Mike's gift to my chest while I blow my nose.

When I've recovered sufficiently, I retrieve the last item, a pristine, pearl-white box that has somehow avoided both crushing damage and grease from the mangled cookies. I pry off the lid and unfold a scarf. The wool is the blue-green of spruce needles, shot through with the navy and grays of the early winter lake, and hints of silver and gold threads that glimmer like sunlight on the snow. I loop the soft wool around my neck and pick up the note that had been nestled underneath.

Flawed, but still functional. —K

When I've recovered enough to continue with my day of loafing around feeling miserable, I move the crushed outer box to the door, ready for recycling. As I'm setting it down, a small piece of paper flutters onto the floor. It's been ripped from a notebook, and around the edges are tiny, detailed sketches of trees, stars, steaming mugs, and snowflakes. In one corner, a sleeping bear dozes, head resting on a gift box.

I am an idiot. Please answer your phone. —Matt

Sometimes I glance through my notifications, but seeing Matt's name in the list of missed calls makes me feel desperate to hear his voice in a way that is deeply unsettling. I swipe it all away and convince myself they were never there to begin with.

Before I begin to sink further into the depression my body is making in the mattress, life beckons. And by beckons, I mean shrieks *YOU'RE BROKE, GET A JOB* through a megaphone.

As the rest of society dives head-on into New Year's resolution season, I edge my way toward productivity, frequenting a café that makes me feel extremely uncool, buying seven-dollar flat whites that I have no business putting on my already bloated Visa.

Ros somehow finds the time to send me link after link to jobs I should check out. These seem to fall into two categories: shoot for the stars gigs I'm not at all qualified for. (*Remember, Kate, the equally underqualified men are lining up for this without a second thought—VP, Global Partners is just a fancy name for Professional Schmoozer. You got this.*) and entry-level admin, including working the front desk at Big Bob's Auto Emporium (*You have a car. You like the word "emporium." How bad could it be?*).

I'm settled at a corner table, picking at the fluffy crumbs of muffin left on the plate and trying to decide what skills Bob would most appreciate, when I hear my name.

"Miz Rigsby!" Josh Meadows beams at me, arms spread wide. "What on earth are you doing here?"

He looks great. Perfectly fitted jeans and an expensive-looking sweater hug his body. His long hair has spent some time with a stylist and manages to maintain his surf-casual look while also being put together. I am immediately aware of how I look—unwashed hair scraped back into a bun, bags under my eyes that no amount of makeup can touch.

"Oh, you know . . ." I laugh awkwardly and trail off, hoping he doesn't ask any follow-up questions. He nods like this is a totally reasonable and complete answer.

"How are things going with you?" I ask, hoping to steer the conversation into safer waters and surprisingly interested in speaking to another human being. I nod to the empty seat across from me and he slides into it.

He takes a deep breath, lets it out slowly, his eyes wandering over the other café patrons.

"Things are good," he says hesitantly, then with more confidence, "Different, but good." I sip the tepid dregs of my coffee and wait.

He leans in, bracing his forearms on the table.

"This is confidential, but . . . Tim's taken a step back. A silent partner, if you will." Josh smiles. "And it's because of you." My eyes widen and I feel my body moving backwards in my chair, making space to flee if necessary.

Josh laughs, waving his hands in a "calm down" gesture.

I relax. "Um, tell me more?" I ask hesitantly.

"The time I spent at Treetops, even though it was short, really, like, altered my thinking on business and what's important. Your man Kev drove home that it's the people we surround ourselves with who inform our decisions and propel us along certain paths. We should be building a community, not a two-man empire." He sighs. "And, well, you know Tim. You might not be surprised to hear we see things differently."

I try to keep my face neutral, but Josh laughs and points at me. "You know it."

"So, what's he going to do?" I ask.

Josh lowers his voice to a whisper and leans in. "Sticker books."

My eyes narrow as I try to process this.

"Adult-focused coloring has been all the rage for years now, but look at the laptops in here, Miz Rigsby. Grown-ups *love* a sticker collection. Timbo is going to curate a selection of luxurious single-sided adhesive images for the over-twenty-five crowd to collect and display in personalized, sustainably made, top quality albums. It's going to be rad." He nods to himself. "And now I'm free to take Party Thyme on an epic, community-centric journey."

I take a moment to bask in the warm, fuzzy feeling that drapes over me like a pre-heated throw blanket. I knew that Treetops was doing something meaningful, but this is my first time witnessing a tangible change in someone's life as a result of their time there and it's kind of mind-blowing. It's also a punch-in-the-gut reminder of what I've lost.

We move on to lighter topics, like the effect of aggressive street-salting on the water table, then Josh invites me to stop in the next day for a tour of Party Thyme's new office. "You can check out the ways we've implemented the key learnings from our time at Treetops." He gives me a quick, professional hug and adds, "Come by at eleven so you can join in the midday meditation!"

"Sounds awesome." I'm not even being sarcastic.

Party Thyme HQ takes up the top two floors of a downtown factory-turned-office space.

When I comment on the sweet digs, Josh explains that "After our Series A closed, the deals just started flowing. Last week we became the official herbal hydration beverage of choice for the NHL."

"The entire NHL has an official herbal hydration beverage?"

Josh runs his fingers through his hair, pushing it off his face. He waggles his eyebrows at me. "They do now."

We go on a tour, past workspace dividers made of reclaimed pallets and walls covered in plants. Along one plant-free expanse of drywall, there's an array of framed articles and photos of celebrities holding Party Thyme swag.

"You were in Oprah's magazine?" I whisper reverently, like I'm speaking the name of a saint.

"Oh yeah, we were part of her favorite things, and then, you know, one thing led to another and we had an herbaceous brunch at her place. Great spot. Have you been?"

"Uh, no. I haven't been invited yet."

"I'll see what I can do. You've gotta try her eggs benny." He does a chef's kiss. "Magic. She says it's a spin on M-Stewy's recipe."

"M-Stewy?" I echo faintly.

"Mm-hmm. Martha stopped in for a mimosa. She's a big fan of Thyme for Pep, our spicy blend. Just wanted to say hi. You know how it is."

"Totally."

We head through a labyrinth of workspaces to a café oasis manned by an actual barista. There's a seating area with couches and floor cushions, all surrounded by individual groupings of potted plants.

"Being downtown, we tried to bring the outdoors in, you know? We don't want to forget where we come from. The roots, the dirt, Mother Earth and science." He takes a deep breath and seems to look inward for a moment of reflection before coming back to the present. "We ask each new employee to build their own indoor garden space, with company budget, obviously, and schedule at least fifteen minutes a day for its upkeep. Good for the brain, good for the creative gains, right?"

I nod somberly. "Of course."

We climb a lengthy set of stairs, Josh effortlessly keeping up a stream of conversation while I puff out single-word answers. At the top, he shoves open a heavy-looking door and a blast of freezing air whooshes into my face.

"Come on! We'll dash it out!" Josh takes off, waving his arm for me to follow.

I bolt after him across twenty feet of rooftop to another door, this one glass.

The door of the greenhouse pulls itself shut quickly, bumping my butt as it clicks closed. I barely notice. The air is warm and humid. Trees in giant pots fill the corners, while raised garden beds accommodate everything from herbs to giant tropical-looking flowers. In the spaces between, people are unrolling yoga mats and getting settled, chatting quietly, but mostly just sitting there, looking blissful. Birds chirp. A giant blue butterfly flutters past my nose.

Josh snags two mats from a shelf and leads me to a spot beside a tinkling waterfall. A giant fern drapes over me and I'm tempted to scooch deeper into its embrace, to hide against its roots.

"VIP area," Josh says, and I can't tell if he's joking.

A gong sounds, pulling my attention to a woman at the front of the group. She's wearing black tights and a crisp white-collared shirt, topped with denim shorts overalls. Her feet are bare on her mat.

"Greetings, my friends," she says in a clear, low voice. She smiles at the crowd with real warmth.

A chorus of cheerful hellos, hiyas, and *bonjours* echo back at her.

"For those of you who don't know me, my name is Gabby, Communications Team Lead, and I am stoked to be leading our meditation today." She gracefully lowers herself until she's sitting cross-legged, hands resting palms-up on her knees.

"Sitting comfortably, close your eyes. Feel your connection with the ground. The beauty of the plants and people surrounding us."

I let my eyelids drop, feeling my connection to my bladder, which is indicating I should have skipped my third coffee. I push the discomfort aside and focus on Gabby's words, and am more than a little shocked to find myself growing calm. My breaths come slower. For the first time in weeks, my mind agrees to be quiet.

Twenty minutes later, Gabby asks us to open our eyes.

"See the world around you through a fresh lens. Feel the possibility of the day." She smiles, nods approvingly, and presses her palms together in front of her chest. "Namaste."

"Namaste," the group echoes. People high-five their neighbors, roll up their mats, and start trickling out.

Josh sighs contentedly beside me and wiggles his toes before standing. He offers a hand and heaves me up.

"Josh, what you're doing here is just incredible. You must be so proud." I slide my boots back on and sling my bag over my shoulder.

"This is all built on the shoulders of the people you see around us. I couldn't do it without the Party Thyme fam." He starts walking along the stone path that loops through the greenhouse. I fall into step beside him and take a deep breath.

"Speaking of the fam, I noticed you have a couple of sales and marketing roles posted. If you think I might be a good fit, I would love to apply. To be part of all this."

He pauses mid-step, very briefly, before continuing. "Everyone here has a different story. We value diverse backgrounds and there's no denying you have that."

I nod enthusiastically. "I feel I have a lot to offer. Not just on the PR side, but in Sales as well. As you mentioned, my experience is diverse."

"There's something else we ask of the Party Thyme crew, and that is that they bring with them a true, deep passion for what we're building." He picks a dried leaf from a hibiscus and rolls it between his fingers, sprinkling the dust onto the damp soil. "The thing is, I've known you a while now. At Regan-Caulfield you did your job and you did it well, but you didn't care about it very much, did you?"

I open my mouth to protest, but he continues before I can say anything useful. Not that I have a lot to say. He's right. I tug at my necklace, suddenly desperate for this to be over. I've made an ass of myself, yet again, and I just want to be back in my apartment, safe from the inevitable embarrassment the outside world holds.

Josh continues. "When we were at Treetops, I saw *you*. I saw the glowing face of a woman who was exactly where she was supposed to be, doing what she was meant to do. You cared about that place, about the people, their growth, their well-being. Heck, you even helped me to see a fresh new path. It was a beautiful thing to behold." He turns and looks me in the eye before wrapping both his hands around my fidgeting ones, holding them still.

"Kate, you're right that we're doing amazing things here

at Party Thyme, and I would be honored to introduce you to Gabby. I'm sure she'll be jazzed to offer you a temporary contract while you get re-centered. One of her teammates just left for a three-month retreat in the Himalayas and she could use the assist. But this is not where you're destined to be. Luxury herbs? This isn't your life's work. You're meant to be in the trees, nurturing the artistic spirit and worshipping the energy of the lake."

I can feel my head nodding, and while a sizeable portion of me is scoffing at the absurdity of this situation, there's another part that knows he's not entirely wrong.

"Now let's get some tea and I'll take you to Gabby's office."

Chapter 24

It takes four days for me to fully accept that Josh was right. I'm not cut out for the luxury herb life. I'm trying to draft a press release announcing the newest Party Thyme product, Zesty Thymes, but just can't channel the necessary energy.

Over my catered lunch of tofu banh mi with a side of sparkling Citrus Thyme water, I spy a glimmer of hope in the form of an ad for a job I actually want. Falcon Ridge, the corporate retreat one lake over from Treetops, is hiring a Growth Specialist. I'm a shoo-in! Local experience, proven success. I crawl out of my self-imposed isolation long enough to text Tania and Jay, who instantly agree to provide references. I even give the wine a night off to craft a top-notch cover letter and polish my résumé before sending it in.

I hold tight to the dream, picturing myself back by the water, taking morning walks, chatting with guests. Except, every time I see it, Mike's walking past with his chainsaw over his shoulder. Kevin makes a disparaging remark about the quality of my work, but he's secretly pleased things are going so well.

Tania's flitting around, making everyone's day run smoothly. Matt smiles when he sees me and wraps me in a hug that chases away so much of the darkness clouding my head these days. Who am I kidding? I want Treetops back, but this is as close as I'm going to get.

On a frigid, gloomy Tuesday morning in late January, I'm taking a break, sipping cinnamon-laced coffee (real cinnamon that I smuggled in after trying Thyme to Cin) in a less rowdy corner of the Party Thyme office café oasis and checking my email. A response from Falcon Ridge has come in. Taking a deep breath, I open it, already planning my enthusiastic yet professional response to their request for an interview.

> *Dear Kate,*
> *Thanks so much for your interest in the Growth Specialist position at Falcon Ridge. We recently restructured and brought in a new management team. While the plan is still to pursue aggressive growth, the hiring managers have requested that this position be put on hold while everyone settles in and we assess current requirements.*
> *Your résumé will certainly be kept on file and when we're ready to revisit this role I will be sure to let you know.*
> *Krista Harper*
> *People Specialist*
> *Falcon Ridge Corporate Lodge*

I send Tania and Jay a quick text to let them know they don't need to worry about the reference thing.

T: Things are going to turn around. I'm sure of it.

K: Yeah, of course. This is a blip. A smudge. By which I mean a total catastrophe that I will never overcome. Ah well. Can't get worse, right?

Gabby calls my name, summoning me to an impromptu team drum circle. I shove my phone in my bag, determined not to worry about what comes next.

After work, I clip on Eric's leash and head out for a walk. He stands by the door wiggling eagerly while I secure my boots and seventeen layers of outerwear. Finally, I'm ready and we hop into the elevator. Bella, the Yorkie who lives down the hall, is in the same car and she and Eric enjoy thirty seconds of passionate sniffing while Bella's mom and I exchange awkward smiles. The doors slide open and we're off through the lobby, Eric trying to drag me after Bella, who's stopping at the mailboxes in the foyer and out onto the nearly empty sidewalk.

It's just starting to get dark and the sky's ablaze with pink and purple clouds. It would be a beautiful moment if someone didn't latch onto my arm the second I clear the building doors. *This is it*, I think. This is the moment I've read about on blogs and in magazines all my life. I have headphones on. There is no key between my fingers. My hair is in a ponytail, perfect for grabbing as I try to escape.

Dimly, it registers that there is no follow-up. There is no longer anyone touching me. Eric is very excited to see my attacker. I spin around, ripping the earbuds from my head.

"I could have maced you!" I shout into Matt's face.

He looks me up and down appraisingly.

"Do you have Mace in your fanny pack? Is Mace even legal?"

"This is a functional cross-body bag, thank you, and that isn't the point. You could be a normal human and use your words instead of accosting me in the street. Try a phone call, Matt! Jesus."

"I did. Many, many times." In my mind's eye, I see my finger swiping away call notifications and texts. Dozens of them. I make a garbled sound of acknowledgment that sounds more like choking.

"Can we talk?" He stubs at the sidewalk with the toe of his black high-top Chucks. Totally inappropriate for this weather, but goddamn he's cute.

I hedge, ignoring the butterflies in my stomach at the sight of him.

"How did you get my address?"

He examines the cracks in the sidewalk, rocks back on his heels as I stare at him expectantly.

"I, um, may have asked Kevin to access the personnel files."

I scowl. This *would* be when Kevin decides to break a rule.

He stuffs his hands in his pockets. "Look, I need to talk to you. I know you don't want to see me, but this is important. Please? Just a few minutes and I'll get out of your hair."

I consider, then nod in reluctant acceptance. "How did you even get here? Is there a helicopter on the roof?" I shield my eyes and peer upward.

"This building is not helipad material." His hand grazes mine gently before he pulls it back to his side. "Please, Kate."

We enter the building, pulling a confused Eric in my wake, then watch the elevator numbers tick past. I try to ignore how close he's standing to me. How good he looks. How much I've missed him. It takes all of the very small amount of willpower I possess not to collapse against him and cry in a decidedly ugly, snot-heavy way.

I'm kicking off my shoes and getting Eric an organic deer antler to tide him over when I realize how strange it is to have Matt in my space. He doesn't belong here, but at the same time my heart is insistently beating in a way that says "Yes, he does." Watching him take in everything that makes this place mine, I plonk into a chair where there's no chance of him sitting beside me unless he perches on the arm. Or my lap.

He paces around the living area, running fingers down the spines of my books, gazing at the photos on the wall.

"Why are you here, Matt?"

I can hear him inhale as he turns to face me.

"We need to talk about what happened with Chaz."

My reaction is visceral and blood rushes through my ears. I

feel sick. "You made your opinion of me clear." I stare at my lap, vision blurring with tears that hold so many conflicting emotions. Anger, of course, but also shame for how I've treated him. Relief that this conversation is finally happening. And hope. So much hope it hurts.

He kneels in front of where I sit. "We need to talk about it. I was so incredibly stupid. I was clearly a complete imbecile and demonstrated nearly every quality I despise in so many men." His thumb strokes the edge of my chin, turning my gaze to his. A tear runs down my cheek and he brushes it away.

"It was completely unfair," he continues quietly, lowering his hand to rest on my knee. "I had all these . . . not plans, exactly, but ideas. Hopes." I raise my eyebrows and his mouth curves up into a smile. "Not those kinds of hopes. At least, not *just* that."

I clear my throat, willing my voice to be steady. "I need to apologize to you as well."

"Not yet. I'm not done. I practiced this the whole way here."

"Even the part where you ambushed me in the street?"

"That was improvised."

"Well, your pre-planned segment is much better." I sniffle, subtly wiping my nose on my sleeve. "Do you want to, I don't know, sit on the couch or something? The Prince Charming kneel is, in fact, very charming, but also looks uncomfortable."

"This is me prostrating myself before you. It's part of the whole thing."

"By all means, then, continue."

"As I was saying, when I thought, for that brief and completely asinine moment, that you were upset because Chaz wouldn't take you back, I was embarrassed. I thought I'd just made a total ass of myself on the lake and you had written me off as pure friend-zone material."

My eyes run up and down his body. "Idiot."

"And when you wouldn't speak to me afterward or answer my calls, I thought I'd really ruined everything. But I had to at least try to explain. To apologize." His hands wrap around mine. "We agreed to wait nine weeks. Today would have been your last day at Treetops if Brooke wasn't the devil incarnate."

Tears are actively leaking down my face now, and I struggle to keep some semblance of control.

"Can I take you out for dinner?" he asks.

"Like a date?" I stand, tugging his hand to bring him with me.

"Exactly like a date."

I lean into him, running my hands over the soft fabric covering hard shoulders, around the back of his neck. His arms come around me and I feel calmer than I have in weeks. I lay my head on his chest and listen to the reassuring, steady thump of his heart. His hand runs over my hair and down my back, settling into the curve just above my waistband. *Lower*, my mind insists.

Running a fingertip over his lips, I lean in, suddenly very certain what I need. It isn't dinner.

Kissing Matt is like coming home, except this home is so, so much sexier than my apartment. My heart thrums at the thought that there's finally nothing stopping us, no cavorting clause, no job goals, no vindictive ex. It's just us.

His lips move slowly, gently against mine as we get reacquainted. One hand dances up and down my ribs before settling on my hip, pulling me closer, the other wraps in my hair. My chest presses against his in an extremely pleasing way, the fabric of my clothes somehow rubbing all the right spots. *Clothes*, I think fuzzily. *Don't want 'em.*

My hands slide under the soft fabric of his sweater, up his back, back down and around to his stomach where the army of abdominals reside. I finger-walk up them, making him squirm. Still kissing me, his mouth opens into a smile and I can't help but do the same. For a moment we stand there, forehead to forehead, grinning like idiots.

"Hi," he says, kissing the tip of my nose.

"Hi," I echo, admiring the flecks of gold in his eyes. "Can we take your pants off now?"

He snorts, charmingly, sexily, of course, and swoops his hands under my ass, picking me up. My legs wrap around his waist and I clutch his shoulders, giggling like a fool as he carries me to bed.

He sets me down on top of the quilt and things suddenly feel very serious as he lowers his mouth to mine, nipping my lower lip before trailing kisses down my neck. My back arches as his breath brushes my collarbone and I curl my fingers around the hem of his sweater, tugging it up. Quickly, he pulls it over his head and drops it on the floor. I can feel my jaw go slack at the sight of him.

"Holy hell, Matthew." He looks smug for a moment, but then I execute a shockingly flawless maneuver that ends with him flat on his back and me straddling him, admiring how his mouth has formed a surprised o.

"Holy hell, Katelyn."

I take a second of smugness for myself before shucking my own shirt and lowering myself to feel the heat of his skin on mine. His hands stroke my back as we kiss, moving higher until he flicks open my bra clasps, sliding the straps down my arms and off. Warm, heavy hands drag slowly, slowly up my sides until I'm practically vibrating with expectation. When his palms brush teasingly over my chest I can't hold back a whimper, needing those hands to be exactly where they are, but also so many other places.

Making use of his inhuman core strength, he shifts to sitting. My legs wrap around his waist and I can't help but move against him, desperate to get rid of the layers still between us. He rakes his fingers through my hair and tugs my head back, exposing my throat to his lips and gentle nips of his teeth. My fingers edge between us and stroke the front of his jeans, making him groan.

I unbutton his pants, lower the zipper, and start tugging the waistband.

"Off. Take them off."

He rolls so I'm lying on my back, taking in the sights as he stands. He watches me as he gets undressed, eyelids low. And, finally, I can see him. *All* of him. I am not disappointed. His hand closes around himself, stroking firmly for a moment as his eyes look directly into mine. I can't form words, but move to kneel on the bed and take his hand in mine, bringing him back to me.

He eases me back and kisses his way from my collarbone to my stomach, running rough palms over my skin and making my back arch as his stubble scrapes against my waist.

His breath is warm on my stomach as he unbuttons my jeans and slides them down my hips, over my thighs, and to the floor. His fingers move under the lacey edge of my underwear and, with deliberate motions, toward exactly where I need him to be. He kisses my inner thigh. I am a puddle. I am a quivering mess of need. And when he pulls the last remaining scrap of fabric aside and glides a finger against me, up and down, and his tongue follows, I am lost.

My fingers twine in his hair and down to his shoulders, pulling him up. He follows my unspoken instructions, but slowly, teasing his way back up my body. When his mouth finally lands back on mine, I'm out of patience. My teeth scrape over his lip as my hands tour his very satisfying anatomy.

"Please. Now," I whisper, nipping at his earlobe. Something like a growl sounds from his throat, which I take as agreement. I rummage one-handed through the drawer of my bedside table, cursing my lack of organization until I find a box of condoms shoved into the back corner.

Logistics taken care of, his body over mine, there's a beat, a moment, an unspoken "Are you sure? We're doing this?" and then, oh. My. God. Yes. We're doing this, and it is an epiphany.

My head is resting on Matt's shoulder as we lie in bed, snuggled under the covers, heads on pillows propped high enough to let us sip the last two beers he found in the fridge. The lights from the cars nine floors down wash across the ceiling. The distant sound of tires on wet pavement leaks in through the window I've opened just enough to let the winter air brush across our flushed faces.

Matt's arm is wrapped around me, his fingertips playing across the smattering of freckles on my shoulder. I am grateful I took the time to change the sheets yesterday.

"I missed you," he says, planting a kiss on the top of my head.

I crook my neck to look up at him in the dim light shining through the bedroom door from the living room. I take a deep breath, clear my throat, and shift around as I try to wiggle the words loose.

"In case it wasn't clear, I'm sorry I ran away. And then didn't answer your calls. And was, uh, terse with you today when you got here."

There. Done. I heave a monumental sigh, feeling weeks of tension flowing out with my breath. "I don't, um, deal well with big feelings. Or failure, which is unfortunate because it seems to be something that comes up pretty frequently for me." Enough with the woeful moaning, Rigsby. You got the man, bask in your sultry, orgasm-filled success.

I roll onto my side, head propped on my hand. It's hard to ignore the six-foot-something swath of man pressing against the full length of my body, but I give it the ol' college try.

"I appreciate you coming here. Your apology was beautiful and clearly effective"—I gesture at our mutual nudity—"It's just . . ."

A large, warm hand trails down my spine, making me shiver.

"It's just what?" he says softly.

I sigh yet again and shrug. "What do we do now?"

His eyes drop to the sheet barely covering my chest.

"I have ideas. Many ideas." He shifts, stuffing another pillow under his head so I'm not looming over him. "But I get the sense you're talking about something different."

"Trust me, I would love to give you the opportunity to nurture your creative spirit as it pertains to bed sport, but yeah, I'm talking about something different." Now it's my turn for the wandering gaze, taking in the unreasonably sculpted shape of his chest, down to a stomach that could bring a lusty tear to the eye. "I'm here. You're way up there, trundling around in the forest. It's not exactly a recipe for success."

"Well, actually, there's something I need to tell you." He looks around the room, avoiding my gaze. "Coming here isn't my entire reason for being in town." I must look as offended as I feel, because he rushes on. "I had a few interviews. For a job. Here. Closer to you."

I sit up, the sheet falling to my waist.

"You what? Where? When?"

"At HIT." He pulls a face. "It's not perfect, but a reasonable next step, I think. Get some more business experience before flinging myself from the nest." He runs his fingers through his hair. "I've been neck deep in output analyses and meetings for a week. Luckily, this branch is run by a different group, reporting to someone other than dear old Dad." He links his fingers through mine and kisses my knuckles. Unluckily, I have a bunch of proving myself to do.

"I need to head back to Treetops in the morning to help out with the Annual General Meeting. I talked to Tania a couple days ago and she's having a panic attack trying to prep everything before the board members start trickling in. It doesn't feel right to leave her and Kevin to deal with it on their own."

"Whoa whoa whoa. The board is going to Treetops? The most underfunded, neglected property in their portfolio?"

"They rotate locations and I guess someone rolled the dice and landed on us. Jay is determined to use this as his stepping stone to bigger and better things. He keeps harping on and on about Lake Louise being his destiny." He looks up at the ceiling, thoughtful. "He might not be wrong. You should have been there for his Christmas feast. The bread pudding was incredible." Matt's stomach growls, the perfect punctuation mark, but my mind is elsewhere.

"You're right," I say, fishing a sweater from the floor and pulling it on. "I should have been there." It could just be the after-effects of great sex and a single beer on an empty stomach, but I'm feeling righteous.

"I should have been there," I repeat forcefully, shimmying into underwear before rising to pace beside the bed. "Admittedly, the bachelorette party was a mistake, but you know what I didn't mess up? Bookings. Revenue. Lead generation." I thrust my finger into the air with each point. "I'd earned my bonus for December *and* January. February was almost locked already. I was doing a goddamn stellar job, Matthew!"

His smile is a beautiful thing, and I take a moment to bask in it before making my wildest declaration since telling Chaz his forearms were better than Chris Hemsworth's. At least this time I'm not entirely full of shit.

"I'm going with you."

Matt's eyes widen. He takes a sip of beer before responding.

"And what are your intentions once we arrive? I'm afraid I can't let you burn the place down."

"Oh no. Oh no no no no, my dear."

"K, now you sound like a wicked witch. You also can't curse them. Or murder anyone. It would be satisfying in the moment, but the regret afterward would be substantial. Also, prison orange isn't your color." He purses his lips, considering. "Or mine, now that I think about it. I would do poorly in a penitentiary setting."

"I'm going to do what I apparently do best. I'm going to sell them on Treetops."

The moment it crosses my lips I know it's one of the truest things I've ever said.

I roll the thought around in my head before realizing what's missing. "And if the opportunity arises, I'm going to throw Brooke in the lake. But don't worry, it'll totally look like an accident. Plus, it wouldn't be murder. I would know, I survived it."

Matt drags his jeans from a tangled pile on the floor and retrieves his phone from the pocket.

"Mission planning of this magnitude requires sustenance."

I crawl back into bed beside him to peruse menu options, my confident indignation fading into moderate panic as we try to decide between pizza and Thai.

Before I can reconsider, Matt sets the phone down to look into my eyes.

"You, Katelyn Rigsby, are the strongest, bravest, most badass woman I have ever met. You will slay them with your might." He kisses me, sending tingles of pleasure through my entire body.

Damn right I will.

Chapter 25

Party Thyme recently implemented what Josh calls "True to You Thyme," which allows employees to work whenever they want, wherever they want as long as the work gets done. He's talking about buying up a bunch of vacation properties for the full-time staff to access when they need a change of scenery, but is still sifting through options. Seville or Laguna? Both? Such tough choices.

While Matt navigates through the chaos of the 401 during morning rush hour, I pop nondrowsy motion sickness pills and draft a blog post detailing the benefits of expressing creativity in the kitchen—using Party Thyme's new Thyme for Dinner Flavor Kit, of course.

"Would you put The Thyme's Cumin in chili? Or on tofu?" A transport truck flings slush at our windshield as it passes. "Can you put tofu in chili?" I mumble as we're reaching the exit for the 400 North.

Matt nearly drives his shiny black HIT Properties company SUV off the road, so involved is he in pulling dramatic faces of disgust.

I sniff, turning my nose up as I silently agree. "You're clearly not cut out for the luxury herb life."

As we roll into Otterburne my forehead stays pressed to the glass while I play an extreme wilderness version of *Where's Waldo?* To my intense disappointment, there are no moose sightings. Not even a fox frolicking in the snow or a bear boycotting hibernation to feel the winter sun on her back. It's hard to mind though, with the frost-covered trees sparkling at me and Matt humming along to the radio, resting his hand on my leg like it's always belonged there.

The back window is cracked and Eric has his nose stuffed through the opening, inhaling deeply. As the kilometers click by my stomach jumps around and I volley between deep calming breaths and desperate excitement to be back at Treetops.

Just before lunch, we pull into a freshly plowed parking area at the side of the road and Matt starts pulling armloads of outerwear from the back seat. I stare at the pile of gear now sitting on my lap, absorbing what I'm about to do. This is insane.

Matt shrugs into his coat and is pulling a hat down over his ears when he notices I haven't made any progress. He walks around to my door and pulls it open. The cold slaps me in the face.

"I can't do this," I whisper, and I'm not just talking about the forty-five-minute hike through the snow. It had seemed like a romantic notion when he suggested it two hours earlier

"This is a terrible idea."

He squeezes my hand, brushes a kiss across my lips, then puts a hand to his ear.

"What's that?" he shouts with much more volume than is required to be heard over the chirping birds and squeaking of snow under his boots. "Can't hear you! So loud! So much nature!"

He slings his backpack on, takes Eric's leash, and disappears into the trees.

I scramble into the rest of my gear, grab my bag and take

off after him, only to discover he's lurking in the shrubbery just inside the mouth of the private road that leads to Treetops. "It's plowed," I observe, bewildered and also deeply relieved. Prolonged high-knees through calf-deep snow doesn't result in a cute look.

"Yeah. Probably took Mike all of yesterday. The board members like to be able to come and go as they please. You never know when an investment emergency will require a hasty departure."

We stroll hand in hand through the woods, mostly quiet, taking in glimpses of the frozen expanse of the neighboring lake through the trees. Thirty minutes later we turn onto the narrower track that will take us to Matt's front door.

The sound of a diesel motor thrums through the air.

Tania's sitting in the utility vehicle in what, in summer months at least, is Matt's driveway. Eric rips his leash from Matt's grip and sprints like the lunatic he is directly into her waiting embrace. I kind of wish I had it on video to do a slo-mo recap with dramatic music.

"Finally! In in in!" She waves one arm like she's directing traffic while continuing to pat Eric's head with the other. "So much to do. So little time. I still need to prep the welcome baskets and temperature check the cabins. Because of course they can't all stay in the Big House. *Of course* they need ample space to internalize the content from each day's agenda. But who's going to be the one doing room service runs at ten at night because there's no support staff? This girl, that's who."

Before I can ask any of the many, many questions I have— like *No staff? Aren't you surprised to see me?* Or, most intriguingly, *Are there going to be leftover welcome baskets?*—Matt holds up a hand.

"Slow your roll. I need to drop this stuff off and get a fire going."

As he says it, I realize we haven't discussed sleeping arrangements. My eyes dart between the Treetops vehicle and Matt's front door. What's the less awkward choice here? Assume I'm invited to stay with him? Reacquaint myself with Employee Hut Four?

He looks at me and raises an eyebrow. "Coming?"

Thank god.

Tania lets out a squeal as I step toward him and his arm comes across my shoulders.

"Finally!" she yells, wiggling joyously and hitting the steering wheel. "I love this. I love you two. I love everything about what's happening here!" She wiggles some more. "You two. Mike and Kevin. What a life!" She nods happily at my wide-eyed stare. "Yeah, they finally figured it out over Christmas. Thank goodness." She nudges Eric with her mitten. "Off you go, big guy."

Though she suggests we should take all the time we need, big wink, before heading to Treetops, I assure her we'll be over to help out imminently.

"Bring Eric with you. Delilah could use a romp."

"Couldn't we all," I say under my breath, but apparently not as quietly as I think.

Matt leans in, breath tickling my earlobe. "That can be arranged."

His arm drops to my waist. "We might need a few minutes extra. Got to warm up a bit."

Tania grins and rumbles away.

In the silence that follows I take a moment to breathe in the crisp air. The sun warms my back. A bird sings from somewhere in the trees. I can feel my shoulders start to relax, a knot in my stomach seems to loosen ever so slightly.

I turn my face into the sun and look up at Matt, unable to hold back my smile.

"This is nice," I say.

He stuffs his gloves into his pockets and cups my face in his warm hands before bringing his mouth down to mine for a long, slow, sweet kiss that seems to both go on forever and not be nearly long enough.

"I know we need to get over there, but I was wondering if you could give me a tour of this place? Last time I was here I feel like we skipped over some key features."

He nods with mock seriousness.

"As you know," he says, leading me toward the door, "I'm an artist, very good with my hands and attention to detail. I have some specific techniques you might be interested in."

The key turns in the lock and we're in the living room, already unzipping our coats and tossing them to the floor. Eric bounds in and disappears into the kitchen, exploring all the new smells.

Matt kneels in front of the fire, striking a match and lighting the pile of newspaper and wood already waiting for him. "The thing is, it's so cold in here. I'm feeling a bit weak," he says, pulling his shirt off. Goose bumps immediately pop up on his perfect skin.

I move in close, fingers already freeing his belt and starting to work on the button of his jeans. "I've heard the thing to do in these situations is huddle for warmth," I say to his collarbone as I lay a trail of kisses along it, leading to the hollow of his throat and up to his mouth.

"Yes, a huddle," he agrees as we lower ourselves onto the floor, tugging every throw blanket within reach on top of us. "I can feel my fingers becoming nimbler already."

"Oh really?" I breathe. "Well then, why don't you show me these techniques you speak of."

He does. Oh, boy, does he ever.

We stroll through the snow to Treetops, loose-limbed and flushed. The area beside the main door has been plowed, and artfully arranged planters indicate each available parking spot.

Matt goes ahead, as I belatedly notice Eric peeing on a tiny, star-topped pine tree nestled in a burlap-wrapped planter on the porch step.

"You better hope no one saw that," Matt calls over his shoulder.

"I have told you time and time again!" Kevin booms from the doorway. "Keep that beast on a leash!"

"Kevin! *So* wonderful to see you. I see the warmth and promise of an impending spring haven't reached your frozen heart. Nice to know there is some consistency in the world."

I spot Mike clearing the pathways between guest cabins, Delilah lying on a blanket in a patch of sun keeping watch. She raises her head to acknowledge us but doesn't trouble herself with a more energetic greeting. "I'll just leave Eric with Mike, shall I?"

"Though I wish you hadn't brought your brutish companion along, it's not entirely awful to see you back here," Kevin grumbles as he moves inside, closing the door firmly behind him.

Leaving Eric running laps around Delilah, I go back to the Big House to find Tania sitting on the floor in a sea of half-filled baskets. Matt's got his boots off and is depositing a trio of steaming mugs of coffee onto the lemon-polish-scented wooden table in the middle of the room.

"Thank God," Tania says, leaning back against the soft brown leather of the couch and heaving a sigh of relief. "Kate, you're on bath bombs and notebooks. Matt, you're in charge of ribbon curling and floral arrangement." She shoves a bucket of creamy white roses in his direction and nods at a spool of silver ribbon that's rolled over against the fireplace. Matt goes in search of another pair of scissors and I grab the bucket to move it to a spot with more space, slopping water onto the gleaming hardwood.

"Barely have your coat off and already causing chaos, I see," Kevin drawls from behind me, where he's come through from the direction of his office. His Treetops polo is topped with a black cardigan with hints of burgundy, navy, and ivory that peek from within the dark fibers like pinpoints of light.

"Tania, I thought you said Kevin was more pleasant now." I sniff a bath bomb and try not to cough as some of the lavender-scented dust lodges in my nose.

Kevin scoffs. "It is impossible to project the rays of social sunshine you seem to expect while we are under such strain. Perhaps you've been too busy making eyes at Matthew to notice how short-staffed we are."

Matt walks in carrying scissors in one hand and balancing a plate piled high with apple slices, brie, and crackers on the other.

"Yeah, where is everyone?" he asks, settling in beside his flower bucket and popping a cracker into his mouth.

"If you get crumbs on this floor, I will be forced to violence," Kevin says menacingly. Then he sighs and perches on the couch arm. "Everyone other than myself, Mike, Tania, and Jay have been released."

"What?" My mouth drops open. "How can they do that?"

"Serge?" Matt asks quietly.

Tania nods, her face crumpling a little. "He's fine, though. He texted us yesterday to say he got a kitchen spot at one of HIT's other resorts."

"When did this happen?" I ask, dropping lavender-vanilla bath bombs into the baskets.

"Yesterday." Kevin's brow furrows in distaste. "Brooke called an all-hands meeting and phoned in to let them go as a group. It was appalling. And with the annual general meeting taking place here! No one has slept. We've been scrambling ever since."

"Did she give a reason?" I start pairing soft black leather notebooks with the HIT logo on the front with Montblanc pens that probably cost as much as a month of rent and sliding them between a bottle of sparkling rosé and a box of delicately colored macarons.

"Cash flow," Tania scoffs, consulting a list so she can add the right size of custom moose-leather moccasins to the basket in front of her. "After you, um, left, she canceled all the bookings except for repeat guests."

"Of which there were very few," Kevin adds. "What a terrible waste of Kate's efforts."

My head whips around in shock.

"Misguided though they may have been," he adds just in time to save himself from being too complimentary.

"Does my dad know?" Matt asks from behind a stunning bouquet of roses and greenery dotted with pinecones.

The sound of slamming car doors reverberates through the room, followed by chatting and laughter from the front porch.

"They're early," Kevin says. "Clean this up immediately." He claps his hands. "Tania and Kate, distribute these baskets and ensure the cabins are up to temperature. Matthew, with me please. You need to greet the guests." He starts to walk away but pauses, turning to give the three of us a long look.

"We are lucky enough to still have jobs. Let us execute this ill-fated mission with precision and grace."

I bite my tongue and get to work.

The eight board members keep us as busy as a group of twenty for the rest of the day. Brooke isn't in attendance, which seems strange, but maybe she didn't want to spend hours in the same building as her ex. Or, more likely, she'll show up just after everyone's gone to bed and make us scurry around in the dead of night to get her settled.

Jay presents a family-style dinner, limiting the rest of us to maintaining the flow of wine and delivering the occasional re-freshed platter to the large table.

I keep myself out of sight, flitting around behind the scenes as much as possible. The likelihood of anyone recognizing me as a disgraced interloper seems slim, but I don't want to chance an awkward confrontation in advance of my big pitch.

At least once an hour I ask myself what I'm doing, but the answer is always the same. I'm helping my friends and show-ing these people how glorious Treetops is, even horrendously understaffed. I want them to understand how special it is. How deeply it can change the people who are lucky enough to be here, even for a short time.

I keep waiting for someone to comment on the lack of staff, or the worn carpet in the dining room. Maybe the peeling mallard-themed wallpaper border running the length of the hall between the lounge and the guest rooms. But no one says a word.

By nine I'm ready for a drink and many hours of sleep. The board members linger in the dining room, sipping wine and the occasional tea, nibbling on small plates of cheese and dried fruit. Matt has been cajoled into having a cocktail with his father, but that's fine. The idea of a few minutes of solitude in the lounge by the fire sounds like paradise.

I put the last of the plates on the drying rack, cursing Brooke for refusing to have the dishwasher repaired. I'm about to go in search of a book to read while I wait for Matt when I hear what sounds like a vehicle crunching over the packed snow of the driveway.

"Poor sap," I mutter, picturing Mike schlepping luggage around in the dark for whatever exec isn't happy with their cabin assignment. I'd practically shoved Tania and Jay out the door a half hour earlier to get some sleep, and Kevin went to the cottage he now shared with Mike to "ensure that canine of yours hasn't completely corrupted poor Delilah."

I slip a half-full bottle of Merlot into a wrinkled canvas market bag I found under the counter, followed by a full bottle destined for Mike as a thank-you for playing dogsitter.

Assuming Matt's place is sorely lacking in groceries after his trip, I add some leftover dinner rolls, a bag of whole coffee beans from the local roastery, and a jar of the house artisanal nut butter—freshly ground peanuts enhanced with cinnamon and local honey.

Someone finds the dining room audio hookup and pipes in the type of soundtrack I associate with student coffee shops. Usually called something like *Low-Fi Beats to Study By*, in this case, it's a verging on cocktail bar volume levels.

A quick scan of the kitchen confirms the oven is off, no water is running, and it's clean enough that I shouldn't be at risk of suffering Jay's wrath in the morning when he comes in to prep breakfast. Hoisting the now weighty bag of contraband onto my shoulder, I flick the lights off.

I drag myself up the stairs to the main level and head toward the lounge to sample some of this wine while I wait for Matt to surface. Lord knows I've earned it.

In the hallway, I notice an empty smoke detector mount, wire dangling. *Weird.* A faint light flickers under the door to Kevin's office and I hesitate at the threshold, hand hovering over the doorknob. My first thought is that he's burning the midnight oil, getting ready for whatever the next day is going to throw at him.

Burning . . . I sniff the air. It's not unusual to get a waft of smoke from the big fireplace in the lounge, but this is different from the sweet smell of aged pine mixed with cherry. It singes my nostrils in a way that activates some prehistoric portion of my brain.

While he's working, Kevin's been known to burn a lightly scented candle, imported from France and sporting a customized label with his initials monogrammed in copper script, but he'd never leave one unattended. I waver. We've been running around like the proverbial headless chickens all day. Maybe he got distracted.

Something thumps from inside the office and my hand stills on the knob. If he's in the midst of some nighttime witchcraft I don't want to just barge in. Lord knows what I'll see.

Just as my hand starts to tighten around the cool metal, *better safe than sorry*, it turns of its own accord, sliding against my palm. The door jerks inward, pulling me with it.

Chapter 26

I stumble forward, instinctively raising my hands to catch my-self and avoid headbutting the other person in the nose. I im-mediately regret it.

"What the hell are *you* doing here?" Brooke demands, hip cocked. She's dressed in black skinny jeans and a red silk blouse with an extremely low neckline. It looks like it's been crumpled under her bed for a week and dark rings of sweat line the arm-pits. A black cropped leather jacket is draped over her shoulders. Her feet are bare and stiletto pumps dangle from her fingertips. Dark red toenails dig into the ivory carpet.

Behind her, a small plastic trashcan jammed with paper is crackling merrily. More crumpled paper and ripped file folders cover the floor. A laptop lies in the middle of the carpet, its in-nards exposed and spilling onto the carpet. Pieces of shiny plas-tic and metal twinkle in the light of the growing flames.

"This is ludicrous," she mutters, running a hand through her hair. It's lost its trademark volume and is sagging limply across her bony skull. "I should have you arrested for trespassing."

She slides her arms into the sleeves of her jacket and pats at the pockets before pulling out a set of keys.

I'm still standing in the doorway, frozen by a mixture of confusion, shock, disbelief, and growing rage. I can hear the deep bass from the dining room and know no one there will hear me if I yell.

She steps closer but stops when she realizes there isn't enough room to scoot around me and my bulging bag of kitchen essentials.

"Get out of the way."

Flimsy pieces of still-burning paper drift through the air, edges glowing, pushed by a draft from the open window toward the carpet. The linen drapes. The walls.

"What are you doing?" I ask, Stupid question. Same thing she's been trying to do for at least as long as I've known her. Destroy Treetops, and, apparently, everyone in it. I let the heavy bag drop from my shoulder until the straps rest in my hand.

"Jesus, you're impossible." She looks back over her shoulder, practically vibrating with tension. A still-burning folder flops from the trashcan onto the floor, lighting the one beside it like a very edgy game of dominoes. Her lips pull back into a tight, ugly smile. "I'm winning, you idiot. Every other ex got a mountain of cash and a polite 'Let's be friends who never speak again.' I have to *work*? And not just work, but report to him? To make this idiotic passion project successful?" She snorts. "What kind of sick mind thinks of something like that? Fuck him." Her eyes refocus on me. "And fuck you too. This"—she waves her hand at the spreading flames—"this is on you. If you'd just *done what I said*"—her voice grows shrill—"we wouldn't be here."

She glances at her watch. The firelight really brings out the glimmer of the diamonds.

I consider making a sprint for the dining room to get backup.

"I don't have time for this." She pulls a bottle of lighter fluid out of another coat pocket and unscrews the cap, and makes to start squirting. Pausing with her hand in the air, bottle tilted ever so slightly, she smirks at me. "You know, maybe this one time you're actually going to be useful. I can see it now. *Disgruntled Former Employee Destroys Luxury Retreat in Fit of Rage.* I'll be in Europe by dinner tomorrow, sipping champagne. And you? You'll be in jail."

The bag of wine connects with Brooke's face, sending her sprawling backward, white-blond hair dangerously close to the flames that are now spreading across the paper trail on the carpet and licking at the baseboards. The haze of smoke builds in the room, threatening to spill out. I drag Brooke through the doorway into the hall, not bothering to check if she's breathing, slam the door shut, and run for help.

I don't have to run far. I crash into Matt at the top of the stairs.

"Fire! Intruder!" I'm panting, shaking, gesturing wildly in a way that is barely helpful but seems to at least indicate the desperate level of concern I have about the situation.

He looks past me to Brooke's prone form crumped in the hallway.

"Is that—"

"Did I mention that THERE IS A FIRE?" A smoke alarm farther along the hall chooses that moment to chime in, proving my point.

After that, it's all a bit of a blur. Matt strides heroically to his almost certain demise. I run to get everyone else out of the building then circle back to sacrifice myself to save Matt. Except, it turns out paper is just really smoky. Matt grabbed a fire extinguisher from the lounge and gotten most of it out, then took care of the rest with the bucket of water conveniently located behind reception. Saved by a leaky ceiling. Who would have thought.

When I get back, preparing to tear my shirt into cloth strips to dunk in water and use as face shields, he's surveying the damage, hands on his hips, apparently oblivious to the now stirring Brooke at his feet.

The office is a wreck.

"Kevin's going to be so pissed."

Clad in navy pajamas accented with a repeating pattern of tiny white sloths dangling from leafy branches, Kevin surveys the group that's gathered in the library.

Mike's lounging on a chaise, slippered feet up, sipping a G and T with a wedge of lime. As soon as it was clear the emergency was over, he seemed inclined to stick around purely for the drama, which is very unlike the Mike I know. "These people are batshit crazy," he murmurs from the corner of his mouth when I stop at his side to ask about the dogs—fine, sleeping at his place, totally tuckered out. "You know, I hardly ever miss being in the city, but the people-watching was always such a joy."

I leave him to absorb the real-life soap opera in which we find ourselves embroiled.

Brooke lies on the leather couch, groaning and probing at the spot where her top left canine tooth used to be. I perch on a bar stool and take the wine from my bag, pouring some into a glass that just happens to be within reach. I sip it in what I hope is a casual fashion, though my hands are still shaking from the fading adrenaline rush. The glass is halfway to my lips when it strikes me that I might be drinking evidence of some sort of crime. *Meh.* I take a generous gulp and glug some more into the glass to replace it.

Matt comes up behind me and rests a hand on my shoulder. I lean my head back against his chest and close my eyes for a moment.

The library hasn't seen this much action since the ill-fated night of the bachelorette. The women and men of the board are milling about, many with a medicinal glass of something in their hands, having quiet conversations I only catch scraps of —*Call the police? Always knew this was a terrible idea. More scotch?*

Graham clears his throat. "Well, that was quite a way to end a lovely supper."

"You're an embarrassment," Brooke mutters from the couch, shoving herself into a sitting position and crossing her legs coquettishly.

Graham's eyes roll to the ceiling and he closes his eyes, taking a calming breath before speaking again. He's sitting on a brown and green plaid wingback chair, feet crossed at the ankles, hands in his lap. I can't decide if he's throwing off king-like vibes, or more petulant-child-in-a-timeout.

"Can you hit her again?" Matt whispers in my ear, and I snort loudly, wine nearly coming out my nose. I elbow him in the stomach, eliciting a satisfying *oomph*.

"You must be wondering what's happened here tonight," Graham says. "Though it pains me to admit it, this does not come entirely as a surprise." Shocked murmurs run through the crowd. Jay and Tania are giving us looks of pure *WTF?!* and I'm sure my face reflects the same sentiment.

"As you all know, Brooke was entrusted with the care and oversight of Treetops as part of an extremely generous settlement upon the dissolution of our marriage."

"Generous, my ass," Brooke inserts. "Someone get me some gin. This tooth is killing me."

Tania, being the stellar human she is, fetches a cut-crystal glass of ice and a bottle of gin from behind the bar, depositing it on the coffee table just far enough away that Brooke can't reach it. She leans precariously across the expanse of walnut, very likely flashing everyone on the other side of the room, until she's all but lying across the table, fingers straining to wrap around the neck of the bottle.

Graham continues, "Unfortunately, despite my best efforts to maintain a civil business relationship, things took a rather nasty turn starting approximately eighteen months ago, and this morning we officially terminated her employment with HIT Properties." He sighs and takes a sip of his drink—decaf coffee laced with a hefty tot of aged dark rum that I think he believes he snuck in without anyone noticing. "I know, I know.

You told me." He shakes his head ruefully, gives us all a self-deprecating smile.

"As I was saying, around a year and a half ago I noticed a distinct drop in bookings, but put it down to a blip. Then, concerning reports started to filter in through the grapevine about lack of upkeep and repeated denial of requests for funds to perform standard maintenance."

A paunchy man wearing frameless glasses and a pale pink polo complete with popped collar chimes in. "Why didn't you bring this forward, Graham?" Others around him nod in agreement.

"I wasn't sure what was going on, Thomas. I wanted to fully understand the situation before troubling anyone else with it. And also, well, part of me wondered if this was just the end of an era." That smile again, and I see others smiling back with understanding.

"This place is a money pit," a dark-haired woman in a navy wrap dress observes. "Always has been. But you love it, Graham. And Lord knows we all have our soft spots for terrible investments." She shoots a look at another white guy in his sixties whose face is hidden jokingly behind his hands. "Yeah, I'm looking at you, Oliver. Mister 'let's get in on the ground floor of the Saskatchewan market.' What a disaster."

A round of chuckles. I give Tania a *Who are these people?* look. She shakes her head, shrugs, and sips some chamomile tea.

Kevin steps forward, clearing his throat. "Mr. Sutherland, perhaps it would be helpful if I summarize?"

Graham takes a step back, ceding the spotlight. "Yes, thank you, Kevin. Please go ahead."

"After a thorough investigation, it was discovered that not only was Ms. Kerrigan purposefully and willfully driving the business downward through untoward business practices."

I sit up straighter. He *knew*?

"But," he continues, his quiet voice carrying commandingly

through the room, "more concerningly, significant funds have been diverted from the business to Ms. Kerrigan's personal accounts." He pulls his phone from a pocket of his cloud-gray robe, tapping open a file.

"Over the past year, we believe Ms. Kerrigan has funneled more than half a million dollars from this business. These funds were acquired through falsified equipment purchases, payroll for staff who are no longer employed by HIT Properties, and neglecting to fulfill the seasonal scholarship awards for the entire duration of her time as General Manager. The scholarship value alone is in the range of two hundred thousand dollars."

I catch movement out of the corner of my eye but am too incensed to register it further. I place my glass onto the bar, stand up and step toward the group.

"How long have you known?" I ask, trying to keep my voice level and directing the question at Kevin and Graham.

"Um, and who are you, exactly?" Graham asks in a politely bewildered tone. "Aside from our savior, this evening, of course!" He raises a glass in a toast, the rest of the group joining in. I can't tell if it's genuine or if I'm being mocked.

"Kate Rigsby, sir. I was employed here as Business Development Director from early November through December."

Instead of being confused about why someone who is no longer an employee is staffing their AGM, he looks pleased. "Ah yes! I've seen your work."

I blink stupidly. "You have?"

"Yes, yes, of course." He looks at the woman in the navy dress who'd called out Oliver earlier. "Carol, this is the young lady whose efforts caught your eye a couple of months ago. With the newly defined ICPs and that shocking bookings spike."

"Oh yes!" Carol nods. "That was excellent. Really, Kate, you inspired this whole thing."

"What thing?" The arson? This incredibly awkward conversation?

"Well, I suppose this wasn't how we were going to reveal it, was it, Graham? But surely this young lady deserves to know just how much her work has paid off."

Graham nods heartily. "I couldn't agree more. Carol and I were going to roll this out as part of tomorrow morning's agenda, but I think this will do just fine." He flicks a look to the nautical-themed wall clock. "Of course, we can delve further into the logistics of it all, in the light of day."

Stepping forward once more, he takes on the presence of the Chairman of the Board. He walks the length of the room, then back again before speaking. "Treetops was born of a love for creativity, to nurture the artistic spirit, and, of course, to fit a market niche that begged to be addressed."

Polite titters. I stare, transfixed, awaiting some grand announcement. *Kate Rigsby for GM! Kate Rigsby gets the half mil Brooke stole! Treetops shall be renamed the Kate Rigsby Institute of Badassery!*

"When I made the admittedly ill-advised decision to pass the reins to Brooke, it was in an effort to keep this project close to me, close to my family." He shakes his head, apparently shocked and dismayed at his idiocy. "So much has happened over the past few years, but one of the most exciting personal progressions has been growing closer to my children as they've become adults, and understanding that they share much of the same passion I do."

My eyes flick to Matt, standing very still by the bar, looking at the velvet stool in front of him with much more interest than it warrants.

"When Kate joined Treetops and started stretching the business to meet the needs of today's modern clientele, she stumbled onto something wonderful."

Sorry, stumbled? It was an expertly planned and executed business effort, thank you very much.

"There is a whole new world of creative geniuses out there

starting empires of their own, just begging, *begging* to be inspired, nurtured, and pampered."

Everyone's nodding except the Treetops staff, who are frozen, statue-like.

"I will share the full financials with you in the morning, along with a market segmentation breakdown and existing versus potential pipeline; however, I think something we can all agree on is that this type of undertaking requires its own visionary at the helm. Someone who has proven their dedication to art. To inspiring the masses. To taking a sprout of an idea and making it break through the canopy to reach unimaginable heights." His hand arcs dramatically above his head.

Not Kate Rigsby for GM, then. My heart flutters a bit as I stare at Matt. Oh my God. He's going to take it over. My knees buckle a little at the absolute magic of everything that's happening. He's perfect for this. The things we could do here together . . . *Slow down, Kate. Pace yourself.* You know, the things we could do if he wanted me here and if I wanted to be here. With him. Long term.

Graham continues, looking composed, confident, and excited. Like he's about to do an *Extreme Makeover* reveal. "Treetops remains close to my heart and always will. What better way to maintain those ties than to keep it in the family?"

Matt's eyes lock on mine, looking deeply pained. He shakes his head ever so slightly. "What?" I mouth back, trying to contain a preemptive grin at the big announcement.

"And so, it is with absolute joy that I can now share my big secret. Effective immediately, my daughter, Christine Morrow, will be stepping into the role of Vice President of Creative Properties. Her first project will be to overhaul Treetops, starting with its complete demolition and a ground-up redesign." He launches into a description of glass and steel. Jet Skis and spray-tan booths.

My mouth is hanging open, collecting some of the dust motes

floating through the air. Christine? The dog-abandoning, improper footwear sporting, angelic social media goddess-slash-demon has been deemed an appropriate figurehead for Treetops?

How dare they.

I'm approximately three seconds away from throwing a fairly epic adult tantrum fueled by wine, exhaustion, residual terror, and general life angst when someone says, "Where's Brooke?"

In the shocked silence that follows we hear an engine gun in the parking lot, followed by the high-pitched whine of wheels spinning on ice.

"Should someone stop her?" asks Thomas of the popped collar.

Matt and Kevin start toward the door, but Graham holds up a hand. "Let her go," he says.

"Um." The sound is out of my mouth before I even know I'm verbalizing my thoughts. Everyone turns, focusing on me. I sigh. Oh well. In for a penny, et cetera. "It's just, she's likely concussed, and the gin bottle's gone. She shouldn't be driving." The tires continue to shriek in the parking lot. "Not that she seems to be getting anywhere."

"She can sleep it off in one of the employee huts," says Kevin. "Lord knows no one will mind if they burn down."

"We'll go," offers Tania, tugging Jay along with her.

Mike, acknowledging that the show is basically over, stands and stretches. As he passes, he gives my shoulder a pat.

"It's not as bad as you think," he says. He's through the door and out of sight before I can request evidence to back up this assertion.

I turn to Matt, who seems to be trying to blend into the bookcase behind me. "Can I talk to you for a minute, please?" The room is still full of execs high on their brush with death, debating whether they should continue with the planned agenda or call the meeting to a close early. I jerk my head toward the door. "Alone?"

Matt nods and heads out, leading me up to the seating area

in front of the fireplace. There's no bar here so we're probably safe from prying eyes.

The overhead lights are off and the room is lit by tabletop lamps that give everything a warm glow. I lower myself onto one of the couches and Matt settles in, bending one leg under him so he's facing me, leaning against the leather-covered arm.

He waits.

"Did you know?" I am furious at the idea that he'd let me come back, intent on proving myself, knowing full well there was no future for me here.

He runs a hand over his face and through his hair, sighing.

"I knew Brooke's exit was in the works. I didn't know it was . . . this." His face reflects the same disgust I feel roiling in my gut. "I haven't really been kept in the loop lately."

"If you had let me storm in there, knowing this was the direction they were taking, that I'd be demanding a job working for Christine . . ." I trail off. A nightmare.

He reaches out, wraps my hands in his. "I swear, Kate. I didn't know before we came. Dad told me after dinner, and I was on my way to find you, but then the fire happened and . . ." He raises our entwined hands and kisses the base of my thumb. He takes a deep breath before continuing. "The idea of Christine running an entire property is, quite frankly, shocking and more than a little terrifying. Imagine the type of staff she'll hire? The guests this place will be brimming with?" He shudders. "I live next door. I'm going to have to form some kind of neighborhood association to keep them in check."

I try hard to hold on to my outrage, but it's past midnight and it's been one hell of a day.

"I know you love it here," he says quietly, stroking my thumb.

I nod, horrified to feel my lower lip trembling and tears burning my eyes. I clamp my mouth shut. I will *not* cry.

"You're going to find something else. Something that feels just as right as this. Probably better because your next boss isn't likely to be into arson and attempted murder."

A smile tugs at the corner of my mouth, but it quickly changes to a jaw-cracking yawn. Matt stands. "I'm going to go check on Brooke. Make sure she isn't conjuring a yeti to tear us all limb from limb, and then we can head to my place."

I lie back on the couch. "I'll wait here."

I'll just close my eyes for a second. Take some deep, calming breaths before walking back to Matt's, which suddenly feels very, very far away. And it's so *cold* outside, but this room is cozy. It's warm and smells ever so slightly of apple cider and woodsmoke. My breathing slows. A heavy blanket is pulled over me. Matt brushes the hair from my forehead.

"You're amazing," he whispers, lightly kissing my cheek before clicking off the light.

"Love you too," my traitorous mouth says.

Goddamn it. I yawn and curl into a ball under the weight of the blanket. Well, Future Kate can deal with that one.

Chapter 27

I wake up with a dry, scratchy throat. My hair smells exactly like someone tried to set it on fire. Living the dream.

Matt finds me a short while later, shoveling waffles and bacon into my mouth while I try to decide who I'm most angry with. Brooke for being a psychopath? Kevin for letting me trundle toward my demise without even the tiniest heads-up? Graham for planning to literally tear my future down and replace it with everything I despise, while also crediting me for bringing this on? My blood boils. Yup. There it is.

It's still pitch-black outside and I'd chosen a seat facing away from the windows specifically to avoid seeing my reflection. I don't even want to imagine the visual that goes along with this odor.

Smelling like the handmade sandalwood and sweet birch guest room soap, Matt's clearly been up longer than I have. Or has, at least, prioritized differently.

I run my hands over my face, parting my fingers wide enough to look at him, shoving the simmering rage aside.

"I assume Brooke didn't resort to Molotov cocktails in the wee hours of the morning?"

He laughs softly. "Nah. By the time they got to her car, she'd passed out. They moved her to a bed and she was asleep when I checked last night. When I got back here at five, she was gone."

I shake my head in disbelief. "What a night."

He puts a bag on the floor beside me and takes the seat to my right.

"Clean clothes," he says, nodding toward the duffel. "I wasn't sure what to pick. Let me know if you want me to run back to my place for something else before the meeting."

My teeth pause along their path through the cream-cheese frosting crust on a mini cinnamon bun. "Ah eedin'?" I mumble doughily.

"The eight o'clock you have with my father to insist on receiving your bonus and being reimbursed for that idiotic bachelorette invoice."

I manage to swallow without choking.

"First of all, I, uh, haven't paid that invoice yet." I take a swig of coffee. "Purely out of spite, you understand. Not due to a lack of disposable income." The waffles have been sitting long enough to have absorbed their first syrup application, so I douse them again before picking up my fork. "Secondly, nope."

He rolls his eyes. "Come on, Kate. Your success here inspired an entirely new business. You earned it, fair and square. Just walk in there, summarize your contributions, and ask for what you deserve. What do you have to lose?"

"Nothing, obviously. I'm fresh out of self-confidence and hope for any sort of career-based future." I drop dollops of fresh whipped cream on top of the waffle resting in its syrup lake. "If they value my work *and* they knew what Brooke was up to, wouldn't they have offered me some kind of severance bonus? A job at a different location?"

The chair directly across from me is suddenly occupied. I blink, wondering if I'm hallucinating.

"You look like a vagrant and smell worse, but Matthew is correct," Kevin says. "After you bathe and do something about"—he waves his hand up and down in my direction—"this situation, you will, in no uncertain terms, let them know you expect to be paid the contractual bonus, plus an additional payment that takes into account your premature and unwarranted dismissal from a role in which you were exceeding all reasonable expectations."

He sips from his mug, then purses his lips for a moment, looking slightly pained. "I would be, well, not happy, but willing, to act as a sort of reference in this respect."

"Kevin, that's . . . I don't know what to say."

"Please, say nothing until you brush your teeth thoroughly." He pushes back from the table and smooths the fibers of today's deep purple fisherman's pullover. "Mike is, somehow, content to continue caring for your ill-mannered canine until after you have completed this piece of business." He sniffs, haughtily (as if there's any other way), and departs.

"I don't wannaaaa," I whine under my breath. It's 7:58 and I'm waiting in the Oak room, the small meeting room just around the corner from where the board is currently gathered. Apparently they'd decided to forge ahead with the morning meetings.

My hair's gathered in a still-damp low bun and I'll admit, for the morning after a near-death experience I'm looking pretty put together in dark jeans, a black turtleneck, and black suede ankle boots. Simple, classy.

"Don't wanna what?" Matt asks, setting a tray of coffee mugs and maple-dipped shortbread cookies on the table.

Laughter floats down the hall. How they can be cheery this early after a night like that, I have no idea, but I guess that's why they make the big bucks. Or they're all still drunk.

"I don't want to face this day. Do adult things." He raises an eyebrow and I shrug, blushing. "With some exceptions, obviously."

"Obviously," he murmurs, face moving closer to mine. My lips part in anticipation.

"Ah, Kelly," Graham says, coming through the door. "I didn't realize you'd be joining us." He shoots Matt a quizzical look.

I also target Matt with a laser stare as I realize there's been some deliberate miscommunication here.

He leans in and squeezes my shoulder. "You are a badass. You've got this. I love you." I don't have time to react before Graham sits down across from me.

Graham dunks a cookie, sploshing coffee onto the white tabletop like nothing out of the ordinary is going on.

Matt straightens. "Oh drat. Must have been a typo during scheduling, Dad. This is actually Kate's meeting." He nods in my direction. "Kate Rigsby? You may remember her as the person who saved our lives last night, and also, more pertinently, as the woman whose dedication to Treetops' success inspired this recent pivot." He backs toward the door, pulling it shut as he slides through. "I'll leave you to it, then."

Graham scrolls through his phone and devours another cookie. A sizeable crumb lodges in his beard.

I clear my throat, take a sip of water.

"Mr. Sutherland," I begin.

"Graham, please!"

My hands are resting on the table and I get the distinct impression he's about to pat them. I retreat, placing them safely in my lap.

"Graham," I start again, smiling in what I hope is a pleasant, respectful way. "Thanks so much for taking the time to speak with me, as unexpected as this is turning out to be." *Stop rhyming.* "I was employed by HIT Properties for only a short while, as you may already know, in late fall through early winter of last year. Based on your comments last night, you are somewhat familiar with my activities during that time."

He nods. "Yes, yes of course! You brought this new business model to light, despite the great adversity you have faced!"

"Indeed." I force myself to stop picking at a hangnail and slide a copy of my contract, conveniently supplied by Matt, across the table. "This is a copy of my contract, which details a variable compensation structure based on monthly bookings goals."

He picks up the stack of paper and flips to where a sticky note flag marks the appropriate page. I pause as he skims it, collecting my thoughts. When he's finished, I slide another page to him, feeling like a bank robber passing over my demands.

"This document summarizes my performance during the time I spent at Treetops. As you can see, I met the necessary milestone for achieving the December bonus, and was well on the way to a record-breaking January and February at the time I was let go."

Graham sets the paperwork down and looks at me expectantly.

I spit it out.

"Sir—Graham. I believe I have met, if not exceeded, the requirements laid out in this contract. And while Brooke asserted that the clientele being brought in was not in line with the traditional Ideal Customer Profile, it seems, based on your plans for this resort, that you recognize there has been a shift. That what was ideal in the nineties is, perhaps, not quite as applicable in today's market." I take a deep breath. *You did the work. You deserve this. You earned it.*

"I respectfully request that I be paid the full value of this contract, with an additional bonus that addresses the untoward nature of my dismissal, and the hardships undergone as a consequence thereof."

I make myself look him in the eye and try not to squirm. I blink first, snagging a mug of lukewarm coffee from the tray and cupping my trembling hands around it. I busy myself swirling in milk I don't want while I await judgment.

A man with a sunburn accentuated by his salmon-toned shirt opens the door without knocking.

"Graham? Christine's here. We're just waiting on you."

Graham stands, brushing cookie debris from his pants. "Be right there, Lester."

He meets my eyes. "You're an astute businessperson, my dear. You have every right to make these requests and I'd be a fool to decline." He picks his phone up from the table and starts tapping out a message. "I'm emailing Georgette, my admin, now. She'll coordinate with finance to ensure you're paid out in full, including a subsequent bonus in six month's time pending your cooperation in keeping the recent events confidential, as is in line with your contract, of course." He smiles charmingly.

"Of course. Thank you."

He plucks the last of the shortbread from the tray, wrapping it in a napkin and sliding the whole thing into his pocket where it will almost certainly be reduced to sugary dust.

"Excellent. Please tell my son I look forward to having our meeting over lunch. It can be served in this room for privacy."

I nod, holding back a reminder that I don't work here.

"Can do, Graham."

As soon as he's gone, I'm doubled over in my chair, taking deep breaths and counting to thirty in French, which is as much as I can remember. I did it. *I did it.*

Sure, Treetops, as it exists today, is gone forever, and I have no idea what I'm going to do with the rest of my life, but this is still a win, right? I got the money. I got the guy. Done and dusted.

I look out the window at the naked trees swaying in the wind against a cloudy gray sky and wonder how long it will take to stop feeling so empty.

After asking Tania to let Matt know about his lunch engagement, I collect an exhausted Eric from where he's supervising Mike's wood collection efforts at the edge of the property.

We retreat to Matt's cabin, feet dragging through the snow along the path, both too tired to pay any attention to the chattering squirrels. When we arrive, the man himself is nowhere to be found, which is okay with me. I need some time alone with my feelings.

The stairs creak under my feet as I climb, Eric clattering along behind me. I flop onto the bed. It smells like fresh laundry and the cold winter air seeping in from the window directly above my head. Eric circles a couple of times before wedging the length of his back against my side, grumbling as he settles in.

Tears burn my eyes, but I try to convince myself it's just a residual effect of the smoke. Despite how exhausted I am, it takes a long time to fall asleep. I can't stop picturing a wrecking ball crashing through the towering stone fireplace in the lounge. Imagining these people I've grown so close to, who have somehow accepted me as one of their own, scattering across the country.

One thought is stuck on repeat: *I just want to go home.* Except I think I'm already there.

The board decides to depart that afternoon, roaring up the driveway like they can't wait to be rid of the place. The sound of so many purring engines and snow being crushed under an army of tires drags me from a fitful sleep.

Heaving the blanket from the bed along with me, I trundle downstairs to find Matt sitting on the couch beside a crackling fire. There's a laptop perched on his knees but he sets it aside when my human-burrito form enters his field of view.

I fall log-style onto the other end of the sofa and tuck my toes under Matt's thighs for warmth. The morning clouds have passed and the late afternoon sun slants in through the kitchen window, throwing a beam of light onto something simmering on the stove. I sniff.

"Do I smell bread?"

"You do. And sweet potato carrot soup." He leans over, wraps strong arms around my body, and hoists me toward him until I'm snuggled against his side, head on his shoulder. I take a deep breath, inhaling the smell of him complemented by warm carbs. His fingers brush some stray hair from my cheek and raise my chin so I'm looking at him.

"Are you going to tell me what happened?"

"I got it. Plus, some mystery payoff in six months if I keep my mouth shut about HIT employing a criminal."

"That's good, isn't it?" he asks carefully.

"It is," I assure him, tracing the lines on his palm with a fingertip. "It's just . . ."

He waits while I gather my thoughts.

"I don't even know. I need the money, so that's great. I feel somewhat vindicated, like people at least know I did a good job during my time here. It's just, it feels like they took that work and twisted it into something terrible and—god, what have I become? I can't believe I'm saying this—they've turned it into something that is not at all in line with the original spirit of Treetops. This new spin is all about money. What happened to the output? The nurturing of the creative passion that lies quietly in each of us, waiting to be awakened?"

"Kevin would be so proud."

"I doubt it." I stare up at the wooden ceiling. "I don't know what I'm going to do, Matt. I'm almost thirty-two and have no idea what I want to be when I grow up. I'm going to end up working the front desk at some midrange hotel, wondering how things turned out so badly." I picture it and shudder. "I'll have to wear a terrible neckerchief like a flight attendant. Orange. And nude pantyhose."

"You've really thought this through."

"I'm out of backup plans."

He pats my thigh and stands, grabbing my hands and pulling me to standing. "Let's eat. You can't snowshoe on an empty stomach."

"How did we get from Kate is a failure to snowshoeing?"

He ignores me, ladling ginger-scented soup into bowls before slicing bread and putting it all on the small table.

"It's all about perspective," he says, covering a piece of still-warm sourdough thoroughly with butter and handing it to me.

"That doesn't make any sense," I mutter. "And I don't know how to snowshoe."

He just smiles.

"They're putting in a pool where the guest cabins are."

Jay is full of information he gleaned while dropping snacks off during the morning meetings. It turns out this outing is a group adventure, but no one will fill me in on our destination. Jay's got a backpack though, and I can see two thermoses peeking out, so I've got high hopes for boozy hot chocolate.

I squint, confused. "Can you even install a pool beside a lake? And why? There's a lake *right there*."

"Where there are endless riches, there's a way. Christine insisted that guests will worry about lake bacteria and there needs to be a low-risk option available for 'hydrophoto-ops.'"

Tania hands me a pair of snowshoes and directs me to sit on a bench by the Gathering Fire while she helps strap them on like I'm five years old.

I'm trying to figure out why no one seems devastated by this turn of events and their impending unemployment, when Delilah saunters over, followed by Mike and Kevin. I blink. Kevin's clad in head-to-toe outerwear, including snowshoes of his own. More shockingly, he moves in them confidently, like an experienced outdoorsperson. Tania finishes strapping me in and heaves me to my feet. I take some tentative steps, raising my knees absurdly high and eliciting laughter from the group at large. Even Kevin's lips twitch in the depths of his glossy beard.

"Shush. Learning a new skill at my advanced age is a complex undertaking. Also, I have a fragile ego." I stop lurching about to stare at them all. "Also, also, remember that time I saved your lives and single-handedly incapacitated a criminal mastermind?"

Okay, maybe that's a bit of a stretch given how terrible Brooke's arson skills turned out to be, but still.

"Speaking of which—" Tania pulls out her phone and turns it to show me the screen. A news site is open.

Woman Arrested After Vandalizing Helicopter

Brooke Kerrigan, a fifty-two-year-old Toronto woman, has been charged with breaking and entering and attempted arson.

Kerrigan was discovered by airport security early this morning, apparently trying to set fire to a helicopter owned and operated by HIT Properties. HIT is the parent company of local luxury hotel Treetops Creative Retreat and sources indicate Kerrigan may be a disgruntled employee.

"She was clearly at a bit of a loss on how to proceed," said Jordan Hampton, security guard at Otterburne Private Air. "When I came through on my normal rounds, she was sitting on the ground, drinking gin from a bottle and googling 'how to destroy a helicopter with fire.'"

Damage was limited to the exterior of the aircraft, on which a crude image had been painted in nail polish.

"Must have taken her ages," Hampton added. "It was a tiny brush and a very large . . . image."

I wipe tears of laughter from my eye with the back of my mitten.

"Googling it!" I double over, delirious.

Matt and Jay exchange looks of mild concern, but Tania just pats my back supportively and puts the phone back in her pocket.

"Let's get going. We're going to lose the light."

We set out across the frozen lake, dogs frolicking ahead of us. Well, Eric frolics. Delilah struts and occasionally loosens up enough to prance a couple of laps around him with a stolen stick.

The fading light casts an orange glow on the expanse of snow and ice. It's quiet aside from the crunching of our snowshoes and my heavy breathing. Occasionally the ice creaks and I have a mild heart attack, but Mike assures me it's perfectly safe.

Just as I'm about to insist someone give me a piggyback, we come around a treed point and stop. I stand there panting, hands on my thighs. A building sits on a rise, looking like a rustic version of a midsize commercial hotel. It's surrounded by outbuildings that remind me of a summer camp.

I look around, waiting for an explanation, or even better, that boozy cocoa to make an appearance. I notice a sign on what would be a small beach in summer months. FALCON RIDGE CORPORATE RETREAT.

"Um?"

Jay crouches and starts pulling small cups and the thermoses from his bag. Tania eyes me with a funny look on her face. Matt's arm settles around my waist.

I see Mike nudge Kevin with his elbow. "Do it," he hisses.

Kevin sighs. "*I am*, Michael. Give me a moment." He steps forward.

"This is Falcon Ridge."

"Ooookay? I actually applied for a job here. Didn't work out though." I think back to the email about their transition to a new management team. Something clicks in my head, but it seems too good to be true. I squint at them suspiciously.

Mike smiles broadly, looking like a kid on Christmas.

Kevin clears his throat and stares at the sun setting behind the trees before continuing.

"Mike and I have agreed to take over management of this venue, effective April first. Falcon Ridge provides a respite for executives looking to refresh their outlooks and come back into the business world sharper, but also more in touch with themselves. All too often these individuals pour themselves into their work without taking the time to check in and understand what kind of fuel their passion requires."

I am hopeful—so, so hopeful that this is heading where I think it is. *Play it cool, Rigsby.*

"Well, that sounds like an excellent next step for you both. And based on how much Tania is vibrating, I assume she'll be joining you?"

"Yes!" she bursts out. "And Jay is coming on as head chef! And Serge is coming back! And—" She stops herself as Kevin catches her eye. "And I am excited," she finishes lamely, looking at the ground.

They already rejected your application, I remind myself, deflating. Who am I kidding? They don't need me here.

"I'm so happy for you," I say truthfully, hoping they take my sniffling to be an effect of the cold air.

"We'll be relocating the Borealis cottage here," Kevin says casually. He points to a spot on the other side of the tree line, away from the main building. I can imagine waves lapping at the shore in the summer. Fairy lights strung along the eaves of the cabin. Sitting on the porch with a glass of wine and the world's most powerful citronella candle to ward off mosquitoes. I press my eyes shut, squashing the image.

"It will get the most glorious morning light," he says. "Far enough to be private while still conveniently located in relation to the central campus. We'll be adding a fence to the rear, of course."

"Oh?" I say, hoping against hope that this means I won't have to renew my Party Thyme contract.

"Well, we can't have this imbecile crashing around all day, harassing guests."

"Which imbecile?" I ask cautiously.

Kevin points a gloved hand to where Eric is attempting to drag a branch the length of a car toward Delilah. It's still attached to the tree.

"We require a staff member to take on responsibility for finding needy souls and their compatriots, and convincing them to sign on for an intensive, soul-opening journey—with premium spa and dining services, of course." He looks at me expectantly. "We can't pay much to start."

"What Kevin is trying to say," Mike chimes in, "is that we need someone to handle business growth, but with a strong understanding of the spirit we're trying to imprint on the Ridge. We'd like to offer that role to you."

I am speechless, staring dumbly at all of them. I don't know whether I want to hug everyone or screech with joy or just crumple into a heap of relieved sobbing.

"Think it over," Mike says as Jay thrusts a steaming mug into my hand. "Kevin will email you a copy of the employment contract for you to review." He pauses. "Thoroughly, this time, yeah?"

Chapter 28

The summer sun beams across a turquoise sky, dotted with fluffy clouds. Heidi stands under an arch weighed down with greenery and dotted with roses in shades from ivory to deep coral. A gentle breeze ruffles my hair and keeps me from fully melting into a puddle of sweat.

We're on the main lawn of Falcon Ridge, surrounded by trees on three sides, and sparkling water on the fourth. A duck glides past with a brood of ducklings paddling willy-nilly behind her. I check the time.

Matt huffs out a breath. "I always cry at these things."

I squeeze his hand, then rummage through the sizeable bag on my lap.

"Don't worry, I brought tissues. And ChapStick, that stuff to get red wine stains out, gum, sunblock, a granola bar."

"This isn't a camping trip. You live five hundred feet away."

"I like to be prepared."

"And I love that you're a thirty-two-year-old Girl Scout." He kisses me softly. For a moment, we bask in the still-new feeling of joy just being with each other.

As it turned out, Christine wasn't the only Sutherland progeny with a new gig. Matt had been offered, and had accepted, the chance to lead HIT's new and improved scholarship initiative. He's heading to Banff tomorrow to meet with the board and pitch a program expansion that would focus on youth in underserved communities.

"Are you packed?" I ask, running my hand down his arm and interlocking my fingers with his. He's wearing a pale blue button-up the same shade as the one I'd marred with lip gloss the day we met. The sleeves are rolled above his strong forearms in deference to both the heat of the day and the casual tone of the wedding. I get tingly just looking at him.

"I have a couple more things to do, but yeah, mostly." He pushes his aviators onto the top of his head and looks me in the eye, suddenly serious. "Are you going to be okay? Wedding aftermath, LifeCycle coming in on Tuesday, and then our trip to see your parents next week? It's a lot."

"Of course. I'll be fine. Tania's going to help with Eric and really, how bad can it be?"

"Classic last words."

I roll my eyes while silently agreeing.

Last weekend, I hosted a trip for some friends from home, taking three days off to personally experience everything Falcon Ridge had to offer. It was amazing to reconnect with Hailey and the other girls I'd grown up with, getting to know them as the extraordinary women they've become.

Off to the side of the crowd, a guitar player switches from acoustic renditions of pop hits from the last three decades to "Over the Rainbow."

"Here they come!" Tania squeal-whispers from farther down our row, bouncing in her seat.

Delilah prances down the aisle, a crown of roses perched

precariously atop her fluffy head. When she reaches the front, she turns and parks herself directly beside Heidi, observing the crowd with her signature disdain.

The song changes again, this time to Beyoncé's "Superpower." Mike and Kevin appear from the trees bordering the ceremony area. The guests rise as one and the couple walks slowly down the aisle, holding hands and looking so damn happy it's blinding. I blink back tears. Beside me, Matt sniffles.

Together, they step up onto the small wooden deck in front of the arbor and turn toward each other, clasping both hands. Mike murmurs something to Kevin that makes him flash a watery smile and dash away a tear with the tips of his fingers.

Heidi steps forward and begins to speak, her gravelly voice accompanied by the sound of lapping waves and the distant call of a loon.

"We are gathered here today to celebrate true love, passion, and inspiration. To embrace one of the greatest joys in life—finding one's true path and following it, over hills and through valleys, until we come to a space that fills us with light, with purpose, with understanding."

Author's Note

Reasonable Adults is a product of serendipity. In November of 2019 I had just returned to work after having my second child. During my maternity leave I'd re-read the Rockton series by fellow Canadian Kelley Armstrong, and wanted to learn more about her writing process. A quick internet search revealed she'd be speaking at a workshop a week later in my hometown.

I showed up that Saturday with no real intention of writing anything, but excited to be out in the world. I had a three-year-old and an eight-month-old at home and could barely form one coherent sentence, let alone three-hundred pages of them.

Scanning the room, I spotted an empty seat near the front and plopped myself down with two other women, unwittingly changing my life.

In that room, at that table, I found my people.

When I got an email the next day inviting me to join their writing group, I was thrilled—making friends as an adult is *hard*. Then I realized I'd have to write something in order to keep showing up. *Reasonable Adults* is that something.

As the world struggled to adjust to pandemic life in 2020, I found I couldn't find anything I wanted to read. Or watch. Or listen to. I decided to make *Reasonable Adults* whatever I felt I needed at the time.

I wanted to be somewhere I love, so I set it in Muskoka, my province's summer vacation destination. I wanted it to reflect the isolation I felt at that time—enter winter. I wanted to talk about the magic you can find in unexpected places, whether that magic is nature, romance, or friendship. I wanted a story about a woman in her thirties who hasn't got it all figured out, because I think that's absolutely okay and normal and sometimes figuring out what you want takes time, or changes, or both of those things. And mostly, at the heart of it, I wanted a romp. A fun, funny read that could be consumed on a cross-country flight.

This book was written in the hallway outside my kids' bedrooms while I waited for them to fall asleep. It was jotted down in stolen moments between meetings and in my car, parked two blocks away from the house. It was a glorious, painful, stunning process, like many of life's most worthwhile things, I suppose.

I hope you find something that feels true in these pages, and that Kate and her ragtag crew bring you some of the light they shared with me when things felt quite dark.

Acknowledgments

I always assumed literary agents were terrifying, unapproachable superhumans. Only one of those assumptions turned out to be correct. Claire Friedman is, as far as I'm concerned, a book-focused superhero. Always supportive, incredibly responsive, the world's fastest reader, and the best champion I could have hoped for. I am forever grateful for everything you do.

Thank you to the entire team at InkWell Management for answering my endless questions and generally being excellent, efficient, friendly people in the face of my panicked requests.

I cannot imagine better homes for *Reasonable Adults* than with Julia McDowell at HarperCollins Canada and Elizabeth Trout at Kensington Books. Your guidance, enthusiasm, and seemingly endless patience with my inability to track time in a manuscript have made this book into its best self. Thank you for loving Kate, Matt, and the whole Treetops gang as much as I do.

In November of 2019, I spur-of-the-moment decided to attend a writing workshop and sat with two hilarious, kind, delightful women. I only started *Reasonable Adults* so I had a reason to join their writing group. Kayleigh, Carolyn, and Kate, thank you for accepting me even though my name breaks the alliteration. And Sandy, I'm so, so pleased you've joined us and embraced the role of my personal pep-talker. Thank you all for never doubting I could pull this off, listening to my rants, talking me off metaphorical ledges, and being some of the best friends a girl could hope for. None of this would have happened without you, and I'll never be able to adequately express how grateful I am that I have you in my life.

Taralyn and Meghan, it's been a journey. One that I don't want to do the math on because I fear we're far older than I feel. Thank you for not batting an eye when I declare things like "I'm writing a novel during the pandemic!" Thank you for checking on me, for asking how it's going, and for continuing to be amazing, thoughtful, wonderful friends despite everything the world has thrown at us. I was going to suggest a Big Night Out, but maybe a light beer (or two!) and an organized line dancing class instead?

Endless thank yous to Mom, Dad, John, Toni, Geoff, and Sukhpreet for their words of encouragement and willingness to show interest in the people I made up in my head. To Shelley and Sherwood (and all Leflers) for giving me time to write without getting yogurt or goldfish crumbs in the keyboard (and also allowing me to maintain my sanity).

To Forrest and Harriet for bringing the best kind of chaos to our lives.

And finally, to Jaron. Thank you for never being anything other than supportive. For giving me the time and space to go on this unplanned adventure. For delivering a drink and my laptop when I'm procrastinating. I love you. Great life team.

Reasonable Adults

Robin Lefler

About This Guide

The suggested questions are included to enhance your
group's reading of Robin Lefler's *Reasonable Adults*.

Discussion Questions

1. When Kate argues with Ros, we learn that the life Kate's been trying to build for herself is based on society's typical expectations for people in their late twenties and early thirties—a home, a steady job, a successful life partner with plans to marry, etc. How do you think external expectations and influences can impact our life choices?

2. Despite Kate's dedication to Being an Adult, she neglects to review her employment contract for Treetops Creative Retreat carefully. Do you think she would have gone ahead with the job if she'd understood the risks? If not, what do you think she would have done instead?

3. The staff at Treetops comes from quite diverse backgrounds (engineer, private investigator, big city chef). What do you think they have in common that draws them to this type of setting?

4. Have you had an experience where you ended up somewhere quite unexpected, but found it to be exactly what you needed? This can be an actual destination or a series of choices that led to a surprising result.

5. Is there a secondary character that you particularly liked or disliked? Why?

6. Matt sees many positive characteristics of Kate that she has difficulty recognizing in herself. Why do you think so many women underestimate themselves?

7. Chef Jay hasn't met a local ingredient he doesn't like. Is there a seasonal food in your area that you can't get enough of?

8. Talking to Eric the goldendoodle is a way for Kate to reflect on her life circumstances. He also forces her to get out and about when she'd rather stay safely cocooned and alone. If you have a pet, do you find yourself having conversations with them? If you don't have animals (or are not a dog person), were you still able to relate to Kate's connection with Eric?

9. Kate seems plagued by terrible bosses. Have you had experience with awful people in leadership roles? How did you handle the situation?

10. Josh and his contingent at Party Thyme start out as a bit of a joke, but end up having quite an impact on Kate's life. How did you feel about Josh's character arc and how it tied into Kates?